The Private Life of Mona Lisa

The Private Life of Mona Lisa

PIERRE LA MURE

LITTLE, BROWN AND COMPANY
BOSTON ❦ TORONTO

FIRST AMERICAN EDITION
T09/76

The author it grateful to Time-Life Books for permission
to reproduce the map of Florence (endpapers) and the
map of Italy (page viii) from Great Ages of Man/ *Renaissance*. Both maps drawn by David Greenspan.

LIBRARY OF CONGRESS CATALOGING IN PUBLICATION DATA
La Mure, Pierre.
The private life of Mona Lisa.

1. Mona Lisa, b. 1479–Fiction. I. Title.
PZ3.L215Pr3   [PS3523.A465]   813'.5'4   76–16811
ISBN 0–316–51300–8

Designed by Susan Windheim

PRINTED IN THE UNITED STATES OF AMERICA

*To Sir William Collins, C.B.E., who
has been my publisher as well as
my friend for over twenty years.*

Acknowledgments

So many people have helped me with the writing of this book that I cannot possibly name them all. Some, however, have been of such invaluable assistance that I must express my gratitude. First among them are Professor Ladislao Reti, a giant among Vincian scholars, translator of the Madrid Codices, the gentlest and most patient of friends; Dr. Elmer Belt, author of several definitive books on Leonardo, donor of the Elmer Belt Library of Vinciana at the University of California, Los Angeles; Mr. Carlo Pedretti, professor of art at the same university; Miss Kate Steinitz; and finally Mrs. William M. Bak, who has shared with me her immense knowledge of Italian Renaissance.

In France, I owe a debt of appreciation to the various officials of the Louvre Museum who have generously given me of their time and advice; in Italy to Count Bino Sanminiatelli of Viamaggio, Greve-in-Chianti (Firenze), and Count Bernardo Rucellai.

I also wish to express my thanks to Miss Terry Carr, Mrs. Mae Kimelman, and Mrs. Patrick Abarta, as well as to the staff of the New York Public Library, the Research Library of U.C.L.A., Padre S. Orlandi, in charge of the archives of Santa Maria Novella, and Dottore Berta Maracchi, director of the Biblioteca Riccardiana in Florence.

Contents

SAVOY

Milan

PALUZZO

GENOA

SENOA

Po R.

Parma

MILAN

MODENA

LUCCA

Lucca

Pisa

FLORENCE

Siena

SIENA

ELBA

CORSICA

to Genoa

SARDINIA

Verona

Mantua

Padua

Venice

Adige R.

Ferrara

FERRARA

Bologna

Florence

Rimini

Urbino

Assisi

PAPAL STATES

Tiber R.

Rome

Ostia

Garigliano R.

VENETIAN REPUBLIC

Drave R.

Save R.

N

ADRIATIC SEA

KINGDOM
OF
NAPLES

Naples

TYRRHENIAN SEA

MEDITERRANEAN SEA

SICILY

SCALE

0   40   80   120 Miles

Foreword

One day in 1480, a young and wealthy wool merchant entered one of Florence's tax offices and filed his declaration of income. In it, he described himself as "Antonio, Maria de'Gherardini, son of Noldo, residing on Via Maggio in the district of San Spirito, father of a daughter named Lisa, aged one, without the beginning of a dowry-senza *principio di dota*."

This child was to become the famous and very mysterious Mona Lisa.

Who was she, this woman who for centuries has intrigued the world and eluded all inquiries with a smile of her soft brown eyes? Why did this patrician and rich girl marry, at fifteen, a silk merchant more than twice her age, burdened with a child and twice a widower? Why did she, at twenty-four (and why did her husband let her), pose for a portrait he had not commissioned, which he never owned and in which she appears without a wedding ring, without a single jewel, and with her hair streaming down the sides of her face, as worn by maidens, but most improper in a respectable matron?

And, while we ponder, how did Leonardo come to paint the portrait of this Florentine housewife, he who was a stranger in Florence and did not seek portrait commissions? Why did he toil so long and hard on this small panel of poplar wood, he who did not like to paint and left his greatest works unfinished? Why did he spend countless hours on this seeming trifle at the most dramatic moment of his life, when he was engaged in an artistic duel with Michelangelo, which all of Florence was watching?

Most puzzling, for whom was the portrait painted?

In October 1517, when he was an old man already in the shadow of death, Leonardo spoke his name. He did so publicly and at great personal risk. That name was recorded for posterity by one who heard it. The disclosure was startling, but had it been false, it would have been immediately refuted.

It never was.

Today, in the light of more extensive documentation, we realize that Leonardo was telling the truth.

In a few words, he not only established the origins of the immortal portrait, but lifted the veil on a tender and poignant Renaissance love affair and whispered to us Mona Lisa's secret.

PIERRE LA MURE
April 1975

BOOK ONE

The Family

Arms of the Noble Family of
the Gherardini. *From the Liber
d'Oro.*

Head of a Child Turned ¾ to the Left by Fra Bartolommeo.
Courtesy of the Fogg Art Museum.

Enter Lisa

In the fifteenth century clocks were rare, costly, and, as they had only one hand, inaccurate. In addition, they were fragile and so complicated that when they broke down, which was often, almost no one knew how to repair them. For these reasons, daily life in Florence was regulated by the pealing of church bells.

On that March morning, shortly before dawn, the portly figure of a monk emerged, lantern in hand, from the cathedral. With the hood of his habit pulled low over his face, he strode the short distance to the Giotto Tower and began climbing its four hundred and fourteen steps, stopping now and then to catch his breath, for he was no longer young.

When he reached the belfry, he eased his bulk down on the sill of one of the slender apertures in the wall and there he sat, puffing, his hands cupped over his knees, the lantern making a puddle of yellow light at his sandaled feet.

As his breathing returned to normal, he pulled back his cowl and revealed a jovial, double-chinned face with a halo of white hair around a pink and shiny pate. Cautiously, like a snail emerging from its shell, he stretched his neck out of the window and peered eastward for the paleness at the hem of the sky that announced a new day. But there was no light over the hills; night still had a few moments to go.

He raised his eyes to the stars gleaming in the indigo sky, marveled at their number, and brightened. Devoutly, he crossed him-

self. Indeed, they were the Lord God's diamonds, and not even
the pope or the Medici had so many of them.

Or such beautiful ones.

A breeze wafted by, gently rustling his wispy hair.

"Spring is here," he mused half-aloud.

Yes, another week and the hills would be green with new grass,
the almond trees white with blooms. People would stop sneezing
and coughing, as they had all winter. The swallows would return
and dance around the cathedral's dome.

And a new year would arrive with the usual festivities: the
guilds' procession in the morning; cockfights, acrobats, and the
annual singing contest in the afternoon and, after supper, dancing
in public squares around bonfires. And for the young ones, a little
kissing and fondling in doorways, as was natural at their age. The
Julian calendar was still in effect, under which the year began on
25 March, Annunciation Day.

How sensible of the Lord to start the year in spring with the
rebirth of nature! There was no end to His wisdom or graciousness. Look how well He had placed Florence precisely in the
heart of Italy, surrounded by the fourteen states of the peninsula,
like a queen by her maidservants, and right in the center of the
beautiful Arno valley which stretched all the way from the snow-
capped Apennines to the sea.

Some people wished Florence were built on the coast, so she
could have a harbor, like Pisa. Personally he did not think much
of the idea. Not that he had ever seen the sea which, after all, was
fifty miles away, but he knew all about it from returning
travelers.

It was a vast expanse of blue water filled with strange fishes,
octopi, mermaids, and scaly-tailed dragons. In times of storm, it
turned green and swelled into liquid, foam-crested mountains that
swallowed ships and the sailors on them. Eventually it would lie
quiet again, but even then it continued to breathe noisily, harassing people with its endless pounding, making them ill or irritable
from lack of sleep.

All told, Florence was better off where she was and no doubt

it was the Madonna who had suggested her location to the good
Lord, for this was the city she truly loved, the only one she personally protected. And when those Genoese ruffians dared to say
she also loved their miserable town, they were liars, Turks, and
blasphemers! But then what could you expect from rogues who
presumed to compete with Florentine wares and Florentine banks!

Jealous, that's what they were. Jealous, like the Romans and
their crumbling ruins, the Venetians and their floating city that
might sink at any moment, the Neapolitans and their smoking
mountain, the Milanese with their flat and dull countryside — all
those foreigners who wished they had been born here, in the City
of Flowers, where everything was more beautiful than anywhere
else.

Like a loving gargoyle, he peered down on the slumbering
town.

"Fiorenza!" he murmured to himself.

There she was, the capital of the Red Lily Republic, with her
web of vassal towns spread all over Tuscany, her immense cathedral, her banks, her mills, her countless churches and hundred
and ten monasteries and nunneries, her great stone mansion where
lived "the fat ones." Soon, at the sound of his chimes, she would
awake and turn into a jumble of brown or reddish houses, a maze
of crisscrossing streets, a swarm of bustling shops, marketplaces
full of haggling housewives. But now, she slept peacefully behind
her forty-foot-high city wall. No one but he ever saw her like
this and for a few moments every morning she belonged to him.

Again he glanced eastward and this time there was a faint glow
over the hills. Night had thinned into a violet mist. The stars were
turning pale. Like a slow-spreading smile, dawn trembled on the
horizon.

Another day was being born.

He got up, walked to a small bell hanging from a beam and
rang the morning prayer. The gentle chimes floated down on the
tile roofs. Lights appeared in windows. Somewhere, a rooster
crowed.

He now stepped to a much larger bell, spat on his palms,

twirled the rope around his fists and pulled on it with all his might, as he scattered his waking carillon through the sky.

That morning, Noldo de'Gherardini, owner of the huge Gherardini Wool Mill and former president of the Wool Guild, awoke in his velvet-curtained four-poster, complaining of painful vapors in the head.

They were due, he declared, to the *campanaro*'s infernal din.

"It seems this fool of a friar wishes to wake the dead as well as the living," he said. "A good flogging, that's what he needs. I shall file a complaint with the Signoria."

"By all means, noble husband," nodded his wife, Lisa, the grandmother of the still unborn Mona Lisa, who had heard the threat before and calmly went on dressing.

Through a gap in the curtains, he watched her fasten her skirt of black serge around her slender waist, and her gestures aroused in him a drowsy, faintly erotic tenderness. Lisa, dear Lisa, still nimble and seemly she was at forty-eight. Or was it forty-nine? A good wife she had been to him, though tricky and a bit mulish at times. But then all females were like that. God had made them that way.

For a while he followed her movements as she walked to the Venetian mirror that reflected her pert and rosy face. He smiled as he saw her slip her white coif over her graying hair.

The years had been kind to Noldo de'Gherardini. A lifetime of orderly and successful living had left his round cheeks unlined and his brow unfurrowed. Time had only bared a patch of skull on the top of his head and hung a small bag of flabby flesh under his chin. At fifty-six, he looked somewhat like a petulant, gray-haired baby.

"People should not be jostled out of slumber," he grumbled on. "Not that I slept, mind you. With all the things on my mind, I did not shut my eyes."

She knew he had slept like a child, for she awoke the moment his snoring ceased, but she sympathized. "Noble husband, why don't you sleep another hour?"

He would not hear of it. How could she suggest such foolishness; had her brains gone down to her slippers? Didn't she know that a thousand urgent matters were awaiting him at the mill, a thousand problems that only he could solve, a thousand decisions that only he could make?

"And with Antonio away, I have no one to assist me," he added plaintively, "no one I really can trust."

Antonio was their twenty-two-year-old son. Three months ago he had left on his wool-buying journey through France, England, and the Low Countries. He was not expected back before October.

"That's why I must get up," he said with a feeble flutter of the coverlet. "And I want no more speech about it."

"What if you overtax yourself and fall into sickness?" she countered while lacing her bodice.

This, he replied, was a risk they must run. All they could do was hope that the Madonna would keep him alive, at least until Antonio's return. She retorted that the Madonna did not help those who insisted on killing themselves.

"I beseech you to sleep another hour."

How nice, he thought, to have someone worry over you, beseech you to do what you wanted to do anyway . . . He must not, however, give in too easily lest she became puffed up with pride and believed she could impose her wishes on him. Therefore, he repeated that his presence at the mill was indispensable, especially now when he was planning to branch into the production of *tintillano:* a very warm and delicate cloth made from the wool of stillborn lambs.

She did not reply, but walked to the bed, took his hand, and raised it to her lips. "God's grace, noble husband. May the Lord keep you well today."

"A good day to you also, wife," he mumbled back.

This had been their morning greeting for over thirty years and time had infused the words and gestures with muted tenderness.

As a rule, she then left the room; but that morning she remained by his bed, arguing that his health came before *tintillano,* and pleaded with him to sleep another hour. Finally he consented to do so.

"But only to please you."

She thanked him with a smile and gracefully fleeted out of the room. Alone, he congratulated himself on his cleverness. Then, pulling the coverlet to his chin, burrowed deeper into the mattress and slid into a shallow doze.

While he slept, Florence started another working day. Hordes of men, women, and children streamed across the four stone bridges to the San Spirito district where stood the great textile *stabilimenti*. In a city of seventy thousand inhabitants, thirty thousand worked in the wool industry alone; sixteen thousand in the silk and cotton trades.

Shopkeepers sorted their wares out in the streets. Masons mixed fresh mortar and their apprentices hauled the first loads of brick up building scaffolds. Girls in pigtails disappeared in the backroom of fashion or novelty shops. Bank clerks gathered around a statue of the Virgin and sang her litanies before scurrying to their quills, ledgers, and money-weighing scales.

On New Market Square, the Stock Exchange opened with the ringing of a silver bell and a short prayer. Then it exploded into a bedlam of gesticulating brokers shouting quotations of stocks, placing orders, hopping about like devils in holy water, for Florence's *Borsa* was then doing a daily business of over two million florins (about eight million dollars): a sum exceeding that of London's Exchange in the mid-nineteenth century.

In churches, yawning, disheveled *dipintori* resumed work on their frescoes of bearded saints, bleeding martyrs, and gold-winged angels. And in Verrocchio's *bottega* — a combination art shop and art school — apprentices in blue hose ground pigments in stone cruets, sanded picture panels, or made charcoal copies of the master's paintings, under the friendly eye of the studio foreman, the handsome, twenty-three-year-old Leonardo da Vinci.

Noldo was awakened by the entrance of Chirigora, a buxom Oriental woman in a yellow turban and blue calico blouse.

"Blessings on you, master," she said.

"The same to you," he replied, watching her set the jar of hot water by the washbasin.

She was in her forties, heavy-hipped and slow-moving, but he recalled how lovely she had been, at thirteen, when she had arrived from Venice where she had been bought at a slave auction. She then had been doe-eyed and soft-lipped; her skin the color of pale amber. For a few years she had given pleasure to his honored father and, on the sly, to him. In time, she had grown fat and flabby-breasted, no longer suitable for lovemaking, but good enough for housework.

"How brief is youth," he sighed, as she padded out of the room.

A moment later his valet, Pandolfo, entered, a smile on his face, his shaving tools under his arm.

"God's grace, master," he said, helping him out of bed and into a long flannel shirt. "Such an amusing story I have for you this morning!"

He had been born in the Gherardini mansion where his father had served as butler. For this reason, he was almost regarded as a member of the family. In addition to being Noldo's valet, he supervised the service at supper.

While lathering the old merchant's cheeks, he told him the story of Cristofana, a parlormaid in the district, who had inadvertently swallowed a devil while eating a lettuce leaf.

Devils were horrid, minuscule red creatures with grimacing human faces, horns in their foreheads, and long, curled tails. They could be swallowed while eating, inhaled while sleeping. They could hide in the fold of a sleeve, a nostril, a tooth cavity. A theologian had calculated their number at 4,405,928, organized in a well-regulated society under the kingship of Satan.

"So there she was, this poor Cristofana wench, with a devil in her belly," said Pandolfo honing his razor, "and it would have made you cry to see what this devil made her do."

Usually a pious and modest female, she had turned into a wanton who shouted obscenities and lifted her skirt high above her waist. The parish priest had been called for and he had come running with a pail of holy water, a crucifix, and a pair of cymbals.

He had held the cross before the girl who had stuck out her tongue at it. He had sprinkled her with holy water, flogged her buttocks, crashed his cymbals in order to frighten the devil out. All to no avail.

Finally a barber-surgeon had been called. He knew what to do. In the twinkling of an eye, he had given Cristofana an enema of onion juice and — praised be the Lord! — this had done the trick. The spectators (for the room was full of people) had clearly seen the devil, weeping and holding his nose, jut out of her nostril.

By now, Noldo had been shaved, and with a little chuckle, he proceeded with his abulations. Methodically he washed his face, rubbed chestnut ashes on his few remaining teeth, scraped his tongue with a double-edged ivory blade, gargled with lemon water. This done, he donned the freshly ironed *lucco* — a woolen kimonolike robe that fell to his ankles — which Pandolfo held out to him. Then, clamping on the red fezlike *berretta* he wore at home, he decorously went down to the dining room.

Lisa was waiting for him, a faint smile in her eyes.

"I see your vapors have cleared," she said, curtsying to him. "This hour of sleep did you much good."

Noldo did not reply, for it was not proper for a wife to address her husband unless invited to, and if you encouraged this sort of thing, you would never breakfast in peace again. He disposed of a vegetable soup, two soft-boiled eggs, gruel pancakes, and fruit. The meal over, he dabbed his lips with the tablecloth and rose from his chair.

Lisa escorted him to the foyer where he exchanged his *berretta* for the formal *cappuccio a foggia* — a round, brimless hat with a swath of cloth on one side. Again she wished him God's grace, as he started down the stairs to the courtyard where Tommaso was waiting, holding a horse by the bridle.

The groom raised Noldo's foot into the stirrup; then, with a respectful shove on his master's backside, he helped him on to the saddle. The merchant straightened his hat, gathered the reins in one hand, and emerged from his house. In a placid clipclop of hooves, he crossed the piazza, lounged along the Arno for a while, rode across the Trinity Bridge and finally arrived at his mill. With Tommaso in tow, he made his way through a vast courtyard and stopped at the door of the administration building where, once again, his manservant helped him down to the ground.

His office was on the second floor, a large corner room with a commanding view of the mill's various structures and, in the distance, a silvery strip of the river. The furniture consisted of a massive desk, several cupboards, and wall shelves on which lay bolts of the firm's various fabrics.

He filled the remainder of the morning with the usual chores of management. He checked invoices and bills of lading, read letters from his agents in Italy and abroad, and replied with long and detailed missives urging them to ever greater feats of salesmanship.

He then summoned the mill's technical director and once again they discussed the *tintillano* project. The venture promised vast profits, but would require the building of a new annex as well as the installation of special machinery. In short, a large outlay of time and money.

For a while his face remained clouded in perplexity.

"A mill must expand or perish," he finally declared and gave the order to proceed with the *tintillano* venture.

Once alone, he planned to set a beautiful statue of the Madonna in the annex and at a place where the workers could see her — and she, them. She would incite them to work hard and, to please her, they would do so. Thus, in a manner of speaking she would be his silent partner. With such an associate, success was assured.

Early in the afternoon he started on his early tour of inspection.

For a while he meandered through the weaving rooms, stopping now and then to shout a few words over the din of clattering looms to some old *tessitore*. He waved at the women tending the carding and spinning machines. They smiled at him, for he was a considerate, though hard-driving employer. Some sang at their tasks. He concluded they were satisfied.

"And no wonder," he thought, "with the wages I pay them!"

He also stopped at the repair shop where hairy-chested men,

naked to the waist, were pounding hammers on red-hot lumps of iron. From there he went to the shipping hangar where he watched the weighing and sealing of bales.

He ended his tour with a visit to the wool-washing shed where, as a boy, he had begun his apprenticeship. Other boys were now kneeling at the trough where he had knelt at twelve. They lifted their little faces at him and grinned. He grinned back, and for a fleeting instant he was tempted to raise their wages. By the time he returned to his office, he had conquered the impulse.

As there was nothing urgent for him to do, he reclined on his chair, his fingers twined over his paunch.

For a while he listened to the muted clatter of his looms rising from the surrounding buildings. Though he had heard it all his life, he had never grown tired of it. To him, it was the heartbeat of his mill. For over two hundred years it had thumped without a pause, growing stouter with the years, and no doubt it would continue to beat like this till the end of time.

His gaze moved to the small adjacent alcove where Antonio used to work. A good boy, Tonio was: respectful, intelligent, and capable in matters of business.

A pang of longing brought a sudden moistness to Noldo's eyes. In vain did he remind himself that Tonio would be back in October. October was still seven months away, and that was a long time, a very long time.

He felt himself growing emotional. Quickly he rang the small silver bell on his desk and instructed his secretary to have his horse brought to the door. On his way back home he stopped at the headquarters of the Wool Guild, where he played two hands of *scartino*, a popular card game, with a retired colleague of his and promptly lost twenty florins.

He did not let this dampen his spirits and still was in a genial mood when he returned to his house.

In the foyer he replaced his *cappuccio* with his red *berretta* and was informed by a parlormaid that Donna Lisa was not at home. Her friend Donna Lucrezia de'Medici had come to fetch her, and the two ladies had gone out together.

With a nod of acknowledgment, he laboriously climbed to the *loggia*, a small covered terrace on the roof. Barely had he eased himself on the wicker lounge chair than the maid reappeared, this time with a tray on which stood a decanter of Spanish wine and a silver goblet. She filled the cup, bobbed a curtsy, and withdrew.

Alone, Noldo gazed at the familiar panorama of steeples and towers rising between the columns of the *loggia*. The afternoon was ebbing to an end and the sky had turned amber with sunshine afterglow. An air of lassitude hung over the town.

He, too, felt pleasantly weary. It was nice sitting like this after a hard day at the office, enjoying the knowledge that all was well with Florence as well as his mill, and that he now was sizeably richer than he had been in the morning.

Noldo was the kind of man who would probably have become rich, even had he been born poor. He had made things easier for himself by being born in one of the town's noblest and richest clans.

Since their arrival in Florence in the year 910, the Gherardini had counted among "the fat ones." In Por San Maria district, near Ponte Vecchio, they owned their family tower, a symbol of financial, as well as social, prominence. It boasted a fine Corinthian capital and two Etruscan lions' heads.

They slept in beds instead of straw pads on the floor, ate from pewter plates, not out of wooden bowls like the *popolani*, the common people. Thirty-eight among them had been granted the privilege of wearing gold spurs, a much-prized distinction. In processions, they rode immediately behind the bishop. Socially, they had achieved the pinnacle of success.

And, of course, they married well.

In those days only the poor married for love (which was one reason why they remained poor) and the Gherardini intended to remain rich. From the earliest days they had made a point to demand from their future daughters-in-law impeccable pedigrees as well as large dowries.

If the dowries were large enough, they had even been known to close their eyes to the absence of pedigree. This had been the case with the Medici who had begun their prodigious ascension as lowly pawnbrokers. When they had become the richest local family, they had acquired social aspirations and one of their first targets had been the Gherardini, who had consented to mingle their blue blood with that of the plebeian Medici heiresses. Not just once, but three times.

In 1351 Guelfo de'Gherardini, Florence's ambassador to the Holy See, and his brother Francesco, Florence's ambassador to Bologna, had wed respectively Leonarda and Venna de'Medici. A few years later Tita de'Gherardini had married the son of Tanai de'Medici, an enormously rich man.

Several Gherardini had entered politics with mixed results. Their fortune fluctuated with that of the Guelf faction. When it came to power, they rose to the highest positions in the state, fulfilled the most important missions. When it lost power, they were thrown in prison, ambushed and murdered at night, or sent in exile to France, England, and even Poland. Two of them had had their heads cut off.

There were also sensible Gherardini who shunned honors and went after money.

Cecco de'Gherardini had been among the first to steal the *Umiliati*'s secrets of fabrication. In 1260 Jacopo de'Gherardini was already president of the Wool Guild and one of the earliest "lords of the looms." With the passing of time, members of the clan had spread into banking and the "noble" trade of winemaking. They had acquired vast fortunes and lived obscure, contented lives.

Noldo's father had been one of these. At his death, the Gherardini Mill had become one of the leading firms in the wool industry. He had carefully supervised his son's apprenticeship, moving him from one department to another, raising him to the position of assistant manager, patiently listening to the innovations he advocated, and finally, in order to have peace, sending him on an extended wool-buying journey throughout Europe.

On his return, Noldo had been wed to Lisa Rucellai, from a great merchant family. She had brought him the freshness of her fourteen years, the sparkle of her eyes, and a large dowry of fifteen hundred florins.

He might have learned to love her, but his father having died shortly after the wedding, he had assumed the management of the *stabilimenti*. Endowed with exceptional business acumen, he had launched various innovations which had proved immensely lucrative. Under his direction, the mill had grown into an industrial complex employing nearly two thousand workers. At forty, he had been elected a director of the Wool Guild; the following year, its president.

Through that period of his life, he had been something of a man about town and maintained an expensive Venetian courtesan, as a matter of prestige more than passion. Then, one day, he had calculated that the raptures she dispensed were out of proportion to their cost and he had severed the relationship.

Henceforth, he had patronized the more exclusive bathhouses where he could wade in a large wooden tub in the company of fetching and naked wenches, partake of a light meal, and later enjoy a relaxing massage as well as the girl who gave it, all for three florins. Altogether much better value than the Venetian strumpet . . .

In time, he had wearied of bathhouse wenches and started spending more evenings at home, especially in winter when it was too cold to go to play cards at the guild. He had begun to notice his wife and what a delightful woman she was. One day after supper he had invited her to keep him company in his den or *studiolo*, where she had never been asked before. Thereafter, they had spent their evenings together by the fire: he, on a capacious leather chair; she, on a three-legged stool.

And so the years had passed. The bare spot on the top of his head had grown from the size of a florin to that of a pancake. His stomach had rounded into a paunch. Stealthily love had entered his aging heart. He did, however, take pains to conceal his feelings, for females were quick to ensnare a man foolish enough to reveal his infatuation.

He was brought out of his musings by the reappearance of the maid, who announced that Donna Lisa had returned and was awaiting his pleasure in the dining room.

They dined in companionable silence, eating from the same

plate, drinking from the same goblet. The service was assured by two table servants under the watchful eye of Pandolfo, now resplendent in white gloves and livery. After dessert, he placed a fresh decanter of Malaga wine before Noldo and filled his goblet. Then, with a discreet snap of fingers he signaled the two maids to withdraw.

No sooner were they gone than the merchant let out a muted belch to signify his appreciation of the meal. Then, pulling a silver toothpick from the purse at his belt, he began picking his teeth, politely holding his hand before his mouth, like the well-bred gentleman he was.

"I hear that Donna Lucrezia came to fetch you," he said to make conversation. "Where did you go?"

"To the Orphanage of the Innocents where I had a nice talk with the mother superior —"

He had learned that talks with the mother superior invariably ended in requests for donations. Rising from his chair, he suggested they repair to his *studiolo*.

It was a small room at the rear of the mansion. It had a hooded fireplace and, on the floor, a Persian carpet with the rich coloring of a stained-glass window. There was also a desk, a painted cupboard in which he kept family papers and his gold chain of office as president of the Wool Guild. A painting of the Virgin with the Babe in her arms smiled down from the wall.

They took their usual places by the fire, and to fill the silence, he told her about the *tintillano* venture. She continued to gaze at the flames and from the rigidity of her features, he sensed she was thinking about Antonio.

She had borne him four children. The first, a boy, had lived but a few hours: an unbroken howl of pain between two eternities of silence; then twin girls who had grown into laughing, babbling tots only to die on the same day from the plague. For the next ten years she had been barren and had nearly lost hope when Antonio was born, but so delicate that he was not expected to live. She had kept him alive by the sheer force of her love. In the end, she had won. Antonio had grown into a tall, robust, and loving boy.

"On his return," Noldo went on, hoping to cheer her up, "I'll put him in charge of the *tintillano* operations."

"No use troubling yourself, noble husband," she said without looking at him, "for he will never return. If pirates don't kill him on the sea, highwaymen will surely kill him on land."

He tried being jocular about it. "Don't make the chickens laugh! There are no more pirates, no more highwaymen."

"And what if some French or English wench makes sheep's eyes at him and steals his purse? What if he falls ill of some foreign fever, if some dragon rises from the sea and swallows the ship he is on?"

He reminded her that he had had three masses said for Antonio's protection. "They cost me five florins and I have the priest's word that Tonio would be adequately protected."

What did that old fool know about traveling in foreign lands, she scoffed, he who had never been further than Prato?

Never had he seen her so overwrought. Nothing remained of the meek and obedient Lisa he knew. Her manner bristled with defiance. "Besides, what kind of protection could you expect for five florins?"

He retorted that five florins was a sizable sum and money did not grow on trees. However, as a conciliatory gesture, he would give her an additional florin to spend on candles to the Virgin.

He expected some mark of appreciation, some expression of gratitude, but none came. Candles, she shrugged, might protect a traveler on a jaunt to Siena or Arezzo, but they were of no use on a long journey in distant lands.

He recognized the peculiar inflection that came into her voice when she went into one of her mulish moods. She then could be very stubborn and there was no telling what she might do.

"What would you consider an adequate sum for Antonio's protection?" he asked.

"Twenty-five florins."

His eyebrows shot up, his mouth sagged. He almost choked. "Twenty-five —"

"The mother superior said —"

He did not let her finish. "I knew it," he exploded, "I knew she was behind this." Then, in a voice heavy with sarcasm, he added, "And what does your dear mother superior propose to do with those twenty-five florins?"

It seemed there was at the orphanage a poor girl — very sweet, very pious — who had a chance to wed a fine young man if only she could bring a dowry of twenty-five florins.

"If she is so pious," he sneered, "why doesn't she enter a nunnery? Better still, why doesn't she become a bathhouse wench and earn her dowry while learning a trade?"

He was beside himself. His face had turned a purplish red. So flustered was he that he interrupted himself to blow his nose into the fireplace, a thing he would never have done in normal circumstances.

"Tell your mother superior she will get not a *lira*, not a *quattrino*, not a *picciolo* from me. And I want no more speech about it."

Like a pall, silence fell over the *studiolo*.

Angrily, he poked at the logs to conceal his inner turmoil. He felt righteous, secure in the justice of his cause. He had been kind, understanding, generous, and she had repulsed his advances. That old hag of a mother superior had put into her head that Antonio needed more protection and frightened her out of her wits.

Furtively, he glanced sideways at her. She looked so heartbroken that his heart went out to her. He wanted to give her the money but his prestige was at stake. He must show her he could be firm, implacable.

At last, she broke the silence.

"Noble husband," she said, looking at him over her shoulder, "I did not know we were so poor. Please, do not torment yourself over the money. I still have the brooch you gave me at the time of our wedding. Tomorrow I shall take it to a moneylender —"

A moneylender! Had she taken leave of her senses? Did she want to ruin him in the eyes of his colleagues? Didn't she know that in the five hundred years that the Gherardini had lived in Florence, no Gherardini woman had ever — ever! — set foot in a pawnshop?

"I don't care," she said, in that mulish voice of hers. "I want Antonio to be protected, really protected."

And not just haphazardly by a busy, absentminded God, but every minute, night and day, by a loving Madonna. For that, she was ready to go to ten moneylenders, make a deal with Satan himself.

"I want him back in good health," she sobbed in her cupped hands.

He placed a hand on her shoulder.

"Do not grieve, wife. Rather than having to go to a money-lender, I shall give you the money myself."

Already, he regretted his impulse, but it was too late. She was peeking at him through her fingers, smiling at him behind her tears. What else could he do but nod?

"Lord God will bless you for that," she said. "And you'll see, the Madonna will watch over your *tintillano*."

Impulsively, she seized his hand and kissed it.

Of course, it was most improper, but for once he did not mind her forwardness. Or the money either. For a fleeting instant, he savored one of the pleasures of the rich, that of giving money away. It was worth all the florins in the world to see her smiling like this and looking so happy.

On March twenty-fifth the new year arrived in Florence with loud and festive morning chimes; but, this time, Noldo did not complain. He bounced out of bed, slipped into a flannel shirt, for people slept naked in those days, and predicted that 1476 would be a fine, prosperous year. He could, he told Lisa, feel it in his bones.

"And it will bring back Antonio," she echoed.

That morning, he was helped by his valet into a formal red *lucco* and his heavy gold chain of office as president of the Wool Guild was slipped around his neck and spread over his chest. One hour later he was walking, together with former officials of the guild, in the traditional New Year's procession, a lighted taper in his hand and singing the Virgin's litanies.

In the afternoon he ambled through the town, stopping to watch cockfights, acrobats, and dancing bears. On his return home, he told Lisa that the festivities had been fair, but in no way comparable to those of his youth.

"Then we knew how to enjoy ourselves," he declared, "but nowadays the young are as zestful as dead fish."

April came with its motley skies and teasing showers. The surrounding hills received their yearly coat of green grass. At dusk, youngsters in feathered *berrettas* plucked their lutes under the windows of pretty girls. Lovelorn maidens left bunches of violets at the foot of statues of the Madonna in street shrines.

Then it was May, and the weather turned so mild that Noldo announced one evening at supper that he would go to Piazza della Signoria and listen to the news.

"You never can tell what those confounded popes may have on their minds," he said ominously, "especially the one now sitting on Saint Peter's Chair."

For centuries, relations between the Republic of the Red Lily and the autocratic Holy See had been strained, oftentimes stormy. On several occasions pontiffs had hurled their armies at the City of Flowers, and the Florentines believed that it was only due to the Madonna's intervention that their state had not become a Church domain.

Although the situation had greatly improved since the accession to power of the Medici, the people of Florence continued to eye succeeding pontiffs with suspicion, none more than the present one, Sixtus IV, better known as *Papa Sisto*.

For one thing, he had been born in Savona, a Ligurian fishing village, and that practically made him a Genoese and therefore a black-hearted, serpent-tongued, treacherous rogue.

A poor fisherman's son, Francesco Rovere had been educated by the local Franciscans, taken the orders, and rapidly climbed the ladder of the Franciscan hierarchy. At fifty, he was General of the Order; three years later, a cardinal.

Having become a prince of the Church, the fisherman's son had proceeded to make himself a prince of the earth, for this *popolano* had aristocratic aspirations. Profiting from a similarity of names, Francesco Rovere had grafted his lowly self on the illustrious family tree of the *della* Rovere, lords of Vinovo, in Piedmont.

This done, he had prepared his elevation to the papacy, bringing to this goal an indomitable will, his Ligurian cunning, and a total absence of scruples. In August 1471, he had achieved his ambition in an election so openly venal that it had shocked the Roman populace, jaded as they were on such matters, and the new pontiff's litter had been pelted with stones.

In the course of his Church career, Sixtus had found time to sire two sons, Girolamo and Pietro, who passed as the offspring of his sister Iolanda. As she had twelve children of her own, the addition had passed unnoticed.

Immediately after his coronation, the Holy Shepherd had called the two strapping young men to Rome, where they had displayed the manners and speech of the Savona waterfront. Garbed in silks and velvets, they had plunged into gambling and low debauchery. In no time they were loathed by everyone. Everyone but their doting father.

By a strange twist of his nature, this cold, scheming monk was possessed of a blind, all-forgiving love for his two worthless sons. In his eyes, they could do no wrong, nor could he do enough for them.

Pietro, he had decided, would succeed him on the papal throne. In no time, the young rake was made Cardinal of Sansisto, Patriarch of Constantinople, Archbishop of Sevilla, Bishop of Trevison, Carpentras, and Avignon. Unfortunately, these honors had not induced the new prelate to change his way of life. He continued to gamble and wench as before, with the result that, at twenty-eight, he died from general exhaustion and a variety of venereal diseases.

When he recovered from his grief, Sixtus had turned his undivided attention on his surviving son, Girolamo, and vowed he would become one of Italy's ruling princes. As a first step in this direction, he had bethrothed the thirty-year-old profligate to

Caterina Sforza, aged eight, the ravishing and illegitimate daughter of the duke of Milan, in the hope that his highness would fornicate himself into an early grave and thus provide Girolamo with an opportunity of seizing the ducal throne.

As the prince showed no sign of fatigue, the Florentines worried that His Holiness might tire of waiting and choose another target, possibly Florence.

"That's why I want to learn what he is doing," said Noldo, draining his goblet of Spanish wine and rising from the table.

A moment later, preceded by his lantern-carrying groom, he was making his way to Piazza della Signoria.

In the orange glow of resin torches, the square looked larger than it really was. Burghers in robes of many hues crowded around returned travelers who brought news from various countries. Off the coast of Spain, a shipment of damask had been seized by pirates . . . In Venice, a comely thirteen- or fourteen-year-old Circassian slave, "guaranteed a virgin," cost you sixty or sixty-five florins . . . The king of Naples, Don Ferrante of Aragon, was waging war on his barons as usual, and placing in his palace the embalmed corpses of those he captured . . .

Noldo joined a group of listeners who encircled a merchant, just back from Rome, who answered as best he could the questions that were flung at him from all sides. Was *Papa Sisto* in a good mood or was he morose, like a man planning some mischief? Was he hiring soldiers? Was he buying cannons or reviewing his troops?

Nothing of the kind, replied the traveler. The pope was having his ugly face imprinted on Roman coins. He was building churches, a bridge, and his own Sistine Chapel. He had just received the king of Denmark, a northern country mainly populated by wolves and bears, and given his blessing to the University of Copenhagen. In short, he was much too busy to plan any mischief.

Reassured, Noldo walked to another part of the piazza and went from group to group, gleaning news along the way.

The silk mill near the San Frediano Gate had received an important order from Portugal . . . In his Sunday sermon, the San Pancrazio priest had railed against his parishioners who dropped counterfeit coins in the collection pouch . . . Complaints had been received about housewives who emptied their slop jars from their windows without looking to see who might be passing by; beautiful garments had been ruined that way . . . The residents of the Por San Maria district had petitioned the Signoria for another public baking oven . . . Stockbrokers were circulating a petition for the building of a public latrine near *la Borsa*. At present, they had to relieve themselves in the streets, which was indecorous . . .

In the center of the piazza, a glove salesman held his listeners spellbound with his description of the French king's entrance in his town of Paris, which he had witnessed. At the city gate, the monarch had been received by the guilds, the clergy, the state officials, the faculty of the Sorbonne University, and three gracious maidens, entirely naked, who had presented him with the keys of the city on a velvet pillow, while dancing and singing most fetchingly.

At last the curfew bell tolled its somber chimes. Groups unraveled. Burghers lit their lanterns and started for their homes, singly or in pairs. On Piazza della Signoria, torches were snuffed out by city employees and night descended upon the town. The streets, so crowded and noisy a few hours ago, now lay still and empty, like furrows of darkness under the starry sky. Now and then, a night watchman walked by, thumping his halberd and chanting his lonely call; then, all was silence again.

Florence had lived through another day.

By mid-July the heat had become unbearable. Anyone who could afford to do so had left for the hills. Only the poor and Noldo de'Gherardini remained in town.

"Noble husband," Lisa remarked at breakfast, "it is so hot that a devil fainted yesterday and drowned in the milk jar. Don't you think we should go to the country? You look peaked and the fresh air would do you good."

He rested on his plate the fig he was about to gobble.

Of course, he looked peaked; of course, the fresh air would do him good, but the *tintillano* annex was being built and he must supervise its construction if he wanted it to be ready by October when Antonio would return.

"So, you see, I have no choice but to stay here," he added, "and I want no more speech about it."

It took her three days to make him change his mind.

She began the following morning. Oh, how they must laugh behind his back, all those young assistants of his who earned enormous salaries for twiddling their thumbs while he, a poor tired man, was killing himself. The next day she let out a sigh and remarked how sad it was to think that their beautiful Montici villa stood empty while here everyone was dying of the heat. Chirigora could not walk anymore, so swollen were her legs. The cook had hallucinations from standing at the stove. The parlormaids lay prostrated, lacking the strength to sweep or dust.

He replied that she could go to Montici if she wished, and take the servants with her. As for him, nothing would deflect him from his duty.

The third morning she predicted he would never see Antonio or the finished annex, for by October he would be dead and buried in the family crypt. He did not say anything, but gave her a dark look.

That afternoon, on his return from the mill, as they sat on the *loggia*, fanning themselves, he announced he had decided to entrust his technical director with the supervision of the *tintillano* annex.

"If some difficulty arises, he will ride to Montici and I shall tell him what to do."

She complimented him on his decision and two days later they left for Montici, where from time immemorial, the Gherardini had been lords. Their crest can still be seen on the façade of the village church.

Upon his arrival at the villa, Noldo abandoned himself to the joys of country living. In a wide-brimmed straw hat and linen *lucco*, he pottered in the garden, took long siestas, roamed

through the vineyard, the orchard, and the olive grove. He even
visited his tenant farmers who lived on the edge of the estate.

This occupied a few days. Then he found himself with nothing
to do and time began to weigh on his hands. He fretted about the
tintillano annex and wished his technical director would come
with some difficult problem, but no one came.

Most of all, he missed Antonio, and so did Lisa. They talked
about him, recalled touching little incidents of his childhood. Occasionally, she would ask him to read aloud the letter they had
received, which had been brought by a returning Florentine salesman Antonio had met in the course of his journey. Noldo would
then remove the rolled parchment from its leather protective
tube, straddle a pair of iron-rimmed spectacles on his nose and begin reading, stopping now and then to make comments.

After the usual introduction to his "most worshipful genitors,"
Antonio described his arrival in *Londra*, an immense English city
with streets narrower and, if possible, fouler smelling than those
of Florence. He and his manservant Battista had been graciously
received by the London Gherardini agent who had insisted on
having him stay at his house during his sojourn. Battista had been
given a fine pad of straw in the servants' quarters.

Accompanied by the agent, Antonio had visited the shops that
stocked Gherardini wares and received many compliments for
their high quality.

English females were remarkable by their comeliness; the men
by their florid complexion which they owed to the large quanti-
ties of meat they ate and hard spirits they drank. People were exceedingly fond of plays and in the city of *Londra* alone, several
theaters operated the year round. He had attended a performance
and noticed that seemly wenches circulated among spectators
during the spectacle selling oranges from Spain.

Antonio went on to say that he planned to depart in a few days
for Scotland, a northern region famous for its wool, its spirits,
and the fighting temper of its people. The letter ended with the
customary salutations and the assurance he would be back in
Florence by October, as agreed.

"This journey will do him a world of good," Noldo remarked

one day, removing his spectacles. "On his return it will be time for him to take a wife, and I shall have a marriage broker show me his list of marriageable girls."

This was the opportunity Lisa had been waiting for a long time and she rested her sewing on her lap.

"How wise of you to think of such a thing!" she exclaimed. "But maybe I can save you the broker's fee for I know of a fine maiden for Antonio."

He darted her a frowning glance. Marriage was a serious business requiring much perspicacity, judicious weighing of pros and cons, protracted considerations over pedigrees, dowries, and other such things much beyond the female intellect. Her remark, however, had pricked his curiosity and he asked who might be this maiden of hers.

"Caterina," she said, "Caterina Rucellai, daughter of my cousin Mariotto."

He let out a good-humored chuckle.

"Haha, a relative! I should've known it. You Rucellais stick together like the two halves of an oyster."

She ignored his bantering tone. "Have you found me such an unworthy wife that you should detest the prospect of one such as myself for our son?"

With a deprecatory gesture, he assured her he meant no offense. As wives went, she had been a good one. "But I have already married you, and one Rucellai is enough. Your suggestion, however, is not without merit and I shall give it some thought."

He did think about it and the more he did, the more attractive it became.

The Rucellais were one of Florence's wealthiest and most distinguished families. The family fortune stemmed from a beautiful crimson purple dye — *oricello* — which had been brought back from the Levant in 1261, the secret of which they had jealously kept for over two centuries.

The head of the clan, Giovanni Rucellai, was a merchant prince as famous for his good deeds as for his wealth. He had paid for the marble facing of Santa Maria Novella Church, and his name was carved on it. He lived in the splendid Palazzo Rucellai on Via

Vigna Nuova. His younger son, Bernardo, had wed Lorenzo de'Medici's sister Nannina in a memorable ceremony which had lasted three days.

Mariotto Rucellai, Caterina's father, was perhaps the most distinguished member of this distinguished family. He was prominent in banking, a profession for which Noldo nursed tender feelings. His success in this field had earned him the presidency of the Bankers' Guild in 1468, at the age of thirty-four.

Like his father, who had been treasurer of the Republic, or finance minister, he joined an interest in politics to his financial activities. At the age of thirty, he had headed the Signoria as *gonfaloniere,* a fact almost unique in Florence's long history. Since then, he had filled important public functions and become one of Lorenzo de'Medici's most trusted advisers.

All this, Noldo reflected, promised well. A former president of the Bankers' Guild would be able to give his daughter a satisfactory dowry.

Caterina Rucellai was becoming daily more attractive. No prospective daughter-in-law could fulfill more completely the Gherardini requirements of lineage and wealth.

She deserved further investigation.

"This maiden of yours," he asked one afternoon with studied casualness, "how old is she?"

"Fifteen, noble husband. Just the right age."

"Is she plain or pleasing to the eye? I should not want an unseemly female for Antonio."

Caterina, she protested, was most seemly, and her beauty was not only of face alone but of the soul as well. Moreover, she was pious, respectful, obedient, even-tempered. She could cook, count on the abacus, plan menus, haggle with the peddlers who came to the kitchen door. In short, she would give Antonio a thrifty, efficient household. And, of course, many sons.

In addition, she played well on the lute.

The thoroughness of her information made him suspicious. "Methinks you know a great deal about this maiden. By chance, did you and her mother arrange this marriage?"

Quickly she resumed her sewing and replied that she and

Donna Filippa Rucellai had touched upon the subject, but in the most casual way.

The autumn rains came early in furious September squalls that tore leaves off the trees and sent the residents of the Montici villas scurrying back to town.

Noldo's first care was to ride to the mill. No one had come to seek his advice and he vaguely hoped for some tragic blunder, some irreparable miscalculation. He found everything in order. The annex was built, the new machinery installed, the statue of the Madonna standing on a corner shelf on the wall.

He went home in a depressed mood. Factories, he brooded, were like children. When they grew big, they no longer needed you.

During the following weeks, he made discreet inquiries about Caterina's father. With delight he learned that Mariotto was even richer than he thought. He attended mass at Santa Maria Novella Church – the Rucellai church – and caught a glimpse of Caterina's profile, as she stood between her parents, reading her prayer book. She was, as Lisa had said, most seemly. Everything was for the best.

That evening he remarked, "Wife, you are a meddlesome female, but if this Caterina is half what she appears, she will make a fine wife for my son."

"Our son."

"All right, our son."

Antonio arrived one October morning, unannounced and followed by his manservant leading by the bridle a baggage-laden mule.

Lisa, who had been discussing the day's menu with the cook, stopped in mid-sentence, whirled on her heels, and fled down the stairs to the courtyard, weeping, laughing, and blessing the Madonna, all at the same time.

"*Tonio, bimbo mio!*" she cried when she saw him.

Raising on her toes, she took the face of the strapping *bimbo* between her hands and pelted it with kisses. By now, the excitement had spread through the house. From various doors, servants emerged and clustered around the returning traveler. On the second floor, a window was flung open. Half-shaven and flustered, Noldo appeared, asking the cause of the *tumulto*. At the sight of his son, he stifled a cry of joy; then, in a stentorian voice he summoned him to his *studiolo*.

A moment later, freshly shaven and wrapped in a maroon velvet lounge robe, he entered the room.

"Welcome home, my son," he said, giving him his hand to kiss. "It is good to have you back."

He sat down at the desk, crossed his fingers over his paunch, and for a few instants considered the tall young man standing before him in his leather breeches and long traveling cloak. His face was bronzed from riding in all weathers. His shoulders seemed to have grown wider. Never had he looked so well. The Madonna had indeed watched over him well.

"Honored Father," began Antonio, "I am pleased to find you in good health."

This was the wrong thing to say. Appearances, Noldo retorted, could be deceptive. He might look well, but the truth was that he was overworked and in poor health.

"While you were gadding about Europe, attending plays and eyeing orange-selling wenches, I was working without respite. But, praise the Lord, the *tintillano* annex is completed and we are ready to begin operations."

He went on to say that Antonio would be in charge of operations. This, of course, in addition to his former duties.

"But let's not talk of such things," he went on with a benevolent gesture. "No doubt you will want to visit with your honored mother and see a few friends. And so you may have the whole day off. Tomorrow morning will be soon enough for you to start working."

Antonio bowed dutifully. As he stepped out of the room, he reflected that his worshipful genitor had not changed. Nevertheless, it was nice to be home.

That evening, after supper, Noldo informed Lisa she might

arrange a meeting with her cousin Mariotto so that they could discuss the matter of Caterina's dowry.

Mariotto Rucellai was one of those men who grow handsome with the years.

At forty-two, an advanced age in the Renaissance, he looked better than at twenty. His graying hair softened the ruggedness of his features. Although deeply lined, his face remained lean, and beneath bushy eyebrows his eyes retained the alertness of youth.

Like many Tuscan men, Mariotto combined a cool, logical mind with an emotional temperament. He had little patience for mediocre or stupid people and was given to violent but brief fits of anger. Born to great wealth, he had the poise that usually goes with it and the optimism of those who are used to success. He laughed easily.

He had married twice. His first wife, Camilla de'Uggucioni, had died in childbirth, leaving him a widower at twenty-one. Five years later he had wed Filippa de'Venturi, from one of Florence's oldest families and a beauty, besides. She had made him a splendid wife and presented him with three sons and two daughters and, only a year ago, to her stupefaction and everyone else's, another girl, who had been named Camilla and was presently sleeping in her cradle.

Filippa's loveliness had been the bait that had attracted him, but she had held him through her qualities of heart and mind. In time, infatuation had turned into love. Each had a great respect for the other. Within the bounds of Renaissance etiquette, he treated her almost as an equal. On occasion he would be unable to contain his admiration of her intelligence and judgment. He would then gaze at her in wonder and declare she had a man's mind. Which was his idea of the highest compliment he could pay a woman.

Since he was extremely busy, he had come to rely on her not only for the management of his household, but also for the selection of the wives and husbands for their various children. Thus, he was not surprised and raised no objection when she announced that Antonio de'Gherardini had just returned from his wool-buying trip and that, in her opinion, he would make a fine husband for their daughter Caterina.

Since the previous year, when Caterina had reached marriageable age, he had braced himself for the news. He would have liked to keep her a little longer, for she was a sweet and obedient child and the house would be lonely without her at supper and at Sunday mass. But the time had come for her to leave the nest and what could he do but bow to the laws of nature?

As the Gherardini name was in itself a guarantee of financial and social prominence, he dispensed with the usual preliminary questions.

"Are you in agreement with Antonio's mother in this matter?" he inquired.

She nodded, and her gesture implied that all problems had been discussed and amicably solved between the two women. Lisa had even promised to coax her husband Noldo into giving Antonio a house of his own, so that Caterina would not have to live in that old and musty Gherardini Palazzo, which did not have any modern conveniences, not even glass panes in windows.

She went on to say that Noldo was ready to meet him and discuss the terms of the marriage contract. Mariotto replied he would be glad to meet him the following Tuesday, early in the afternoon, on Piazza della Signoria.

And so the two men met, as if by chance, and expressed surprise at running unexpectedly into each other. Both wore a *cappucio a foggia*, their gold seal rings on their thumbs, and, over the *lucco*, a sleeveless, fur-lined cloak, for it was a chilly November day. They exchanged a few remarks about the weather. Then Noldo suggested they repair to the Snail's Inn for a tankard of hot wine.

The room was deserted, yet they selected an isolated corner table to ensure their privacy. Covertly, they studied each other while the serving wench set between them a single tall and lidded pewter mug. When she was gone, each took a sip from his side of the tankard and remained silent for a few instants.

Mariotto opened the conversation with a wistful statement about the passing of time. Years, he declared, flew faster than swallows. It seemed only yesterday that his little Caterina was a happy *bimba* trotting through the house. Now, here she was, an accomplished maiden of fifteen, about to be wed.

Already he was harassed with demands for her hand. The town's most eligible young men whirled around her, like flies around honey. So keen was the competition that already some of their families had offered to forego even the mention of a dowry, for nowhere in Florence could be found a more pious, obedient, comely, soft-spoken, well-educated, thrifty, kind-hearted girl than Caterina.

"I am afraid I won't be able to hold out much longer," he concluded with a look of apprehension. "Any day now, some fortunate youngster is going to take her away."

It now was Noldo's turn to speak.

He began by saying that Florence was overrun with pious, obedient, comely, thrifty, kind-hearted maidens and their parents were desperately trying to get them off their hands. What was rare, rarer than hen's teeth, rarer than pearls in oysters, were boys. For one such as Antonio, who was handsome, dutiful, hardworking, well traveled, any maiden would gladly give her right eye.

He let that sink down in Mariotto's mind and comforted himself with a sip from the tankard.

Not that he denied Caterina's seemliness, he went on with a soft smacking of lips. No question, she was a fetching female, but beauty was like the morning dew and lasted about as long. A maiden must bring something more substantial than looks; she must bring a dowry.

"Say two thousand florins."

Surely his good friend, Noldo de'Gherardini, was speaking in jest, Mariotto remarked with a forced smile. One thousand was all he could possibly afford.

"Don't make the chickens laugh," retorted the merchant. "Everyone knows you are a rich man."

This, insisted the banker, was an incorrect notion. People were always confusing him with his cousin, Giovanni Rucellai. Here was a truly rich man. "But I barely make ends meet."

How strange, chuckled Noldo, that such a poor man should have been chosen as president of the Bankers' Guild! How strange that he should live in the beautiful Casa Rucellai on Via del Giglio, in the most fashionable and expensive district in town! How strange that Donna Filippa could afford to give such brilliant festivities during the social season!

"And that fine Rucellai bank on Via dei Tavolini, does it belong to you, yes or no?"

It did, sighed Mariotto, it did; but it wasn't doing well. If people knew the truth, they would not think of him as a rich man. "But to show you that I am not one to haggle on my daughter's happiness, I shall give her twelve hundred florins. Let's shake on it before I recover my senses."

"Two thousand."

This time, Mariotto pretended to lose his temper. "Noldo de'Gherardini, it is a stone you have in place of a heart. By the Holy Virgin, you are a Turk!"

It went on like this for a long time. They haggled, glared at each other, fell into hostile silences. In this fashion, the bidding rose to fifteen, then sixteen, and finally seventeen hundred florins.

"Seventeen fifty," demanded Noldo.

"Agreed."

They shook hands and it was over.

At once, the atmosphere became one of extreme cordiality. They began calling each other "cousin." Laughingly, Noldo confessed he had been ready to accept fifteen hundred florins; Mariotto to give two thousand. Both were pleased with their bargains.

Another tankard was served.

Mariotto rose, bowed, raised the mug to his lips, and drank the health of the Gherardini clan. No sooner had he sat down, than Noldo rose, bowed, lifted the mug to his lips, and drank the health of the Rucellai clan. For the next half hour the procedure was repeated as they toasted their future grandsons (there was no mention of granddaughters), their respective guilds, the Gherardini mill, the Rucellai bank, and, finally, the Republic. It was late in the afternoon when, arm in arm, they left the inn and unsteadily made their way home.

The following morning Caterina was summoned to her father's study. She curtsied and waited for him to finish the letter he was writing. After a while Mariotto rested his quill on the desk and looked at her with a fatherly smile on his lips.

"Daughter," he began, "time has come for you to be wed, and I've found you a good husband."

Antonio de'Gherardini was handsome, of an amiable disposition: one of the most eligible young men in Florence. The wedding had been scheduled for June, which gave her eight months to purchase a trousseau, select her bridesmaids, and attend to other preparations.

He then handed her a velvet-bound, silver-clasped copy of *Dalla Famiglia*, a book which listed the various qualities expected from an ideal wife and served as a manual guide to prospective Florentine brides. "It will tell you all you have to know to please your husband. If you need more information, ask your honored mother."

With a small dismissing gesture of the wrist, he terminated the audience.

She met Antonio, two weeks later, at the dinner which followed the signing of the wedding contract. She thought him very handsome, though somewhat reticent. But several times she felt his eyes resting tenderly on her and they exchanged a few furtive smiles across the table. By the end of the meal, she was already half in love with him.

Shortly after Christmas, she began gathering her trousseau. Accompanied by her mother — sometimes by Tessa, her personal maid — she went to "The Moor's Head," a fashionable apothecary shop where one could buy drugs, toiletries, eyebrow pluckers, ivory combs, silk stockings of various hues, bed and table linens, and practically everything else, while comely youngsters in skin-tight hose circulated among customers offering candies and re-freshments. Ears were pleasantly tickled by lute music wafting from an orchestra hidden behind greenery.

In a painter's *bottega* they purchased beautifully decorated chests, or *cassoni*. And of course, the conjugal bed with a head-board of gamboling cherubs.

At home she perused *Dalla Famiglia* and learned that a good wife should laugh at her husband's jokes, even if they were not funny or if she had heard them a thousand times; should discover his favorite dishes and have them served frequently; should keep herself clean and appetizing, lest he should conceive a great dis-gust of her and seek the company of bathhouse wenches.

She must not provoke his wrath by her prattle when he wished her to be silent, or be silent when he wished her to be merry. In the act of love, she should not depart from modesty — or, at least, the appearance of it — so that he would have to use " a little lov-ing force." Another thing: men, and husbands in particular, were prone to think of themselves as great lovers. The perfect wife must never fail to let him keep his illusions on this point. Tact-fully, she should extol his amorous prowesses and he would love her for it.

While Caterina was learning how to become a good wife, An-tonio was being indoctrinated by his father on his rights and privileges as a husband.

"As soon as possible, impress on your wife that you are her lord and master," he expounded, "and your word is law in the house."

He warned him to refrain from verbal endearments, loving glances, or caressing gestures, except at night in the privacy of the bed, lest such cajoleries induce Caterina into forgetting her-self and displaying indecorous expressions of love at all hours of the day.

Antonio must also remember that females were cackling crea-tures. They simply could not hold their tongues. Should Caterina prove a chattering wife, he must first reprove her gently. Should she persist, he would then be justified in taking a stick to her. As the great San Bernardini had so eloquently said, "I do not object to your beating your wife, but you must choose the proper time."

This, Noldo felt, was true Christian wisdom.

While this went on, Lisa did not remain idle. Of course, she told her husband, she rejoiced at the prospect of Antonio's wedding, but the prospect of his and Caterina's living in the house filled her with dread.

"And why should it?" asked Noldo archly. "Generations of Gherardini brides have lived happily here."

"True, noble husband," she agreed. "But have you thought of what it will mean for us?"

She painted a harrowing picture of what their life would become. Howling infants keeping them awake all night; countless and costly physicians' visits at all hours, for babies were always sick; the stench of medication permeating the house.

By the end of the week she had achieved her objective. Noldo informed Antonio that as a wedding present he would give him the money to buy some small house where he and Caterina would live during the first years of their marriage.

"Then," he added, "when your children have grown into reasonable beings, I shall expect you and your family to come and live here."

Antonio reported the good news to his mother who went in search of a suitable home.

She found it on Via Maggio, in the San Spirito district. It had bright and airy rooms, glass panes in windows, heat ducts in the walls, and other such modern conveniences. A small garden with a few fruit trees, a tiny pond, and a chicken yard extended at the back of the house. In the basement there was a fine bathroom equipped with a large wooden tub that could accommodate two persons. Thus, Caterina could invite her husband or some lady friend to share a bath with her, if she so wished.

Noldo approved of the house; Caterina fell in love with it at first sight. Early in spring, curtains were hung at the windows and pictures on the walls; carpets were laid on the floors. Jars of olive oil and barrels of wine were stocked in the cellar, together with lard, salted fish, and a few precious pounds of sugar.

One April morning Mariotto Rucellai came to the Gherardini mansion.

"Cousin Noldo," he said, "has it occurred to you that we have as yet made no arrangements for the religious ceremony?"

It had been agreed they would share the cost of the wedding banquet and they had held several meetings with caterers, musicians, and entertainers of various kinds. They had spent much more than they planned and were determined to use restraint in the church function.

"By all means, Cousin Mariotto, we must do so without delay. But let's remember that clerics are skillful at sucking money out of your purse."

"We shall be on our guard," remarked the banker. "After all, we are men of affairs and we won't let ourselves be befuddled by some honey-tongued priest. Personally, I favor a tasteful but simple ceremony."

"I see with your eyes on this point. Ostentation is a great sin. Besides," he added in an afterthought, "it attracts the attention of the tax assessor."

Thus they were of one mind when they called on the arch-priest at the cathedral's chancery.

"We wish a tasteful but simple ceremony," began Noldo who, being the older, was entitled to speak first.

"How wise of Your Magnificences," exclaimed the cleric. "Nothing pleases the Lord more than tasteful simplicity."

There were, however, limits to simplicity. Surely Their Magnificences would not want some paltry ceremony in conflict with their social standing. Therefore, the service should be simple and tasteful, but also adequate.

"And the first requirement of an adequate ceremony," he went on, fixing his gimlet eyes on them, "is candles."

Lots and lots of candles. Candles everywhere: on the main altar, in the side chapels, the apse, the transept, on the pillars, before the statues of the Virgin and saints. The whole church must

be aglow with candles. And, since the cathedral measured five
hundred feet in length and three hundred in width, this meant
quite a few candles.

"Let's say four thousand," he suggested, quill in mid-air.

They gulped, but nodded. He wrote the figure in the ledger.

"Now," he pursued joyously, "we come to the matter of
flowers."

Ha, flowers! How sweet and appropriate they were in a church
dedicated to Our Lady of the Flowers. Nothing touched the Madonna, nothing impressed guests like flowers. On the wedding day
the cathedral should be a gigantic basket of flowers.

"Blooms, blooms everywhere," he cried, as though in a vision.

Again he suggested a figure, and again they nodded.

"Now, let's talk about incense," he pressed on.

Incense, he declared, was God's perfume. It delighted His
sacred nostrils. The Almighty never tired of inhaling incense. Its
fragrance prompted Him to grant favors He would never grant
otherwise. A wedding without incense was like a day without
sunshine, a meal without wine.

"I entreat Your Magnificences," he said with pathos in his
voice. "Stint on everything else, but not on incense."

And so they did not stint on incense. Nor on music and singing, nor in the number of officiants, cross bearers and thurifers.
With each new item, they exchanged troubled glances, but they
nodded.

"That priest was a Turk," hissed Noldo, as they were coming
out of the chancery. "He spoke with the tongue of serpents."

"I'm afraid we fell into the sin of ostentation."

They felt depressed by their extravagance and lack of will-
power. To bolster their spirit, they repaired to a nearby wineshop. As they sipped from a tankard of wine, their optimism
revived. They began groping for excuses. After all, they had to
uphold the honor of their clans, had they not? What would their
guild colleagues think of them, if they had consented to some
shabby ceremony?

"Personally, I do not regret a single *picciolo*," said Noldo.

"Neither do I. Mark my word, this is going to be the finest wedding of the year."

And it was.

In the sunniness of the June morning, the bridal cortege emerged from Casa Rucellai and wound its way towards the cathedral, preceded by beribboned trumpeters and one hundred flower girls, aged from five to eight, all dressed in white, who tossed rose petals from wicker baskets. Caterina looked lovely in her red damask gown as she rode sidesaddle through the streets, waving and smiling at the crowds. Behind her came her twelve bridesmaids, also on horseback.

Antonio, in a doublet of blue brocade, was waiting on the church square surrounded by his twelve assistants. As the bridal cortege halted before the cathedral, he helped Caterina dismount, and together they made their entrance into the flamboyant nave.

The priest had kept his word.

The immense building was ablaze with candles and fragrant with flowers. Amid torrents of organ music, mass began and unfolded its ancient choreography. Officiants and acolytes shuttled back and forth with hands joined before their faces. They bowed, traced large signs of the cross in the air, swung billows of incense, exchanged brotherly kisses.

The nuptial banquet was held at the Gherardini mansion.

An awning had ben spread over the inner courtyard where the newlyweds, their immediate relatives, and twenty-four assistants sat at a long and festive table. Each course was announced by a blare of trumpets and ceremoniously sampled by a food taster. Entertainment was provided by lute players and acrobats.

Guests were scattered through the house according to age and sex. Elderly ladies convened in a room of their own so that they might take their ease, remove their dentures of shark's teeth and, if need be, clap their hands to summon their women slaves to bring their silver chamber pots. Men enjoyed their own company and talked business. Children were relegated to the upper floor where they gorged themselves on roast chicken and cake, while watching a buffoon and his trained monkey.

It was late when Antonio and Caterina were escorted to their house on Via Maggio. As they were approaching it, he climbed down from his horse, lifted her from her saddle, and, flinging her over his shoulder, carried her over the threshold.

Guests trouped in after them. They watched the bride cut the cake, while a round of laurel wine — the wedding wine — was being served. A male infant from the neighborhood was brought in and placed in her arms, as a token of future sons of her own. A gold coin was slipped into her shoe to entice prosperity. Then bride and groom were hugged, blessed, kissed by tearful parents and relatives, and, at long last, left alone.

Later that evening they undressed, and in a state of complete nakedness entered the bedroom, each holding a candlestick. After placing the candlesticks in the middle of the floor, they knelt by the bed and prayed God to grant them many sons. This done, Antonio blew out the light and followed Caterina to bed.

Dawn was graying the window when they fell asleep, lips to lips and legs entwined. They did not hear the morning chimes and it was past noon when they finally awoke, surprised at finding themselves in the same bed. He kissed her mouth; she kissed him back, and soon in the full flood of daylight they reopened the passions that had first been kindled by the flicker of the votive lamp.

Then they dozed again for a while. When he awoke, he saw her, looking and smiling at him. Without a word, he took a gold ring from the night table and slipped it on her third finger of the left hand. This signified that he was pleased with her and they now were truly man and wife.

Through the following months she discovered the man she had wed: his gentleness, his judiciousness, his quiet sense of humor.

He was, she found, a competent executive without his father's passion for money. He liked his work, discharged his responsibilities; but, after a day at the office, he could forget the mill. She became expert at guessing his moods, learned his favorite dishes, shared his pleasure in lovemaking, and discreetly let him know it.

He, in turn, grew accustomed to her "God's grace, revered

husband" greeting in the morning, the pressure of her young lips
on his hand, the sight of this sixteen-year-old matron running
about the house in a dress of black serge with keys dangling from
her belt, prodding servants, sorting linen in *cassoni*, dispensing
salt and spices to the cook.

They had adopted the modern style of eating and drinking
from individual plates and goblets. During meals he would covertly watch her daintily pluck food from the salver with three
fingers of her right hand, chew small mouthfuls behind closed
lips, and, dessert over, discreetly signal the maids to withdraw.

Then she would tell him about the day's events. A neighborly
lady had brought her a jar of jasmine preserve . . . One of the
parlormaids had gone that morning to the barber's to have a tooth
pulled. The cook had seen a devil in the kitchen. Could she buy a
quattrino of sulfur and have it fumigated?

Of such things married life was made.

Early in July Noldo transferred the direction of the Gherardini Stabilimenti to Antonio.

He did so in his office, a few days before leaving for the country, in a touching ceremony. He began by reviewing his career
and that took a long time, for he started with his apprenticeship
at the age of twelve up to his latest and crowning achievement,
the *tintillano* venture. Now, after a life of unremitting toil, time
had come for him to withdraw from earthly pursuits and devote
his few remaining years, perhaps months, to prayer, meditation,
and the preparation for his journey across the Great Sea.

Henceforth, the mill and its two thousand workers would be
Antonio's sole responsibility. It would be his turn to know the
sleepless nights that went with the supreme command of a large
industrial concern.

"Of course," he added, "emergencies will surely arise and then
you may turn to me for guidance."

He then announced his departure for Montebuoni where he
owned a modest country house. There he would spend the summer in spiritual endeavors. As he was about to be hoisted on his
horse, he said that on his return to town, he hoped to learn that
Caterina was with child and that a grandson was on the way.

Antonio omitted these last remarks when, on his return from the office, he reported to Caterina on the morning scene. He then asked her if she would be willing to forego the summer at Montici, which Nodo had deeded to him. "I should like to profit by his absence to familiarize myself with the management of the mill."

She assured him that the small garden at the back of the house would make an excellent substitute for the country estate. And it did. They supped in it during July and August, enjoyed the cool breezes that arrived after sunset, lingered at the table until the appearance of the first evening star. On Sundays, they spent lazy afternoons under the single cherry tree, talking of this or that and simply enjoying their nearness.

The autumn rains sent them back into the house. They also brought Noldo back from Montebuoni. One day he dropped in at the mill, pored over ledgers, checked invoices and went on a tour of inspection. He seemed to be in excellent health and not once did he mention his imminent journey across the Great Sea.

The next week he reappeared. And the next and the next. Gradually his visits grew longer and more frequent.

"Wife," said Antonio one evening, "what am I to do with him? He comes nearly every day, checks the books, criticizes everything, upsets everybody, spends hours in the *tintillano* annex. Then he calls for his horse and goes to play cards at the guild."

She caught the tinge of exasperation in his voice and tried to soothe his feelings. "Be patient, revered husband. The mill was his whole life. He can't get used to having nothing to do."

The winter evenings by the fire brought them closer still. She had a pleasant voice and played the lute well. Her singing made the hours pass swiftly before the curfew chimes. He learned a few more things about her happy childhood at Casa Rucellai: the dancing festivities and garden parties at "The Farm," her father's country estate; her games and quarrels with her brothers and sisters. She remembered her tutor who had made her read Petrarch's sonnets. Her piety was sincere, her faith unquestioning. If you burned enough candles to her altars and gave enough alms to the poor, the Madonna vanquished all difficulties, overcame all obstacles.

February brought Carnival and its rowdy frolics ending in the gloom of Lent. Every pulpit in town had its Dominican monk in white robe and black cloak, reminding their audiences that only one out of every hundred thousand Christians ever entered heaven, while purgatory was crowded and hell packed to the rafters.

The impact of these homilies created a flutter of repentance among the population. Women gave up almond cake and stopped plucking their eyebrows; men also made good, but short-lived resolutions.

Then everything returned to normal.

By mid-March, preparations began for the New Year festivities. On Piazza della Signoria, the "Old Palace" sported a flag at every window. Acrobats' booths, refreshment stands, strolling-players' wagons sprouted on the square, which assumed the appearance of a country fair.

New Year had always been a festive occasion, but in recent years it had become a tribute to Lorenzo de'Medici who was born on New Year (March 25th) 1450. It offered the population an opportunity to express its affection and gratitude to the young man who, for the past eight years, had been ruling Florence.

Antonio suggested to Caterina they celebrate the arrival of 1478 by joining the crowds that convened on Piazza della Signoria on this occasion. "It will give us an opportunity to hear Cousin Lorenzo compete in the singing contest and sing his songs in his off-key voice."

Hand in hand, they meandered through the throng, stopping here and there to watch a cavorting buffoon, a sword-swallower, a dancing bear. At a refreshment stand they had a goblet of lemonade, for the afternoon was sunny and already warm. They also bought a slice of almond cake on which they nibbled while resuming their stroll.

For a while they stood before the platform of a storyteller, or *narratore*, who stood beating an iron pot to attract listeners.

"O people of Florence, famous for intelligence and generosity, come and listen to Beppo's stories. Nobody has stories like Beppo. Stories that will make you laugh, cry, melt your heart like wax in the fire."

That day he told the story of Santa Reparata, one of Florence's patron saints. At the age of twelve she had had her budding breasts torn off her chest. Afterward, naked and blood-stained, she had been dragged through the streets, flogged, disemboweled, and finally decapitated: all on account of her attachment to the Christian creed.

"As her head fell to the ground," wailed Beppo, tears running down his cheeks, "a dove flew out of her neck and soared straight to heaven. Such a wondrous thing it was that the axman fell to his knees and became a Christian on the spot. And so, he also had his head cut off."

At this point the *narratore* climbed down the three steps of his platform and circulated, *berretta* in hand, among the audience. Back on the stand, he told the touching story of Parthenope, the lovelorn mermaid who had fallen in love with Ulysses.

Antonio dropped another coin into Beppo's *berretta* and led Caterina to another part of the square where, suddenly, they came upon Lorenzo de'Medici standing, like the storyteller, on a wooden platform.

On his twenty-eighth birthday, he cut a striking figure: tall and gaunt, with an angular face that seemed hewn into a block of cherry wood. He had a crooked nose, jutting cheekbones, a square jaw, and a thin, wide mouth. His ugliness, however, was of the kind women found attractive, and they readily fell in love with him — and he with them. Which further complicated his already complicated life.

Besides being ugly, he was extremely intelligent, good-natured (though implacable in vengeance), courteous, and sensitive. In an age when everyone rode surpassingly well, he also was an expert swordsman (a fact that was soon to save his life), a genuine poet, a Greek and Latin scholar, a compulsive collector of ancient manuscripts, dutiful son, a devoted brother, a loving father, and an unfaithful husband.

And, of course, the richest man in the world.

When Antonio and Caterina spied him on his platform, he was singing a ballad of his composition, titled *"Giovinezza."*

In his tuneless voice, he went through the first stanza:

"How fair is youth, but how quickly it flies!
Be merry while you may;
Of tomorrow none can say."

The song over, he addressed in Florentine dialect the men and women who pressed around him. He assured them that his greatest ambition was to win the singing contest, but he never would because everyone in Florence sang better than he. Perhaps, if he took singing lessons, he might win some day, but he had no time for lessons. And why? Because he and his brother Giuliano were killing themselves on their behalf, working all night while they snored contentedly on their straw pads.

And were they grateful? Not in the least. They always wanted more public fountains, more baking ovens, more public latrines. And where was he going to find the money for these things when they cheated in their income declarations, hiding their money in jars of oil where tax collectors could not find it?

In short, they were ungrateful wretches and not worth the trouble they gave. He and his brother had talked the matter over and had decided to give them one last chance. They would continue to work one more year, just one more year, for them. If by then the situation had not improved, he would take his family to the end of the world where he would never hear of the Florentines again.

They laughed, for they knew he loved them and would never leave them; they, in turn, loved him and would remain faithful to him, come what may.

One month and three days later, on Sunday, 28 April 1478, Lorenzo was attacked in the cathedral by two priests who rushed at him, dagger in fist, at the end of the mass and wounded him in the back of the neck. At the same moment and in the same place, his brother Giuliano was stabbed nineteen times by Francesco Pazzi, who, in his frenzy, gashed his own thigh.

Shortly afterward, Archbishop Salviati, who had been officiating at mass, leaped on his horse and, followed by a contingent of fellow conspirators, galloped to the Old Palace. Still in his sacramental robes, he flounced by the sentry and burst upon the members of the Signoria as they were having lunch. Striding to the head of the table, the archbishop informed the *gonfaloniere* that the Medici brothers had been killed. In His Holiness's name, he demanded the councillors' immediate resignation, adding that anyone who refused would be immediately hanged.

As he spoke, he glanced over his shoulder and, to his horror, discovered he was alone. His companions had lost their way in the building and had inadvertently locked themselves into a room that could not be opened from the inside. He blanched, stammered, tried to bolt, but the *gonfaloniere* was too fast for him. He seized the prelate by the hair, jerked him around, and crashed his fist in his face.

This done, he asked questions.

Thus, the pitiful plot, known as the Pazzi Conspiracy, came to light. Its purpose had been to deliver Florence into Pope Sixtus's hands by murdering the Medici brothers in one single stroke and seizing the Signoria. After which the tower bell was to be rung, calling the citizens to the piazza, where they would be informed that the Republic was abolished and Florence and her territory had become a Church state. A week or so later His Holiness would make his entrance and, misty-eyed, watch the coronation of his son Girolamo as Duke of Tuscany.

This sinister and grotesque plan had been lovingly hatched by Francesco Pazzi, member of a great Florentine banking family and a Medici relative. A few years before he had vied with Giuliano for the favors of the blonde, exquisitely beautiful Simonetta de'Vespucci, who has come down to us in Botticelli's "Birth of Venus."

When she had chosen Lorenzo's brother, Francesco had fled to Rome with rage in his heart. There he had become Girolamo's gambling companion and the pope's private banker. Even Simonetta's death in 1476 had not healed his wounded pride or slaked his thirst for revenge. When Sixtus's hopes for the crown of Milan for his son had come to naught, Francesco had suggested his plan, which had been heartily endorsed by the holy father.

All this was told by the archbishop in frightened stammers, to the accompaniment of slaps and kicks from the magistrates. As he was finishing his story, people were running out of the cathedral and gathering under the window of the Medici Palace.

Lorenzo appeared, grim-faced, a bloodstained bandage around his neck. Yes, he announced, Giuliano was dead. His murder had been part of a plot against Florence, of which he himself was also to be a victim.

"Please go home," he asked. "The culprits will be found and punished as they deserve."

For once, they would not obey. Their grief and anger demanded the outlet of violence. They turned into an uncontrollable, rampaging mob.

The manhunt began.

Their first quarry was Francesco Pazzi. After killing Giuliano, he had managed to slip unnoticed from the church and sought refuge at his uncle's house. They found him in bed, moaning in pain from his self-inflicted thigh wound. Grappled by a hundred hands, his face clawed by women's nails, he was dragged out in the street, pushed and kicked all the way to the Signoria's dining room, just as the archbishop was about to be hanged.

A rope was slipped around Francesco's neck; then both men were flung out of the same window. For a few moments they swung together as they strangled side by side. At this point, a gruesome thing took place. In a supreme spasm of fury, the archbishop threw himself at his companion and with his teeth tore a lump of flesh from his chest. He died with it in his mouth.

For a week hysteria held the population in grip. One after another, every member of the conspiracy was ferreted out of his hiding place and butchered on the spot. The two priests, Antonio Maffei and Stefano Bagnone, who had wounded Lorenzo, had taken asylum in a monastery. But no sanctuary could save them. Their noses were slit, their hands hacked off, their loins slashed.

The archbishop's followers were discovered in the self-locking room and let out, in pairs, only to have their skulls bashed open as they emerged.

At one time, twenty-six corpses hung from the Old Palace's windows while sixty-eight more swelled and rotted below on the piazza in the spring sunshine. All in all, two hundred and seventy-two people paid for Giuliano's murder.

At last, their anger spent and ashamed of themselves, the Florentines returned to their homes, wondering what *Il Papa*'s reaction to their savagery would be.

They did not have long to wait.

In a bristling message, Sixtus called Lorenzo "a suckling of perdition" and placed the city under excommunication.

This meant that all religious life came to a halt. Bells could not be rung, with the result that no one knew what time it was. Weddings could not be performed, nor could baptisms. Confessionals were shut and people had to go about with their sins on their consciences. When they died, they were buried without prayers, candles, or the laments of hired weepers, like dogs.

Worse, excommunication extended to Florentine wares. Throughout the world, their textiles, their shoes, their fashion novelties became pestiferous. Anyone who bought a yard of San Martino cloth or entered a Florentine bank became "a suckling of perdition," a moral leper.

Goaded into open rebellion, the Signoria convened a congress of Tuscan bishops to study the validity of Sixtus's excommunication. The holy men examined the holy father's brief and found it written in such atrocious Latin that it couldn't possibly have come from God. They proclaimed it null and void and enjoined the Tuscan clergy to pay no attention to it. Church bells would continue to be rung as before; parents would christen their children, confess their sins and marry in churches, die with the usual sprinkling of holy water and the cries of professional weepers. As a parting gesture, the bishops excommunicated – the pope.

Sixtus's answer to this impertinence was war.

Only then did the Florentines realize the folly of their ways. They had no army to oppose the papal troops and those of his ally, Don Ferrante of Aragon, king of Naples. By July they were already entering Tuscany and approaching Florence, who lay helpless in her luscious valley.

But, as in the past, the Madonna was watching over her favorite city.

Clearly she had no love for popes, and through centuries she had taken the Florentines' side against them. As a rule, she suggested to the Signoria to bribe the papal *generalissimo:* a practice which was invariably crowned with success.

This time, however, the general in chief of the pontifical and Neapolitan armies was unbribable. Duke Federigo of Urbino was the ruler of the tiny state of Urbino in the Apennine vastness and a very rich man. His previous campaigns as *condottiere* had brought him an immense reputation as a master tactician, as well as a drawerful of decorations, including the English Order of the Garter.

And so, this time, the Madonna arranged for Duke Federigo to be a decent person and an old friend of the Medici family. With disgust, he had learned of the part played by the pope in the Pazzi Conspiracy. At the beginning of the hostilities, he had asked to be excused from duty. Sixtus's reply had been a thunderous command to rejoin his headquarters under penalty of excommunication.

The *generalissimo* had obeyed, but with the firm intention of thwarting his employer's designs.

A glance at the map of operations showed him that Florence lay wide open before him and victory – total, inescapable victory – was staring him in the face.

Without hesitation he ordered – a strategic retreat.

Ignoring the pope's furious messages, he turned his back on the target and went in search of distant villages to besiege, none of them of the slightest military importance. By mid-November he was standing before Monte Sansovino, a town so small that its name is omitted from most maps of Italy.

It took him three weeks to set his bombards in position.

Then, on 8 December 1478, just as the first salvo of round, hand-hewn stones was about to be fired, the inhabitants of Monte

Sansovino hoisted a white flag and requested a four-month truce that was immediately granted.

In Florence, news of the armistice sent people dancing in the streets.

"It will give Lorenzo time to reach an agreement with the pope," said Antonio. "By spring, we'll be able to sell our wares again."

The strain of the past six months had left its mark on him. Sixtus's excommunication had nearly ruined the Florentine trade. Many textile mills along the Arno had closed. The Gherardini Stabilimenti was still open, but limping along on reduced operations, its warehouses bulging with unsold goods and the prospect of a shutdown growing daily more inevitable.

Suddenly, there was hope again.

"You see, revered husband, the Madonna has protected us," said Caterina.

Never had she doubt that she would, and her trusting faith brought a smile to his lips.

"She has, indeed, and you may burn as many candles to her as you wish."

It was good seeing him smile again, she thought. Now they would resume their contented evenings by the fire, she would again sing and play the lute for him, as she had the previous winter.

Her heart went out to him, and to make his happiness complete, she told him she was with child.

"Are you certain?" he asked, not daring to believe his good fortune.

She nodded. She had visited the midwife, who had predicted the *bimbo* (for, of course, he would be a boy) by the end of summer, probably in August.

For a while he looked at her through eyes full of love. At last his sweet, loving wife was going to give him the son he had longed for since the day of their wedding, eighteen months ago.

"I look forward to your breasting our son," he said innocently.

To his stupefaction, she shook her head.

"As much as I should like to please you in this matter," she said with lowered lids, "I am afraid I shan't be able to do so."

Since the beginning of time, women have accepted motherhood as unavoidable, with feelings ranging from rapture to resignation. They have, however, stubbornly shirked suckling their young whenever they could and delegated this chore to poor, healthy farm girls. Professional nursing may not be the oldest career in the world, but it comes a close second.

In the Renaissance, ladies of wealth and "high degree" did not like breasting their young either, and, to avoid doing it, they had invented a number of excuses, which they passed on piously to their daughters from generation to generation.

Caterina had learned them from her mother and she now presented them to her noble and confused husband.

Oh yes, she explained, farm women could feed their litter and soon return to household tasks. God had made them strong for just that purpose. Noble ladies, on the other hand, were delicate creatures. Their milk was weak and watery, just good enough to raise a pup. And this, she added, she was prepared to do, but to ask her to nurse their son would be to condemn them both to a certain and untimely death.

"Is this what you want, revered husband?" she asked, raising to him her beautiful brown eyes.

Before he could reply, she pressed on. Nursing would ravage her figure. Although only seventeen, she would turn into a prematurely old, haggard-looking, flabby-breasted crone. She would become an object of repulsion to him, and he would carouse with bathhouse wenches, just to avoid the sight of her.

Feebly, Antonio argued that the Virgin was always represented suckling the Babe and she looked beautiful. Caterina was prepared for that one. The Madonna, she replied, may be God's mother and all that, but the fact remained that she was the wife of a poor carpenter, therefore a *popolana*, one of those robust plebeian females who could breast-feed their brood and keep their looks.

Having disposed of his objection, Caterina went on to say that nursing their son would mean social disgrace. It would publicize the fact that Antonio was too poor or niggardly to pay the two florins per month (about eight dollars) which constituted a *balia*'s wages. People would say, "There goes Antonio de'Gherardini, of the illustrious Gherardini clan, but such an avaricious man is he that he condemns his poor wife to an early death, just to save a nurse's wages."

"Is this what you want?" she asked, blinking back the tears.

By now, he was thoroughly mystified and took refuge in generalities. He accused her of speaking with the tongue of serpents, threatened to take a stick to her. Finally, stomping out of the room, he told her to do whatever she liked.

She spent the following two weeks looking for a nurse with the proper requirements.

She must be pious, jovial, industrious, in perfect health, and a brunette, for blondes were anemic and redheads had a violent temper. Her milk must be abundant and sweet-tasting, not rancid or granulous. Her breasts should not be too large, for the *bimbo* might choke on them, nor too small, for then he might not find them. Neither must they be too hard, lest he crush his nose on them, nor too soft, for then he might refuse to suckle "out of sheer disgust." One last thing: the nurse must have good teeth and a pleasant breath.

At last Caterina found this pearl of a *balia* and engaged her for a period of one year. She paid the woman a month's salary in advance and told her to keep herself ready to enter her functions some time in August.

As news of her pregnancy spread through the district, neighboring ladies, friends, and relatives began stopping at the house, bringing toys, rattles, and goatskin blankets.

They also gave her the benefit of their experience.

If she ate fish or pork, her baby would be born with round, glassy eyes or with a snout instead of a nose. She must not sneeze, lest she sneezed him out of her. At all costs, she must satisfy her cravings, outlandish as they might be, for they were warnings sent by the *bambino* of some urgent need. Miscarriages could be averted by rubbing a small emerald on the stomach every morning.

Above all, Caterina must stop sleeping with Antonio, because, in the drowsiness of slumber, he might forget her condition and fondle her, might arouse her, and before they knew it, some agile devil might sneak inside her. And when a devil got into your belly, it was virtually impossible to get him out without losing the child.

Every week the midwife came to visit Caterina, for doctors were of no earthly use in childbirth. Pregnancy was women's business and men had no place in it, except at the very beginning.

One day the parish priest called. He, too, had heard the news of Caterina's pregnancy and was coming to congratulate her.

"So, Your Ladyship is going to make a little *bimbo*, eh?" he said with the forced joviality of poor clerics before rich parishioners. "Well, that's what females are for."

Unlike the lazy and lecherous monks who went begging from door to door and impregnated kitchen wenches, parish priests had won the respect and affection of the population. They brought solace to the sick, hope to the bereaved, forgiveness to the dying. Ill-paid, often not paid at all, they eked out a pittance from a never-ending round of masses, baptisms, funerals, and visits to expectant mothers.

"Motherhood," he proceeded, "is woman's crown of glory."

He had said it a thousand times, and that morning he said it again. Yes, motherhood was the sign of God's predilection for women, but it entailed suffering, for it was written that females would conceive in pleasure and confine in pain. It entailed also a certain amount of danger, as God sometimes chose to snuff out a life while creating another. For these reasons, it was prudent to enlist the Madonna's protection with some small donation to the parish church.

To Caterina, the request seemed perfectly natural. She had been taught that Heaven protected those who helped the Church, and in exactly the same proportion. Much money, much help; little money, little help. No money, no help at all.

Caterina gave the priest a gold florin, a smoked ham, a chicken, and some eggs. He went away with his bounty, grinning, stammering thanks, showering blessings over her, the household, and the forthcoming *bimbo*.

In June, the midwife declared that confinement was now only three months away, and Caterina must take to her bed. She did so and at once became an object of solicitude on the part of her mother, mother-in-law, sisters, lady friends, neighbors. They spent much time by her bedside and by their chatter or singing tried to keep her mind away from the approaching ordeal.

The huge wooden tub was hauled up from the basement and set in the center of the room. Twice a day it was filled with hot water and Caterina was carried into it for a long, hot bath. On occasion, some barren woman would bathe with her, for the bathwater of an expectant mother was regarded as a powerful remedy against sterility.

While this went on, Antonio was all but forgotten: a stranger in his own home. Servants paid little attention to him. He dined by himself, slept alone in another room. On his return from the mill, he was allowed to visit his wife for a minute or so, exchange a few words with her. Then, politely but firmly, he would be ushered out.

By the end of July, when confinement was judged only three weeks away, some of Caterina's closest friends moved into her house, bringing with them their wardrobe, cosmetics, mattresses, and chamber pots. Some slept in her room; the others, wherever they could.

The parish priest called again. He assured Caterina of the Virgin's protection. However, as an additional precaution, he urged her to secure also the protection of Santa Margherita, who, though a maiden herself, was the matron saint of women in labor. Caterina gave him a half-florin and he went away happy.

No sooner was he gone than the astrologer appeared: a spindly bearded old man in a square bonnet and star-spangled mantle with a moth-eaten fur collar. He pressed his ear against Caterina's stomach and listened intently. He then stepped to the window and squinted at the sky for a long while. When he returned to the bed, he announced that the baby would be a boy. Yet, because of a rare conjunction of planets, he might well turn out to be a girl. In either case, he or she would bring much honor to the Gherardini clan.

So saying, he handed her a goblet of mule's urine, and immediately afterward a slice of baked apple to eat. He then collected his fee, bowed to the ladies, and decorously departed.

In mid-August the midwife came every day. Finally, she installed herself in the house, crotchety and self-important. She sorted her instruments, phials, unguents, amulets, and magic powders on the bedside table and took charge of everything.

When labor began, she tied a snakeskin belt around Caterina's stomach to frighten any devil that might scheme to sneak inside. During the next hours, she pressed wet linens on Caterina's brow, held a flask of vinegar to her nostrils, and let her clutch her hand.

As birth appeared imminent, she scooped her in her arms and carried her to the "birth chair" and plunged into work, while the visiting ladies sank to their knees and intoned the litanies of the Virgin.

Thus, in the summer of 1479, amid the chanting of prayers and screams of pain, Lisa de'Gherardini — the future Mona Lisa — was born.

Lady with an Ermine by Leonardo da Vinci, *c.* 1483. *Courtesy of Museum Czartoryski, Cracow.*

The Making of a Renaissance Lady

Like a pall, disappointment descended upon the room. The ladies exchanged dejected glances, stopped singing, and began gathering their belongings. The birth of a *bimba* did not call for rejoicing.

Girls, it was agreed, were inferior, troublesome creatures sent by God as a trial to their parents, and a source of expense. To men they were an instrument of temptation, as Adam could testify, an inducement to sexual depravity and economic ruin.

Theologians, who knew about this sort of thing, as about everything else, taught that girls "received their souls ninety days after conception" while boys got theirs much sooner. A Roman midwife, charged with infanticide, was acquitted by the Church tribunal because the fetus she had thrown into the Tiber was that of a girl, less than three months old, and therefore soulless, a mere object. Had it been that of a boy, she would have had both hands cut off.

Inferior or not, Lisa had arrived and must be attended to. Her *balia* sprang into action. She washed her with a lotion of rose water and aromatic herbs, poked a finger into her tiny mouth and rubbed her gums with wine and honey. This done, she laid her down on a goatskin blanket and let her dry by the fire.

Just then, Antonio arrived from the mill and entered the room. A glance at the naked infant told him of his misfortune. Yet he tenderly kissed Caterina on her moist brow and assured her he was well pleased with a daughter. In a drowsy murmur, she begged his forgiveness and promised to do better next time. He comforted her, kissed her again and went out to break the sad news to his father.

Noldo de'Gherardini received his son in the *studiolo*. He gave him his hand to kiss and heard of the birth of his granddaughter with Christian resignation. Removing his red *berretta*, he crossed himself and declared that, since it had pleased God to send him this new affliction, he would bow to His will. Without protest, he would endure the pitying glances of his guild colleagues, the downhearted compliments of neighbors.

"Not that I have anything against females," he added.

Except that they cost a fortune to feed, dress, and educate; then, when they reached fourteen or fifteen, another fortune to find them a husband.

Which led him to speak about Lisa's dowry.

It was not too soon to think about it, he said, for girls grew like weeds and before you knew it, you had to get them off your hands. Fortunately, Florence had a dowry bank or *Monte delle doti* for just that purpose. By paying a specified monthly amount, a father could provide a suitable marriage portion for his daughter. As the bank paid an interest of eighteen percent on deposits, it was considered a sound investment.

"In normal times," Noldo proceeded, "I would advise you to go and make a first payment, but these are not normal times. It is prudent to wait and see how things will turn out."

Contrary to all expectations, Pope Sixtus had resumed military operations at the expiration of the truce. Florence had been forced to raise an army and it was feared that its cost might induce the dowry bank to reduce its interest rate.

Antonio agreed and, leaning over his father's hand, took his leave. He walked to the Battistero, the small octogonal church with the famous bronze doors, and there he dropped a white bean into the "birth box" fastened to the outside wall. This informed the authorities that the town's population had increased by one female. No further information was required.

This done, he proceeded to Piazza della Signoria where the *banditori* or town criers loitered by the Old Palace, with their drums slung over their shoulders. For the sum of eight *soldi*, one of them agreed to go about the city, beating his drum (with one hand) and stop at every street corner to announce that "a daughter, named Lisa, was born to Antonio Maria de'Gherardini and his wife, Donna Caterina."

In one of the goldsmith shops on Ponte Vecchio, he bought a bracelet of gold and ivory: a modest, but adequate bauble to thank his wife for having given him a daughter. Of course, had the baby been a boy, the gift would have been a much costlier one. On his way back to the mill, he stopped at a flower stall and had a bouquet of red roses delivered to his house. (The Gherardini were Guelfs and would have only red roses in their homes; in turn, Ghibellines had only white ones.)

Late that afternoon, on his return from the mill, he learned that Caterina was peacefully sleeping under Tessa's watchful eye. He climbed to the top floor where the nursery was situated and there he found Lisa, bound from head to foot in swaddling clothes, asleep in her cradle, a drop of milk still gleaming on her lower lip.

For a few instants he gazed at her wrinkled little face framed in a white coif. She wasn't much to look at, he thought tenderly, and she had chosen a bad time to be born, with Florence still excommunicated and at war; but at least she had chosen a good home. Unlike so many other white beans in the birth box, she would never be cold or hungry. And she would be loved.

The following day preparations began for the postnatal festivities. The tub was removed from Caterina's room, which was transformed into an elegant parlor with red silk drapes at the window, red bed curtains, red coverlet, and red pillowcases. Antonio's red roses stood on a corner table.

In this flamboyant decor, Caterina lay in state, her hair elaborately dressed, her eyebrows carefully plucked. For the next three weeks she received friends, neighbors, and relatives who brought fruits and cakes on exquisitely painted "birth plates." Nuns and monks also came, bringing smiles and blessings.

When Lisa was one month old, she was dressed in a cloud of lace and carried to the Battistero Church where all Florentine infants were baptized, whatever their district. A priest in surplice prayed over her, sprinkling her with holy water while she was being undressed. At last, naked as the day she was born, she was plunged headlong into the baptismal font, a ceremony from which she emerged howling, water-dripping – and a Christian. Whereupon parents, grandparents, godparents, and friends, led by four beribboned musicians, returned to Via Maggio in joyous cortege, tossing hard candy to street urchins.

The baptism marked the end of the postnatal festivities.

Down came the red curtains and the red window drapes. The room assumed its customary look. Servants went back to their usual tasks. Caterina resumed the management of the household; Antonio regained his status as lord and master of the family and his place in the conjugal bed.

And Lisa remained in her cradle.

For the next year she continued to be bound in swaddling clothes, lest she twist herself into some horrible shape. Or, worst still, turn into a quadruped.

She did little but sleep, suckle, gurgle, burp, excrete, and, now and then, beam at nothing in particular, as infants are wont to do. She learned to make her wishes known by screaming at the top of her lungs and discovered that it did not do any good, for in the Renaissance the crying of children was regarded as a fine lung exercise, and nothing else.

Once a day she was brought to her mother, who held her for a few instants, inquired about her health and behavior, and returned her to her *balia*. Her father came to visit her after work. He talked to her, tickled her chin, kissed the tip of her nose, and sometimes got a smile as a reward.

Thus, her first winter went by.

In May, the weather turned sunny and warm. She was taken to the garden, released from her swaddlings, and laid down on a blanket on the grass. In the sunshine, the little mummy became a lively human being. She rolled on her stomach, bounced on her back, shook her silver rattle, nibbled at her big toe, or stared in wonder at the tiny crater of her navel.

While this went on, her nurse engaged in calisthenics of her own. She skipped rope or lifted weights, for athletics were supposed to improve a woman's milk. In large households, *balias* were made to ride horseback. Nothing like a brisk canter to stimulate "the lacteous secretion."

In August, Lisa was one year old. She had learned a great deal about the world in which she had arrived and was learning more every day. Already she had a little past, about as long as the wake of a very small boat. Her nurse was discharged, as agreed, and her place taken by her mother's personal maid, Tessa.

Tessa was in her early twenties: a splendid, buxom Turkish girl with gleaming white teeth between pulpy, scarlet lips. She had onyx-black eyes which could send beams of motherly love or lightning flashes of disapproval. At the age of twelve, she had been bought at a slave auction in Venice and brought to Casa Rucellai, first as Caterina's companion and playmate, later as her personal maid. When her mistress had married Antonio, she had followed her in her new home.

During the Renaissance, rich Florentines had Turkish, Egyptian, Circassian (but no black) women slaves. In their adolescence, they usually served their masters as "objects of pleasure" and, later, as household servants. They were well treated as a rule, and often refused to be freed and returned to their country of origin.

It took Lisa several days to get used to this gigantic, terrifying creature, her broad ocher face, her yellow turban, the tinkle of her brass jewelry. In due time, she began communicating with her through a vernacular of grunts, gurgles, and occasional full-throated yells which Tessa understood perfectly, but often chose to ignore. Then, the conflict between the two females turned into a clash of wills, an endurance contest as to who could yell or remain deaf the longer.

Lisa discovered that her *bambinaia* or governess could remain deaf an awfully long time.

One of Tessa's convictions was that girls had no other purpose but to grow into shapely women, capable of luring a rich husband. Her first care in entering Lisa's life was to free her from her swaddlings, except at night. Every morning she bathed her in warm rose water and let her dry by the fire, so that the fragrance would seep through her skin so that, in time, she would smell like a rose. Afterwards, she gently massaged her limbs, buttocks, and even tiny fingers. By the time she was two, Lisa's education as a temptress was well advanced.

After the bath and massage came a hearty breakfast of bran porridge sweetened with honey and diluted in milk — the rich, creamy milk a farmer brought every morning to the house in a goat-driven cart. Lisa would dip one hand, sometimes both, into the wooden bowl, scoop some mush in her palm and raise it haphazardly to her mouth. It was an unreliable, untidy procedure, but on it she grew into a sturdy baby.

Her energy was boundless. She crawled for hours on the nursery floor. One day she tried standing up and instantly found herself sitting on the floor. But she was stubborn and had all the time in the world. She repeated the performance many times with similar results. After countless defeats, she managed a few lurching steps. In time she mastered a sort of drunken gait which got her across the room and into Tessa's ample and downy bosom.

At about the same time, she bubbled her first words: *mamma* and *babbo*. Rapidly she acquired a vocabulary of her own. From that moment onward, she never ceased talking either to Tessa or herself.

As her legs grew sturdier, she embarked upon forays that took her farther and farther away from Tessa. Soon, she was sneaking out of the nursery and wandering through the house. Looking for all the world like a diminutive housewife in her voluminous skirt and white coif, she went from room to room, crawled under beds, peered into drawers, broke a few things. Once she lost herself in the cellar, where Tessa finally found her in tears and trembling from fright.

With the return of spring, she ventured into the garden, which became for her a magic land full of new sounds and smells. She chewed grass, lunged after butterflies floundering about like flying flowers, studied her reflection in the pond, and watched wiggling tadpoles.

That summer, she accompanied her parents to the family estate in Montici.

Systematically, she began exploring the vineyard, the olive grove, the cow pasture, the orchard, and the vegetable garden. She walked almost as far as the end of the estate where stood the house in which lived the Gherardini farmer and his family. She sneaked into the stable and the pigpen and became acquainted with the long-eared donkey who pulled the manure cart.

In August, she was told she was now three years old, which meant nothing to her; but she was given an extra slice of *berlingozzo* cake, which meant a great deal. After that she wanted a new birthday every day, but when she learned that it would take many, many days before she got another one, she lost interest.

Autumn brought the family back to town. Now she stood at the nursery window gazing out at the leaden October sky, following with her eyes the rivulets of rain trickling down the glass panes. Then came the excitement of winter: the rattling of shutters, the crackling of burning logs, the snowflakes falling gently on the rooms, the chestnuts Tessa roasted for her in hot ashes.

It all was very new and interesting.

In August 1483, she celebrated her fourth birthday playing hostess to a number of little girls and boys from the neighboring villas. They had cake, fruit, and lemonade, yelled and played in the garden's alleys to their hearts' content. Then everyone went home, and life returned to normal.

A few days later, as she was crossing the cow pasture where the four Gherardini cows grazed, she noticed a boy in a tattered straw hat sitting under a walnut tree and playing a reed flute. She noticed that his feet were bare and none too clean. Clearly, he did not take a bath in rose water every morning, as she did.

He paid no attention to her and went on blowing into his flute while she studied him from afar, for she still was shy with strangers. After a while, she trussed up her skirt and ran to the house where she asked Tessa about him. She learned that his name was Nino and that he was the youngest son of the Gherardini farmer. Tessa, who like all servants of great families was a snob, stressed the fact that Nino was a lowly peasant boy, a *villano*, and that a proper young lady should have nothing to do with him.

The following morning Lisa ran to the pasture and, sure enough, Nino was there in his tattered straw hat and dirty feet. This time she walked close to him, making certain he saw her. After a while, he signaled her to come and sit on the grass by his side.

She did so, spread her skirt about her ankles, and launched into a stream of questions. He went on playing his flute as though she did not exist, and it finally dawned on her he wanted her to be silent. She stopped babbling and listened to his simple tune. When he finished playing, she said it was very pretty. He smiled at the compliment, and she thought he had the prettiest smile in the world.

After that, they became friends. He told her he was six years old and showed her how to make music by blowing into the reed and closing or opening the holes. He also taught her to sing a country song in dialect.

During the remainder of summer, they saw each other every day, even though Tessa disapproved of the relationship. What was the use, she wailed, to try making her into a lady and bathing her every morning in rose water, if she returned in the afternoon stinking of manure and singing songs in dialect, like a *villana?*

Lisa did not care whether she ever became a lady or not. She liked being with Nino and told him about Florence which he did not know. At sunset they walked, hand in hand, behind the four cows, back to the stable.

Then the rains came, and it was time for her to return to Via Maggio. She wept when she said goodbye and, on an impulse, kissed him on the cheek. He looked at her as though she had taken leave of her senses. Then, slowly, with the back of his hand he wiped off the kiss. She was a little hurt, but he smiled at her and she forgave him. She promised to think of him every day.

And she did — for nearly a week.

Shortly after her arrival, she was told that her honored grandfather Gherardini wished to see her.

He had never come to see her, and she could not understand why she should go to see him. She said so to Tessa, who told her to be quiet.

The following day she was dressed in her best gown and taken to the Gherardini mansion. Along the way, Tessa lectured her on how to ingratiate herself with the old merchant. She was to give him a big smile, pretend to be pleased at seeing him, and say nothing until spoken to.

"And remember, you must let him kiss you, if he wants to," whispered the slave, as they were climbing the stairs to the *studiolo*.

The encounter was a disaster.

She forgot to smile, froze on the threshold to examine the stranger behind his desk. When he grinned and leaned forward to take her in his arms, she was seized with fright and hid behind Tessa's skirt. Hurt by her behavior, he straightened up in his chair and signified Tessa to remove this uncouth *bimba* from his sight.

She was taken away in disgrace and reprimanded all the way back home. But, as *Mamma* did not reprove and that evening her *babbo* played with her as usual, she soon forgot the incident.

Anyway, another winter was arriving and all sorts of things demanded her attention: the dancing of flames in the fireplace, the rain that made people run in the street below, Tessa's chestnuts. Sometimes a gust of wind swirled down the chimney and filled the room with smoke. Then Tessa would rise, puff her cheeks, and, with a great waving of arms, try to push the smoke back into the chimney. Lisa would imitate her. For a few instants the air would bristle with excitement.

Somehow, that winter she caught cold.

She was put to bed with a hot brick at her feet, wool blankets up to her nose, and Tessa at her side, like some monumental, turbaned guardian angel.

The family doctor, an *algebraista* of great renown, was sent for. He came, double-chinned and dignified in his black robe, black gloves, and four-cornered hat. She peeked at him with circumspection while he stood, silent and ominous, peering at her over the rim of his spectacles. He then asked to see her tongue and she stuck it out. After looking at it, he told her to pull it back into her mouth. He seized her wrist and counted her pulse by the hourglass his assistant held before him. This done, he glanced into her chamber pot and assumed the deep and knowing expression doctors have assumed since the beginning of time.

Finally, he turned to Caterina and informed her that her daughter was suffering from noxious vapors in the head and pernicious humors in the chest. The patient must be kept in bed for three weeks and bled in the left foot.

"And her hair must be shaven," he added.

So saying, he bowed and walked away, followed by his assistant carrying his instruments and syringes.

The barber-surgeon appeared the next day, stubbly cheeked and hairy-armed in his bloodstained leather apron.

A mirthful fellow he was, with two front teeth missing and a stock of amusing stories. Lisa eyed him with apprehension as he sorted his instruments and told how he had bled a mule that morning, and a sillier, more contrary beast God had never created! It kicked, it reared, it bit, and made so much to-do you couldn't help laughing. By the time he finished his story, he had Lisa giggling, unaware that her foot was oozing blood into a basin of warm water.

She did, however, cry when he shaved her head as smooth as an egg. Tessa soothed her feelings by promising it would grow again and so beautiful that all the little girls of the neighborhood would be green with envy. Lisa felt much better after that.

For the next three weeks she remained in bed dozing, drinking herb potions. Twice a day she was carried to the fireplace and her head held close to the flames in order to dissipate the noxious head vapors. Then back to bed and another potion.

To while the hours away, Tessa told her about witches.

They were toothless, craggy-faced hags with long pointed noses and claws instead of nails. They were blind, but could see through artificial eyes, which they put in or took out as they pleased. They could make themselves invisible and no one noticed them when they came to town with their bags on their shoulders, poking their long noses into houses and looking for naughty children. When they found one — generally a little girl — the *strega* shoved her in her bag, took her to her house deep in the forest, cooked her with mustard and garlic, and ate her for supper.

Illness, Lisa discovered, was a shortcut to popularity. People felt sorry for you and brought you presents.

Her *babbo* gave her a silver bracelet that was worth catching a cold for. Even the parish priest, who sprinkled holy water on her bed, gave her a holy medal. Her grandmothers Gherardini and Rucellai brought her candy. Her honored grandfather Rucellai sent her a beautiful doll all the way from Pisa where he was serving as governor. Thereafter, she slept with her "child" in her arms — his name was Lappo — and she worried so much about his catching cold that she forgot about her own illness.

Only her grandfather Gherardini sent her nothing.

The three weeks went by and she was allowed to get out of bed. By New Year, the vapor and humors had gone, and she was as good as new. Once again she went trotting about the house. There were more places to explore, more drawers to peer into, more beds to crawl under.

And her hair had started to grow back.

In July, the family moved to Montici for the summer, as usual. Her first care on arriving at the villa was to go in search of Nino. He was not at his usual place in the cow pasture, or anywhere else. At last she found him, his bare chest shining with sweat, pitching hay in the mangers. She almost failed to recognize him, so tall had he grown. He had changed in other ways as well. Gone was the proud, taciturn boy she had known.

At the sight of her, he stopped working, took off his straw hat (that had not changed), and waited for her to speak. When she suggested they go and sit under the walnut tree, he shook his head and said it would not be proper. It had been all right for them to talk and sing last summer. They had been children then; but now she was almost five and the master's daughter, while he was seven and must help his father.

He said it all in one breath, as though he had rehearsed every word during the past months.

She went away brokenhearted.

That evening she wept in bed and fell asleep with tears still moist on her cheeks. For a few days she watched him working in the field by his father's side. She missed him and felt lonely.

Fortunately, the neighboring villas were filled with children who did not have to help their fathers, and they were eager to play with her. By the end of summer she had almost forgotten about Nino, but she had learned her lesson. Even children were not equal: some had to work while others could play as much as they liked.

Lisa returned to town prepared to spend another carefree winter. Alas, her carefree days were over. She was now five and five-year-old Renaissance girls must begin their education by learning about the Christian religion.

One morning an old nun dressed all in black climbed to the nursery. She walked in a shuffle, leaning on a cane. She had watery, red-rimmed eyes and no teeth. A black cloth covered her head and fell down the sides of her wrinkled face. Her name was Sister Perpetua and she belonged to the Order of the Ladies of Faenza.

Without a word, she took Lisa by the hand and made her sit on a footstool in front of her. Then she crossed herself and began the lesson. That day, she told her about a little boy named Gesù who was born in a stable with nothing but a little straw to sleep on and only a cow and a donkey who breathed on him to keep him warm.

"Didn't he even have a *coperta?*" asked Lisa goodheartedly.

No, said the nun. He did not have a blanket, for his parents were very poor. Lisa said she had many blankets and would be glad to give one to Gesù. The nun told her to stop talking and thereafter Lisa kept her thoughts to herself.

Sister Perpetua came every morning.

When it rained she dressed in a long cloak of *pignatolo*, a water-resistant cloth, and walked on high wooden socles to cross safely over puddles. She wore an eagle feather at the back of her head as a protection against lightning, for in the entire history of the world, no eagle had ever been struck by lightning.

She would remove her mantle, warm her hands at the fire, and begin.

That winter she told Lisa how Gesù had grown into a beautiful obedient little boy who helped his honored mother in the kitchen, fetched water at the public fountain, and gathered dead wood in the nearby forest for the stove. He also swept his honored father's shop. He also helped with his work for, although of royal blood, Joseph was only a poor carpenter.

As a diversion, Sister Perpetua would tell her how Lord God had created the sun, the moon, and the earth with Florence plumb in the middle of it; how Jonah had lived three days inside a big fish; how the king of Egypt's daughter had picked up Moses's cradle as it went floating down the river.

She was a superb storyteller with a flair for drama and a gift for mimicry. She imitated little Moses's wailings as he sailed down the Nile, the stomach rumblings of the whale after he had swallowed Jonah. With waves of her ample sleeves, she showed how God had flung fistfuls of stars across the sky. Then she would close her eyes and lean her cheek on her hand to show how He had taken a restful siesta after creating the universe.

Her faith was total, unclouded by doubt. A lifetime in a convent had kept her mind as naïve as that of a child. Mentally, she and Lisa were the same age.

Thus winter wore on. Then in February Lisa became aware of strange goings-on in the house.

Mamma had become invisible. She no longer came to the nursery or asked to see her. No longer did she run about the house with keys dangling from her belt, prodding servants, sorting, discussing menus with the cook. Stranger still, although in good health (for the doctor had not been sent for), she had retired to her room and taken to her bed. The bathtub had been brought up from the basement, set in the room, and, judging from the servants rushing back and forth with buckets of hot water, she took an unconscionable number of baths. The house was full of visiting ladies. On top of everything, *Babbo* ate by himself, and nobody spoke to him.

It all added up to something intriguing and mysterious. Tessa was of no help. She merely said that an angel was about to come down and bring Mamma a beautiful baby. Lisa took to squinting at the sky for a glimpse of some white-robed angel floating down to Via Maggio with a bundle in his arms.

None appeared while she watched, but one morning she was awakened by a blubbering Tessa who said the angel had come during the night and brought the most beautiful baby boy in the world.

That afternoon she was taken to visit her brother, whose name, she learned, was Francesco. All she saw was a cocoon of swaddlings about the size of a small fire log with a shriveled red little face at the end of it. She did not think much of it, but tactfully refrained from saying so.*

For days the house was the scene of joyous agitation. Streams of visitors came bearing gifts and clamoring to see Francesco. Even Grandfather Gherardini arrived, moist-eyed, demanding to see his grandson whom he actually held in his arms for a few instants. He then declared that his last wish was fulfilled and he now was ready to cross the Great Sea.

Lisa did not remember anyone making so much fuss over her. She grew weary of hearing Tessa say how wonderful Francesco was. Deep in her heart, she was jealous. She sought refuge in the garden, laying flat on her stomach and confiding her grievances to the tadpoles in the pond.

Her father gave her a pony for her sixth birthday, and that summer she received her first riding lessons. With little girls from neighboring villas, she took small rides sidesaddle through the hills.

One morning early in September, she awoke to find the vineyard abloom with farm girls in brightly colored blouses and wide-brimmed straw hats gathering grapes in wicker baskets.

---

* Little is known about Francesco de'Gherardini, except that he died in 1537. He had a son named Antonio Maria who, in turn, had one named Francesco who married Faustina de'Medici.

This branch of the Gherardini family, to which Mona Lisa belonged, became extinct in the eighteenth century with Amedeo de'Gherardini, who died on 1 June 1797.

Winemaking time had come to Montici.

Wine was one of the few things of which the Church approved. Had not the Savior changed water into wine at a wedding banquet? Didn't He turn His blood into wine at mass? Beside being a "noble" trade, the culture of grapes was almost a religious rite. In spring, priests blessed the budding grapes. Harmful insects were duly excommunicated. In summer, statues of saints were carried through vineyards to intercede for rain and if rain did not come, the statues were often thrown into the Arno.

The vintage, or *vendemmia*, brought a brief spell of Christian brotherhood to the Florentine countryside. Feuds were forgotten. Farmers who did not speak during the year helped one another. To Lisa, it provided an opportunity to have her father to herself for a few days. She walked by his side as he strolled through the vineyard, stopping to exchange friendly remarks in local dialect with the grape-gathering girls.

Along the way, he would explain how wine was made, how it got its color from the skin of the grape, how it was purified with whites of eggs and left to sleep for a long time in cool and dark cellars.

Later they walked to the shed where coopers hammered strips of iron around casks and girls would trample grapes in huge vats with their bare feet. To Lisa, this represented supreme happiness. Discreetly, she would tug at her father's sleeve, give him imploring glances until at last he would consent. In a flash, she would truss up her skirt, climb into the vat and join in the girls' bouncing to the strains of bagpipes.

That autumn her education began in earnest.

Sister Perpetua resumed her lessons. From her Lisa learned that God had created the world on a Wednesday at around nine o'clock in the morning and that Gesù had left his honored parents to roam about the countryside, preaching to peasants and fishermen. He cured the sick, walked on water, made loaves of bread and little fishes fall from the sky, and other such wondrous things.

Lisa asked why he had not stayed home and helped his poor

father. Impatiently, the nun told her to hush up and went on to describe how Gesù would make everybody sit on the ground and would tell them to love each other and if somebody slapped you on one cheek, you should quickly turn the other cheek. Then, once again, the first one – and so on.

Lisa did not think much of the idea, but did not say so.

She also learned about the saints who usually lived in caves, mossy grottoes or burning deserts, and were always hungry. On occasions, saints ventured to the nearest town where they would proclaim the glory of God, tell the king, governor, or chief of police to get rid of the bad women who lived in the city. They also would exhort crowds to repent and stop cheating each other. This got them in trouble. They were disemboweled, roasted over a slow fire, skinned alive, boiled in oil, or beheaded like Saint Denis, who after his decapitation had walked away with his head under his arm.

In addition to the nun's lessons, Lisa also was taught how to read and write by her mother.

On the fire bench of Mamma's sitting-room, she learned the alphabet. With a chalk stick, she wrote capital letters on a slate which she wiped clean with a rag. Three months later she could read and write simple words. That Christmas, her father gave her a crow quill that she might learn to write on paper. She also was shown how to make ink by pounding charcoal into dust and mixing it with soot gum, and a little water.

Mamma was very strict.

"Blessed Madonna," she would exclaim when Lisa did not apply herself, "this is not a Florentine girl, but some Roman simpleton!" In Florence, Romans were regarded as the most stupid people on earth. Or she would clasp her hands and cry, "Sweet Mother of God, what have I done to deserve this Sunday child?" Children born on Sunday had no salt on their brains or tongues, since the salt shops were closed that day.

Besides reading and writing, Lisa was taught the rudiments of etiquette.

First, the curtsy.

In an age when a girl must curtsy to her parents, grandparents, adult relatives, and practically everyone else, the reverence was the cornerstone of manners. But how difficult! It required much practice. But no sooner had she achieved a correct reverence, which her mother rewarded with a kiss, than already there was something else to learn.

"No use curtsying well, if you don't know how to wash your face properly," Mamma said.

A farm girl might be content to dip her face into a fountain or a brook. Not so a lady, who must scrub her cheeks, ears, and neck for at least five minutes.

Then came the brushing of teeth.

There also you could notice the difference between an uncouth country girl and a proper *signorina*. The first rubbed her teeth with her finger dipped into a solution of water and her own urine while the *signorina* used marble dust or finely ground eggshell. Wealthy patrons had their apothecaries prepare individual toothpastes made of honey, ginger, and crushed pearls.

"Now," remarked Caterina one day, "suppose you are at a friend's house and suddenly you want to blow your nose. What do you do?"

Until now, Lisa had held her nose between two fingers and blown hard into the fireplace, like everyone else. Well, this also was wrong. A young lady who wanted to blow her nose must excuse herself to her hostess, run to another room, lean out of the window and empty her nostrils. This done, she casually returned to her friends and joined in the conversation, as though nothing had happened.

There seemed to be no end to the things you must do if you were to become a lady. At times Lisa wondered whether it was worth the trouble.

She was glad when July came and the household prepared to leave for Montici, and all lessons were suspended for the summer.

When she returned to town in October, she was seven years old and resigned to becoming a lady.

Sister Perpetua now came only twice a week. The other days, her place was taken by a tutor, Mestro Bernardo. He was an old-looking young man with the gentle, defeated eyes of the unsuccessful intellectual. From his patched *lucco* and frayed sleeves, Lisa judged he must be very poor; from his wine-smelling breath, a drunkard. But he was patient, soft-spoken, and they got along well.

From him she learned that the sun revolved around the earth, and the earth was round and flat as a pancake. If you kept walking or sailing in one direction, you would fall off it and that would be the end of you. She memorized a few Latin verbs and became expert at counting on the abacus. Geography was her favorite subject. She was delighted when Maestro Bernardo told her that in the Indies there lived men and women with long curled noses, like cats' tails. In Ethiopia, a savage country where people had black skin, the inhabitants of this nation had an eye in the belly, at the spot where everybody else had an *ombelico*.

Sister Perpetua looked more wrinkled than the previous year. She walked more slowly. She told Lisa how Gesù had gone to Jerusalem, where he had been flogged, crowned with thorns, spat upon, and finally nailed to a cross. Lisa felt that nothing of it would have happened if he had remained home, but she did not say a single word.

She did, however, give a start when the old nun informed her that He had died because of her.

"Yes," she cackled, wagging a bony finger. "He died because of your sins."

This was news to Lisa, who, however, held her tongue while Perpetua launched into a tirade on what a great sinner she was, and all because her great-great-great- a thousand times great-grandfather, a certain Adamo, had eaten an apple. It sounded so far-fetched, so *ghiribizzoso* that she suspected that her teacher's brains had gone down to her slippers.

She was sure of it when she learned that she had two fathers beside the one who lived in the house.

One was the pope, *il Papa*. He lived in a grand palace, sat on a throne and you must kiss his foot before addressing him. The other one lived in the sky and knew everything about everybody, especially Lisa de'Gherardini. Each time she committed a sin (and she committed one practically all the time) He wrote it down in a big book, so He wouldn't forget about it. He was awfully strict. Did she put out her tongue at Tessa, that was a sin. Did she pretend not to hear when called, that was another sin and down in the big book it went. The littlest thing sent Him into transports of wrath. A lie, even a tiny one, got you thousands of years in the purgatory; a big one, an eternity in hell.

Neither of these two fathers appealed to Lisa and she did not dwell on them. Anyway, she had other things in mind, for, on top of everything, Mamma was now teaching her how to eat properly, as a lady should.

If you grabbed food with your hand instead of plucking it daintily with three fingers from the salver, you are like a pig. The same applied if you took big mouthfuls and chewed noisily like a horse. Or if you licked your fingertips or wiped them on your sleeve. The thing to do was to dip your fingertips in the silver bowls of warm water that servants passed between courses and discreetly wiped them on the tablecloth (napkins being unknown). Chicken bones could be tossed under the table, but not in your neighbor's lap.

A young lady was not supposed to belch or scratch herself in the course of a meal. Only old ladies could do that. Nor were you permitted to spit on the floor or rub your nose with the back of your hand.

"If you ever did such a thing," Mamma would lecture, "people would say, 'This Lisa de'Gherardini is most uncouth. She eats like a pig. She is a shame to her clan and we'll never invite her in our house again.' "

And so Lisa applied herself, and in time acquired good table manners. That spring, as a reward, she was allowed to sit at dinner with her honored parents.

Gone were the happy-go-lucky nursery days when she could grab a broiled pigeon with her two hands and gnaw her way through it, her cheeks smeared with gravy. Gone were the finger-licking, the giggling and chatting with your mouth full.

Now all was silence and propriety. She curtsied to her father when he entered the dining room and took his place at the head of the table. She picked up food with three fingers, as prescribed, and chewed behind closed lips, also as prescribed. Through the meal she felt her mother's eye on her, caught an occasional frown or approving nod. Now and then, her *babbo* would give her a wink of encouragement.

That spring she also began escorting her parents to Sunday mass.

It meant getting up earlier than usual, hurrying through her bath, skipping massage, gulping down breakfast, dressing in her best brocade gown, and sedately walking with Tessa, a few steps behind her honored genitors.

Churches were meeting places used for poetry readings, literary lectures, and sacred plays as well as for religious ceremonies. Mass was regarded as a dutiful weekly call paid on some rich and influential relative. It provided ladies with an opportunity to show off new dresses, gather around *braseros*, and indulge in gossip. Because of the absence of pews or benches, men paced back and forth to keep warm, talking business in reverent whispers. Children romped under their nurses' watchful eyes.

One Sunday, at the end of the service, Antonio turned to his daughter and said, "It's a very beautiful day. My little fish, how would you like it if we took a walk together, just the two of us?"

And so a tradition was born. From then on every Sunday, Caterina and Tessa would return home while Lisa and *Babbo* would stroll, hand in hand, through the town. Along the way, he would point out places of interest: the Giotto Tower whence came the chimes that woke her up in the morning, the Battistero where she had been christened, the Old Palace with its slender tower and one-handed clock, usually out of order.

They also went to the zoo, where they looked at wolves, bears, parrots, monkeys, and the giraffe which the sultan of Egypt had sent Lorenzo de'Medici. Most of all, they gazed at Marzocco, the lion that was the living emblem of the Republic. Most of the time he crouched in his cage, whisking flies off his back with his tufted tail or yawning in the visitors' faces. Occasionally he would let out a roar and then Lisa would clutch her *babbo*'s hand.

In this way she came to know Florence's landmarks — and her

father. Until then he had been a hazy figure in the background of her life; suddenly he stood in the center of it. She loved walking alongside this tall, distinguished *signore* at whom ladies smiled and men doffed their hats. To all, he would bow and smile in return, even though he did not always know who they were.

"They're probably cousins of ours," he would say with a chuckle. "You see, my little fish, we've lived in this town so long that we have more relatives than a dog has fleas."

He was, she felt, a *babbo* to be proud of.

As to her other two fathers — the one who lived in Rome and the one who lived in the sky — they receded into insignificance. The man who held her hand and called her "my little fish" was the only one she wanted, the only one she loved.

That October Antonio was elected to the Board of Directors of the Wool Guild. This distinction prompted his father to summon him and, in an emotional oration, demand that he and his family come to live in the family mansion. No longer was it proper for a director of the Wool Guild to live in a modest house in an unfashionable district.

That evening after supper, Antonio informed Caterina of his father's request. She did not protest, but her expression betrayed her dismay.

"We've been happy in this house, haven't we?" she said, holding back her tears.

For nine years it had been their home. Here their two children were born; here their love had grown deeper with each passing day.

"My election to the board is only an excuse," he went on. "He is lonely and wants his grandson about him for his few remaining years."

She understood. "We shall feel the same when Lisa and Francesco go away. Do not fret, revered husband, so long as we have each other, we shall be happy anywhere."

And so the dismantling of the house began. She attended to everything, was everywhere at once. Down came the window curtains, the birthplates on the dining room wall, the picture of the Madonna over the headboard. Linen was sorted into painted chests, the kitchen utensils removed from their shelves. One morning two painters from the Brotherhood of Saint Luke whitewashed the whole house.

Lisa had not yet learned resignation. Sniveling and muttering under her breath, she laid down her "children" in a big wooden box, as in a common grave. She hated her grandfather Gherardini and she told Tessa he was the worst *nonno* in the world. What right had he to upset her life and everyone else's? Never, never would she be nice to him; never would she give him a smile.

The day before they were to move, she walked through the garden. It was a quiet autumn day with a pewter-gray sky and the hint of approaching winter in the air. Silently, she said goodbye to the trees, the chickens, the tadpoles. It occurred to her that she was saying goodbye to her happy childhood and, with tears running down her face, she ran back into the house and into Tessa's arms.

She arrived at the Gherardini palazzo with the firm intention of hating it — and she did.

A cursory exploration convinced her it was damp and smelled musty. It lacked all modern conveniences. There were no heat ducts in the walls, no glass panes in the windows, but a glazed linen that shut out the light and let in the cold. There were no carpets, but rather straw on the floor; there was no garden, no pond.

"It is awful," she told Tessa.

More awful still were the suppers in the candlelit dining room with her grandfather enthroned at the head of the table and Pandolfo, forbidding in livery and white gloves, at his back. She was mortally afraid of him and so, apparently, was everyone else. Her honored mother and grandmother curtsied to him when he entered the room and even her beloved *babbo* bent down to kiss his hand. Everybody ate in silence and waited for him to finish chewing his food, which took forever, as he had only a few teeth left.

Now and then she would feel his eyes resting on her and once or twice she thought he was smiling at her. But she did not trust him and pretended not to notice.

Her education progressed on several fronts at once. She was given music lessons by her mother, who made her sing simple songs while accompanying herself on a small lute. Her tutor patiently instructed her in Latin, French, astronomy, and arithmetic.

As for Sister Perpetua, she told Lisa about heaven and hell and how you got into *paradiso,* if you bought enough indulgences. They were sold at street corners, like lottery tickets, or from house to house by monks. When you died and arrived at the Heavenly Gate, you showed Saint Peter your sheaf of indulgences and if you had bought many of them, he had no choice but to let you in.

At the same time, she was learning about housekeeping. Every morning she accompanied her grandmother to the Old Market Square and was taught how to choose a ripe watermelon, and haggle with cart vendors. Before leaving the piazza, she followed her honored *nonna* to the stocks and slapped the face of the cutpurse clamped in the stocks.

In addition to all this, she helped Tessa with the beds, the dusting, waxing, sweeping, emptying the chamber pots in the streets. She assisted the cook by peeling onions or pounding garlic in stone cruets.

With so many things to do, she had little time to complain about the house or hate her grandfather; and before she knew it was Christmas.

At the crack of dawn she ran to the fireplace and found her shoes filled with a fine doll from her parents, many toys, and a lovely silver flower wreath, like the ones maidens wore on festive occasions. When she learned that it came from her grandfather, some of her hostility subsided. Anyone who gave you such a lovely and expensive gift could not be all bad.

She began to answer his smiles across the table. She even felt sorry it took him so long to chew his food. It was sad to be old and have only a few teeth.

One afternoon, as she was racing up the stairs, she collided with him.

"And wither are you running, my child?" he asked gently. "Is the house on fire that you should be running like a hare before the huntsman? Have you got an urgent message for someone?"

No, she replied with a sketchy reverence. She was just running to her room because she liked it better than walking. He remarked that he, too, had been a boy once, long ago, and had liked to run. Since she had nothing better to do, would she like to visit his *studiolo?*

They climbed the stairs together, stopping now and then for him to catch his breath. When she entered the small room, she was surprised to find it had glass panes at the window and a carpet on the floor. Why didn't he have glass in every window and carpets in every room, she asked. Because it would cost too much money, he replied, and he was too old to make changes.

"When I cross the Great Sea, your honored father will make all the changes he wants," he said.

He showed her his gold chain of office as president of the Wool Guild and hung it around her neck. She laughed and the sound of her laughter brought a smile to his lips. He invited her to sit down and told her about the time when he was an apprentice at the mill and washed raw wool on his knees.

The visit opened a new era in their relationship. She took the habit of dropping in on him whenever she had a free moment. She would sit on the floor at his feet, raise her face to him, and wait for him to tell her a story. He would smile, feast his eyes on her coltish grace, clear his throat, and tell her about her noble ancestors.

According to him, all had been men of the utmost integrity, civic spirit, and kindness of heart. Whenever they had been thrown in jail, banished, or beheaded, it had invariably been due to some fearful miscarriage of justice. For all, he had some excuse: even Baldovinetti de'Gherardini who had murdered Antonio da Panzano in a political discussion; even the Gherardini of Montagliari, those splendid rural lords who had tried to starve Florence by cutting the legs of the mules who brought food to the town; even Andrea de'Gherardini who had been exiled for dipping into public funds.

The only one for whom he had words of indulgent censure was Francesco de'Gherardini, Florence's *gonfaloniere,* who, in 1409, had received the Golden Rose from the sacred hands of Pope Martin V. This rare distinction had gone to his head and unhinged his mind. The poor man had not been the same after that. He had added "della Rosa" to the family name, forsaken the ancient Gherardini crest, and designed a ridiculous one of his own showing a lion standing on its hind legs and holding a rose in its paw.

"He had lost his reason," said Noldo, implying that the same thing had happened to all the Gherardini della Rosa.

But the ancestor for whom Noldo reserved his highest praises was Dominus Otho de'Gherardini, son of Gherardo and Jollita who, in 1057, had been expelled from Florence and found refuge in Normandy.

There he attached himself to Edward the Confessor and followed him to England where he became a British nobleman. He anglicized his surname from Gherardini to Geraldine, and his name from Gherardo to Gerald. By one means or another, he acquired great riches and vast domains. At his death, he possessed three lordships in Surrey, three in Buckinghamshire, three in Berkshire, four in Middlesex, nine in Wiltshire, ten in Hampshire, three in Dorset, one in Somerset.

Otho's son Walter succeeded to his father's lands, titles, and money. In addition he became constable of Windsor. In the course of his career he joined the Norman barons who conquered Wales. With them, he moved to this beautiful, rugged land. For his part, Walter conquered Gladys, daughter of the prince of North Wales. His son Gerald married equally well when he married the lovely Nesta, daughter of Rhys-ap-Tewdr, prince of South Wales.

So fetching was Nesta that as a young girl — almost a child — she had been abducted by Prince Henry of England, who was at war with her father. Henry visited her between battles and she gave him a son. Thus she was no longer a maiden when she was returned to her parents and married to Gerald Geraldine.

Her husband, who was greatly in love with her, chose to ignore this. She, in turn, began cuckolding him almost immediately after the wedding with various Welsh knights. Whenever he returned from the battlefield, Gerald, on hearing of his wife's misconduct, would fall into terrible rages. As he could not challenge the entire Welsh knighthood, he solaced himself with his rivals' wives. Thus, some sort of a delicate balance was struck and life went on in the days of the chivalry.

Nesta had a favorite lover: Owen, prince of Cardigan. She dreamed of spending the rest of her life at his side and he said it would be heavenly. So together they arranged her kidnaping. As it was to take place while she lay in bed with her husband, the matter required careful planning.

Owen set fire to Gerald's castle in the middle of the night. When smoke filled the bedroom and the air resounded with the crash of falling beams, Nesta awoke Gerald and suggested he go and see what might be the matter. She even helped him out of the window with a stout rope she had stored for just that purpose.

No sooner had her husband reached the ground and started fighting the flames, then Nesta signaled Owen to come and fetch her. He burst into the room, and carried her out of the blazing manor.

They had a few ecstatic weeks together until she returned, unexpectedly, to her husband, who thrashed her within an inch of her life and finally forgave her. But he never pardoned Owen, whom he had the pleasure of killing before he himself died in 1135.

Between lovers, Nesta presented her husband with a daughter, Angharet, and three boys. The eldest, Maurice Fitzgerald Geraldine, was to annex Ireland and make it part of England.

He crossed the Irish Channel with thirty men-at-arms, one hundred archers, and ten knights. For two years he skirmished with the natives. Then one summer day he came upon King Rory O'Connor as he was bathing in the Liffey River with his general staff while nearby his men relaxed in a meadow. Maurice pounced on Rory, who barely had time to scramble out of the water and in regal nakedness take to his heels followed by his army and generals. The pursuit lasted until sunset and broke the resistance. Two months later, in October 1171, King Henry II of England arrived with five hundred knights and four thousand archers, who were no longer needed.

For his share of the loot, Maurice appropriated the two adjoining kingdoms of Leinster and Munster, roughly a fourth of Ireland. At his death, he left Leinster to his elder son, Gerald Fitzgerald Geraldine, who became the forefather of the earls of Kildare, later dukes of Leinster. Munster went to his younger son, Thomas, who begot the earls of Desmond.

The Gherardini clan of Florence now had a flourishing branch in Ireland.*

One February afternoon Lisa knocked at the door of the *studiolo*. When she received no invitation to enter, she peered in and saw her *nonno*, hunched on his chair and shivering by the fire. He explained he had spent the morning at *la Borsa* watching the fluctuation of stocks. The *loggia* was drafty, and he had caught cold.

"I am afraid I've sickened with some pernicious fever," he said through chattering teeth.

Lisa informed her grandmother, who took matters in hand. For once she paid no attention to his frowns or protests. In a minute she had him in bed with blankets up to his chin, a hot brick at his feet, and a hot brew in his stomach. That evening, Lisa prayed for him on her knees.

Noldo recovered in a few days, but he did not regain his cheerfulness. He regarded his illness as an omen that his time on earth was coming to an end and he must truly prepare for his journey across the Great Sea.

The torments of hells, once remote and hazy, suddenly became very real. He could hear the screams of the damned amid the hissing of flames, smell the stench of roasted flesh, see the grimacing red devils with their pitchforks in hand.

Memories of old sins haunted him.

---

* About the conquest of Ireland and the Irish Gherardini, see *The Geraldines* by Brian Fitzgerald, and other books listed in the bibliography at the end of this volume.

He recalled his nightly meetings with Chrigoria while his father slept peacefully; he remembered the Venetian courtesan, the bathhouse wenches with their expert caressing hands. And what of his sarcastic remarks about the orphanage's mother superior, his distrust of Pope Sixtus? What about his boastfulness, his gambling at the guild, his fits of anger? Why, according to Dante, anger alone got you in the fifth circle of Hell: a marshy, foggy place where naked and perpetually angry men bit and struck one another for all eternity.

And there was more, much more.

On occasions, he had loaned money at usurious rates, and that brought you to the seventh circle of Hell. There you hopped through flames until the end of time, with little money bags tied to your neck. Was this the way he, Noldo de'Gherardini, former president of the Wool Guild, was to spend his eternity?

The prospect made his thinning gray hair stand up. He became very pious, gave huge alms, bought an enormous number of indulges, and arranged for masses to be said on his behalf. He tried to read the Fathers of the Church and fell asleep on them. He then turned to the Bible, but when he learned that the only man who had been chosen to survive the Flood was Noah, a notorious drunkard, he doubted God's wisdom. Neither did he find solace in Saint Paul's Epistles. That this *popolano*, this lowly tentmaker should presume to give advice to a Gherardini outraged his sense of propriety.

Nowhere did he find peace.

"Such a great sinner I've been," he told Lisa, who spent much time with him for she sensed he derived comfort from her presence.

He worried he might not have bought enough indulgences and would have to spend several thousand years in purgatory, a place almost as bad as hell.

All he asked was to be admitted into Heaven, no matter where or how far from the Almighty's throne. Nor did he care whether he ever saw any angels, saints, or virgins. He would be content with any little place in the remotest region of paradise.

"Anywhere, anywhere at all," he said humbly.

He lost his appetite. His round and smooth face guttered down in folds of waxen flesh. For the first time in his life, he slept badly.

"Noble husband," remarked his wife one evening, "you look as sad as a willow in the rain."

"I am, wife, I am — and with good reasons."

"Have you bought indulgences?"

So many, he replied, he now was a poor man.

"Repentance is more expensive than the sin," he lamented.

"Have you thought about making a pilgrimage?"

He hadn't, and the idea appealed to him at once.

Pilgrimages were a feature of Renaissance life. They came in various lengths of duration, degrees of hardship, and cost. Pilgrimages to the Holy Land were so long and arduous that few people ever returned from them. They were intended for murderers or husbands who wanted to get away from their wives forever.

There were also beneficial pilgrimages to famous shrines.

A Roman church rescinded 48,000 years from a purgatory sentence, just by entering it. The German town of Wittenberg possessed 17,000 relics, including a straw from Jesus's manger, a drop of Mary's milk, and 204 bone fragments of the children slaughtered by Herod. Exeter Cathedral in England had the candle which had lit the tomb of Christ and a sprig of the Burning Bush from which God had spoken to Moses. A Durhman monastery treasured the Virgin's shirt and showed it to pilgrims on receipt of a small donation.

"They are all too far from me," sighed Noldo. "I would be dead before I arrived."

Fortunately, there were pilgrimages which did not venture farther than fifty miles from Florence and lasted only nine days. They were guild-sponsored and popular among bankers and rich merchants who were permitted to bring their valets and large stocks of delicacies. On such terms, pilgrimages turned into convivial outings.

This was the kind Noldo had in mind. He made inquiries from

his "cousin" Mariotto Rucellai and learned that the Bankers' Guild was sponsoring a pilgrimage to Arezzo in late April. Mariotto then arranged for him to be included among the pilgrims.

Thus, one morning Lisa was treated to the sight of her unshaven grandfather dressed in a white robe with a rope around his waist and a large cross of red felt over his chest. His feet were shod in sandals. In his purse he carried the ritual "needle and thread" purportedly to mend his garments; in his hand he held a shepherd's crook. This last was intended for him to lean upon, ford streams, and defend himself against farm dogs. It gave him a faintly biblical look. On his head he wore the conical hat that was part of the pilgrim's uniform.

Lisa thought he looked ridiculous and touching at the same time. She gave him a smile and a fine curtsy.

In the courtyard Noldo bid farewell to his household with the solemnity of a crusader leaving for the Holy Land. He traced a large sign of the cross over the kneeling servants, gave his wife his hand to kiss, a blessing to Antonio, and to Lisa a pat on the cheek.

Turning around, he thumped his staff on the ground and marched out of his house followed by his groom Tommaso, driving a cart heaped with hampers of food and camping equipment, for pilgrims were supposed to sleep in the open air.

He joined the bankers waiting for him in the middle of the square. Like him, they were dressed in white penitents' robes and wore the same kind of pointed hats. He took his place among them and they started crossing the piazza, two abreast, singing the ritual lament, "Mercy, Eternal God! Have mercy on the sinner!"

Nine days later Noldo returned from his pilgrimage, whitebearded, pink-cheeked and looking much better. Once again, his face was round and smooth. He told Lisa about his journey: the violets along country lanes, the nesting birds at work in the trees, the cypress-studded Umbrian hills, the early morning masses in rural chapels, the afternoon siestas on the grass, the superb meals, the card games afterward with his new banker friends.

And he told her about his vision.

One night when he was lying under his tent, thinking about

the devils who were awaiting him in hell, the Madonna had appeared to him. "Noldo," she had said, "stop fretting." She had not forgotten the twenty-five florins he had given the orphanage during Antonio's wool-buying trip and the statue of herself he had placed in the *tintillano* annex. This and the indulgences he had bought had made up for most of his big sins, leaving only a few venial ones. Somehow she would arrange to smuggle him into a distant part of Heaven, through a wooden gate nobody knew about.

Kindly, she had described the region to him. It looked much like the Arno valley and it had a nice river in which he could fish whenever he felt like it. No saints, angels, let alone the Almighty ever visited there. It was sparsely populated and the few houses could not compare with the mansions in which saints, martyrs, hermits, and other heavenly "fat ones" lived. But she had found for him a nice little villa, half hidden in an olive grove. Nothing ostentatious, but with a good tile roof and a working fireplace. There he would wait for his good wife to join him, and together they would spend their eternity in peace and modest comfort.

"By the time I woke up, the Madonna was gone," he said. "But I am not afraid any more."

He died in his sleep three days later.

From the nursery window (children did not attend funerals), Lisa watched as he was carried out of the house at dusk, unshrouded, on a bier borne by four black-hooded men. In the glow of torches, the mourners followed, silent amid the wails of hired weepers. People in the streets crossed themselves; women knelt on the cobblestones and wept.

Lisa could not understand this display of sorrow. To her, death was merely the ultimate feature of old age. First you lost your hair, then your teeth, then your eyesight, and your face wrinkled up, like that of Sister Perpetua. Then one day you died.

"Why do they weep?" she asked Tessa. "He is happy in his little house and waiting for my honored grandmother to come and join him."

He did not have long to wait.

Three weeks later Donna Lisa died from no apparent cause.

The doctor was puzzled, but not Lisa. She knew that her *nonna* had worried about her noble husband, wondering if he had his Spanish wine over dessert, someone to help him dress in the morning, sensing that he was lonely and missed her company after supper by the fire.

So, she had prayed to the Madonna to let her die, and the Madonna, who loved her very much, had obliged.

Lorenzo de'Medici by Andrea del Verrocchio. *Courtesy of the National Gallery of Art.*

The Hour of the Lion

 Reassured over the fate of her grandparents, Lisa turned her attention to the changes that were taking place in the old Gherardini mansion.

Glass panes replaced glazed linen in windows. Heat ducts were installed in walls; carpets were laid on floors instead of straw. Sunshine burst into the damp palazzo. The musty smell vanished. One room adjacent to that occupied by her parents was transformed into an elegant bath, with a beautiful carved oak tub and a vanity table.

Her father now presided at supper and sat at the head of the table. All the house servants now called him "Master." Mamma went to Old Market Square in the morning with a maid and Lisa. They passed from cart to cart and all three slapped the thief who happened to be in the stocks that day.

In the afternoon Lisa accompanied her mother on her round of visits. Dressed in her best gown and holding one of her dolls in her arms, she was duly presented to ladies of all ages and performed for them the curtsy she had so laboriously practiced.

Some patted her cheek; others spoke a few words to her. Then they clapped their hands and summoned a maid or a turbaned woman slave who led Lisa to the children's quarters on the top floor of the house. There she played until she was brought back to the living room and rejoined her mother. Again she curtsied and decorously made her exit.

In the course of one of these visits, she met Contessina, Lorenzo de'Medici's youngest daughter.

Their friendship was immediate. One hour later they knew everything about each other. From that day onward, they visited each other constantly at one or the other's house.

They occasionally went with Tessa or Barnaba, Contessina's nurse, to Piazza Firenze, to listen to Beppo the storyteller.

From him, they learned about early Christians and how they were eaten by lions or roasted on pits, like chickens. They also became acquainted with pagan gods and goddesses, for Beppo varied his programs with stories of saints as well as mythological personages.

They came to know Jupiter intimately. He was the king of gods and very fond of beautiful females. He often came down on earth in search of some lovely girl who had caught his fancy, and started courting her. Then he would pull big clouds across the sky so that his wife Juno, who was very jealous, would not know where he was or what he was doing.

Lisa soon became familiar with Contessina's house, the big Casa Medici at the corner of Via Larga: its colonnated inner courtyard, walled-in garden in the rear, stately rooms hung with beautiful paintings and tapestries.

She met Contessina's mother, Donna Clarissa, who came to the nursery one afternoon unannounced. She sat, panting, while Lisa plunged into a reverence. She was a pale, stout lady with sad bulging eyes. She spoke with a strong Roman accent and wore the traditional Roman headcloth instead of the transparent Florentine headveil.

She complimented Lisa on her curtsy and said she would write Donna de'Gherardini for permission to let her daughter come and visit Contessina that summer. She did not remain long for she started coughing.

"Mamma has devils in her chest," said Contessina when her mother was gone.

Now and then, Lisa caught a glimpse of Contessina's older sisters and brothers — and, once, of Lorenzo himself, who smiled at her and patted her cheek. She also got to know Contessina's younger brother, Giuliano. He was nine, tall for his age with hazel eyes and light chestnut hair. Never had Lisa known such a mischievous boy. He instantly adopted her, which meant that he pulled her pigtails and forced her to wrestle with him. She hated him and swore never to speak to him again. Then, unexpectedly, he would bring her a flower from the garden and she would not hate him any more.

Early in July a groom in the white and purple Medici livery rode to Montici with a message for Donna de'Gherardini in which Donna Clarissa de'Medici begged Caterina to let her charming daughter spend a fortnight at Careggi with the Medici family.

Although the distance between the two villas was only a few miles, it took Lisa most of the day to make the journey. The sun was about to set when she reached Careggi on her pony with the family groom at her side and followed by a baggage cart on which sat a stable boy and Tessa in full regalia and orange turban.

Contessina was waiting at the door of the villa, which, spacious as it was, was packed with relatives and houseguests. Lisa and Contessina slept in the same bed, which gave them an opportunity to chat in whispers after the candle had been blown out. The days were too short for all the things they had to say and do. After the morning bath in the two-seat tub and a substantial breakfast, they would disappear into the garden, where they waded in the large circular pond and attended to their dolls. Sometimes, in the afternoon, they would ride to neighboring villas for picnics or fishing parties.

Occasionally they would spy Lorenzo strolling pensively along an alley or reading a book under a tree. When they succeeded in attracting his attention he would signal them to come and join him. In a flash, they would sit at the right and left of him and tell him about their "children's" misbehavior. Chin in hand, he would pretend to mull over the problems and threaten to call a witch,* then, after a while with a sigh, he would rise and return to his study where he resumed his never-ending work. For hours he would pore over papers of state, tax records, statements from the

* In an age which frowned upon familiarity between parents and children, Lorenzo's playfulness was severely criticized. Several ambassadors' letters mention "His Excellency's 'inordinate love for his offspring.' "

Medici bank, petitions of all sorts or, pacing the floor, he would dictate replies to the unbroken stream of messages which arrived at the villa from every part of the world.

He now was thirty-seven, at the peak of his fame and power, and everyone, it seemed, wanted a moment of his time. And so he would work without respite every day until he felt too tired to go on. Then he would dismiss his secretary, Niccolo Michelozzo, who was also his childhood friend, and in the deepening dusk he would brood over the twist of fate that, for three generations, had chained the Medici family to Florence's destiny.

In the early days of the Republic, like the true democrats they were, the Florentines distrusted any public servant the moment they elected him to office. They lived in dread one of them might steal their precious liberties and make himself dictator. To parry this danger, they elected a brand new Signoria every two months.

Only then did they feel secure.

They were an industrious people and very keen on money. From dawn to dusk, they sat at their primitive looms weaving a cloth they made from the sheep grazing outside the city walls. It wasn't much of a cloth. It scratched, it frayed, it did not keep one warm. But it was the only cloth they knew how to make and they sold it through the villages of the Arno valley, as far as Pisa, some fifty miles away.

In this way, life went on in Old Florence: busy, laborious, reasonably happy. Had they remained poor, the Florentines would have lived in peaceful obscurity, content to weave their wretched cloth and talk politics. But it was their destiny to become rich.

Very rich.

In 1238 a group of saintly monks, the Humble Brothers of Saint Michael, or *Umiliati*, petitioned for permission to build a small wool mill in the city. They were told to erect it on the pasture across the river, which they did. Then, singing hymns, they sat at their looms and proceeded to manufacture the softest, warmest, strongest, most beautiful cloth in the world. They called it *panna di San Martino* or *San Martino*, for short.

The local wool men looked at it and were amazed. Promptly,

they pirated the monks' manufacturing processes; and a cloth rush was on, as frantic as any gold rush. The grazing meadow turned into a bedlam of hammering, sweating, shouting men building makeshift mills in which they turned out San Martino cloth, as fast as they could.

In no time they had given a bad name to the newborn wool industry. Complaints poured in from everywhere to the Wool Guild. Its officials passed draconian rules of manufacture and levied crushing fines against transgressors. Several landed in jail; two were hanged.

The others saw the light.

Purged of its malefactors, the wool industry grew to gigantic size and became the "noblest" of all trades, open only to families of the highest standing.

Before long, there was not enough wool in Italy to feed the mills along the Arno. The Florentine wool men or *lanaiuoli* began sending representatives, usually their sons, to Spain, France, England, where they bought raw wool which was shipped to Florence where it was converted into San Martino and sold back to their countries of origin at a profit of four hundred percent.

At this rate, the "lords of the looms," as they were called, had more money than they knew what to do with. They began looking for some other profitable endeavor and found it in banking.

They plunged headlong into finance as they had in textiles and proved as successful at one as at the other. Their shrewdness and daring stupefied Europe's old countinghouses. To avoid the transfer of bullion, always a risky procedure in those days, they reinvented the letter of credit, thus throwing highwaymen out of work.

Banking became an international paper game at which they excelled. Behind the double doors of their unpretentious offices (ostentation was bad form) they sent coded messages to their agents by swift ships or galloping couriers and moved huge sums of money across the chessboard of Europe with deft and rapacious hands.

Now Florence had two suckling breasts: textiles and banking.

In 1252, only fourteen years after the arrival of the *Umiliati* monks, the first gold florin was minted and immediately accepted as standard European currency. By the middle of the fourteenth century, the small Tuscan town had become very rich; by the beginning of the fifteenth, the world's richest.

Sudden and colossal wealth is a mixed blessing to an individual, as well as a community.

Money begets temptations from which the poor are spared. It provides ever-fresh opportunities to make costly mistakes, and the Florentines made so many simply because they had so much money to make them with. Once again, they proved how difficult it is to be both wise and rich while it requires no brains at all to remain a pauper.

With their coffers full of florins, it dawned on them that they should have "an empire." Their Republic should rule over every foot of Tuscan ground, from the Apennines to the sea.

They launched a policy of frantic territorial expansion. Some towns they bought, for you could buy a town simply by paying the local lord to move out; those they could not buy, they took by force. For nearly half a century, the Florentines were engaged in permanent conflict.

Fortunately, in those days war was a gentlemanly game played according to urbane, intelligent rules. As patriotism had not yet been invented and national armies did not exist, military operations were left to prudent and experienced *condottieri* – soldiers of fortune with troops of their own – who offered their service to the highest bidder and whose main concern was to keep their men – and themselves – alive. Thus bravery was frowned upon. Headlong flight was accepted as a clever tactical maneuver on the grounds that who fled today lived to fight (or flee again) another day.

In the early Renaissance, Italian warfare was divided into campaigns of movement and campaigns of attrition.

Campaigns of movement began with the opposing generals taking to the field in late spring, ostensibly in search of each other. A few weeks passed in marches, countermarches, flanking movements, forays, feints, counterfeints, and strategic retreats. At no time did the adversaries come within striking distance of each other. Every afternoon the *condottieri* sent a message to their respective employers describing the activities of the day. These messages were read to the populations, thus keeping their war fever at peak temperature.

Finally, by mid-August, the campaign climaxed in one — sometimes two — great battle. The enemy armies converged to a suitable, previously agreed-upon spot, usually a vast meadow. Furious preparations for the forthcoming encounter began. Patrols reconnoitered, crawling on their bellies, missing each other by inches. Armor was polished; swords honed.

At last, one morning at sunrise (sooner, it was too dark to see; later, too hot to fight) cavalrymen were hoisted on their well-upholstered horses. Amid the blares of trumpets and the waving of flags, they charged, flinging themselves at their foes, making horrible faces, shouting deadly insults, whirling their sabers over their adversaries' heads, where they could do no harm. Behind them, archers aimed their arrows to the sun.

In this way, the most violent frays resulted in few casualties; often none at all. At the Battle of Anghiari, one of Florence's greatest victories, the sole fatality had been that of a cavalryman who had fallen from his mount and been trampled to death by his fellow horsemen.

The battle over, warriors retired to their tents for a well-earned siesta. At sunset, prisoners — if any — were escorted back to their camp under a flag of truce. Then came one or two weeks of rest during which the opposing generals exchanged greetings, baskets of fruit, and camp girls.

If the weather remained fair, another battle was scheduled. By then the autumn rains had usually arrived, sending adversaries to their winter quarters. Rain was the natural enemy of the Italian soldier. It rusted armor, blurred archers' aim, caused horses to stumble. Mercenaries saw no point in fighting in the rain when they could fight better in sunshine.

Campaigns of attrition were to besiege cities and crumble their ramparts through artillery fire.

To do this, guns must first be set in position, a slow and laborious procedure, for Italian artillery mainly consisted of bombards, weighing about twenty-five thousand pounds and requiring two hundred oxen to be moved about, probably the most cumbersome war engines ever devised.

They were fearsome to behold, these bombards, and fittingly they were given fearsome names: "the Desperate," "the Cruel," "None-of-your-Jaw," and such. They fired round, handhewn stones that weighed about fifty pounds and seldom reached their objectives. As these stones were costly and hard to chisel, they were given much care. Whenever they fell short of their targets, artillerymen ran to retrieve them in order to fire them again and again until they finally crashed into the enemy ramparts or exploded, usually in the bombarders' faces. Because of the risks they ran, artillerymen received double pay.

Either by campaigns of movement or attrition, the Florentines always won. As they had the most money, they could hire the best generals, raise the largest armies, buy the biggest bombards, chisel the most stones. In the end, they always got what they wanted.

By 1429, they owned every town in Tuscany except Siena and Lucca, and they were next on their list. Without a pause, they began preparing an expedition against Lucca. It was calculated to last three weeks and, of course, to end in a great victory.

Three years later, the war was still on and going badly.

By now, the Florentines had spent over fifteen million florins, accumulated an astronomical national debt, and accomplished the feat of bringing the world's richest town to the brink of bankruptcy.

A tall, silent, stoop-shouldered man was watching these developments with increasing alarm. At forty-two years of age, he had close-cropped gray hair, baleful eyes, and a long, thin nose in a long, narrow face.

His name was Cosimo de'Medici.

Because he was a realist and had few illusions about men, people thought him a cynic. He knew it, but cared little what people said or thought of him. He asked only to be left alone to run his bank — the gigantic Medici bank with its sixteen branches from

London to Constantinople – collect paintings and ancient manuscripts, and now and then spend a few pleasant hours with one of his luscious Circassian slaves, for he loved beauty in the flesh as well as in art.

As the Lucca war dragged on, Cosimo became convinced that the fools on the Signoria were leading Florence — and his bank — to ruin. As he loved both of them, he decided that something had to be done before it was too late. This meant entering politics, which filled him with dismay for he had no taste for posturing or verbiage. He comforted himself with the thought that the emergency would not last long and he would be able to return to his books, his roses, his slaves.

He went to work in his own secretive way, financing antiwar riots in the slums. The Signoria retaliated by having him arrested and banished for ten years. With his son Piero, his valet Matteo, his architect Michelozzo, his slaves, and his paintings (but not his wife), he departed for Venice where he was welcomed with open arms, as the very rich usually are.

In the October mist, the miracle city of marble and water was a vision of loveliness. He moved into a palazzo on the Grand Canal, strolled through the narrow streets, continued to direct his bank through its Venetian branch, and prepared to enjoy his sentence.

Meanwhile, in Florence, the situation was becoming desperate. People were sick of war taxes and victory bulletins. A new Signoria, favorable to Cosimo, was sent to Venice. On 6 October 1434, one year to the day after his departure, he was back in Florence.

This time as her master.

He declined all titles, made no speeches, promised nothing. From his office at the bank, he began taking action. He immediately ended the war with Lucca, reassured neighboring states of his pacific intentions, loaned enormous sums to the treasury at no interest, and watched over public finances as though they were his own.

As he had neither the time nor the inclination to indulge an opposition, loyal or otherwise, he drew a list of his most implacable enemies and had them quietly banished for life by the Signoria.

Although an autocrat, he had the wisdom to maintain the trappings of democracy. Knowing the Florentines' passion for oratory, he let them talk to their hearts' content. He merely paid no attention to what they said. The Signoria continued to be elected, but somehow only his supporters seemed to receive a popular mandate.

Of course, it was all undemocratic, illegal, unconstitutional; but it worked. On Sundays, laborers fished in the Arno, sang in taverns, or watched cockfights instead of listening to war bulletins. The poor began smiling again.

A few years went by. Prosperity returned. The emergency which had forced Cosimo to seize the power had passed. Cosimo was growing old. The double burden of running the state and his bank were beginning to tell on him. He longed for his books, his roses, his slaves. He wanted to go back to private life.

To his stupefaction, he discovered he could not.

To rule is to make enemies, and he had made many. The troublemakers he had banished were impatiently waiting for him to step down so they might return, foment agitation, and perhaps seize power again. He knew that if they returned they would have his head, confiscate his bank and his beautiful new house on Via Larga, persecute his friends, and resume their stupid, ruinous wars. Nothing would remain of his years of toil.

And so he never laid down his burden. Thirty years he ruled, sternly and well. He was sincerely mourned when he died at seventy-four on a fine summer day. He, who had refused all titles while alive, was given a noble one at his death: Father of the Country.

Time had been on his side. A generation had grown under his rule and wanted no other. At his death, it seemed natural that his son should succeed him. There was no election, no public referendum. The members of the Signoria merely went to Casa Medici and asked Piero to continue his father's work.

Crippled with arthritis from boyhood and confined to his bed most of the time, Piero de'Medici managed to govern creditably,

both Florence and the family bank, with the assistance of his remarkable wife, Lucrezia.

He had the good sense to follow Cosimo's policies in most
things. Only on one point did he depart from them, and it nearly
cost him his life. A kindly man, he rescinded several of his father's
banishment sentences. Sure enough, the old troublemakers flocked
home, ambushed his litter on the road to Careggi, and almost succeeded in murdering him. He owed his life to the courage and
presence of mind of his elder son, Lorenzo.

The morning after his funeral, the members of the Signoria
again went to Casa Medici in their red robes and gold chains of
office. They were greeted by Donna Lucrezia, queenly in her
widow's veils. Flanked by her two sons, Lorenzo and Giuliano,
respectively nineteen and sixteen, she curtsied to Their Magnificences who in turn gravely bowed to her.

The *gonfaloniere* launched into a flowery address in which he
recalled Cosimo's great deeds and Piero's virtues. He ended by
urging Lorenzo to follow in their footsteps.

Head bowed and tight-lipped, the young man listened with
misgivings to this proposition. He had seen his father and grandfather work by candlelight while the Florentines snored contentedly in their beds. Only too well did he know the dangers,
the thankless, grueling toil entailed in the high-sounding but
hollow title of "Chief of the Republic" that was held out to him.
But he also knew he had no choice but to accept, no alternative
but to remain in power or be destroyed.

And so he thanked the *priori* and pledged to devote his life to
the welfare of his fellow citizens. He then walked to the window
and waved at the cheering crowd below. But that evening, in the
privacy of his diary, he revealed his true feelings:

They [the magistrates] condoled with us on our bereavement and
offered me the direction of the government. I hesitated on account of
my youth and the responsibilities, as well as the dangers I should incur. I only accepted to safeguard our friends and our property.*

* *Archivio Mediceo.*

At first, there was some doubt over the judiciousness of entrusting the leadership of Italy's richest state to one so young. On the assumption that wisdom comes with age, elders predicted catastrophes. None occurred. Rapidly, Lorenzo de'Medici proved himself a brilliant statesman and won not only the respect and trust but the love of the population.

Housewives began to wave from their windows at the new ruler who went about town without an armed guard. They called him "Lauro" in almost maternal affection, for they remembered him, as a boy, walking by the side of his grandfather Cosimo, or wrestling with youngsters on Piazza Santa Croce.

From boyhood, he had been trained for the position he was to occupy. At fifteen, he had been sent on his first diplomatic mission as his family's representative to the wedding of Ippolita Sforza, daughter of the duke of Milan, to the crown prince of Naples. He had given an excellent account of himself on this occasion, treating his fellow ambassadors to sumptuous banquets and, on the sly, winning the caresses of the bride-to-be.

On his return to Florence, he had met Lucrezia Donati, the fifteen-year-old wife of Piero Ardinghelli, a rich merchant who was imprudently traveling in the Orient on business. While Piero sold bolts of damask to sultans, Lorenzo and Lucrezia fornicated to their hearts' content and shared the rapture as well as the torments of adolescent love.

At the peak of his affair with Lucrezia, he was betrothed by his father to Clarissa Orsini — a plain, pious, dull, and consumptive Roman princess. In those days, a father's command was not to be questioned, and in June 1469 he had duly married Clarissa. After the wedding banquet, he unburdened in his diary the bitterness that filled his heart.

Today, I, Lorenzo, took Donna Clarissa, daughter of Jacopo Orsini, to wife. Or rather she was given to me.*

He had tried loving her and found it impossible. The differences between them were too great to be bridged. She could not

* *Archivio Mediceo.*

forget that she was a Roman princess and regarded as "lowly merchants" the Florentine millionaire bankers or "lords of the looms." Unable to adapt herself to local customs and costumes, she remained *la straniera*, "the foreigner."

He was courteous to her, but sought elsewhere the happiness he did not find at home. Gently, he pushed her out of his life by the simple expedient of keeping her permanently pregnant. Everybody in town knew of his amours for, like his grandfather, he did not care what people said of him and did not stoop to deceit.

In the end, he found his most enduring solace in work. With his brother Giuliano, he shouldered the burden of leadership. As a result, Florence grew ever more prosperous. With his hand on the helm of the ship of state, she became the world's capital of trade as well as culture. Like a windblown caravel, she sailed the high seas of her brief but dazzling Golden Age.

It had come to an abrupt end with Pope Sixtus's war and excommunication, which followed the Pazzi Conspiracy in which his brother was killed and he himself had barely escaped with his life. Through two successive campaigns, Florence had been saved by the stubborn refusal of the papal generalissimo to enter the city. But the excommunication had achieved what war had failed to do. With their wares outlawed on all European markets, the Florentines had come to the end of their endurance and were about to sue for peace. Secretly, Lorenzo had sailed for Naples and induced King Ferrante of Aragon to abandon his ally and sign a separate peace. Unable to wage war alone, Sixtus had held out the olive branch of peace.

Peace had returned and, in time, prosperity.

But Lorenzo could not forget his brother's murder in the cathedral. He had named after him the son who was born to him shortly afterward. His mother's death on New Year's Day, 1482, had increased his solitude. Loneliness had closed in on him with his passing years.

His prestige grew and spread all over Europe. Monarchs sought his counsel on matters of state; the sultan of Egypt wrote to him for advice and sent him jars of perfume and a giraffe in sign of appreciation. In appearance, his life did not change. He still re-

ceived ambassadors, still enjoyed the company of witty and
erudite friends, still collected ancient manuscripts and occasionally still wrote a poem. But his gaiety was gone. He no longer
sang on Piazza della Signoria. He did not trust life anymore, and
he feared the future.

On that summer afternoon of 1487, he was standing at the open
window of his study, hands behind his back, lost in thought and
gazing absently at Lisa and Contessina playing with their dolls in
the garden below. Now and then the ripple of their laughter rose
to him, and a wistful smile would pass over his gaunt face. Was
there anything in the world lovelier than the sound of children's
laughter?

He was about to return to his desk when his attention was
caught by the sight of his son Giuliano stealthily approaching the
two girls from behind, looking exactly like a nine-year-old boy
about to commit some mischief.

Having reached a distance that he judged adequate, he plunged
his arm into the pond, scooped a palmful of water, and sent it
splashing on them, letting out a yell of triumph while his victims
rent the air with their wails. Clearly, he was delighted with himself and about to repeat the performance when he heard his name
called from above.

Cain apostrophized from Heaven by a wrathful God could not
have looked more surprised. Turning around, he saw his honored
father frowning ominously on him. With considerable reluctance,
he made his way into the house.

It was a subdued Giuliano who stood before his genitor, head
bowed, water dripping from his arm.

"Aren't you ashamed of yourself?" asked the ruler of Florence.

With a nod, Giuliano signified that he was. His expression reflected repentance as well as dismay at having been caught.

"Is this the way to behave towards your sister and her honored
guest?" Lorenzo went on.

The answer came in the form of a contrite shake of the head.

Wasn't he aware that Lisa de'Gherardini was a young lady of

noble birth, that several of her ancestors had married into the Medici family, and she was therefore a distant kinsman of his?

The culprit nodded repeatedly and braced himself for the forthcoming sentence.

After which Giuliano rejoined Lisa and Contessina, apologized for his uncouthness, and pecked the two girls on the cheek as he had been told by his father. This done, he ran off. As he was about to veer into a side alley, he glanced over his shoulder, thumbed his nose at them, and vanished from sight.

Lorenzo did not have the heart to call him back. It was just the kind of thing he would have done as a boy. How wonderful to be nine years old with a whole lifetime spread out before you, like a feast.

He was jolted out of his musings by the sound of a galloping horse and a courier's horn. "Another message," he sighed wearily, returning to his desk.

A few moments later a decoding clerk handed him a rolled parchment.

"From our ambasador in Rome," he said and withdrew.

Lorenzo leaned back on his carved oak chair, crossed his long legs, and began reading.

His Holiness, Innocent the Eighth, had suffered another fainting spell, more alarming than any previous one. For over an hour he had lain lifeless on his bed. His Jewish physician, Maestro Solomon, gave him only a few months to live.

As Lorenzo perused the dispatch, his heart sank. Something must be done at once or his fondest dream would collapse; the countless letters of advice he had written to the pontiff in the last three years would have been in vain. His second son, Giovanni, would never become a cardinal and, therefore, never be pope.

This had been his overriding ambition, the very goal of his life for the past nine years, since the late Pope Sixtus had launched his war against Florence. As a matter of fact, his resolution to gain the papacy for his son had stemmed from this war. He was convinced that peace in Italy depended upon the man who sat on the papal throne, and also that the Florentines needed peace for their trade. They would remain faithful to the Medici only so long as he and his successors could keep them at peace.

From that moment onward, he had had no other thought than for Giovanni, then aged five, to wear some day the Triple Crown.

This was not an impossible dream, for the highest dignity on earth was elective. Not only elective, but notoriously venal. A pope was merely a cardinal who had bought the votes of his twenty-two colleagues. With the tranquil cynicism of a Renaissance man, Lorenzo reasoned that no one would be better equipped to buy twenty-two consciences than a Medici with the resources of the world's greatest bank at his command.

He swore that nothing would stop him from achieving his plan.

No sooner had Sixtus made peace and taken back Lorenzo — the former "suckling of perdition" — into the bosom of Mother Church than a flowery correspondence took place between the two men. Sixtus now called him "his beloved son," assured him of his esteem "on account of your great virtues," occasionally solicited a loan or requested that a few Florentine artists be sent to decorate his newly completed Sistine Chapel. These effusions did not prevent Sixtus from having a hand in two more attempts on Lorenzo's life: one by poison; the other by assassination, and again in a church, the Carmine Church, this time.*

For his part, Lorenzo replied by granting loans, sending Botticelli and other Florentine artists to Rome. At the same time, he began alluding to Giovanni's unusual piety, his delight in catechism and precocious gravity: all signs of a manifest religious vocation. If only the holy father would bestow some small papal distinction on such a deserving boy, there would be much rejoicing in the Medici family.

Sixtus, of course, had no intention of fostering the plans of the man who had shattered his own. He limited himself to sending a profusion of blessings, a swarm of indulgences, but nothing else. As time went by, Lorenzo understood he would never obtain anything from Sixtus.

He had about lost hope when help had come to him from the

* See *The Medici* by Col. C. F. Young, C.B. Vol. I.

most unexpected source: Louis the Eleventh, king of France, known to his subjects as "Old King Spider."

This most remarkable of French monarchs had welded the various baronies of his realm into a united France at the cost of immense ingenuity, infinite patience, and treachery. He also had sinned in various other fields, indulged his taste for very young girls, and broken nearly all of God's commandments.

Now, at sixty-two, he suffered from gout, asthma, fainting spells, recurrent loss of speech, epilepsy, and a cruel skin disease called herpes which represented lechery. Anyone else with so many complaints would have laid down and died, but not "Old King Spider." This brilliant man had retained a childlike faith in the torments of hell. Already he saw himself hopping in the ever-boiling cauldrons of hell. This prospect spurred in him the desire to remain alive.

Towards his end, he paid astronomical fees to his doctor, drank tumblers of turtle blood which the French fetched from Cape Verde, wore little lead statues of holy men on his hat. He even lured a saintly Italian hermit, Francesco da Paola, from his Calabrian forests to come and pray at his bedside for his recovery. Most of all, he surrounded himself with miracle-working relics, which he bought wholesale from his friend the sultan of Turkey, who possessed thousands of them and, as a Moslem, had no use for them. Louis's bedroom was cluttered with teeth, hairs, toenails of martyrs and virgins, bedside clocks, magpies, hunting dogs, and his beloved canaries.

Somehow he heard about the ring of San Zenobio, Florence's bishop in the sixth century, as an infallible remedy against skin diseases. At once he dictated a letter to Lorenzo imploring him to obtain the loan of this ring, so that he might wear it for a while. Obliging as ever, Lorenzo obtained the relic from the Girolami family to whom it belonged and sent it by special courier to the ailing king who received it on his knees, tears streaming down his hatchet face.

Immediately, he felt better.

His gratitude was immense and immediate. On 10 May 1483 a royal courier burst into the courtyard of Casa Medici, bearing a document sealed with yellow wax which made the seven-year-old Giovanni abbot of the splendid Fonte Doulce Monastery.*

Sixtus had no choice but to confirm the royal decree and reluctantly appointed the boy papal protonotary, which entitled him to wear a fine cassock of violet silk and a large amethyst on his hand.

Meanwhile, the ring of San Zenobio continued to work wonders. "King Spider" felt better and better. On 9 June another courier brought another parchment. This time, His Majesty was pleased to appoint Giovanni archbishop of Aix-en-Provence, a charming little town in the south of France.

Lorenzo's joy was unbounded. His son's clerical career was now properly launched. News of this extraordinary preferment spread through Florence. There had never been a seven-year-old archbishop. Crowds congregated under the palace's window asking for Giovanni's blessing.

Suddenly, disaster struck. It was learned that the titular archbishop of Aix-en-Provence was still alive. Feeble, in his dotage, but still breathing. He died shortly afterwards, but by then it was too late. The king was no longer able to repair his mistake. The ring of San Zenobio had lost its miraculous powers and Louis stood at death's door. He died at sunset one August day, clutching his rosary and praying "my good mistress, Madame la Vierge." For five days, every church in France tolled his passing.

One year later, almost to the day, it was Sixtus's turn to exit from this world. Appropriately, he died in a fit of rage, making a last attempt at stealing another ducal crown, this time that of Ferrara, for his precious son Girolamo. His demise was not lamented. He was buried amid sighs of relief. Even the Sacred College of cardinals had had enough of him, his schemes, his wars, his worthless son.

As his successor, they elected a man who was in every way his opposite.

Francesco Cibo was an amiable, pot-bellied monk with a wreath

---

* By the Pragmatic Sanction of 1438, the king of France could appoint to all ecclesiastical offices in his realm.

of graying hair and a permanent smile on his wattled face. His good nature was equaled only by his obtuseness. People who knew and loved him best described him as "one of the finest men God ever created and one of the most stupid."

He chose the name of Innocent the Eighth and it suited him well. Although, as usual, he had bought his election, everyone liked this fat, easygoing man. He endeared himself to the population by the love he displayed for his son, Franceschetto, and two daughters, Battistina and Teodorina. He would have none of the fiction which passed off papal offspring as nephews and nieces, but publicly acknowledged his children as his own. He had them visit him at the Vatican, even eat with him. This shocked his entourage but pleased the populace who approved of a pontiff who was also a good family man.

Being self-indulgent, Innocent had the grace of being indulgent towards others. When an overzealous cardinal tried to reduce the number of practicing prostitutes, His Holiness told him to mind his own salvation and leave the poor sluts alone. This made him popular among the local dregs and turned the holy city into a vast and flourishing brothel. Unperturbed, the pontiff remarked that the Romans were now doing openly what they would have been doing anyway in secret.

Incapable of grasping the complexities of political problems – or any problem for that matter – he had the good sense to place himself in the sagacious hands of Lorenzo. At all hours, galloping couriers brought pleading messages to the Medici Palace during most of the year and in summer to the Careggi villa.

It did not take Lorenzo very long to measure the simpleton who was now occupying the papal throne. Here, he exulted, was the man he had been praying for, the one and only person on earth who might fulfill his dream and make Giovanni a cardinal. Of course, it would take time, but he would be patient. After all, Giovanni was only twelve; he could wait a few years.

Meanwhile Lorenzo held Innocent in his grip, loaning him money, advising him in political and even religious matters. Tirelessly he sent him long and detailed letters which he signed

"Your humble and loving servant, Laurentius, who commends himself to Your sacred feet."

But time was getting short, and Pope Innocent might die at any moment. At all costs, he must be made to create Giovanni a cardinal.

Lorenzo turned this thought in his mind as he tapped the ambassador's dispatch on his knee. Somehow he must find some irresistible lure, bait his hook with some irresistible morsel for which Innocent would stifle his qualms of conscience, defy the censure of the world's clergy.

After a while, the solution flashed through his mind. A wedding! He would offer his daugter Maddalena in marriage to Franceschetto Cibo, the pope's son. For that, the holy father would do anything.

What if Maddalena was barely fourteen and Franceschetto thirty-nine, a nonentity and a gambling fool? He was reputed to be good-natured like his father, and uncommonly handsome. Since females set great story by looks, Maddalena would probably fall head over heels in love with him and be a very happy wife.

He was about to congratulate himself when his jubilation vanished like a pricked balloon. His wife would never consent to her daughter's marriage to "a priest's son," even if the priest happened to be the supreme pontiff. As a member of the princely Orsini clan, she would arouse half of the Roman aristocracy against this marriage. She might even curse it publicly, and not even a pope would dare to defy a mother's curse.

And so Clarissa would have to be won. She, too, would have to be enticed into acceptance by some irresistible bribe. He would pay whatever price she demanded, accept any terms she might impose, but he would obtain her acquiescence.

He rang the silver bell on his desk and sent a page to ask his wife for the favor of an interview. The page returned an instant later, saying that Donna Clarissa would be honored by his visit any time, at his convenience.

She rose to curtsy when he entered.

"God's grace, *magnifice conjux*" ("magnificent husband" in

Latin), which was how noble Roman ladies addressed their husbands, and how she still addressed Lorenzo after sixteen years in Florence.

It was a long time since they had been alone together, and for a few instants they faced each other in silence across the gulf of their estrangement. As he looked into her feverish consumptive's eyes, he hoped that some belated understanding, perhaps even some tardy forgiveness might have grown during the winter of their solitude.

He soon discovered how wrong he was.

With hands folded in her lap, she calmly listened to his plan. Contrary to his apprehensions, she did not object to her daughter's marriage to "a priest"s son." She merely proposed another wedding in exchange: that of their elder son, Piero, to her Neapolitan cousin, Alfonsina Orsini.

This was her price, her long-awaited revenge. Their son would not wed some "lowly millionaire merchant," but the daughter of the Great Constable of Naples, a princess like her.

He looked at her with helpless anger. Desperately he wanted their elder son to marry a Florentine girl, for he was aware of the population's antagonism to any "foreigner." But he also knew that any plea would be useless.

He rose and said, "It will be done as you wish," and, without kissing her hand, strode out of the room.

Wedding negotiations began at once, both in Rome and in Naples.

On 20 November 1487 Maddalena de'Medici was duly married to the pope's son in the presence of his father, the entire Sacred College of cardinals, and the entire Roman aristocracy. As Lorenzo hoped, his daughter fell in love with her husband almost thrice her age, and became a fulfilled and contented housewife.

Piero de'Medici's wedding took place seven months later at the Medici Palace, in June 1488. It was not a joyous occasion. Alfonsina Orsini turned out to be short-necked and most unremarkable in looks. Although her noble father was debt-ridden, she made up for her poverty by an abundance of Orsini pride. As Lorenzo watched her during the banquet, he sensed that she would prove even more unpopular than his own wife had been. Fearfully, he asked himself whether he had not paid too high a price for Clarissa's consent.

His eyes rested on his wife. She seemed to be the only person who was enjoying herself, and well she might, for this wedding was her crowning achievement. The flush in her cheeks betrayed her jubilation. Did she know that she was dying, he wondered. Her physician had told him that she would not see the end of summer. She probably knew and did not care. Her dream had come true.

And, indeed, Piero's wedding was her last joy on earth. She died five weeks later, on the last day of July. Her death went unnoticed. Most ambassadors in Florence failed to mention it in their dispatches.

Winter confirmed Lorenzo's apprehensions over Piero's marriage. Alfonsina made herself promptly disliked by her haughty manner, and the Florentines labeled her "the foreigner," as they had Clarissa. No great love materialized between her and her husband. After performing his conjugal duty, Piero began looking around for convivial mistresses as soon as his bride became pregnant.

Shortly after Christmas, Lorenzo suffered the first arthritic pains in his hands which were to torment his remaining years.

His physician, Maestro Leone, prepared complicated potions that brought little improvement. From Ferrara, the world-famous Petrus Avogardus advised him to have "a stone called sapphire" set into a gold ring and wear it on the third finger of the left hand, for "this stone has the specific virtue of preventing the return of these gouty pains and the formation of evil humours in the joints."*

Lorenzo had the sapphire ring made and dutifully wore it, as prescribed, without appreciable benefit. Henceforth, his life alternated between periods of intense suffering and relative well-being.

On top of all this, he worried about the pope. His Holiness still

---

* The full text of this letter is given in *The Lives of the Early Medici, as Told in Their Correspondence,* by Janet Ross.

hesitated at making Giovanni a cardinal. In his messages, he feebly argued that the boy was still too young to be raised to such lofty eminence. But Lorenzo was not to be cheated out of his bargain. He threatened to call back a loan of 90,000 gold florins — which His Holiness owed him.

In March 1489 a papal courier brought to the Medici Palace a beribboned parchment signed with the Fisherman's Ring conferring upon the thirteen-year-old Giovanni the title of Cardinal Santa Maria-in-Domenica.

Yet even then the distraught Innocent tried to conceal his shame at such an appointment. In stately Latin sentences (written by his secretary), he specified that the boy's elevation must remain secret for the next three years. Until March 1492 he must wear no red hat, no red cassock, no red silk mantle. As in the past, he would be simply called "Monsignore" instead of "Your Worshipful Lordship."

In short, Giovanni was in fact a cardinal, but no one was to know about it. As an additional measure of discretion, Lorenzo packed his son off to the Pisa University where the new prince of the Church would learn something about theology and canon law.

Certain at last that Giovanni would some day sit on the throne of Saint Peter and maintain peace in Italy, Lorenzo abandoned himself to his happiness. He cancelled the pope's debt, commuted several death sentences, took a new mistress, and wrote a play.

It was called *La Rappresentazione dei Santissimi Giovanni e Paolo*, or *The Story of Saint John and Saint Paul*. Despite its title, it had little to do with either apostle, but delved into the relationship between Princess Constanzia, Emperor Constantine's daughter, and her cousin Julian. A visit to the tomb of the two saints had cured Constanzia of leprosy and converted her into a fervent Christian. Julian, on the other hand, had remained a worshiper of old pagan gods. They argued a great deal, and their discussion constituted the burden of the play.

La Rappresentazione was to be a strictly amateur production with Lorenzo himself in the part of Julian. Contessina and Giuli-

ano were also included in the cast. The other roles were eagerly
sought by members of the social elite.

At Contessina's coaxing, Lorenzo prevailed upon Lisa's parents
to let their ten-year-old daughter take part in the play. At once
she became an actress and behaved like one. Her daily lessons
were set aside and she virtually disappeared from home. Accompanied by Tessa, she went every morning to the headquarters of
the Brotherhood of Saint John where the rehearsals were held.

Like Contessina, she was assigned several parts, small but dramatic. In the prologue, she escorted Angel Gabriel, who floated
down to the stage on a wire, barefooted and dressed in a transparent white robe with large golden wings. On touching ground,
the angel curtsied to the audience and recited the opening poem.

Lisa would have loved to be Gabriel, but angels were blond
and she was not. The part had been given to Agnoletta de'Landi
who was flaxen-haired, blue-eyed, and pretty as an angel.

"Isn't she awful?" Lisa would hiss in Contessina's ear while
Agnoletta rehearsed. "She will ruin the play."

When she noticed that Giuliano paid much attention to the
angel, Lisa felt the first pangs of jealousy.

"For the life of me, I can't imagine what he sees in her," she
would remark with forced casualness. "From afar she may look
pretty, but the closer you get, the uglier she becomes."

In the first act, Lisa and Contessina were among Constanzia's
maidens-in-waiting. Lisa was in charge of the princess's parasol;
Contessina, of her fan. The parts were silent, but the two friends
discussed them at length, in order to extract from them every
possible drop of drama.

Lisa's great moment came in the second act, as one of Lorenzo's
Oriental slaves. As such, she was dressed in a skimpy leopard skin
to make it clear that she was a jungle creature. The prince, now
emperor, reclined on a fur-covered couch under his tent, in a
despondent mood and talking to himself.

At one point, he sighed and said, "How often does the man that
envies me not know that happier far than I is he!"

This was her cue to steal into the tent, kneel before the im-
perial couch, and offer Lorenzo a silver tray piled high with fruit

from the Careggi villa. For an instant, the brooding monarch appeared to hesitate between his slave or a slice of watermelon. Then, with a languid flip of the wrist, he dismissed both from sight.

The play was a success and ended in a storm of applause.

After the show, the cast repaired to the Medici Palace. Lorenzo thanked his fellow players and promised to write another play the following year. Lisa and her friend reviewed (favorably) their performances and criticized everyone else's while devouring slices of almond cake. Giuliano, who sat at a nearby table, came to compliment her on her acting. For that, she forgave him his attention to the angel.

"He thought I was marvelous," she told Tessa that evening, as she was getting ready for bed.

Apparently, so did everyone else. Her *babbo* patted her cheek; Mamma gave her an approving smile. Wherever she went, people congratulated her. During the week that preceded the family's departure for Montici, she basked in the sunshine of fame.

The Card Players, attributed to French follower of Caravaggio.
Courtesy of the Fogg Art Museum.

The Choppy Seas of Adolescence

 That summer, the eleven-year-old Contessina de'Medici was betrothed to Piero Ridolfi, member of a great Florentine banking family, and Lisa attended the engagement banquet which took place early in July in the garden of the Careggi villa.

It was a sumptuous affair enlivened by the singing of musicians and the capers of buffoons. But neither the usual toasts nor the jolly speeches could conceal the quivers which passed over Lorenzo's face with each new spasm of arthritic pain.

The day after the festivity, he departed for the Spedaletto baths which seemed to bring some improvement to his condition.

No sooner was he gone than Contessina began inquiring about his return, harassing everyone in the house with questions. Ten times a day, she and Lisa would run to the garden gate and stand on the Careggi Road for a glimpse of some news-bearing courier. Now and then, a letter from her father would arrive and she would read it aloud between heartbroken sobs.

"I hope the devils in my *babbo*'s hands will drown in the Spedaletto baths," she would say and start weeping again.

One of these letters has come down to us. Although nearly five hundred years old, it still retains the fragrance of the tender relationship between Lorenzo de'Medici and his youngest daughter.

My dear little Contessina,
 As I hear that every hour thou askest after me, how I am and when I am coming back, I write to tell thee that, thanks to God, I am very

well and have greatly improved since my departure. These continued baths suit me excellently. If it pleases to God, I shall leave very soon and come to stay with thee.

During the remainder of her sojourn at Careggi, Lisa quarreled with Giuliano, called him *una bestia*, an animal, a shame to his clan. A thousand times she swore never to speak to him again. For his part, he continued to treat her as if she were a boy, pulled her pigtails, forced her to race or leapfrog with him. Yet, whenever he invited her to go riding with him on a pillion attached to his saddle, she would accept with alacrity. Either in love or hate, he occupied her thoughts most of the time.

One day she spied Giovanni de'Medici, the youngest cardinal in the history of the Church, playing the lute under a tree. In deference to the pontiff's wishes, he still wore a cassock of violet silk and an amethyst ring on his finger. Unlike his two brothers, he was fat, with the beginning of a double chin and the unctuous gestures of a seasoned prelate.

She thought he looked so lonely that she stopped racing her hoop and asked permission to sit beside him for a moment. He flushed from pleasure and soon they were chatting like old friends. From that day on, she made it a point to spend a few moments with him. He let her play on his lute; she let him race her hoop. For a few instants, the Cardinal Santa Maria-in-Domenica would grin and run like a normal boy.

Returning to Montici, Lisa began to ponder over the consequences of Contessina's engagement. It meant that her best friend would soon vanish from her life, and so would Giuliano.

"But you tell me all the time how much you hate him," said Tessa perplexed.

Of course, she hated him, countered Lisa. He was *una bestia*, he was *stupido*, he was a shame to his clan, but she did not want him out of her existence. In fact, she wished he would come and ask her honored father to pledge her to him before it was too late. After all, she was practically ten, and she might get wed any day.

"I don't want him to lose me," she said, bursting into tears.

For a few days she felt misunderstood and unwanted. She brooded and wept at night in bed before falling asleep. Even her birthday party failed to dispel her gloom. Curiously, she found comfort in the company of her brother Francesco, now five. He was gentle and looked at her with a mixture of awe and devotion which she found most pleasant. After Giuliano's rough ways, it was nice to shine in someone's eyes, if only a small boy's.

And so she hugged and kissed him and said she loved him better than anyone else in the whole world.

She was feeling better by early September. Once again, the vineyard bloomed with straw-hatted girls in colorful blouses gathering grapes in hampers; once again, Lisa walked among them by her father's side. But this time he did not invite her to join in the grape-trampling in the huge wooden vats, and deliberately ignored her imploring looks.

"I know what you want," he said finally, wagging a finger at her. "You want to get into the vat, don't you?"

She nodded.

"But don't you see you are now too big to be jumping about like a cricket, with your skirt trussed up! It is time you behaved like a proper young lady."

She did not protest, but her eyes blurred with tears. He kept his gaze away from her.

Brusquely, he turned to her.

"Oh, all right," he said with a smile and shake of the head. "You won't be a child much longer. Get into that vat, my little fish, and hop to your heart's content."

Through the winter, Caterina sensed that something was worrying Antonio.

She had grown used to silences; it did not create a barrier between them. But now his silence had a new brooding quality. At night, she knew he lay awake by her side, staring in the darkness. She asked no questions, for experience had taught her that in his own time he would confide in her.

Thus, she was not oversurprised when on an April Sunday afternoon, 1490, as they sat on the roof *loggia*, he suddenly said,

"Wife, our wool industry is dying. In a few years, most of our mills will have shut down."

She looked at him incredulously. Wool was the rock on which Florence had grown rich.

"Couldn't it be a temporary setback?" she asked.

No, he said quietly, it was not. It was the beginning of the end. Florence's hour of the lion was almost gone. After two and a half centuries of textile supremacy, the Florentines had lost their wool monopoly.

"How could such a thing come to pass?" she asked incredulously.

A rueful smile passed over his lips. "Foreigners have grown tired of buying from us wares they can make themselves. They stole our methods of fabrication, as we stole those of the good *Umiliati* monks. Now they make San Martino cloth as good, if not better, than ours."

In turn, the silk trade continued to flourish. The silk mills were working at capacity while the wool *stabilimenti* barely made ends meet.

After a pause, he went on. "I may have to convert our factory to the manufacture of silk."

This time, her mouth opened in a gasp of unbelief. He was speaking sacrilege. "You must be jesting, noble husband."

"I may have to."

Oh yes, he knew that the wool trade was more prestigious than that of silk . . . He knew that the Gherardini had been identified with wool for over two hundred years . . . He knew that his honored father would have a fit in his grave.

"But I have two thousand people to think about and I cannot feed them on prestige."

He remained silent for a few instants, his gaze resting on the cathedral's pink dome, standing like a gigantic rosebud between two of the *loggia*'s columns.

"I shall decide what to do after my return from Venice," he said at last.

"Venice!"

He nodded. "I wish I didn't have to go, but I don't see how I can avoid it."

A Turkish merchant, an old and loyal Gherardini client, had paid for a recent cloth shipment partly in bales of paper and gallnut, partly in cash, and partly in slaves, who were currently used as currency. Doctors accepted them in payment of their services; priests, as fee for masses.

The paper and gallnut had already been sold at a profit by the Gherardini agent in Venice.

There remained the matter of the slaves.

"How many are they?" asked Caterina.

"Eight," he replied. "One male and seven females."

The man was a Russian, by the name of Dimitri: a blond giant, strong as an ox and of a good disposition. He would fetch a high price at auction, for he was intelligent and would make an excellent steward.

The women were a motley lot. Five of them were Anatolian country girls, suitable for farming or housework. The other two were Circassians, respectively thirteen and twelve, most pleasing to the eye and well suited for wenching. Both had been "guaranteed" virgins at the departure, but they had been raped in transit by Venetian sailors: a fact that considerably impaired their value on the slave market.

"Of course," Antonio explained, "I could sue the shipping company, but virginity is a difficult thing to establish."

Affidavits would be required. A trial would ensue; lawyers would appear on the scene and their fees would be greater than the amount the girls might bring. "All told, I think we'd better let the matter rest."

To make things worse, Venice was at present glutted with slaves of every description. The seven females sent by the Turkish merchant could be sold only at a severe loss. The Gherardini agent suggested they be sent to Spain where they would fetch a much higher price. Unfortunately, two of them had fallen sick and he was unwilling to ship them to Spain on his own authority.

"He insists on my coming to Venice and making the decision."

To soften the blow, Antonio added, " It should not take long. I plan to leave in May and return in time for the vintage."

She did not plead or raise objections. She belonged to a merchant family and understood that a man might have to travel on business. She merely asked permission to move to Montici earlier than usual and wait there for his return. He readily granted her wish, and they spent the first spring days at the villa.

They spoke little, for they thought of the long separation ahead. He left one morning at dawn when the sky was mauve and the trees droned with the twitter of nesting birds.

Caterina stood in the porticoed doorway between her children, a forced smile on her ivory-white face. They watched him climb on his horse and ride down the sanded alley, followed by his groom Battista leading a baggage-laden mule.

At the gate, he turned on his saddle and waved in farewell. Francesco waved back; Lisa, weeping, blew him a kiss. Caterina tried to smile. Then, taking the children by the hand, she returned into the house and the waiting began.

Caterina received a long and affectionate letter from Bologna. The crossing of the Apennines, the most arduous part of the journey, had been effected without difficulties. The weather was turning very hot, but he and his manservant remained in good health and spirits. He counted the days until his return to Montici.

A month later another letter arrived at the villa, this one from Venice and brought by special courier. The heat was oppressive, the canals fetid. More than ever, he longed for the cool Montici hills, their lingering suppers on the terrace, her singing or playing of the lute. He had seen the slaves and decided to follow his agent's advice. In Spain they would fetch a much higher price. Already he had started making inquiries about traveling insurance rates; but in Venice everything took an immense amount of time. Yet he still hoped to be home by early September.

Then, for a whole month, she had no news.

At last, two days before Lisa's eleventh birthday, a third letter arrived from the Gherardini agent. It said that Messer Antonio was in fine health, but too busy to write. At once she knew that something was wrong. She wanted to go to Venice, but her father would not hear of it. The autumn rains were due any moment, making the crossing of the Apennines nearly impossible.

"And what if he returned while you were away?" he added.

He was right, as usual, and she remained at Montici. But now each day became an eternity of anguish and uncertainty. Before going to bed at night, Lisa prayed on her knees for her *babbo*'s return. Winemaking time came and went without any of the usual merrymaking. The ghost of Antonio hung over the estate and the grape-gathering girls did not sing.

The autumn rains came, as Mariotto had predicted, and Caterina decided to return to town.

In the old family mansion, the atmosphere became one of despair. Caterina no longer gave Lisa her music lessons, but spent most of her time in church praying before a statue of the Madonna. Pandolfo, Noldo's former valet, went from inn to inn in search of anyone who might have news of Antonio. From a Venetian glassware salesman, he only learned that Venice had suffered a severe malaria epidemic.

Antonio returned, unexpectedly, in an October downpour, bent double on his saddle and shaking with fever. He had to be helped down from his horse and carried to his room. For the next three days he lay in bed, hanging between life and death, unconscious most of the time. Caterina did not leave his bedside.

He awoke one morning feeling weak, but clearheaded. As he looked at Caterina, he was shocked by her appearance. Her face had turned ashen, her cheeks hollow with fatigue.

"What have I done to you?" he sighed. The words came out in a whisper of grief.

Their hands touched on the coverlet, and for an instant they remained silent as though they feared that the sound of their voices might shatter their happiness.

"You are here," she said with a fearful smile. "Soon you will be well."

After being shaved and fed some broth, he felt strong enough to tell her about his journey.

Venice had been sweltering in moist heat, her canals stagnant under a broiling sun. He was settling the matter of the traveling insurance when he had been stricken with malaria. After that, everything dissolved into a blur in his mind. He vaguely recalled being transferred from the inn to the house of the Gherardini agent where the man's wife had nursed him with devotion. Early in September he was out of danger but facing a long convalescence. He would not wait for spring, as his doctor advised, and had started on his way home.

The return journey had been a nightmare. The seasonal rains had rutted the roads, swelled the brooks into raging torrents. This time, the crossing of the Apennines had taken two weeks.

"I swear I'll never leave home again," he said.

Then he asked to see the children.

Francesco was ushered into the room. He removed his *berretta*, walked to the bed, and kissed his father's hand. With loving pride, Caterina remarked that already he could read and write like a scholar. Next year he would be ready to take lessons from a tutor.

"It is all very well," said Antonio, "but a true Gherardini must also be a fine horseman."

He then gave the boy the silver spurs he had bought for him in Padua. "You will use them next summer when we go riding together."

Again, Francesco kissed his father's hand and was taken away by his *bambinaia*.

It was now Lisa's turn to enter.

At the sight of her *babbo* propped against pillows, looking pale and drawn, she forgot to curtsy and with a sob ran into his arms. Caterina apologized for her bad manners, but Antonio did not seem to mind.

"Don't weep, my little fish," he said, gently stroking her hair. "Everything is going to be well."

He made her sit on the edge of the bed and told her what a beautiful city Venice was and how it wondrously floated on water. Nobody rode horseback in Venice. People moved about in long narrow boats called gondolas.

He was getting tired, but insisted on giving her the present he had bought for her birthday.

It was a "writing box" of cut glass with a compartment for

the powdered charcoal, another for the arabic gum, two more for the drying sand and sealing wax. There was also a long and narrow division for two beautiful swan quills. The box itself had a lid of solid gold embossed with dancing cherubs.

Lisa held it in her hand, slowly running a finger over it. It must have cost a great deal of money, she thought, and that proved how much her *babbo* loved her.

"I'll keep it always," she said at last.

Her happiness brought a drowsy smile to his lips, but already his lids were closing. Her mother signaled her to leave.

When, once again, she was alone with Antonio, Caterina resumed her place by Antonio's bedside. Again their hands touched on the coverlet, and he fell asleep.

He died that evening without regaining consciousness.*

Lisa refused to believe he was dead. Even after she had seen him being carried out of the house in the glow of funeral candles, she continued to say he merely was asleep. When she finally admitted to herself that he was gone, she broke into choking, rebellious sobs. She who had accepted without protest the demise of her grandparents because they were old revolted at the unfairness of Lord God for taking away her *babbo* before his time.

"He was not old," she kept repeating.

She swore never to pray again or ever ask God for anything. Tessa let her rant and weep in her arms, as when she was a little *bimba*.

Caterina's grief did not express itself in sobs or revolt, but in a traumatic daze, a frozen stupor that kept her hour after hour, day after day, gazing into the fire of her sitting room, dry-eyed and stony-faced. She shut herself out of the world. Visitors were denied admittance. She who had so diligently dismantled the Via Maggio house paid no heed to the problems resulting from her husband's death.

"She might as well have died with him," grumbled her father to his wife, three weeks after Antonio's death.

* The death of Antonio Maria de'Gherardini in 1490 is recorded in *The History of the Noble Family of the Gherardini* by E. Gamurrini.

"She loved him very much," said Donna Filippa. "Give her time to recover."

He would give Caterina all the time she needed, he declared, but meanwhile decisions had to be made, a new director had to be appointed at the mill, dispositions had to be taken regarding the house servants.

Obviously the old Gherardini palazzo would have to be sold. It was not proper for a seemly, twenty-eight-year-old widow to live by herself in this huge house. She would have to come and live with her parents until she married again.

"She will have no trouble at all finding a husband," he added confidently. "Young and comely widows with large fortunes are at a premium on the market."

Filippa doubted his optimism. "Don't call the wedding broker as yet, noble husband. Something tells me that it will take a long time before Caterina gets over Antonio's death."

He assured her he would be most patient and give her six months, even a year if necessary, to get over her grief.

At the same time, he took matters in his capable hands. He appointed a temporary director to the Gherardini mill, pensioned off the older servants, dismissed the others.

He had the good fortune to sell the Gherardini palazzo to a member of the clan, Girolamo de'Gherardini della Rosa, formerly Florence's ambassador to Hungary.

By Christmas, Caterina, her two children and, of course, Tessa, moved back to Casa Rucellai where she had been born.

It was a large stone house on Via del Giglio — Lily Street — with an elaborately carved doorway and wrought-iron lanterns at the corners. Inside, it managed to be both stately and informal. The furniture still bore scars from the games of the Rucellai children. All were married now and with families of their own, except Camilla, the latecomer, who was only fourteen and still unmarried.

She had beautiful light-brown eyes and blond hair. She led Lisa to a wing of the house and opened a door.

"This will be your room," she said.

Located on the first floor, it opened on a small balustraded terrace on which stood a number of potted plants. A flight of brick stairs curved down to a walled-in garden. It had been the room of Maria Rucellai, one of Camilla's sisters, and her flowery-curtained four-poster as well as her vanity table recalled her occupancy.

It was perfect, Lisa thought, except that it adjoined Tessa's room, thus squashing all hopes of privacy. But a door separated the two rooms and a door could be locked. All in all, it was much better than the huge nursery room of the old Gherardini house.

Camilla proved to be the friend she needed at this time in her life. (Contessina was spending much time with her fiancé or at the bedside of her father, whose condition was steadily deteriorating.) Lisa turned to Camilla for solace. She showed her the writing box her father had brought her from Venice; she told her of their Sunday strolls after mass and how he called her "my little fish" and let her trample grapes in the Montici vats.

It so happened that Camilla was equally miserable and in search of a confidant. She revealed to Lisa that she was to be wed in June to Messer Francesco del Giocondo, an old silk merchant of thirty-one, thick-waisted, bulky, and unromantic-looking. Not that he was a bad man — he was very rich and considerate — but he simply was not the kind of man with whom a girl could fall in love.

Nevertheless, her honored father persisted in forcing her into this dreaded marriage, although he knew that she loved Cipriano del Pace. Ah, Cipriano! He was sixteen and a half with melting, long-lashed eyes and an irresistible smile. Last summer they had gone on picnics and fishing expeditions, and he had let her ride pillion on his horse, with her arms around his chest. It had been heaven . . .

"Does he love you?" asked Lisa.

Of course he did, at least most of the time. He swore that no other female existed for him; three times, he had strummed his lute under her window. Yet she had caught him giving soft glances to other girls.

This was too much for Lisa. She could no longer contain herself. In one long breathless sentence, she told Camilla about

Giuliano and how much he loved her, though he was not aware of it. On occasions, he had brought her a flower from the garden. Yet during the rehearsals of *La Rappresentazione*, he had made sheep's eyes to Angoletta.

"Twenty times I told him to hurry and ask his honored father to have me pledged to him before it is too late. But he says his father has many things on his mind and much pain in his hands. Meanwhile, he does not even notice how much I've changed and still treats me as if I were a boy."

Their common problem constituted a new bond between the two girls. Lisa talked about Giuliano; Camilla about Cipriano. They agreed men were fickle, stupid, heartless. Yet they could not conceive life without them.

Camilla wept at the mere thought of her forthcoming wedding to Francesco del Giocondo. Her mother was her last hope to avert this calamity. Donna Filippa had promised to plead her cause with her father and attempt to make him change his mind.

"If she fails, I shall kill myself or enter a nunnery," said Camilla with the impetuousness of youth.

Thus Lisa and her fourteen-year-old aunt comforted each other in their wretchedness.

That evening Mariotto Rucellai sat in his study, idly poking at the firelogs while waiting for his wife. An hour ago she had sent her personal maid to ask when it would be convenient for him to see her. Instinctively, he had guessed what she wanted to talk to him about, and in his mind he already rehearsed how he would refute her arguments.

He walked to her when she entered and courteously led her to a velvet-backed chair. The formality of these proceedings implied that both were aware of the solemnity of the occasion.

In true Florentine fashion, he opened the conversation by broaching a subject which had nothing to do with the manner at hand.

Caterina's sorrow over Antonio's death was, he declared, immoderate.

"Mind you, I have no quarrel with a wife mourning her husband, but enough is enough. It is nearly three months since she came to live in this house, but she might as well lie in the cemetery for all we see of her. She has even stopped giving music lessons to Lisa. The poor child has no mother anymore. She is practically an orphan."

Donna Filippa replied calmly that Lisa might be momentarily neglected by her mother, but she could hardly be called an orphan. She had become a member of a loving family and gained an elder sister in Camilla.

"The two are inseparable."

Moreover, she had arranged for Lisa to take *spinettino* lessons.*

"It will keep her busy. Anyway," she pressed, turning to him, "I did not come to see you about Lisa or Caterina, but about Camilla."

"She is as bad as Caterina, and I feel like taking a stick to the two of them."

"You can't blame her for looking sad when you are forcing her to marry a man she does not and never will love."

He shrugged impatiently. "At her age, a girl has the brains of a maggot and knows nothing of love. A female begins to know the man she has married only after sleeping with him for a few months."

As to the romantic drivel poets wrote about, it was much too erratic and ephemeral a feeling to build a lasting relationship on it. "Believe me, wife, in time she will learn to love Giocondo."

"Perhaps, but she does not love him now. To begin with, he is too old, much too old for her."

True, he readily admitted. Giocondo was more than twice Camilla's age. But middle-aged men made the best husbands. For one thing, they usually had more money than young men, and females were very fond of money. It was a wondrous sight how their eyes sparkled at the sight of beautiful dresses, furs, gems — all things that cost a great deal.

Furthermore, and strange as it might seem, middle-aged men also made the best lovers. From past experiences they had learned

* The *spinettino* was a portable, small-keyboarded percussion instrument, the ancestor of the spinet, clavichord, and today's piano.

many ways to please a woman and their expertise stood them in good stead in the intimate moments of married life. They were patient in their caresses, took time to fan a girl's lust while most of those swaggering cockerels could not rein in their impatience and were bent only on their own selfish gratification. After which they turned on their sides and started snoring, leaving their poor wives tense and tearful in the flickering glow of the votive lamp.

History, he went on, abounded in young females who had lost their hearts to older men. Cleopatra had loved passionately, at least for a while, Julius Caesar, who was bald and twenty-five years her senior. Of course, he was a general and that might have had something to do with it, females being notoriously partial to uniforms. And what about the thousand wives, not counting occasional houseguests like the queen of Sheba, who had lovingly shared Solomon's bed? And more recently, what about Maddalena de'Medici who had become exceedingly smitten with her oaf of a husband, twenty-eight years older than herself?

"So you see," he concluded, "you needn't have any fears about our daughter's happiness on that ground."

He felt he had neatly disposed of her argument and was rather pleased with himself.

"So much speech has parched my throat," he said. "I should relish a goblet of Malaga wine."

Fondly he watched her rise to pull the bell rope. In her youth, Filippa had been a great beauty, and traces of it lingered in the delicacy of her profile and the slenderness of her neck.

While sipping his wine, he noticed that she remained lost in thought, which meant that she proposed to resume the debate. She was using the interval to marshal new arguments.

"Well," he said, resting his cup on the small table at his side, "what else do you have against Giocondo?"

She took the plunge.

"No doubt he has a fine mind and good character, but the gap between him and Adonis is rather wide. You cannot expect Camilla to be smitten with such a boorish, plain-looking man."

No question about that, Mariotto agreed with a conciliatory chuckle, Giocondo was not exactly a romantic figure, but looks didn't matter much in matrimony. After a while, husbands and wives stopped looking at or even seeing each other.

"I wager I could grow another nose and you probably wouldn't notice it." Challenging her, he pressed on, "Anything else?"

"Yes, noble husband," she said with sudden petulance. "There is something else. He is in silk!" She almost flung the words at him.

He knew this had been on her mind for a long time, and it finally was out.

"Yes," he said quietly, "he is in silk. As a matter of fact, this is one of reasons why I want Camilla to marry him."

In plain terms he told her about the decline of the wool industry. It was not yet being talked about openly, but it was being whispered about in banking circles. Many of the great wool mills along the Arno found it difficult to meet their financial obligations. The days of the four hundred percent profit on San Martino were over. Lorenzo de'Medici worried about the loss of revenue to the public treasury. On the other hand, the silk industry was flourishing more than ever.

"Antonio, who was a farsighted man, came to see me before leaving for Venice and told me he was considering going into the manufacture of silk."

He caught the look of stupefaction on her face.

"Yes, wife. He was about to go into silk when he died. Do you now understand why I want Camilla to marry Giocondo?"

At once he knew he had won her to his views.

"Noble husband," she said simply, "you will hear no more from me on this matter. I realize you have acted in our daughter's best interest. It may take her some time to admit it, but someday she will thank you for it."

Her cheeks dimpled into a smile. "Would you spare me a sip from your cup?"

They were at peace again . . . That was what he liked about her. She was sensible, open to reason, not one of those females who continue to cackle and argue when there is nothing more to argue about.

"Wife," he said, holding out the goblet to her, "I've said it before and I shall say it again, you should have been a man."

When Camilla learned of her mother's "betrayal" and her acceptance of her father's plans, she was crushed with despair and inflamed with the desire for revenge.

"There is nothing left for me but to kill myself," she announced calmly, brushing a strand of blond hair from her face.

Lisa agreed, but suggested that she wait a few days. "You can always do it in a week or two. Besides, you must decide how you will kill yourself."

Together they examined the various suicide procedures. They discussed self-stabbing, hanging herself, slashing her veins, drowning in the tub, diving into the Arno. None appealed to Camilla. As her main purpose in killing herself was to punish her parents for their cruelty, she felt it was unfair that she should have to strangle herself just to make them feel miserable.

"I shall enter a nunnery," she declared one day.

She would be alive, yet dead to the world: a living corpse, haunting her parents with the memory of their heartlessness. Gradually, however, the prospect of spending the rest of her life without male company, attending mass every day, never wearing pretty dresses anymore or going to dances, became too much to bear. Then it occurred to her that she would need her father's permission to enter a convent. This put an end to her nunnery plans.

"There seems to be no way out of your wedding to Messer del Giocondo," concluded Lisa, in her role of adviser. "Perhaps you'll get used to him in time, even if he is old and fat."

Besides, she went on, all hope was not lost. A man of his years would not live long or he might have to travel in foreign lands, and there was always a chance that his ship might sink or be seized by pirates. Thus Lisa reasoned in her eleventh year.

"Then you would be a widow and could marry Cipriano."

The situation no longer appeared so desperate as it had first seemed.

By degrees, Camilla grew accustomed to the idea of marrying the man she did not love. With the coming of spring, she began gathering her trousseau. Soon she had so much to do she no longer had time to think about the approaching ordeal.

When Lisa was not advising her aunt or accompanying her on errands, she complained to her about Giuliano's blindness.

Here she was nearly twelve, the product of countless rose-water baths and massages, already arousing flattering comments when she walked in the streets, and the stupid Giuliano continued to treat her as a younger sister.

"He is blind as a mole," she would say spitefully.

It was now Camilla's turn to bestow solace and advice. Boys, she would explain, were exasperatingly slow to mature. She had actually known fifteen- and even sixteen-year-old *giovanotti* who paid no heed to the most attractive maidens and preferred wrestling or playing *calcio* on Piazza Santa Croce.*

On a sunny April morning, while Lisa was helping Camilla with the writing of wedding invitations, the sound of a piping young voice rose in song from the garden below.

> *"How fair is youth, but how quickly it flies!*
> *Be merry while you may; of tomorrow no one can say."*

The ballad wafted into the room accompanied by the strumming of lute.

"It's Giuliano," said Lisa, quill in mid-air. "Let's not pay any attention."

An instant later the pane tinkled with the sound of a striking pebble.

"That fool is going to break the glass," she exclaimed.

Rushing to the window, she leaned over the sill, and as she had expected, Giuliano stood in the garden, his face raised to her, his *berretta* at a rakish angle on his head.

* *Calcio* was a distant forerunner of football requiring twenty-one players in each team.

"Go away," she cried. "I have no time to listen to your silly songs. Besides, you sing like a frog."

"I have a message for you. *Importantissimo.*"

"What is it?"

He could not say. Not only was the message *importantissimo*, but *privatissimo*. The neighbors might hear it, and that would be terrible. If she wanted to hear it, she must come down in the garden.

"I don't believe you have any message," she replied, suspecting a trap.

"As you wish, fair cousin."

He slung the lute over his shoulder and started walking away in the direction of the gate.

Curiosity got the better of her.

"Wait," she cried. "I'll come down, but if it is another of your tricks, I'll never speak to you again."

The garden with its brick wall and weedy alleys was drenched in sunshine when she came out of the house. He was nowhere to be seen; his voice rose out of a thicket of laurel bushes over a strumming of lute. She spied him sitting on the ledge of the well, a long silk-hosed leg swinging in cadence with the song. She noticed how handsome he looked with his face in repose.

She strode towards him and stopped a few feet away. "Well, here I am. What's the message?"

"Ssh!" He raised a finger to his lips. "I'm composing a song."

The impudence of him! "I knew you had no message. You are a shame to your clan."

"If you speak so much a fly will get into your mouth."

He stopped playing and declared he would deliver the message in exchange for a kiss.

He had kissed her before, but never asked for a kiss.

"I'll eat grass before I kiss you."

He did not argue, but slung his lute over his shoulder, vaulted over the wall and walked away.

She ran after him and pecked his cheek. "Here's your kiss. Now, the message!"

He clasped his forehead. "The message! What message?"

He had forgotten the message . . . She had wearied him so much with her prattling that it had escaped his mind. She called him a rogue, a black-hearted snake, *una bestia*.

Suddenly he grinned. The message had returned. "We're going fishing tomorrow and Contessina would like you to come with us. If you give me another kiss, I'll let you ride pillion with me."

She was furious. So, this was the *importantissimo* and *privatissimo* message that could not be overheard by the neighbors! The message for which he had made her come down to the garden and demanded a kiss!

"Well, it so happens that I have more important things to do than stand by a river with a pole in my hand and wait for some silly fish to bite."

As she spoke, she felt his lips on hers. The scoundrel had kissed her again!

"We'll fetch you tomorrow, after the morning chimes," he said, dashing towards the wall.

She bent down to scoop up a few pebbles and hurled them in his direction, but already he had climbed over the wall and was out of sight.

The following morning she was waiting for the fishing party, in her bottle-green riding suit, a smile on her face and revenge in her heart. They arrived in a clatter of hooves, the boys holding reins, the girls sitting behind on pads attached to their saddles.

They were members of Florence's gilded youth, sons and daughters of "fat ones" every one of them: great merchants, bankers, state dignitaries. Giuliano hoisted Lisa on his horse and she circled her arms around his chest. At his signal, the joyous cavalcade clattered out of the courtyard and made its laughing, singing way to the appointed spot on the bank of the Mugello, a tributary of the Arno. Throughout the ride, Giuliano behaved like a perfect gentleman; Lisa, for her part, was graciousness itself, gay and kittenish.

After a picnic meal on the grass, the grooms in the white and purple Medici livery baited the fishing hooks and distributed the fishing poles. Giuliano pointed to a wooden bridge standing a short distance upstream.

"Fair cousin," he suggested, "let's go and fish there. The water is deeper and I shall teach you how to cast a line properly."

She was still thanking him a moment later as he stood on the ledge of the bridge, precariously raised on his toes, as if about to take flight, and twirling his line in the air.

"You see," he said, "this is the way —"

He did not finish the sentence, for at that precise instant she gave him a slight shove that sent him headfirst into the Mugello. Alas, in a lightning reflex, he managed to grasp her skirt and took her with him in his fall.

Oh, the shame of it all! The splash down, the floundering in the river, the mouthfuls of water, her hair glued to her face — and Giuliano, the beast, laughingly watching her drown . . .

"He is the most awful man I've ever known," she told Tessa that evening. "I'll never, never speak to him again."

Two days later she was summoned to her grandfather's study. For a while he considered her in silence while she stood before him, her eyes riveted to the carpet.

"What is this I hear about your pushing Giuliano off the bridge?" he asked, his bushy eyebrows knit in a frown.

She launched into a voluble explanation from which it resulted that she had not done such a thing. A sudden gust of wind had caused Giuliano to lose his balance. Casting about for support, he had inadvertently clutched her skirt and carried her down with him.

"In other words," said the banker in a tone of extreme incredulity, "you were both victims of circumstances beyond your control. An act of God, so to speak."

She nodded eagerly. That was it: an act of God.

"Well," he went on with a twinkle in his eyes, "this is what we shall say, and if we say it often enough, we may even come to believe it."

His face relaxed into a smile.

"Get yourself gone, my child, and pray the Madonna to forgive our sins."

She bobbed a curtsy, turned on her heels, and ran out of the study.

That afternoon Mariotto called on Lorenzo de'Medici at his home on Via Larga.

"Cousin Lauro," he began, easing himself down on a chair across the desk, "I've come to invite you to the wedding of my daughter, Camilla. But first, I should warn you that my granddaughter Lisa tried to drown your son Giuliano."

Lorenzo's bony face creased into a grin. Yes, he had heard about the bridge incident and tried to get to the bottom of it without success. Contessina had given him an account of it that was so involved that he could not figure out who had done what to whom. As for Giuliano, his explanations had been even more confusing.

"But I know my Giuliano, and you may rest assured that whatever Lisa may have done, she had ample provocation. By the way, have you pledged her to anyone yet?"

"No," replied Mariotto, somewhat taken aback. "It's still too early to think about it. She is not even twelve and, frankly, she has become very dear to my wife and me, and we would like to keep her to ourselves for a few more years. The house is going to seem quite empty after Camilla goes." After a pause he added, "Why do you ask?"

"As you know, I was forced to marry my son Piero to a foreigner and I regret it bitterly. Alfonsina is not popular and I fear she will prove a great liability to him when the time comes for him to succeed me. I swore that Giuliano would marry a Florentine girl, and it occurred to me he could not get a finer bride than Lisa." He shrugged indulgently. "Oh, I know they quarrel like cat and dog and call each other names. But I suspect they like each other a great deal. If you look favorably upon this notion of mine, we might discuss it again in two or three years."

Mariotto declared he was greatly honored by the suggestion. A wedding between the two youngsters would indeed tighten the bonds of friendship already existing between the Medici, Gherardini, and Rucellai clans. "Meanwhile, can we count on your presence at Camilla's wedding?"

For an instant, Lorenzo twirled the sapphire ring on his finger.

"Frankly, it all depends on the condition of my health," he said at last. "Some days, like today, I feel reasonably well; others are a torment. But, in either case, you may rest assured that my family will be well represented."

After Mariotto's departure, he sent for Giuliano.

"It's such a lovely day," he began, "why don't we walk to the San Marco Gardens and have a little chat?"

The gardens were located a short distance from the palace, and shortly afterwards they were sitting on a stone bench under a linden tree. A fountain splashed softly nearby. At the end of an alley, a statue of Diana stood out against the dark green background of a cypress hedge; the bustle of Florence expired at the garden's gate.

"Your honored great-grandfather Cosimo created this park and gave it to the people so that they would have somewhere to enjoy silence, rest, or think, and for a moment forget their troubles amid beautiful things."

He pointed to the statue of Diana glowing white in the sunshine. "See how graceful she is, and how young! Yet she is much older than our cathedral or Ponte Vecchio or Christ himself. Like the Parthenon, the writings of Plato, Homer's poems, or Phidias's statues, she belongs to a civilization that long preceded Christianity and in many ways was much superior to it." Although Lorenzo observed the outward practices of religion, he was an agnostic, and had expressed his lack of faith in verse:

> *O Dio, o Sommo bene, or come fai*
> *Che te sol cerco e non ti trovo mai.*

"O God, O Supreme Good, why do I seek Thee and do not find Thee."

After more than a thousand years of oblivion, they were coming to light again. Nations were not remembered by their battles or their banks, but by the beauty they left behind. In the end, only art endured.

"If ever you have an opportunity to help a great artist, don't fail to do so. It will repay you a thousand times."

He gave a last glance at the statue and laboriously rose to his feet.

"About this bridge incident," he said suddenly as they were returning to Casa Medici, "is there anything you might have done that could have made her take her revenge?"

"She didn't push me, I fell."

"Well," smiled his father, "whether she did or not, the thing for you to do is to go and apologize."

"Apologize!" The word burst out in a gasp.

Certainly, his father argued. That's the logical, gracious, and clever thing to do. If she had not pushed him off the bridge, she would be impressed by his proclaiming his guilt; if she had shoved him in the river, she would be overwhelmed by his generosity. In either case, she would be most favorably impressed.

"This, my son, is diplomacy," he added, taking a coin from his purse. "Flowers make excellent and inexpensive gifts, and females love them. Go and bring her some."

He found her practicing on the *spinettino* in the music room.

Despite its elegant name, the "music room" served as a storage place for garden tools, broken furniture, and odds and ends of all descriptions. At one time it had been a servants' chamber, and a derelict four-poster testified to that fact. It was on the ground floor and opened directly on to the rear garden. A shaft of green sunlight filtered through a sycamore into the room through its single window. No sound from the music room reached the upper floors of the house. Thus people were spared the nerve-jarring dissonances of Lisa's practicing.

She was laboriously negotiating an arpeggio when she saw Giuliano's face half hidden behind a large bouquet of spring blossoms.

"Will you ever forgive me for pushing you off that bridge?"

he pleaded from the threshold. "It was a beastly thing for me to do."

"I've already forgotten about it," she said, running to him. "Please, come in."

As an additional inducement, she gave him a big kiss on the cheek. As her face remained close to his, he had no choice but to give her a tender kiss, which happened to fall on a corner of her lips. This time she did not object, did not call him names, did not throw pebbles at him. That night, she slept with a flower from his bouquet under her pillow.

Giuliano's apology opened a new era in their relationship. No more wrestling or quarreling. His blindness had vanished as if by incantation: no longer did he treat her as though she were a boy. His visits became more frequent and increasingly intimate. The isolation of the music room encouraged the exchange of confidences.

They told each other what great friends they were. With her head on his chest, she would seek his advice on various imaginary problems while listening to the beat of his heart. Inadvertently, his lips would brush her hair, her cheeks, her mouth.

It did not occur to her to protest, for they were great friends and of such things friendship was made.

In June 1491 Camilla Rucellai resignedly married Francesco del Giocondo.*

The house did seem empty after her departure. Lisa missed her and their confidences. Never had she needed her so much, never had she so much to tell. Giuliano was proving himself the most attentive and tender friend. He let her cuddle up to him, stroked her hair while she whispered endearments, but he never mentioned marriage. One of these days, he would kiss her lips, circle his arm around her shoulder and announce he was marrying someone else. Probably Agnoletta de'Landi . . .

---

* This marriage, which explains so much of Mona Lisa's later life, is confirmed by a score of historians and scholars: E. Muntz, A. C. Coppier, C. Peladan, E. Staley and the great Florentine Renaissance expert Gaetano Milanesi, whose manuscript can be consulted at the Riccardiana Biblioteca in Florence.

The mere thought of it sent her into fits of anguish.

Thus she almost wept from joy when, one evening at supper, her grandfather announced that the newlyweds would spend the summer with them at "The Farm," the Rucellai country house.

"Francesco feels it will give Camilla time to adjust herself to her being married to him," he told Filippa after the meal.

"Which proves he is an intelligent and considerate man, just as you said. I look forward to having them with us in the country."

Two days after their moving to "The Farm," they welcomed Giocondo and his bride. The entire household gave voice to expressions of happiness at seeing Camilla again. Lisa thrilled at the prospect of resuming confidences with her beloved aunt.

The following morning Mariotto invited his wife to join him in the *boshetto*, a small oak forest that was his personal domain on the estate. Recurrently he would proclaim his intention of tending it himself, on the grounds that exercise was beneficial to health. And, indeed, for a few days he would wear a cotton *lucco* with a wide-brimmed straw hat and meander about the *boschetto*, hoe in hand, pretending to weed an alley or two. Then he would give up, return to mull over banking or politics in his favorite chair, or simply doze over a book.

That morning, however, there was a certain solemnity in his manner, an unusual gravity in his voice.

He began by saying that he was now fifty-seven and deep in his sunset years. No doubt, his time on earth was approaching its term. He thanked God for giving him the pleasure of having seen his youngest child married to a good and honorable man. Now nothing remained for him but to prepare for the journey across the Great Sea.

"This summer 'The Farm' is going to be full of people. What with Camilla and Giocondo, Caterina, Lisa, and our other children who will surely come to visit, you won't have a minute to yourself. Would you object to my going on a pilgrimage?"

She looked at him with amused surprise. He looked ruddy-cheeked and clear-eyed as ever. Never, in all their years of married life, had he ever expressed any desire to join one of the

Bankers' Guild pilgrimages. He must have some idea in the back of his head, she thought.

"Not the slightest, noble husband," she said smiling. "The camping and walking will do you a world of good. How long will you be away?"

"Two, at the most three, weeks."

He stayed away all summer.

From time to time couriers arrived from various Tuscan towns with brief, affectionate notes from which she deduced he was traveling a great deal and enjoying himself. Before long there appeared a string of carts heaped high with dilapidated objects: bronze shields, dented helmets, broken kitchen utensils, black and orange oil amphoras, most of them damaged. She wondered what on earth he planned to do with this bric-a-brac.

He returned in late September, hale and leather-skinned, richer by thousands of years of indulgences and hundreds of florins won at cards from his fellow pilgrims. After bathing and shaving his beard (pilgrims were not supposed to shave), he joined his wife in the *boschetto* and inquired how things had been at "The Farm" during his absence.

Fine, she replied; everything had been fine. Various sons and daughters of theirs had paid their customary visits with their children, nurses, and tutors. Lisa had seen a good deal of Giuliano and gone with him on picnics and fishing parties. He had given her swimming lessons, in case she should fall off another bridge. In short, they had had a happy summer. For her birthday, Giocondo had given her a beautiful coral rosary and that had mollified her opinion of him.

"What about Caterina?"

Filippa hesitated. Caterina was the only cloud in the picture. Oh yes, she had tried to be cheerful, played with her nephews and nieces. But her heart had not been in it. Her thoughts remained turned to the previous summer and the last days she had spent with Antonio before his departure for Venice.

"No use deceiving ourselves," she said at last. "Some women can love only once and she is one of them."

He let out a sigh and shrugged helplessly. Then he asked, "And Camilla?"

A wondrous change had come over her. Not only had she reconciled herself to the idea of marriage, but she clearly had become fond of her husband.

"More than fond, I should say, from the way she looks at him." Softly she added, "I believe she is with child."

Mariotto could not resist crowing a little as he recalled his predictions of a few months ago. "Didn't I tell you that middle-aged men have a way with females?"

She agreed and conceded his superior wisdom. "And now, noble husband, tell me about your summer."

The pilgrimage had been a great success. In San Gimignano they had visited the shrine of Santa Fina, a local fifteen-year-old saint who had spent the last five years of her life lying on a board and having heavenly visions of God and the popes. Each year, on the anniversary of her death, violets sprouted of their own accord on the board where she had lain so long.

After their visit to the shrine, they had repaired to the town's brothel, which appeared to be the most popular meeting place and was run as a public service by the city council.

Filippa inquired about the shipments of knickknacks that had arrived at the village. She was told they were Trurian artifacts he had collected in view of a book he planned to write about the Etruscans, this ancient and mysterious tribe who had lived in Tuscany in distant times.

Yes, he declared, he longed to leave some lasting memento of his passage on earth. Not as a banker or public servant, but as the man who had unlocked the Etruscan enigma. Henceforth, he would renounce all business pursuits and divide his few remaining years between meditation and the writing of his book.

The Etruscans proved extremely disappointing. The more he studied them, the more mysterious they became. As their mystery increased, their fascination waned. On close examination, he also discovered that most of the artifacts he had bought were forgeries.

Dejectedly he told his wife he had had enough of the Etruscans.

"I am afraid I'll never be anything but a banker."

She assured him there were worse fates. The next day he found that the Etruscan bric-a-brac, which had cluttered his study, had been discreetly removed to the music room. She was, he thought, a pearl of a wife.

And so, having foresaken the Etruscans, abandoned the fathers of the Church and his literary aspirations, he returned to the unquestioning faith of his ancestors and regained his peace of mind. He deserted the obfuscating world of theology and returned to the simple world of money. Again he spent the morning in the *loggia* of the *Borsa* and watched the fluctuation of stocks. He made a great deal of money, gave some of it to the poor, and kept most of it.

While her grandfather was recovering from his religious and literary crises, Lisa was sailing the choppy seas of adolescence.

For some months she had already experienced the tremors and anxieties of that stormy period of life. For the first time, she tossed in her sleep. Her dolls, her beloved "children," once so lovingly dressed, undressed, scolded, spanked, and nursed, now lay about the room like abandoned orphans.

One single day would see her go through a whole range of moods. In a few hours she could pass from exuberant singing to silent gloom. For some time she had become aware that changes were taking place in her body, and this knowledge filled her with delight one moment and despair the next. The gentle swelling of her breasts, the rounding of her hips stirred her rising femininity, only to plunge her, shortly afterward, into pits of alarm. Devils were at work within her. What if they never stopped inflating her breasts, turning them into enormous balloons? What if her hips never ceased widening?

Somehow she became convinced that Giuliano knew about the devils and this was the reason why he never mentioned marriage. He kissed her out of compassion, caressed her out of kindness. In his heart, he knew she was doomed.

Her worst fears were confirmed when hair appeared where there had been no hair before. What made it even worse was that

Tessa did not even comment on it and calmly shaved the silky down. This operation became a weekly feature of her bathing routine to which she submitted in cringing shame and with eyes tightly shut.

Her inner turmoil also expressed itself in recurrent fits of all-embracing suspiciousness when even Tessa became suspect and a potential enemy. Lisa now saw her as an informer who reported her every word and gesture to her mother.

One day she announced that henceforth the door between their rooms would remain closed, admission to be gained only by a gentle knock.

"So, now *la signorina* wants to be alone," said Tessa.

"I have things to think about."

"What things?"

"I won't tell you. You'd only run to Mamma and tell her everything."

The slave did not press the point and promised to knock on the door. Lisa was able to brood in privacy. She soon grew tired of it. To her surprise, she found herself missing her *bambinaia*. It was she who knocked at the door and pitifully asked to be let in and allowed to sit by the fire.

Tension grew through October and most of November. Giuliano's visits had become infrequent, for he was now working in his father's decoding office. Lisa concluded he had abandoned her to her fate and she wept silently while eating Tessa's roast chestnuts.

Then one morning she noticed blood smears on the bedsheets. The end had come. This time, terror shot out of her in a wail that brought Tessa rushing into the room.

"What is it, *bimba mia?*" she asked, hugging her against her bosom.

Pointing at the blood smears, Lisa sobbed she was going to bleed to death, one drop at a time.

In a flush of repentance, she begged Tessa's forgiveness for her past misdeeds. "Deep inside, I really love you."

In an unbroken stream of words, she disposed of her earthly belongings. Her "children" were to go to some poor orphan girl.

The silver wreath her grandfather Gherardini had given her she bequeathed to Contessina; her father's ink box to Camilla. As to her dresses —

Finally, Tessa shook her into silence. "You are not going to die, you silly goose."

All females bled at a certain time of the month. It was just part of growing up. It meant nothing, not a blessed thing.

"And what about the hair?"

Meant nothing either . . . Just some kind of decoration, one of God's little jokes. Boys were even worse off. They had hair sprouting out of their faces which forced them to shave every day.

The episode marked the end of Lisa's wretchedness. On learning she was not going to die, her past fears turned to complacency. She studied her reflection at length in the vanity-table mirror and decided she was very pretty and shapely. She vowed to make Giuliano realize it by making herself irresistible.

She became extremely fashion-conscious and complained that her wardrobe did not do her justice. She plagued Tessa into adding a bit of lace to her sleeves, a ruff to her neck, a knot of ribbons on her bodice. She tried plucking her eyebrows and Tessa caught her at it. They had a violent scene. They had an even more violent one when Tessa caught her rouging her nipples, a fad encouraged by extremely low necklines. This time, the slave threatened to call a witch, but Lisa said she could run faster than a witch. Then Tessa declared she preferred to see her dead at her feet than going about with rouged nipples like a bad woman.

Frustrated as she was in her endeavors, Lisa noticed that young men, and even old ones of twenty and more, eyed her with increasing relish when she walked about in the streets. She did nothing to discourage them. On the contrary, she gave them furtive smiles, under lidded glances, which prompted Tessa to say she had as much modesty as an alley cat.

Suddenly it was wonderful to be alive and twelve years old in that autumn of 1491, a maiden of high degree and a budding beauty. Her happiness soared still higher when, in December, her grandfather announced he was taking her with him on his journey to Pisa, and Giuliano would also come with them.

"The situation in Pisa is getting daily more difficult," Mariotto explained to his wife that evening. "The Pisans hate us, and with good reasons. They can't forget how we starved them into surrender, branded their women on the cheeks, and slashed old men's noses. I know it was very long ago, when we were dreaming of an empire, and many years before the Medici came to power. Lorenzo has done everything in his power to conciliate the Pisans. He has lived in their town for long periods of time; he has sent his son, Giovanni, to their university. But the Pisans continue to wait for an opportunity to rise against us. Meanwhile, they stab our tax collectors and throw them in the Arno; they ambush our sentries, harass our garrison."

Lorenzo, he went on, had asked him to go to Pisa and attempt a last effort at conciliation. "While I was governor in that city, I made some influential friends and he feels they will trust me. It is to be an unofficial mission, and this is why he suggested I take Lisa and Giuliano with me. As you can imagine, I do not relish the prospect of riding to Pisa in December, but the matter is urgent, and I simply could not refuse his request. Lorenzo is dying. Illness has spread through his entire body and I don't think he will see summer again."

The mission, he wound up, should not take more than two months. He would be back in March in time for Camilla's confinement. "This is one thing I do not want to miss."

During the few days preceding the departure, Lisa bought several new dresses. She also visited her young aunt and was struck by the change that had come over her. No longer did Camilla talk about killing herself. Not once did she mention her hope that Giocondo might go on some distant journey and never return. Instead, she extolled his kindness and patience. It was clear that she had become hopelessly in love with her fat and old husband. Not once did she mention Cipriano. Marriage did accomplish wonders, Lisa thought.

Excitedly, she talked about her forthcoming trip to Pisa and her plans to maneuver Giuliano into realizing what a fine wife she would make.

Camilla did not approve of such self-advertisement. "Do not be like the shopkeeper who stands on the step of his *bottega* and cries to passersby, 'Look at my wares! See how fine they are!' Let Giuliano discover how pretty you are."

Lisa assured her she would be very subtle and clever.

"On my return, I'll tell you everything," she said, slipping on her fur-lined gloves.

"I'll be in bed by then," smiled Camilla, "waiting for my baby to come. He will be a boy, I am sure of it. Already we've chosen his name, Bartolommeo. It was the name of my husband's father."

On the eve of her departure, Lisa was told that her honored mother wished to see her. It was a long time since she had had a private encounter with her mother and she had some misgivings as to her reception.

"You are about to go on a long journey," said Caterina. "Remember that in Pisa customs differ from ours and make sure not to give offense either by word or gesture. From heaven, your honored father will be watching you." Suddenly her eyes filled with tears. "He will be expecting you to behave like a true Gherardini lady."

Softly she added, "He loved you very much."

Then she recalled the house on Via Maggio: the reading and writing lessons, their singing and playing the lute together.

"We were happy then, and on your return we shall resume our music lessons."

She kissed her tenderly and Lisa felt that at long last the chasm between them had disappeared.

The journey to Pisa was effected without incident. The weather was cold, but crisp. They rode the fifty miles in two days, with Tessa following on the baggage cart.

At Lorenzo's request, they lodged at the Medici Palace along the Arno. The sixteen-year-old Giovanni, soon to be installed as a cardinal, received them with genuine pleasure. He gave Lisa his hand to kiss and recalled their pleasant moments in the Careggi garden.

Whenever Giuliano's presence was not required by Mariotto, he accompanied Lisa on her tours through the city. Together they visited the admirable cathedral that seemed carved in ivory. They climbed the Leaning Tower, walked hand in hand through the cemetery where the dead slept in earth brought from Jerusalem.

They attended several functions given in honor of Mariotto. Giuliano proved an attentive escort and Lisa enjoyed the gleams of envy she caught in the eyes of the flower-wreathed Pisan maidens. Everywhere she behaved like a true Gherardini lady and was a source of pride to her clan. She knew that her *babbo* smiled on her from heaven.

Whenever she found herself alone with Giuliano, she brought the conversation around to the subject that was dear to her heart.

"I am worried about you," she remarked one rainy day in January, as they sat by the fire in one of the rooms of the Medici Palace. "Very worried."

"What about, *cocolina?*" he inquired, gently drawing her head onto his shoulder.

"Have you ever thought about taking a wife?"

No, he hadn't, he replied, giving her a very tender, very friendly kiss. It simply hadn't crossed his mind. He felt he was still too young to think about taking a wife.

"That's where you're wrong," she corrected.

Youth lasted but a moment. Soon he would be too old and decrepit to find a suitable maiden. "I just wanted to warn you, that's all."

He thanked her for her solicitude with another tender and friendly kiss on the lips, and changed the subject.

Despite this inauspicious beginning, she did not give up. On several occasions she described how lonely and unwanted he would feel as an aging bachelor, bereft of the love of a good wife.

"Someday you will remember my words," she predicted darkly.

Another time, she listed the qualities he should seek in a wife. She should be well-born, poised, stylish, polished in manners — and a brunette. Blondes, she explained, turned a mousy gray in their early twenties and redheads were violent-tempered.

"She also should be rather tall," she wound up, "have beautiful brown eyes and shapely hands." As she spoke, she flapped her long lashes at him and rested her well-massaged fingers on his sleeve.

Between kisses, he promised to think about what she had been telling him.

The first three weeks of January wore on in constant rain. For the remainder of the month, the sky remained gray with billowy, sodden clouds almost touching the roofs.

It was February before they dared ride the seven miles to the sea, which neither of them had ever seen.

Even before they reached the shore, they could hear the pounding surf. They dismounted and walked to the edge of the water. Afraid and hugging each other, they stood, their hair windswept across their faces, as waves came rushing at them like fearful dragons, their jaws open and filled with foam.

They had planned to spend the day at the shore, but it started raining and they rode back to Pisa. Both were drenched to the bone when they reached the Medici Palace.

At once they were led to Mariotto's study.

"We must leave immediately," he told Lisa. "Your honored mother is very ill."

They rode without respite through the ceaseless drizzle. Even then, it took them two and a half days to reach Florence. As they neared Casa Rucellai, they saw that the doorway was festooned with black cloth and knew that Caterina was dead.

The previous week she had gone to mass in a pelting rain, Filippa said in faltering sobs. She was shivering on her return from church. One hour after going to bed, she had become delirious and had died during the night.

"Don't weep, wife," said Mariotto, placing a hand on her shoulder. "Tears are out of place for one who did not want to live. Caterina had died a year ago, with Antonio."

When a few days later he reported to Lorenzo on his unfinished mission, he was led not to his study, as usual, but to his bedroom on the second floor. There he found the ruler of Florence hunched by the fire, holding his skeletal hands to the flames.

Mariotto was shocked by the change in his friend's appearance. His hair was streaked with gray. At forty-one, the Magnificent looked old. His face, once etched with lines of laughter, had become a dolorous mask of jutting bones and hollowed cheeks, occasionally contorted by a twinge of pain.

He waved the visitor to an armchair at the opposite end of the fireplace.

"Forgive me for giving you this distressing spectacle," he said with a semblance of a smile. "You have before you a man in process of disintegration. Every organ in my body is about to collapse. Gout has now spread to my legs as well as my hands, and I cannot walk any more. Liver, kidneys, bladder have nearly ceased to function, and I'm waiting for that huge strawberry bouncing in my chest to grow tired and come to a halt."

With a visible effort, he went on, "Now tell me about Pisa."

Mariotto mentioned the meetings he had had with various personalities in view of reaching some sort of understanding, but he soon became aware that Lorenzo was not listening.

"I see you are in great pain," he said. "I shall return tomorrow or some other day at your convenience."

"Please, don't go. I shan't be any better tomorrow or any other day."

There was no self-pity in his voice, merely the final acceptance of defeat.

"I used to think that the world was divided between rich and poor, young and old, weak and strong. I was wrong. It is divided between the sick and the healthy. When you enter the Brotherhood of Pain, you take leave of your fellow men. You no longer care about what goes on in the world, whether or not the Pisans will ever forgive us for what our ancestors have done to their ancestors. You think only of the next spasm, the next throb in knuckles or knees and how long it will last. And you find yourself praying God for the mercy of death."

Suddenly his face contorted in agony. For a few instants he was unable to speak and sat rigid, his eyes shut, his hands clutching the arms of his chair. Sweat glistened on his brow. Then his face relaxed and his chest heaved with returning breath.

"Cousin," he said at last, "I've learned of your daughter's death and it increases my reluctance to ask another favor of you." Again a wan smile floated over his lips. "I swear it will be the last."

In a rapid stream of words, as though he feared he might die before saying what he wanted to say, he explained that he did not expect to live more than a few more weeks. He only wanted to see his son Giovanni duly installed as cardinal, and make sure that his eldest son, Piero, would be named his successor by the Signoria, as he and his father had been.

Piero was not yet twenty, intelligent, but impulsive. His wife, Alfonsina, was not popular. Worse still, the times were filled with problems that would tax the most experienced statesman.

"Our economic decline is becoming more serious every day. A quarrel is brewing between Naples and Milan which threatens to set Italy afire." His voice broke off in a muted sob. "I'm dying when I could have been most useful."

Tears gleamed in his eyes as he forced himself to go on. "It would give me great peace of mind if you would head the Signoria during the coming term of March and April."

His eyes rested on Mariotto. "Please."

"Rest your mind at ease, Cousin Lauro. I shall do as you wish. Now lay down and have your physician make you some sleep-inducing potion."

To Mariotto's relief, his wife approved of his promise to Lorenzo.

She felt that the duties and responsibilities of government would keep him from brooding over Caterina's death and Camilla's imminent confinement.

And so Mariotto donned once again the red *lucco* with its long-trained, star-embossed mantle and close-fitting, ermine-fringed coif. And, of course, the splendid gold chain of office.

On the first of March, he moved to the Old Palace where he

took possession of the *gonfaloniere*'s room with its enormous hooded chimney, its large desk, its few chairs and, in a corner, the velvet-curtained four-poster to which was still fastened the Red Lily standard of the Republic.

He and his colleagues spent the morning, after mass, discussing matters of state, voting on each issue by placing a white or black bean on the green-felted table. In the afternoon he performed many of the duties Lorenzo could no longer perform and received Piero de'Medici, who came to ask his advice and report on his father's condition. Donna Filippa brought news of the household and Camilla's condition.

Supper over, the councillors gathered in his room for a last goblet of wine and some informal talk by the fire. All were prominent merchants or bankers; all had known one another since youth. They were aware of Lorenzo's desperate illness as well as the accelerating economic decline of Florence and disintegrating political situation in Italy. They shared the same apprehension over the future without Lorenzo at the helm of the government.

"He's leaving us when we need him most," they said.

To everyone's surprise, he continued to live, and on 9 March he knew his last joy on earth.

The three-year delay imposed by His Holiness had ended, and that day Giovanni was officially installed as Cardinal Santa Maria-in-Domenica. By special dispensation, the ceremony took place in the abbey of Fiesole, a suburb of Florence. Lorenzo was unable to attend, but a string of galloping couriers kept him informed of the unfolding investiture service.

The ritual over, the new prince of the Church in the scarlet regalia of his rank rode to the Medici Palace on a white horse, escorted by a swarm of clerical dignitaries and an immense cortege. He knelt by his father's bedside and asked for his blessing. Then, in response to the popular clamor rising from below, he appeared at a window, traced a large sign of the cross in the air, and, on a youthful impulse, tossed his beautiful red hat to the crowd.

That night every window glowed with burning candles. An atmosphere of carnival replaced the religious fervor of the morning. On Piazza della Signoria slow-moving carts decorated with greenery, plaster emblems, and flimsily clad girls representing angels or virtues lumbered among the revelers. Fireworks spangled the sky with luminous, short-lived blooms.

The following day, a Sunday, a solemn mass was sung in the cathedral. Eight elderly bishops knelt to kiss the hand of the seventeen-year-old cardinal. The rest of the morning was taken up by a banquet at which Lorenzo appeared on a litter borne by four liveried grooms. He managed to smile, spoke a few gracious words, raised a gold cup in toast to His Holiness, and withdrew.

This was his last public appearance.

In the afternoon the presentation of gifts from the Signoria, the guilds, the diplomatic corps, and high dignitaries, as well as from the Florentine Jewish community — a splendid silver table service — was held in the Audience Room.*

On Tuesday, 12 March, Cardinal Santa Maria-in-Domenica bid farewell to his dying father, his brothers and sisters, and the Medici servants and set out on his journey to Rome. In spurred boots, plumed hat, black velvet doublet and travel cloak, the new cardinal emerged on horseback from the family house and made his way to the southern city gate, followed by a large retinue of clerics, personal attendants, men-at-arms, and a long baggage train.

That afternoon Lorenzo dictated his last letter. In it, he warned his departing son against the dangers of Rome, "that cesspool of iniquities"; he urged him "to use his ears more than his mouth," advised him to have little truck with his fellow cardinals "because of their lack of virtue," to avoid ostentation and be content "with a few good antiques and fine books" and finally to entertain His Holiness "only of amusing matters, for this will be in accord with his nature."

---

* Jews enjoyed religious freedom as well as commercial prosperity under Lorenzo de'Medici. On several occasions he intervened on their behalf with persecuting rulers. In a letter to the duke of Ferrara, he threatened to recall a loan owed to him if the extortions "against my friends, the Jews" were not immediately stopped.

All gifts presented to Giovanni de'Medici on his elevation to the college of cardinals were returned the next day with thanks.

He pressed his seal ring in the blotch of hot wax and, closing his eyes, reclined on the pillows. He had seen his dream come true. His son would some day sit on the papal throne and keep Italy at peace. It had been worth all the years of toil it had cost, the compromises, the maneuvers, the bargains. Now there remained only to wait for death.

A week later he was still alive.

In Mariotto's room, the members of the Signoria marveled at his tenacious hold on life. During their convivial evening discussions by the fire, they wondered how long he would endure his lingering agony.

"But we know there is no hope," remarked one of the magistrates. "In a few days he will be dead. Then what will become of us, of Florence, of the Medici?"

He turned anxiously to the *gonfaloniere*, but his questions remained unanswered. Mariotto sat on his chair, gazing into the flames, lost in thought. An hour ago a message from his wife had told him that Camilla had entered labor and confinement was imminent. She had promised to let him know the moment the *bimbo* arrived. Nothing had come, and he was becoming impatient, vaguely apprehensive.

The councillors understood that he wished to be alone and discreetly they drained their goblets and made their way out of the room. Mariotto did not detain them. From the doorway, he watched them recede through the lantern-lit gallery.

He returned to his chair. Fretfully he glanced over his shoulder at the hourglass on his desk. By now the *bimbo* should have arrived. It was already unreasonable of him to pick such a blustery night to be born on; the least he could do was to hurry and appear so that his tired and worried grandfather might go to bed and get some sleep. And why wasn't Filippa keeping him informed? She knew he did not like to be kept waiting. What on earth were they doing at the Giocondo house?

He rose and, hands behind his back, began pacing the floor, followed by his tall shadow on the wall. Memories of Camilla as a babbling child alternated in his mind with visions of her lying in bed, screaming, her face contorted in pain.

He paused in front of the window, trying to peer through the blackness outside. In hissing gusts of wind, snowflakes splashed against the glass panes. It truly was a cruel night, and to him it became the portent of times to come.

At last, shortly before dawn, Filippa's long-awaited message arrived. God had given him another grandson, but Camilla was dead.

BOOK TWO

The Invasion

Warrior; study for
the *Battle of Anghiari*
by Leonardo da Vinci,
c. 1503. *Museum of
Fine Arts, Budapest.*

Charles the Eighth and his signature. *Courtesy of the Bibliothèque Nationale, Paris.*

The Little King

 One year had passed since Camilla died, and on the anniversary of her death a requiem mass was sung for the repose of her soul.

After the service, Mariotto and his wife returned home and sat by the fire of his study, for it was a chilly morning. They remained silent, each lost in thought.

Then abruptly Mariotto blurted out, "It's all so unfair! She was so young and wanted so much to live. What kind of God is this who allows such a thing? If he must have a life, why not take mine?"

She knew he spoke from the extremity of his grief and forgave his anger.

"My sorrow would have been even greater," she said without looking at him.

A moment later a maid brought a letter from Giocondo in which he asked permission to come and talk to them that evening.

"Tell his groom he will be welcome." After she had gone, Mariotto added, "What can he possibly want?"

The silk merchant arrived shortly after supper. He was still portly, but his cheeks were no longer florid. Little remained of the jovial man who had spent the summer at "The Farm" almost two years ago. He bowed to Donna Filippa and raised her hand to his lips. With Mariotto, his manner was one of unaffected, almost filial, deference.

"Please do not misjudge me or think ill of me for what I am about to say," he began. "I have not forgotten Camilla and never will. If I only listened to my feelings I would remain a widower for the rest of my life, but Camilla herself would want our son, Bartolommeo, to have the love and guidance of a mother. This is why I've decided to marry again."

Filippa gave an involuntary start. Her eyes blurred; yet she managed to say, "You are right. Meo will need a mother."

This was her nickname for the infant who had already endeared himself to her, even though he had cost Camilla's life. Her heart melted when the child beamed at her from his cradle. In the course of her visits to Casa Giocondo, she had feared, for her grandson, the prospect of growing up in a motherless home. Yet she had not contemplated the possibility of her son-in-law marrying again.

"Who will be your new wife?" she asked, trying to control the quivering of her lower lip.

Her name was Tommasa de'Villani, and she belonged to an old and honorable Florentine family.

"Tell her she will always be welcome in our home," continued the elderly lady with some effort. "I hope she will let me come and see Meo now and then."

She could not trust herself to go on. She rose and with a brief nod hurried out of the room.

"Perhaps, I shouldn't have come," remarked Giocondo after she was gone.

"She had to learn it some time," said Mariotto. "It is proper that she should hear it from you. In her heart, she knows you are right. The boy needs a mother."

Over their goblets of hot wine, they talked about Camilla. Giocondo spoke of her with moving tenderness and Mariotto realized that his grief would endure a long time. Then the conversation veered to a review of last year's events.

Lorenzo de'Medici had died at Careggi three weeks after Camilla, on a rainy April night. The Florentines had not yet recovered from his loss. Obscurely, they sensed that an ominous era was about to start and that he would no longer be there to protect them.

Ironically, Pope Innocent, the perpetual moribund, had outlived him by nearly four months. At last, in August, news had come from Rome that he was dying; and this time it was true. No longer could he swallow the woman's milk on which he fed. As a last recourse, three ten-year-old boys had been killed to provide draughts of youthful blood for the ailing pontiff. Even this desperate measure had remained without effect.

The funeral ceremonies had lasted nine days, as prescribed by etiquette. Then the twenty-seven cardinals — including the young Giovanni de'Medici — had met in solemn conclave to elect his successor.

They were duly locked in. Sinking to their knees, they called on the Holy Ghost for guidance in the performance of this most portentous of their duties. A stirring address was pronounced by the cardinal-bishop of Nardajoz in which he compared the Church to "The Whore of Babylon," a metaphor popular at the time.

"However," he intoned in conclusion, "the Church will survive, for it is written 'Rejoice not, o mine enemy, for when I fall, I rise.'"

Having mulled over this profundity for a while, the prelates then settled down to business. It was brisk, shameless, and lasted five days.

A few lightweight candidates were promptly eliminated. Soon the choice hung between two deadly enemies: Cardinal Giuliano della Rovere, nephew of the unlamented Pope Sixtus, who had received 200,000 gold florins from France to spend on his election, and the Spanish Cardinal Rodrigo Borgia, Vice Chancellor — or business manager — of the Holy Church, who had only his own immense fortune.

The moment came when Borgia needed only one vote to have the required two-thirds majority. The deciding ballot belonged to the ninety-five-year-old Cardinal Gherardo, Patriarch of Venice, who held out his trembling hand for an additional 5,000 gold florins as the price of his conscience.

By now, Rovere had run out of funds; Borgia had not. He paid and was elected under the name of Alexander VI.

In his capacity as Vice Chancellor of the Church, the portly

Borgia had revealed himself a surpassing executive. In his hands, everything turned to gold. Every ecclesiastical office had been for sale; every papal dispensation for the bidding. For 24,000 gold florins, he had forged a papal brief authorizing the French Count Jehan d'Armagnac to marry his own sister. Reasonably enough, Borgia had kept a third of that sum as his commission in this transaction.

In addition to exceptional business acumen, the new pontiff was a born lecher. At the sight of a pretty girl, any pretty girl, he became "marvelously excited." In turn, his soft Spanish eyes "set females afyre" and melted the staunchest virtues. At sixty-two, when he ascended the papal throne, he was fat, majestic-looking and endowed with a virility that was the envy of the Sacred College.

From an old liaison with Vanozza Catanei, he had acquired three sons and one daughter, Lucrezia, whom he loved tenderly. Some said too tenderly. Recently, he had taken a new mistress, the sixteen-year-old Giulia Farnese, who was regarded as the most beautiful girl in Rome. His old concubine, Vanozza, approved of his choice, and the two women, as well as the papal children, lived in harmony in the nearby Palace Santa Maria — in Portico, which could be conveniently reached from the Vatican by a secret passage which opened in the Sistine Chapel.

At the time of his coronation, Alexander had ordered the glittering cavalcade to pass under Giulia's window, so that she might see her aging lover in full sacerdotal regalia. It was the kind of delicate attention which endeared him to women.

His superb command of Italian politics and diplomacy soon revealed itself in stately messages to the world's rulers. Six months after his elevation to Saint Peter's Throne, it was acknowledged throughout the world that the holy father was a sinful, but re-markable man.

"Let's hope that this Alexander will be able to keep Italy at peace," sighed Mariotto. "Another war like that of Pope Sixtus would complete our ruin."

A few weeks before, a traveler from Spain had brought news that had sowed the gravest fears in Florentine banking circles.

A navigator by the name of Cristoforo Colombo, in the service of the king and queen of Spain, had just returned from a long journey, in the course of which he had discovered strange and beautiful lands where men and women went in shameless nudity, with only a few flowers or feathers in their hair. Although they had never heard of Gesù, the pope, or the Holy Church, they appeared content, and swam, danced, and fornicated as if they had been created to enjoy themselves instead of repenting their sins.

Not only did these distant countries abound in delicious fruits, new vegetables, and "smoking leaves," but in gold, which the natives seemed to despise and called "the excrement of the gods." From his journey, Colombo had brought nine natives who had been duly baptized and forced to dress, as well as coffers of this "excrement of the gods." Their Catholic Majesties had been enthralled with it. Already there was talk of a second expedition, this time with soldiers and missionaries.

"If large amounts of gold go to Spain, it will mark the end of Florence as the money capital of the world," Mariotto remarked, after taking a sip from his goblet. "Already we've lost our wool monopoly, we shall also lose our preeminence in banking."

He lapsed into thoughtful silence, gazing at the smoldering logs.

"To think that only a few years ago we were at the peak of our prosperity," he said, turning to Giocondo. "Now we are facing economic disaster. I truly feel sorry for Piero de'Medici. He couldn't have chosen a worst time to head the government. His father knew, and that's why he died a heartbroken man."

Yet all in all, Piero had given a better account of himself than expected. He had successfully completed one year as the head of state when most people had predicted he would not last three months. His brother Giuliano had become his assistant and also proven himself a serious, hard-working boy.

"Of course, he has little time to visit Lisa and this makes her furious," Mariotto went on with an indulgent chuckle. "She would like him to spend all his time with her, take her to the storyteller and sing serenades under her window. But he comes to see her whenever he has a free moment, and I truly believe they love each other. That is, as much as youngsters can love. In a year or two, if things remain more or less as they are, I may let them marry, as Lorenzo wished."

"They should be very happy," said Giocondo, draining his goblet and rising from his chair.

Mariotto escorted him to the street door. On the way he inquired whether he wished a groom to light his way home, but Giocondo replied he had brought a lantern and would not need any assistance.

The two men took their leave.

As they went their separate ways, neither of them suspected that at this very moment, many miles from Florence, a misshapen, half-witted young man was about to change the course of history, bring ruin to Italy, and shatter Lisa's adolescent dreams.

At twenty-two, Charles the Eighth, king of France, was a drooling, spastic, adenoidal, short-sized, short-sighted, six-toed caricature of a man with tufts of russet hair that sprouted on his cheeks, a huge head that shook on his small neck, hands that trembled, and an enormous nose, pointed and long-nostriled, which was much too big for his face.

His brain was on a par with his physique.

Sickly from birth, he had never received a formal education and had spent most of his childhood in his velvet-curtained four-poster, bouncing from excitement at the accounts of Charlemagne's great deeds or weeping at the romantic chivalry romances which his tutors read aloud to him. He had remained illiterate and could barely sign his name.

Most of all, he thrilled at the chronicles of the Crusades. With bated breath, he listened to the reading of the stirring speech Pope Urban II, a Frenchman, had addressed to his countrymen in 1905 to send them on the first of these harebrained expeditions.

O Franks, race beloved and chosen by God, the Holy Sepulcher is now held by an unclean and accursed race, wholly alienated from God. . . . It befalls upon you to avenge this wrong and wrest the royal city of Jerusalem, this paradise of delights, which is situated at the center of the earth and implores you to come to her aid. Let none of your possessions keep you back, nor anxiety for your family affairs. Undertake this journey eagerly, and be assured of an imperishable glory in the Kingdom of Heaven.

Naturally, those heady words that had aroused Frenchmen nearly four hundred years earlier now went to Charles's big, empty head. In his dreams he saw himself in shiny armor and plumed helmet, leading his army into Jerusalem, slaughtering the wicked Moslems, and liberating Our Savior's beautiful, empty tomb. At other times he imagined himself to be Tristan or Lancelot or some other gallant knight jousting in tournament or rescuing damsels in distress.

In this way he had survived childhood and strengthened his grip on life.

He was thirteen when his father, the genial "Old King Spider," had died amidst his relics, his magpies, and his canaries. The following spring, Charles had been crowned king of France at Rheims Cathedral.

Clad in a red shirt, he had been anointed with the sacred oil — it had been brought down from Heaven by a dove — on the lids, lips, shoulders, armpits, hands, feet, navel, and, finally, the loins. This done, he had been dressed in kingly regalia. Swaddled in an ermine mantle, the crown askew on his shaking head, the scepter in one trembling hand, the orb in the other, he had received the oath of fealty from his lords. He then had walked out of the church and been presented to his clamoring subjects.

Back to his turreted, immense Chateau of Amboise on a bank of the Loire, the thirteen-year-old monarch had revealed the first symptoms of a devouring, pathological lubricity. The drooling, palsied runt proved to be a sexual giant. Single-handedly, he tackled the battalions of the palace's scullions; then he graduated to the legions of ladies' maids. By the time he was fifteen, he was converging on the ladies themselves. The chateau's galleries resounded with the patter of galloping feet, as nubile countesses fled before the pursuing sovereign.

Thus, life was merrily rolling along in the royal palace when the duke of Brittany, the last great independent French lord, rebelled against the Crown. Soon Bretons and French were at one another's throats, and Charles was having the time of his life.

His person was, of course, too precious to be exposed to the dangers of battle, but he now wore shiny armor and a plumed helmet, as in his childhood dreams. He slept under a tent, took part in the meetings of the general staff. He hobnobbed with his towering knights, drank, swore, urinated in the open like the best of them. Now and then he was hoisted on his horse and he reviewed troops. Between military functions, he mounted farm girls his valets provided for him.

It lasted five years, five wonderful years, and came to an end with his marriage to Anne of Brittany, the daughter of the rebellious duke.

She was sixteen and consented to marry him only with the greatest reluctance, for she could not endure the sight of him. Tears rolled down her cheeks when her ladies-in-waiting undressed and laid her in the royal bed to await the arrival of the bridegroom. Her weeping increased when he made his entrance, naked and shaven, except for his hair and beard, holding a candlestick in his trembling hand.

Soon, however, his peculiar brand of magic worked its wonders on her. As he repeatedly led her to the inexhaustible font of his virility, her repulsion vanished and turned to delight. That night, Anne fell in love with her husband. By morning, "she had become so smitten with him that she insisted on his sleeping with her every night." Neither of them suspected that "in order to establish she was marrying him of her own free will," six burghers were concealed behind the bed curtains and witnessed the proceedings of the wedding night. Their report, couched in terms of candid ribaldry, testified to the queen's entire satisfaction.*

He should have been happy.

In due time, the queen presented him with an heir, Orland, thus assuring the future of his dynasty. Duchesses now fell with clocklike regularity in his rose-spattered bed. His wife, recalling the exuberance of her wedding night, continued to love him. Despite

* It is at the Bibliothèque Nationale in Paris.

his ugliness and stupidity, he was popular with his subjects. They called him *"L'aimable,"* for he was reputed to be good-hearted.

Yet he was not happy.

Anne's modest charms (she limped and had bad teeth) no longer stirred up his lust. He missed his lovely war: no more shining armor and plumed helmet; no more sleeping under a tent and reviewing troops. His melancholy vented itself out in ceaseless agitation. He walked in a ducklike waddle, which on occasions could reach high speed, and he would dart hither and yon in various directions like a wound-up toy. As he talked while he walked and did not see where he was going, he bumped into people and things. Yet badminton was his favorite game. He loved nothing more than to dash about, racket in hand, after a shuttlecock he did not see.

To kill time, he dabbled in government, presided over cabinet meetings, improved the gardens of the royal palace. But time weighed on his hands. His life, he felt, was empty, purposeless. He would never be Charlemagne or Lancelot, never lead his knights into Jerusalem, never deliver Our Savior's tomb. He sank into despondency.

"Your Majesty should apply his great talents to some vast and glorious undertaking," suggested his confessor one day. "A crusade, for instance."

At the word, Charles pricked up his ears. A crusade — but where?

"To Jerusalem, my son," proceeded the holy man. "Jerusalem, where Our Savior's tomb awaits your arrival."

Unbelievable as it sounded, the Holy Sepulcher had not yet been delivered. Four hundred years after Pope Urban's speech, despite eight military expeditions, it still remained in Moslem hands. Why? asked Charles . . . Because none of the previous crusaders had been able to sail from Naples, which was the logical point of departure for all attacks on Jerusalem.

"And it happens that Naples belongs to Your Majesty," continued Francesco da Paola, with a quivering of his long white beard. "Yes, my son, you are king of Naples, as well as king of France."

This was news to Charles. He wanted to know more. Naples
— where was that? . . . In the southern region of Italy. A beautiful harbor city surrounded by a sunny kingdom abounding in
flowers and golden oranges . . .

Charles had heard enough. He drooled at the thought of his
beautiful sunny kingdom. When he learned that, in addition to
flowers and oranges, Naples abounded in luscious girls with
pulpy red lips and fire in their loins, he grew impatient to meet
his new subjects.

Unfortunately, the throne of Naples was presently occupied by
an elderly king, Don Ferrante of Aragon, who had a strong army
and showed no disposition to relinquish his realm. Charles began
dropping hints about launching an expedition against Naples and
pushing Don Ferrante into the sea. To his dismay, his suggestions
failed to arouse any fervor. Nobody seemed to care about Naples,
a dirty, sun-baked town at the tip of the Italian peninsula, in-
habited by the laziest population on earth.

Nobody except Charles. He stopped talking about marching
against Naples and regaining his lost kingdom. But in his heart he
believed that God would come to his help.

And curiously, in the spring of 1493, He did.

Four distinguished-looking Milanese noblemen, headed by
Count Belgiojoso, arrived at the court of France with mouths full
of compliments and coffers full of gold. The count was presented
to His Majesty, played badminton with him, and soon won his
friendship. In the course of a private conversation, he mentioned
that his master, Ludovico Sforza, duke-regent of Milan, was one
of Charles's most fervent admirers. So fervent, in fact, that he
would regard it as a privilege to contribute the sum of 200,000
gold florins should His Majesty decide to march against Naples.

This was a great deal of money, yet the little king saw nothing strange in the proposition. It merely proved that this Ludovico Sforza — whoever he was — was a fine, generous man.

At the same time, the count's companions were making friends
at court and influencing influential people. Gold-filled purses discreetly changed hands; court ladies began to appear at functions
wearing splendid jewelry and gowns of the finest Italian brocade.

High officials who until now had scoffed at the notion of a Neapolitan expedition now judged it necessary and statesman-like. Even the prospect of another Jerusalem campaign no longer seemed absurd. Suddenly, French dignitaries grieved over the fate of Our Savior's tomb. Even Stuart d'Aubigny, commander of the king's Scottish Guard, who had fiercely opposed the campaign, changed his tune when (by his own admission) he received 8,000 gold florins, and his wife a splendid pearl necklace.

The war fever grew steadily through the summer and autumn of 1493. Generals looked upon a Neapolitan campaign as a brief and pleasant *promenade*, as well as a source of profit and promotion. Courtiers dreamed of sunny Neapolitan estates given them by a grateful monarch. As for Charles, he anticipated fervid dalliances with those gorgeous and passionate southern females.

Yet something held him back. In his heart, he waited for some unmistakable "sign" that God wanted him to go to Naples and, later, Jerusalem. The "sign" appeared in February, when he learned that the seventy-one-year-old king of Naples, Don Ferrante of Aragon, had climbed down from his horse and collapsed, lifeless, to the ground.

Now Charles had no more doubts: God was on his side. At once, he dictated a letter to "his cousin, Ludovico" informing him of his decision to regain his Neapolitan throne and announcing his arrival in Italy for April. He also sent an urgent message to Pope Alexander revealing his plan to lead a crusade to Jerusalem and "return to the Christian faith the lands now occupied by the Turks."

As he intended to sail from Naples (which belonged to him anyway) he would appreciate it if the Holy Father would dispatch to him a brief of investiture to the kingdom of Naples, by return courier.

The cavalier tone of the missive did not go down very well with the pope who, however, replied by approving of the crusade and sending a profusion of blessings, indulgences, and even the Golden Rose. As to the throne of Naples, it was already occupied by the late King Ferrante's son, Don Alfonso of Aragon. Nevertheless, if Charles would submit proofs of his claim to the Neapolitan kingdom, they would be examined with fairness and speed by a papal tribunal.

The "Little King" was furious. No, he wasn't going to submit any proof of his claim. God and his confessor had told him that he was king of Naples, and that was enough for him. In fact, Charles did have feeble claim to the Neapolitan crown. In 1421, Queen Joanna II, the Mad, a half-demented nymphomaniac, had formally bequeathed her throne to a Spanish prince of Aragon, only to change her mind shortly afterward and bequeath it to a French prince of Anjou. After her death, the Aragon prince had defeated the French who had returned to France, but had never renounced their claim.

Without hesitation, he had himself crowned "King of Naples and the Two Sicilies, King of Jerusalem, King of Constantinople," and, for good measure, "Emperor of the Orient." This done, he had himself fastened in his shiny armor, hoisted on his horse, and made a grand entrance into the city of Lyons.

Now the days were too short for all the things he had to do. He discussed strategy and logistics with his generals, watched his troops drill, extorted enormous war credits from the *Assemblée des Bourgeois* representing *le petit peuple*. He barely had time to copulate and he only did so in an absent-minded sort of way, from habit. He could not wait to cross the Alps with his 40,000 men and invincible artillery. By May, he would sit on the Neapolitan throne.

Then suddenly he lost interest in the campaign. No longer did he wear his helmet with the beautiful purple and yellow plumes. Naples meant nothing to him any more. The flowers, the oranges, even the fiery southern girls had lost their appeal.

He had fallen in love.

The object of his affection was a young Italian woman of great beauty and no virtue whatsoever. She eked out a modest living as a prostitute, catering to the genetic needs of the Italian male colony established in Lyons. She was good-natured and wondrously expert at her craft.

Two French court officials, still in the pay of the Aragon

prince, sampled her, marveled at her resourcefulness, and agreed she represented their last chance to swerve His Majesty from his war projects, at least for a while. They duly briefed her on what she was expected to accomplish and warned her that the king was the most inconstant of lovers and that the most beautiful court ladies could hold his interest only a few short moments. The Italian wench nodded understandingly and in her delightfully accented French promised to do her best. She was paid half of her fee and returned home, a hovel in the slums where she lived with her aunt.

There she studied the situation, decided on the strategy she would adopt, and peacefully went to sleep.

The moment Charles saw her, his loins tensed. He drooled profusely as he ran his bulbous, short-sighted eyes over her. From habit, he tried plunging his hand into her bodice, but she eluded his grasp. Rising on his toes, he then lunged for her mouth and found himself kissing the air.

By now, he was becoming annoyed — and intrigued. No woman ever dared to evade his caresses.

"What is the matter?" he asked in a shower of spittle. "Don't you like me?"

She did — very much. But because she was poor, he wanted to make sport of her, rob her of the thing she valued most, her honor. As a little *bimba*, she had sworn to bring her virginity as her dowry to the man who would marry her. And now here he was, handsome and clever — and the king, besides — making it very difficult for her to keep her vow.

"Already I feel the love for you," she said, looking at him through her splendid gold-flecked brown eyes. "But the love, it is like a flower, no? It must have time to grow, yes?"

This charade succeeded beyond all expectations. By the end of the first interview, Charles was trembling with frustration, but he had swallowed the bait. As a parting gesture, she gave him a devastating smile, a peck on the cheek and the address of the house where she lived.

"With my aunt," she added piously.

She did not mention that her aunt was her procuress, and also dabbled in fortune-telling, aphrodisiacs, and witchcraft.

"I shall be there tomorrow," said His Majesty Charles the Eighth.

Sure enough, he arrived the following morning, dressed in his finest clothes and reeking of perfume, for he had a passion for scents. As he wanted to make a good impression, he rode in the ceremonial royal coach drawn by eight white horses, escorted by the helmeted and breast-plated men of his Scottish Guard. Heralds in the royal red and gold livery blew their silver trumpets to announce the approach of the august visitor.

The carriage came to a halt in front of the aunt's house. Charles climbed down and gingerly made his way among the dunghills that dotted the courtyard. Late that afternoon, he drove back to the palace, more frustrated and enraptured than ever.

Henceforth, he spent most of his time with his wench at her aunt's house. He even started to hold cabinet meetings there. Crown dignitaries convened in the hag's kitchen and patiently waited for the king to emerge from the adjoining room.*

Forgotten were Naples and Jerusalem, the Savior's tomb, the troops who idled away the hours by plundering houses and raping women. At court, consternation reigned among the war advocates.

But Charles was happy. Vainly he had been told that his virtuous girl was a slut; her aunt, her procuress. He did not believe it, or perhaps he did not care. She had opened to him a world he had never known, a world of informality, laughter, and tenderness. He was weary of duchesses who called him "Sire" during intercourse. Instead his wench called him Charles or Carlo, let him sit on her knees and play with her breasts, and slapped his knuckles when he went too far.

She sensed he would remain a child all his life, and out of some obscure motherliness, at times she almost loved him. She hugged

---

* The girl's name has not come down to us, but her affair with the king and the cabinet meetings at her aunt's house are described at length in Belgiojoso's dispatches to Ludovico Sforza. See also the scholarly volume, *L'expedition de Charles VIII en Italie* by H.-F. Delaborde.

and kissed him, occasionally gave herself to him to appease his satyriasis. When he ate, she would hold his shaking hand, help him lift food to his mouth.

Like ordinary lovers, they had noisy quarrels when she called him names and said she never wanted to see him again. He would threaten to call his guards and have her hanged. Then there was the joy of reconciliation, the promises of eternal love, the special caresses granted as a reward.

Thus spring wore on. By the end of April 1493, the French army still waited for its marching orders.

When May arrived, and "the barbarians" remained behind their mountains, the Italians regained their natural optimism and felt sure that the terrible French *écorcheurs* would never appear. The Florentines, whose territory lay across the road the king would surely follow on his march upon Naples, breathed a sigh of relief.

In vain did Piero de'Medici argue with the members of the Signoria that the monarch might momentarily postpone his expedition but would not renounce his plans to "regain" his stolen Neapolitan throne. His pleas for funds to reinforce the Florentine frontiers fell on deaf ears. The councillors agreed that all danger was past and the strengthening of frontier garrisons was a foolish expense.

Forgetting their fears of the past few months, the burghers met on Piazza della Signoria after supper and chuckled over the Little King: his ugliness, his stupidity, his six toes. In their hearts they were proud that an Italian woman held back the invasion with the sole resources of her pelvis. Once again, the Madonna was protecting her favorite people, and this time she had chosen this fine young slut as her instrument.

The spring social season which had been held in abeyance because of the threat of invasion exploded belatedly in a flurry of functions and dancing festivities that kept the windows of mansions aglow with candlelight until dawn.

Women's fashions reached peaks of frivolity. Never had dresses been so daring — necklines so low, skirt-slits so high. Bosoms vacillated on the edges of bodices and occasionally spilled out. From Milan had come the fad of wearing a precious stone on the forehead, and now every Florentine lady of fashion went about with a ruby or emerald dangling between her eyebrows.

Makeup became a form of art at which women spent much time and money. Poultices of mashed beans and mare's milk were guaranteed to improve the complexion. Unguents of various hues were applied to various parts of the face: cerulean blue to the lids, black to the lashes, pomegranate red to lips, nostrils, nipples. Every woman became an artist and painted her portrait every morning.

Men's fashions were just as capricious. Dandies spent hours at barbers' having their hair washed, dyed, curled in a thousand ringlets, *a la zanzara*. Their garments became as ornate and provocative as ladies'. The noble *lucco* became the badge of old age and was supplanted by doublets of silk or velvet, with trunk hoses as sheer as headveils. The sight of men's buttocks became as common as that of women's breasts.

In that spring of 1494, young blades stressed their virility in their apparel. To this end, they enclosed their genitals in padded pubic bags which simulated permanent erection. These receptacles often turned into minor works of art. Some sparkled with shards of colored glass or small gems; some glinted with gold or silver embroideries. Some were made even more festive with tiny bells that tinkled with every step. These bells had a vocabulary of their own and could convey amorous messages. A slight tintinnabulation at the approach of a pretty girl was meant as a courtly sign of appreciation, a ripple of desire. A robust chime betrayed a violent emotion; a protracted carillon, an uncontrollable lust.

In this atmosphere of strenuous gaiety, Lisa escorted her friend Contessina in the gathering of her trousseau. Contessina's wedding to Piero Ridolfi, so long deferred, had finally been scheduled for the end of the month. Together the two friends went to "The Moor's Head," where they bought cosmetics, linens, and a dozen handkerchiefs or *fazzoletti*, a novelty that had just been adopted by the social elite.

For centuries Florentine ladies had ignored the stench of their streets. Offal, rotting garbage, the contents of slop jars on pavements had left them unmoved, but not so any more. Suddenly their delicacy was affronted by such things. The mere sight of a man relieving himself in a doorway sent them into a blushing trot, their *fazzoletto* pressed to their nostrils.

Thus, Lisa and Contessina rushed from one shop to another, handkerchiefs fluttering in their hands, like the stylish young ladies they were. As the weather turned hot, they refreshed themselves with an occasional dip into the pool of the very proper and exclusive ladies' bathhouse on Watermelon Street. Wrapped in ankle-length white shirts that ballooned in water and made swimming nearly impossible, they splashed and giggled among other bathers to the strains of an invisible lute orchestra. From behind a wrought-iron railing, society matrons watched the scene, waved to acquaintances while sipping lemonade or *sugo d'arancia*.

Lisa also assisted Contessina in the display of her wedding trousseau in one of the palace's rooms, as required by tradition. Diligently, she draped on life-sized and lifelike wax dummies the rare hunting tunic made of "a lion's skin edged with crimson" which had been sent by the sultan of Egypt, the "rustic" dresses suitable for picnics, fishing expeditions, or garden parties, the sober black serge "house" dresses to go marketing in, the "visiting" dresses, and finally the gem-embossed gala gown to be worn at formal functions. The luxuriousness of some of these gala dresses was almost unbelievable. One, displayed on this occasion, was valued at 14,000 gold florins (approximately 55,000 dollars), while the Careggi villa with its garden, arable lands, vineyard, olive grove, orchard, and farm houses cost 800 florins.

For two days the local gentry circulated amid the gorgeously garbed dummies with Lisa and the other bridesmaids acting as hostesses. Wedding gifts filled another room, each properly identified with the donor's name. Donna Filippa noticed that her silver tureen had been advantageously set up on a background of purple velvet by her granddaughter.

On the eve of the wedding, Contessina and her financé, Piero

Ridolfi, gave an informal supper party for their assistants, twenty-four in all.

It was on this occasion that Lisa met her cousin Jacopo de'Gherardini della Rosa. He had flaming red hair and gentle porcelain-blue eyes in a freckled face. She judged him to be seventeen, although the dimple in his cheeks made him look somewhat younger. He sat next to her and in almost no time she had pried from him all she wanted to know.

He had just returned to Florence after graduating from Pisa University, which explained why they had not met before.

"Ha, Pisa!" she exclaimed. "Such a charming little town!"

She made some offhand remarks about the Leaning Tower and the Church of the Thorn to show him she had gone to Pisa and was a well-traveled young lady.

And what, she inquired, was he doing in Pisa? . . . He had been studying law, which was a mandatory requirement for the diplomatic career he planned to embrace. His honored father had been Florence's ambassador to Hungary and he wished him to follow in his footsteps.

"I've been promised a small clerical position at our embassy in London," said Jacopo, "and I am to join my post shortly after Christmas."

To this end, he was taking a daily lesson in the English language from a private tutor.

It all was most interesting, Lisa declared, and no doubt he would soon be promoted to ambassador. With a deprecatory gesture, Jacopo replied he would probably spend the next two or three years at the embassy's decoding room or some similar obscure department.

She half listened to what he said, for she was watching Giuliano who was chatting across the table with the very pretty — and very stupid — Esmeralda Malaspina. Although her attention was divided, she soon became aware that her fiery-haired, freckled-faced kinsman was looking at her with eyes glazed with nascent love. It was, she decided, a most pleasant sensation to be an object of unattainable desire on the part of this well-mannered, promising young diplomat. In some recess of her mind, the notion took form that Jacopo might become useful. As Giuliano was often too busy to accompany her to the storyteller or some dancing festivity, Jacopo might make an excellent substitute.

Meanwhile, across the table, Giuliano seemed enthralled with Esmeralda. There just was no limit to men's stupidity, Lisa reflected. They had no appreciation of charm, culture, femininity. With them, only looks counted.

Taking aim, she shot a small hazelnut which caught Giuliano on the tip of the nose. He swiftly veered around, but by then she was raptly smiling at Jacopo.

"Yes," she remarked, "the English language will be most useful when you live in the English nation."

A moment later she learned that he lived with his family in the old Gherardini mansion. At once she plunged into reminiscences. She recalled her grandfather's *studiolo* where they had spent many happy hours.

"It is now my study room," said Jacopo. "That's where I take my lessons in the English language."

Over dessert, they were calling each other "cousin" and she made him promise to come and visit her before long.

Supper over, the guests passed into a small ballroom where they danced *il branlo* or "kissing dance." Its popularity rested on its simplicity. No intricate steps, no complicated figures. You skipped and hopped as you pleased, inventing routines as you went along. Couples danced facing each other, dissolving at will after exchanging a kiss, joining new partners only to part again after another kiss. By the end of the evening, everybody had kissed everybody.

It was late at night when a lantern-bearing groom accompanied Lisa home. She slept like a child, without a dream, until it was time to dress for the wedding. A moment later, on the morning of 24 May 1494, she stood among Contessina's bridesmaids as her childhood friend married Piero Ridolfi.

The nuptial banquet lasted most of the afternoon. Over dessert, a silver tureen was brought in and set before the newlyweds. The bride lifted the lid, and a dove flew out into the room, as a potent of happiness. Lisa made a mental note that, when she married Giuliano, she too would have such a dove.

Now it was June, and the news from France continued to be reassuring. The wench still held the king in her tender grasp. The terrible French army remained behind the Alps. Already it was too late, said the Florentines, to launch a military expedition. They shrugged off their last remaining fears and turned their attention to local events.

One of these, the decapitation of a highwayman — an event of small importance in itself — aroused much comment because of the unusual circumstances surrounding it. As usual, the day before the execution, the town criers had gone about the city, beating their drums and stopping at every street corner to announce the hour of the beheading. Thus, a number of housewives had gathered on Piazza Santa Croce to watch the beheading on their way from the market.

As the criminal was a man of no account, a poor devil of a bandit, his beheading had been entrusted to an apprentice executioner, the *capo carnefice*, or chief axeman, attending only to wrongdoers of rank. This apprentice was a well-meaning but inexperienced young man. To make things worse, this execution was the first he was to perform. The hood which covered his face concealed his pallor. Duly, he knelt before the condemned man and asked his forgiveness for what he was about to do to him.

The *bandito* nodded and told him to get on with it. He then put his head on the block and began reciting the litanies of the Madonna while waiting for the fatal blow.

Once, twice, three times the heavy sword descended upon his neck, but the head would not drop.

Such clumsiness incensed the housewives, who hurled eggs, cabbages, and salami at the apprentice, who took to his heels. Someone ran to the house of the *capo carnefice* who was enjoying his breakfast. Without even taking time to slip the hood over his face, he brought the head down in fine style.

People were still reproving the bungling apprentice when

another local event — this time, a romantic tragedy — captured their attention.

The nude bodies of an eighteen-year-old Carmelite nun and of a young Franciscan monk were found enlaced in a final embrace on a pallet of straw. A bloodstained dagger lay nearby on the floor.

The double suicide had clearly been motivated by a mutual and hopeless passion and it revived the usual comments made on similar occasions. Once again, the prohibition of clerical matrimony was given as the main cause of the rampant misconduct in monasteries and nunneries. When the abbess of the San Nazzarro di Nebulesco Convent gave birth to her fourth child, the archbishop of Milan finally brought himself to reprimand her, stating in his letter that "her institution had been conducted for forty years like a brothel."*

On Piazza della Signoria, burghers wondered once again: why did the Church stigmatize so violently something that Christ had approved in the first pope, Saint Peter? Why this rage against decent matrimony, when a swarm of pontiffs had sired large families out of wedlock? In guilds, taverns, and homes, heated debates were held over the famous statements of Pius II, one of the greatest pontiffs of the Renaissance and himself the father of two charming Scottish children, "There are good reasons for enjoining the celibacy of the clergy, but there are better and stronger ones for enjoining them to marry."

Even Lisa took part in the general controversy. Staunchly, she stood on the side of the young lovers.

"I know where they are," she told her cousin Jacopo as he was escorting her to the storyteller. "The Madonna has smuggled them to a region where Lord God never goes, the same region where my honored grandfather Gherardini is. They are living happily in a little house of their own."

Tentatively Jacopo wondered whether the Virgin would publicly encourage living in sin in heaven, but Lisa swept his objections aside. By the time they reached the *narratore*'s stand, he had surrendered to Lisa's theory.

* See *Leonardo da Vinci* by Antonnina Vallentin.

"Fair cousin, I now see this matter entirely with your eyes," he lied to please her.

They took their places before the stand as the storyteller beat his iron pot to attract listeners. He had lost a few teeth and his face was furrowed with wrinkles. But his voice retained his resonance as he pronounced his familiar harangue. "O people of Florence, famous the world over for intelligence and generosity, come and listen to Beppo's stories."

The address over, he set the pot on a table and launched into the story of Aurora, the goddess of dawn.

Having finished with great verbal flourishes, he removed his *berretta* and circulated among the listeners.

"Fair cousin," said Jacopo with a gentle tugging at Lisa's sleeve, "couldn't we go now? My English tutor must be waiting for me."

She gave him a beseeching look. "Please, *cocolino*, let's listen to another story. A short one."

Giuliano would have grabbed her wrist and pulled her away, but Giuliano knew himself to be loved and could do whatever he wanted. Jacopo, instead, was timid, as the unloved ones usually are. He hesitated and this was his undoing.

Already Beppo was back on his stand.

"Then let's hurry," said Lisa, taking Jacopo's wrist. "I wouldn't want you to be late for your English lesson."

Hand in hand, they ran across the square.

Since meeting her kinsman, Lisa had made much use of him. Aware of his infatuation, she practiced on him her feminine wiles. His subservience to her wishes gave her a delicious sense of power she seldom, if ever, experienced with Giuliano. It was exciting having this future ambassador at her beck and call, always ready to answer her calls and accompany her wherever she might want to go and, best of all, never ask anything in return. It was very nice indeed.

Also very wicked, in Tessa's opinion.

"A shame it is the way you make eyes at him," she would say, "when all the time you think only of Giuliano."

The truth was that Tessa had lost her heart to **Jacopo**. She loved everything about him: his fiery hair, his blue eyes, even his freckles.

She never tired of singing his praises. Such a fine *signorino*, such gentlemanly manners! Always ready with a smile and a few gracious words to her. "And you talking to him with the tongue of serpents, taking advantage of his good heart."

"Is it my fault if he finds me fascinating?" Lisa would retort.

Was it her fault if he found her clever, if he thought she had the most wonderful smile in the world, if he loved being seen with her?

Tessa would walk away, shaking her head and muttering to herself.

And so June wore on in a series of blue-skied days. In town, tapestries were hung on balconies and sand spread over the pavement in anticipation of the *palio*, the annual horse race through the streets, which took place on 24 June, Saint John's feast day.

One morning, when she was watering the potted plants on her bedroom's terrace, Lisa heard the sound of footsteps in the garden. Lifting her eyes, she saw Giuliano, who had just climbed over the brick wall. She let out a hoot of surprise and, setting down her water bucket, raced down the flight of stairs. He took her in his arms, kissed her lips, but declined to follow her to the music room where they usually met in privacy.

"I just came to tell you that my brother, the cardinal, is giving a hunting party tomorrow," he said. "Piero has given me the day off, and I should like you to come with me."

He read the delight on her face and proceeded in rapid whispers. "I'll fetch you after the morning chimes and, please, don't be late."

Another kiss and he was off.

The day seemed endless. She tried on her bottle-green hunting dress to make sure no last-minute alterations would be needed. She was awake before the morning chimes and was waiting in the courtyard when he arrived. He helped her mount her horse and together they rode through the wakening town.

They turned to a lively trot as soon as they passed the city gates and found themselves in the country. One hour later they were entering the Settignano Woods, and the barking of the cardinal's hounds led them to the clearing where the huntsmen were to meet. Most of them had already arrived and they stood at a respectful distance from a lace-covered table where His Most Worshipful Lordship sat alone, eating a roast chicken.

He now was nineteen, tall, bulky, with a slablike face and soft, short-sighted eyes. For the occasion he had discarded his scarlet robes for a suit of black velvet, high leather boots, and a wide-brimmed, red-plumed black hat. Only the gold cross on his chest identified him as a man of the Church.

At the sight of Lisa, he fastened a gold-rimmed monocle in his left socket and welcomed her with a smile of genuine pleasure. For her part, she almost did not recognize the lonely boy in the violet cassock she had played with in the Careggi garden. Dutifully, she bent down over his hand and kissed his ring.

He ate with gusto, tossing chunks of meat to his dogs, addressing an occasional remark with them. At last he dipped his fingertips into a silver bowl of warm water and signaled a page to remove his lute from the velvet-lined case in which it rested. He took it from the kneeling page, cradled it in his lap with a loving gesture, and began tuning it.

"He keeps it by his bed," whispered Giuliano to Lisa. "He plays it at night when he cannot sleep."

In a clear tenor voice, the Cardinal Santa Maria-in-Domenica sang a tender and wistful ballad. He kept his eyes closed as he sang and the love of music illumined his rather coarse face. The man who from childhood had been trained to be pope was born to be a troubadour.

Graciously he acknowledged the applause, handed the lute back, and, rising to his feet, lumbered to his mount. Once in the saddle, the artist of a moment ago became a figure of command. Standing in his stirrups, he raised a long spear in his fist and made a forward gesture. With a pounding of hooves and barking of dogs, the boar hunt began.

Lisa had never attended a boar hunt before and soon fell

behind. To her relief, Giuliano reined in his horse and brought it to her side.

He suggested they dismount and stretch out on the grass instead of breaking their necks chasing after a wild hog.

"We shall rejoin the hunt for the midday meal," he said, helping her down to the ground.

For a while they lay side by side in the sun-shafted stillness of the forest, listening to the receding sound of the hunting horns and the hounds' barks. Then he lifted himself on his elbow, leaned over her face and gently kissed her lips. She kissed him back and before long they were kissing each other hungrily, at random.

A delicious helplessness overwhelmed her as his fingers unlaced her bodice and caressed her breasts.

It was all new and wicked and wonderful.

On 17 July 1494, an extraordinary event took place at the court of France.

The Milanese ambassador, Count Belgiojoso, dared remonstrate with the king on the scandal of his conduct. With unparalleled temerity, he reminded His Majesty of his unfulfilled promise to march upon Naples in the spring. He described how his master, Duke Ludovico Sforza, had generously offered to help him regain his kingdom of Naples and thus incurred the wrath of the Neopolitan monarch who was about to make war upon him. Yet the great Charles the Eighth, this paragon of all knightly virtues, had remained indifferent to his friend's plight.

The reason for this unworthy behavior was, alas, only too easy to find. In a letter to Ludovico Sforza, the ambassador repeated the words he had addressed to the king:

One woman has stopped Your Majesty from passing in Italy. Christendom has its eyes on Your Majesty and I let you imagine, Sire, what disrepute will be yours if it can be said that for a female you have failed to succor the Lord Ludovico who has placed himself in great danger to serve His Majesty.

For one month of pleasure you have derived from this amour, you expose yourself to lose the pleasures of a lifetime, as well as honor and credit.

These remarks created stupefaction among the courtiers. For a moment the king drooled in silence and his head shook on his neck. It looked as though he might have the diplomat expelled from France. Instead he blushed, sputtered apologies, and swore he would leave for Italy at once.

"Tell our cousin Ludovico that we shall go and speak to him," he replied, "and no one will be able to sway us from our decision."

It took him twelve days to keep his word. At last he was hoisted on his horse, and in armor and plumed helmet he led his army out of the city. Two hours later he had reached the charming village of Vienne, five miles from the city. The weather was hot. He felt tired and ordered a halt.

The halt turned into a visit; the visit into a three-week sojourn. Commandeering the local castle for his personal use, he sent for his wench and made himself at home. From 29 July to 22 August, he remained deaf to the pleas of his confessor, the tirades of the Milanese ambassador, the advice of his generals, and the sermons of the Cardinal della Rovere who had come all the way from Rome to induce him to invade Italy, take Naples, and, on the way, stop in Rome just long enough to depose his deadly enemy, Pope Alexander.

Charles played badminton, watched tournaments, and frolicked with his mistress.

Then, abruptly, the plague broke out in Vienne. He regarded this as a sign that God truly wanted him to start on his crusade. When he explained this to his wench, she begged him not to disappoint the Almighty. The poor girl had reached the end of her endurance and was tottering on the brink of a nervous breakdown. He was driving her mad. She had lost much weight and her fine Italian eyes glowed feverishly in their sockets.

After a last, exhausting night of love, she watched him depart, from her bedroom window, with tears of relief. When he disappeared down the road, she climbed back in bed and slept peacefully for the first time in weeks.

On 17 August Charles said goodbye to his queen who had escorted him to Grenoble and provided him with the ugliest women she could find for his personal service.

Luck was with him. Guided by two Italian muleteers, the French crossed the Alps with miraculous ease. In four days, churning torrents were forded, cannons lifted up vertiginous slopes, baggage wagons lowered down mountainous slides. By 3 September the Great Crusader, as he now called himself, set foot in Italy behind a silver coffer containing a bone of Saint Denis, patron saint of Paris, and one of the Thorns of the Holy Crown.

The first French invasion of Italy, one of the most fateful and grotesque events in Europe's history, had begun.

The king of France was followed by the general staff, the members of his Scottish Guard, the clattering squadrons of his armored knights on their clipped-eared horses. Behind came the endless horde of Swiss, Germans, Spaniards, Gascons, Normands, Bretons, and other mercenaries who constituted the French army, and eight hundred prostitutes with open blouses and flowers in their hair.

Along the roads, wine-growers waved their straw hats and stopped in the middle of *la vendemmia* to watch them pass; women blew kisses at them. They did not know what these bearded foreigners were doing on their land, but they had heard they were on their way to deliver the Holy Sepulcher, and they wished them well.

As he approached the city of Turin, Charles was met by the duchess of Savoy and her court, all splendidly garbed and riding silver-bridled horses. That evening, Her Highness entertained the traveling monarch and his staff at a ball. For the occasion, she wore a gown of gold cloth and her famous emerald necklace.

This last was a mistake.

Already short of funds, the Great Crusader could not take his short-sighted eyes from it. While dancing, he suggested that she would greatly oblige him by loaning him the little bauble around her neck. In two weeks, at the latest, she would have it back — with interest. She had his word on it, the sacred word of honor of a king.

Taken by surprise, the duchess had no choice but to unclasp her necklace and hand it to Charles, who promptly sent it to Genoa as collateral for a loan of 12,000 florins, at forty-two percent interest. Whether she ever recovered her necklace is unknown.

From Turin, he proceeded to Asti, in the province of Piedmont, where he received the visit of his "cousin," Duke Ludovico Sforza, who had come from Milan to look at the man he had lured to Italy and to get a glimpse of the famous French army, of which he had heard so much.

He was enthralled with the army, which was stronger than all the Italian armies put together, but disappointed in the king. He had been warned about Charles, but he was not prepared for the tapirlike proboscis, the bulging, vacant eyes, the drooling, the spatulated feet, the imbecility.

Yet he felt he owed Charles a glimpse of Italian superior culture and courteously invited him to some *divertimenti* that his master of revels, Leonardo da Vinci, had prepared at the nearby Castello d'Annona.

Two days later Charles arrived at Annona with a few members of his entourage. In the entrance courtyard he was greeted by the duke's nineteen-year-old wife, surrounded by her eighty-three ravishing ladies-in-waiting. At the sight of the Great Crusader, Beatrice and her attendants plunged into a deep reverence. Whereupon he was hoisted down from his horse, gallantly removed his white-plumed toque, and gave each lady a long, slavering kiss on the mouth.

What with games of badminton, banquets in the gardens, dancing and plays at night, and rapid copulations with the ladies-in-waiting who proved as obliging as they were lovely, time flew on gossamer wings. A week later Charles was still at Annona. Forgotten were Naples, Jerusalem, and the Holy Sepulcher.

Tactfully, Ludovico reminded him of these. "The road before

Your Majesty is still long and your loving Neapolitan subjects yearn for your presence."

Charles promised to leave for Naples immediately. Casually he asked his host for a loan of 50,000 gold florins, once again kissed Beatrice and her ladies on the lips, and departed.

Barely had he left Annona when he was seized with fever chills. On his arrival, he was carried to his room where his doctor diagnosed a sunstroke.

It was smallpox.

In those days, smallpox was regarded as the plague's first cousin and dreaded almost as much. When it became known that His Majesty had contracted the fearsome disease, masses were said for his recovery, processions meandered through the town; but no one came near him. His physician examined him from the doorway, his face covered with a mask, his gloved hand holding twigs of burning thyme. His confessor refused to walk to his bedside and Charles had to shout his sins across the room. Even his faithful *compagnon de lit*, Comte de Ligny, was excused from duty. (When the king did not sleep with the queen or some women of his choice, he slept with one of his knights who served as his *compagnon de lit* and was expected to protect him with his life. This office was highly prized among courtiers.)

Miraculously Charles recovered.

His face was now pockmarked, but it was better than being dead. Soon he could sit at the window and listen to the royal fanfare being played below. As his health improved, state officials reappeared. Alas, they had only bad news. From France dispirited messages told of the growing unpopularity of his Italian campaign. Farmers greeted tax collectors with pitchforks. The queen, devoured with jealousy, wrote tearful letters begging him to return.

Only two months had passed since his men had set foot in Italy and already they had made themselves loathed by the population. The pretty seashore village of Rapallo, near Genoa, had been given a taste of French warfare. In a few hours it had been turned into a heap of charred ruins. Women and children had been burned in church. Raped girls had been left to die in the streets; hospital patients had been killed in their beds. The commander of this slaughter, Duke Louis of Orleans, the king's cousin and brother-in-law, had earned the sinister nickname of "the butcher of Rapallo."

In these few weeks, "the crusaders" had become "the barbarians." In Genoa, tavern wenches refused to serve "the foreign devils"; French sentries were stabbed at night. Hated by everyone, their pay in arrears, the invaders were deserting in droves. Even officers longed to return home before winter.

This was not all.

Charles was also learning disturbing things about his "friend and cousin" Ludovico. He discovered that the duke's contribution of 200,000 gold florins had not been motivated by generous sympathy for his cause, as he had naïvely believed. Instead, it had been a sordid maneuver to lure him and his army to Italy and have the French remove the king of Naples who was then threatening to march upon Milan.

A flicker of understanding gleamed in Charles's foggy mind. He realized that he had been brought to Italy to fight Ludovico's war. In short, he had been used. A petty, illegal, Italian ruler (who, incidentally, was the grandson of a Romagna peasant) had made sport of the king of France.

The more he thought about it, the angier he became.

In a sputtering rage, he dictated a letter to "Messer Ludovico" — no more "friend" or "cousin" — announcing his arrival at Vigevano where the duke and his court were spending the remainder of summer. On 9 October he left Asti and started on a long trek through Lombardy. This time, however, he brought with him a contingent of seven thousand men and forty cannons.

Ludovico blanched on receipt of the king's letter. The prospect of this second, unexpected visit filled him with foreboding. When he learned that Charles was arriving with men and guns, his apprehension turned to desperate fear. For the first time he berated himself for having listened to his wife Beatrice, who had engineered the plan of bribing the French court officials and enticing Charles to Italy. God only knew what the drooling half-wit might do. He might forget about Naples and take Milan instead. Or the whole of Italy, for that matter. With forty thousand men and an invincible artillery, there was nothing he could not do.

It was with a strained smile that Ludovico welcomed Charles on the stairs of his Vigevano Villa. The king's first request was to demand that all the keys to the house be given him. French sentries were placed before every door. The visit turned into an occupation.

These measures were not calculated to rekindle the conviviality of Annona. Charles's request for an additional "loan" of 57,000 florins did little to relax the tension. Ludovico looked at the soldiers' tents and the cannons. Reluctantly, he handed over the money.

Under these conditions, the visit to Vigevano was not a success. In vain did Beatrice's ladies blink their lashes at him and give him their most inviting smiles; in vain did Leonardo da Vinci organize dazzling *spectacoli*. Three days after his arrival, the king announced his departure.

On 16 October he arrived, tired and discouraged, in Piacenza. There he paused and reviewed the situation. It was desperate, growing daily more hopeless. Already Ludovico's money had melted to pay the long overdue wages of the mercenaries. No more money could be expected from France. His credit was gone. This man whose income was eleven million livres could not raise a florin on his royal and illegible signature.

Moreover, the pope had proclaimed the legitimacy of the Aragon dynasty and even married one of his sons to the king's daughter. On top of all, Piero de'Medici, Florence's young ruler, had courteously but firmly refused the French free passage through Florentine territory on their march against Naples. His argument had been that Naples and Florence had been allies for many years, and honor forbade him to betray their treaties of friendship. It meant that the invaders would have to fight their way along the Tuscan coastline through a marshy region where artillery and cavalry would be of little use.

And so there was no choice but return home before it was too late, before the population turned against the invaders and destroyed their baggage and their guns.

Charles was about to have his trumpets sound retreat when, on 19 October at sunset, a traveler galloped across the city gate's drawbridge as it was about to draw up for the night.

His name was Giovanni de'Medici. He was not the cardinal, Lorenzo's second son, but belonged to the junior branch of the family. He and Piero had been boyhood playmates. Then they had fallen in love with the same girl, and their friendship had turned to bitter rivalry. When she had chosen Piero, Giovanni had sworn vengeance. To achieve it, he had journeyed all the way to Piacenza, a four-day ride.

No sooner had he crossed the city gate, than he solicited an audience from the king on a matter of extreme urgency. Because of his famous name, it was instantly granted.

The Florentines, he began after the three ritual genuflections, loved none more than His Majesty. They longed for a glimpse of his sacred person and deplored Piero's anti-French policy. They deeply regretted the humiliations and delays that their unworthy ruler had inflicted on the glorious king of France and emperor of the Orient. Gladly they would pay a large sum of money to atone for the harm which had been done him.

At the sound of the word "money," Charles pricked up his ears.

"Proceed," he said, trembling with excitement on his chair.

Encouraged, the traitor pressed on.

If His Majesty would only come to Florence, he would discover how deep was the love of the population and at the same time collect a large indemnity which was righteously his due.

By now, Charles was convinced. Why hadn't he thought of it? Of course, it was Piero's refusal to grant passage to his troops that had ruined his expedition. It was only fair that the Florentines, who were known to be the richest people in Italy, should reimburse him. In fact, they should be made to finance the remainder of his campaign.

All at once his despondency vanished. He would not return to France, but regain his Neapolitan throne. Later, much later, he would attend to the matter of the Holy Sepulcher.

The following morning couriers were dispatched to all French commanders to converge with their troops on the small town of Pontremoli, on the Florentine frontier. There they would be joined by the king, his seven thousand men, and his forty cannons.

Two days later Charles was back on his horse, in armor and plumed helmet as usual. At the city gate he was presented by the local authorities with "several excellent cheeses, as big as millstones." He was touched by this token of devotion and had the cheese sent to the queen with assurances of his eternal love.

And now, on to Florence!

Giuliano de'Medici by Michelangelo. *San Lorenzo Church, Florence.*

The Errant Hour

"And so," remarked Mariotto after a long pause, "because of a foolish rivalry for the love of a girl, the French will soon be here and take our money to pay for their absurd campaign."

He spoke evenly, without anger. Now that all hope was lost and his predictions had come true, he had become very calm. He, who for months had raged against "the blind fools on the Signoria" for refusing to strengthen the frontiers, seemed almost reconciled to the approaching disaster.

Without transition, he added, "The sun feels good, doesn't it?"

Summer that year would not die. October was coming to an end, but instead of the usual gusts of rain, the weather remained sunny and warm and the sky spread blue as a lake. After the midday *colazione*, he had said, "Wife, let's go to the roof and enjoy the last thing we still have to enjoy."

And now they sat on the *loggia*, gazing at Florence's landmarks which they knew so well, slowly running their eyes over them with a new tenderness, as though they might never see them again.

"Many people are already leaving," she said. "They say the French will sack our town, as they did Rapallo. What do you think, noble husband?"

"That's the question Giocondo asked me this morning. He has some relatives in Bologna and wanted to know whether he should send Meo to them for safety."

"How did he look?"

The elderly banker shrugged in a gesture of helpless despair. "Like a man who does not want to go on living."

Giocondo had lost his second wife, Tommasa, the month before. The young woman had died in the complications of a premature childbirth. She had been buried with her stillborn baby.

"Sometimes," Mariotto went on, as though talking to himself, "I think it is more reverent to say that life goes along haphazardly, like a rudderless ship, than to say that it is planned and directed by all-wise, all-kind God who permits things like that."

For a few instants he gazed absently at the small cupola of the San Lorenzo Church where Lorenzo de'Medici was buried; then he turned to his wife. "It seems that our grandson will grow up motherless after all, for I doubt very much that Giocondo will marry again."

"What did you tell him?"

"He could send Meo to Bologna if he wanted to, but personally I intended to remain here. After all, this is our town and if we leave it at the first sign of danger, we don't deserve to keep it."

"You don't believe the French will sack Florence?"

They might, he replied, but he did not think so. As a rule, sacking was committed against defenseless villages. The French would think twice before trying to sack a city of nearly a hundred thousand people where an ambush could be staged at every street, where every house was a fortress.

"Moreover, the presence of the king will be a deterrent to any large-scale raping and plundering. I understand he has no salt on the brain, but he is not a cruel man. Besides, he only wants our money; once he has it, he and his men will be on their way. As a matter of fact, I am less afraid of the French than of our own people."

"Our own people?"

"Yes, wife, our own people. They will be told that Piero could have kept the French out of our territory, and they will believe it."

"But you said he did everything to keep us out of war."

"True, but the Signoria will blame him nevertheless because officials are cowards and never admit their own blunders. Piero has committed the crime of being right while they were wrong. They will not forgive him."

The truth was that Piero had revealed a statesmanship and a foresight that were hardly expected from one so young. He had done exactly what his father would have done, if he had been alive. He had pleaded to reinforce the Sarzanella garrison and stop the French before they could enter Tuscany. The Signoria had shrugged at his arguments. In fact, King Charles's chamberlain, the great French historian Philippe de Commines, later wrote: "If only Sarzanella had been strengthened to hold out, the French would have been broken."

"Piero warned the Signoria," Mariotto explained, "that if they let the French cross our territory even once, they would never get them out of it, for the army would need an open line of communication for munitions, reinforcement, provisions. Troops and guns would pass through our land a thousand times and we might as well give France our entire coastline. Yet the members of the Signoria refused to believe him."

As a last recourse, Piero had called on the magistrates' sense of gratitude. He had reminded them that the king of Naples had saved Florence from the grasp of Sixtus IV by signing a separate peace and had ever since proven a loyal ally. Even that had failed to move Their Magnificences. He then had explained that granting passage to the French army would certainly lead to retaliations upon the thousands of Florentines established in Naples. Likewise it would bring down on Florence the wrath of Pope Alexander.

"Nothing he said had any effect. Finally, as he was about to leave, he turned around and, pointing his finger at the councillors, predicted that if they let the French set foot in Tuscany, Florence would lose Pisa, our main harbor and vassal town. And, mark my words, this is exactly what is going to happen."

Yet, Mariotto went on, and this time there was bitterness in

his voice, Piero would be blamed for not keeping the Florentines out of the war. The population would be systematically
aroused against him.

"And, once aroused, God knows what they may do to him,
his family, and his friends." Hesitantly, he added, "And that
means you and me, our children, Lisa, our servants, even our
house."

"Do you mean there may be a revolt?"

"Yes, wife," he said slowly. "I do."

She stared at him, unwilling to believe his words. She had
braced herself for the sight of bearded foreigners running
through her house, smashing cupboards, tearing tapestries off
the walls, forcing chest lockers with daggers, stealing jewelry
and silverware; but not the Florentines. To her, Florence was
home, a community of friendly neighbors, respectful tradesmen,
good-natured cart vendors haggling on Old Market Square. It
was hard to imagine them as a rampaging mob attacking Casa
Rucellai.

"But we have done harm to no one," she said.

"It makes no difference. We are related to the Medici; we
have served the Medicis for a long time. My father was State
Treasurer. I was governor of Pisa and twice I served as *gonfaloniere*. It is enough for us to be among their first targets."

A smile stole over his lips and he placed a reassuring hand
over hers. "But fear nothing. They will find us well prepared."

Like the methodical man that he was, he had made plans for
the safety of his household. He had sent to "The Farm" for five
cartloads of stones to be stacked by every window. The entrance
door would be reinforced to withstand the blows of a ram.
The silverware coffers would be buried in the garden. At the
first approach of the mob, every servant, male and female,
would take his assigned post. Kettles of water would boil on
every stove and every fireplace, and would be poured on the
assailant's heads. Every male servant would be given a weapon.

"In about ten days, we should be ready for any eventuality,"
he said in conclusion.

"What about Lisa and Francesco?"

Her question sent his eyebrows up in his forehead. "They will be with us, of course. After all, it's their house, and they should defend it. They can stand on the roof and throw stones. By the way, where is Lisa? I haven't seen her all day."

"Giuliano came to fetch her this morning and I gave her permission to ride with him to Fiesole. It's such a lovely day."

He gave an approving nod, but his brow remained knitted in perplexity. "It may be a long time before they go riding together again."

"What do you mean, noble husband?"

"Since they were children, we have taken it for granted that they would marry some day. It was Lorenzo's wish and ours as well. But the coming of the French may bring many changes to our plans."

"They love each other."

"Yes, I guess they do," he echoed wearily. "As much as one can love at their age. She has just turned fifteen and her head is full of romantic notions. For Giuliano, also, it is the age of adolescent infatuation. There is nothing wrong with that, and in normal times I would pledge them to each other and marry them in a year or two. But times are not normal and many troubles lie ahead of us. For one thing, we don't know if the Medici — or ourselves, for that matter — will survive the crisis which is bound to explode one of these days. As I said, we may have a rebellion; a new government may come to power. As Piero's brother, Giuliano will certainly be included in any sanction against the Medici family. Even we may find ourselves banished from Florence."

She had turned very pale, and he hastened to comfort her.

"All this is much in the future. For the moment, we must think of some place where Lisa will be safe while the French occupy the town. Have you any suggestions?"

"The Carmelite convent on Via Ghibellina," she said.

The mother superior was a childhood friend of hers and might consent to take Lisa as a temporary novice. The idea appealed to Mariotto, for the Signoria planned to surround nunneries with city guards.

"As a matter of fact," he said, "I should breathe easier if you, too, would go to a convent."

She looked at him with amused surprise and for the first time broke into a peal of laughter. She thanked him for his concern, but assured him that no Frenchman would waste a glance on her.

"Besides," she hurried before he had time to argue, "you will have need of me in the house. French dignitaries will certainly be billeted in our home, and someone will have to look after their comfort."

Slowly, her hand crept over his. "We've been wed many years and have known much happiness together. If, as you say, we are facing somber days, I want to face them with you."

Thus, Filippa and Mariotto Rucellai talked on that afternoon of 26 October, on the *loggia* of their house, finding reassurance in the sound of their voices and each other's nearness.

While her grandparents were discussing the advance of the French on Florence, Lisa and Giuliano were riding along the sloping lanes to Fiesole.

Around them the countryside basked in sunshine. Every tree, every bush, every blade of grass shared in that belated autumnal embrace.

Usually they chatted gaily in the course of their rides together, but today Giuliano was silent and brooding and Lisa sensed that he, too, was thinking about "the foreign devils."

It was still early in the afternoon when they entered the village, deserted at this hour, with the men working in the fields and the women spinning wool in their houses.

He helped her dismount, hitched their horses at the fountain in the center of the square, and, taking her by the hand, led her into the chapel of the abbey. It was cool and dim, the air thick with incense. Candles burned in clusters of yellow rosebuds before a statue of the Madonna.

They crossed themselves, knelt side by side, and it flashed through her mind that they would kneel and pray like this on the day of their wedding. A moment later they rose and strolled about the chapel, looking at the carved pulpit, the colored statues of saints.

"This is where my brother Giovanni was made a cardinal," he said.

He also told her how his great-grandfather Cosimo used to come here and rest for a few days in the adjoining monastery to read one of his beloved books and forget about affairs of state.

A moment later they left the church and were back in the afternoon sunshine. They climbed back on their horses and started riding in silence, gently swaying on their saddles to the ambling gait of their mounts.

"Let's stop here," he said suddenly, as they came upon an olive grove. "I have things to tell you."

He lifted her by the waist. As her face slid down close to his, he kissed her lips. Then they stretched out on the grass under a gnarled old tree, looking at the shards of blue sky between silvery leaves.

He did not speak, and finally she turned on her side and whispered, "You're thinking about the foreign devils, aren't you, *cocolino?*"

Yes, he said quietly, looking into her eyes. He and his brother had done nothing else in the last two days. The thing their father dreaded most had come to pass, and he no longer was there to guide them. With his usual foresight, Lorenzo had written, "May God grant that the idea of trying his strength in this country never enter the head of a king of France. When that happens, all will be lost."

"He left us when we needed him most," he said.

She saw the tears in his eyes, and suddenly he seemed as young and helpless as she was. Both were children engulfed in a vortex which they could barely comprehend, let alone control.

He told her how Piero had pleaded with the Signoria to stop the French before they entered Tuscany, but Their Magnificences had refused his request.

"They wouldn't have done that with our father, but they said that Piero was too young to have much judgment. Instead it was they who showed they had none. The French will be here in two

or three weeks, and nobody knows what to do. Now is too late to
fight or even negotiate. Already several frontier towns have surrendered. Others will soon follow. The butchery of Rapallo has
stifled any attempt at resistance.

"And so Piero has decided to go and meet the king at his headquarters, reach an agreement with him and try to persuade him
to bypass Florence, and proceed directly on his way."

"And you?"

"I'll go with him, of course."

Barely had he spoken the words, when she was in his arms, lying over him and sobbing on his shoulder. The foreign devils
would kill him. She knew it, she was sure of it. In vain did he
assure her that the king was not a cruel man. Surely she must
see that his duty was to be with his brother. She did not see it.
Why couldn't Piero go to see the king by himself?

"Then if the French devils come to Florence, you and I can
die together."

She was now lying over him and he felt the pressure of her
body upon his as she unfolded her brave plan in sobbing whispers.
She had it all clearly arranged in her mind. On the day the French
entered Florence, she and Giuliano would ride to some nice place
in the country — this olive grove, for instance. They would lay
down on the grass and kiss and kiss and kiss. Then at sunset he
would plunge his dagger into her heart and he would stab himself
afterwards. A day or so later they would be found still in each
other's arms, their lips sealed in a farewell embrace, like the young
monk and Carmelite nun a few months ago.

"Then we'll live in our little house in heaven and be happy
forever."

He did not have the heart to shatter her dream, and agreed with
her. Gently, he laid her on the ground and it was his turn to lean
on her. He kissed her wet cheeks as she spoke, but already her
words slurred in a drowsy murmur. She offered no resistance
when his hand crept under her dress. Her lids closed, her lips
parted. She stopped talking as she felt they were becoming one.
With a sigh of delight, she slid into a well of bliss.

The sky was mauve when she awoke and saw him, stretched out at her side, his head resting on his arm, smiling at her.

"We must go back," he said softly. "But first I want to give you something."

While speaking, he unfastened a small gold medal and clasped it around her neck.

It was called a *santelena* and had been brought from the Holy Land. His honored great-grandfather Cosimo had bought it in Venice where he had been sent in exile. When he was recalled to Florence, Cosimo found he had misplaced the medal. An agitated correspondence took place between his wife and Matteo, the family butler, for its recovery. It finally was found and Cosimo wore it all his life. It was guaranteed to protect "against dagger and poison."

"I want you to have it till I return."

It meant they would not die together after all, but she did not have the strength to argue any more.

They rode back to town in silence. At the door of Casa Rucellai, she made him swear to come and see her the moment he and his brother were back, "any hour of the day or night."

He promised. They kissed once more, and he was off.

That evening Piero and four companions rode secretly out of town. It was almost dawn when they reached Empoli, where they halted at an inn. While his friends slept, Piero wrote to the Signoria giving the reasons of his journey and what he hoped to accomplish "by this act of despair."

His letter split Florence wide open. Some regarded his going to meet the king as a noble, selfless gesture. They recalled that fifteen years before his father had likewise gone to meet the king of Naples and gambled his life to save Florence. Others called it a sordid maneuver to seek the invaders' protection for himself.

During the following days, Lisa learned of the mission's progress from her grandfather's comments at the dinner table.

On 30 October, Piero had come in sight of the French camp and was courteously brought to the king's tent by His Excellency Guillaume Briconnet who, in addition to being minister of finance, was a bishop. Contrary to all expectations, Charles greeted Florence's young ruler with kindness. Their fathers had been friends and the monarch recalled the San Zenobio ring which had eased "Old King Spider's" sufferings in his last weeks on earth.

In a few days Piero and the Great Crusader had reached an agreement.

Realizing the futility of any haggling, Piero had readily consented to the temporary surrender of various towns, most of which were already in French hands while the others were eager to capitulate. (Fivizzano, a mountain village, had tried to fight and had paid dearly for its bravery. Its two hundred defenders had been slaughtered by the fourteen thousand invaders, its houses burned, its streets littered with corpses.)

He also promised to pay an indemnity of 200,000 gold florins in three installments.

In turn, the treaty stipulated that all towns would be restituted the moment Charles entered Naples and it guaranteed the safety of "all houses, monuments, works of art" as well as the lives of the 650,000 people living on Florentine territory.

"Not a bad treaty at all," remarked Mariotto at supper, "under the circumstances. Of course, 200,000 florins is a great deal of money, but consider the value of our cathedral, the Battistero's doors, the Leaning Tower, let alone the lives of an entire nation."

He recalled that in 1375 the Florentines had gladly paid a sum of 130,000 florins to the papal generalissimo to induce him to withdraw his army from the city gates.

Sir John Hawkwood, a former Surrey tailor, had been commander in chief of the papal army. Not only did he accept the bribe, but for an additional 30,000 florins, he volunteered to defect and lead the Florentine troops against his own. Thus the City of Flowers had won another great victory against the Holy See. For this double betrayal, Hawkwood was buried in the Florence cathedral with his portrait on horseback painted by Paolo Uccello.

"Under the circumstances," he went on, "it was the best possible treaty he could make."

From these observations, Lisa concluded that Giuliano had not been killed after all and would soon be back. On the night of 8 November she heard his footsteps in the garden. Her heart leaped in her chest. He had kept his promise and come to see her. . . .

In a flash, she was out of bed. Slipping into a woolen robe, she tiptoed to the balcony. In the moonlight, she recognized his slender silhouette. With a little cry of joy, she raced down the stairs and they were in each other's arms.

The next day, a Sunday, Florence exploded into a well-prepared revolution. Piero's thirteen-day absence had been put to good use by the enemies of the Medici regime. On his return, everything was in readiness.

Exhausted by the fatigue of the journey, he slept late that Sunday. It was mid-afternoon when he rode to the Old Palace with Giuliano and a small retinue to report to the Signoria on his encounter with the king.

He was told by the sentry that Their Magnificences were having a light meal and could not be disturbed. They would, however, receive him later in the afternoon, if he came alone and used the service entrance.

This insult to the chief of state had been carefully rehearsed, and so had the events that followed.

As Piero emerged from the Old Palace, he saw people were running into the square from all adjoining streets, as upon a signal, brandishing fire pokers and hurling stones. The attack was made to simulate a "spontaneous" outburst of popular indignation; its intent was to kill him and his friends on the spot.

Vaulting into his saddle, he shouted to Giuliano to seize the San Gallo city gate and keep it open at all costs.

This decision saved his life.

Spurring his horse and swinging his crop, Giuliano and a few fellow horsemen ploughed their way through the threatening mob and galloped to the Porta San Gallo. After a scuffle with the city guards, he and his followers managed to capture the cranking device that operated the drawbridge and kept it lowered long enough for Piero and his retinue to thunder over it. A moment later they were receding figures fleeing in the early November dusk.

The Medici regime which had lasted sixty years and one month, had collapsed in less than an hour.

Frustrated in their designs upon Piero and Giuliano, the populace converged on the Medici Palace. In the glow of torches, they forced their way into the stately mansion, slashed tapestries, hurled onyx and alabaster cups through windows and sent them crashing down on the pavement. Glass cabinets filled with antique coins, Tanagra statuettes were smashed to bits. Precious manuscripts were stolen. An iron coffer containing 22,000 gold florins was forced open, its contents divided among the thieves. The Signoria encouraged the looting. City guards in uniforms helped drag Donatello's admirable "Judith" out of the courtyard and set it at the entrance of the Old Palace "as a warning against the enemies of liberty."

Lisa saw none of it. Forbidden to go out because of the turmoil in the streets, she had spent the afternoon at the window of Tessa's room watching men run aimlessly with knives or clubs in their fists. At supper she learned that Giuliano had managed to escape and she let out an inward sigh of relief. At least he had not been killed, and in time, they would meet and kiss and make love again.

As for Cardinal Giovanni de'Medici, he had sought refuge among his brethren and knocked at the door of the San Marco Monastery, an institution which his great-grandfather Cosimo had built at his own expense and given to the Dominican Order. For three generations it had been funded by the Medici family. Yet the San Marco monks had slammed their door in the cardinal's face and refused him sanctuary.

"So much for Christian charity as practiced by the Dominicans," concluded Mariotto with joking bitterness.

No one knew where the prince of the Church was at the moment. Some feared him dead. In fact, he managed to escape two days later, disguised as a lowly Franciscan monk.

Mariotto then described the sacking of the Medici Palace. For a while he excoriated people's ingratitude. He recalled Cosimo's endless toil which had saved Florence from bankruptcy, his eight-million-florin philanthropies, Lorenzo's desperate journey to Naples in order to bring peace to Florence, and finally Piero's foresight for which he had been rewarded by expulsion and the looting of his house.

"And now," he said, draining his goblet of Spanish wine and rising to his feet, "it is time for us to take our posts and prepare to defend our home."

Once again, his predictions had proven true. After sacking the Medici Palace, the rampaging mob was turning against the mansions of the Medici officials. The damages inflicted on various residences that evening would amount to over 100,000 gold florins.

Mariotto rang the courtyard bell, as the shouts of the approaching crowd could already be heard. At once the reinforced entrance door was shut. In a flash, grooms, menservants, maids, and scullions as well as members of the family stood at windows ready to drop heavy stones or pour kettles of boiling water on the assailants' heads. Lisa and her brother crouched behind the roof balustrade with rocks in their hands.

The assault on Casa Rucellai was violent, but mercifully brief. The ladders which had been leaned against the façade were pushed back with hooks and grapnels. The entrance door shook under the blows of a battering ram, but did not break. A few burning torches that had been tossed inside the house were quickly snuffed out with sand before any serious damage had been done.

Surprised by this unexpected reception, pelted with stones, tumbled down from ladders, scalded by boiling water, the assailants did not persist and retreated in haste. A few moments later the street was silent and dark again.

"I believe they've had enough and won't come back," Mariotto said to the assembled household with a satisfied grin. "Let's thank the Madonna and go to sleep."

Lisa tried to stay awake after going to bed, for it seemed callous to sleep while Giuliano was fleeing through the night. But too much had happened that day and fatigue was stronger than grief. She slept peacefully, tears drying on her cheeks.

Neither had she time to think about him the following morning, for King Charles had entered Pisa the day before and the Florentines expected him to march immediately upon their town.

Lisa was taken to the Carmelite convent on Via Ghibellina by her grandmother. Arrangements had been made for her admission as a temporary novice. After being graciously received by the mother superior, she was led to the cell she was to share with two other spurious novices. They giggled as they slipped off their stylish dresses and were fitted into black regulation garments. To them, the arrival of "the barbarians" was turning into a sort of masquerade.

Tessa was also included among the kitchen lay sisters, which entailed her forsaking her turban and brass jewelry and adopting the Carmelite robes.

The convent, usually so peaceful, was presently the scene of great agitation, as other "maidens of high degree" arrived, escorted by their personal maids or turbaned *bambinaias*. They, too, were rapidly transformed into young nuns. Lisa found several friends among them, and in excited whispers they discussed what the French would do to them. Would they respect their sacred garments or would they tear them off their backs and leave them, raped and dying in puddles of blood, as they had the girls of Rapallo and Fivizzano?

The convent's schedule left Lisa little time to ponder the question. She discovered that nuns did an enormous amount of praying, most of it on their knees. When she was not in the chapel, she was expected to help in the kitchen, pray some more in her cell, and work in the garden. This left her practically no time to think about the Fiesole olive grove and her last afternoon with Giuliano.

Meanwhile, at Casa Rucellai preparations were made to receive the French dignitaries who were to be billeted there during the king's sojourn in Florence.

One of the royal quartermasters had visited Mariotto and courteously informed him that the bishop-minister of finances, His Excellency Guillaume Briconnet, had solicited the favor of being lodged in his house, for he had been a banker before entering the Church. The other "guests" would be high-ranking officers and a handsome, twenty-one-year-old nobleman, Pierre de Bayard, who spoke perfect Italian, having been a page at the court of the duke of Savoy.

With her usual efficiency, Donna Filippa had taken matters in hand. Under her direction, the house buzzed with the shuttling of maidservants. The cook was told to try her hand at French cooking. Fresh silk curtains were hung on the bishop's bed, a decanter of Trebbiano wine set on his desk. A comely maid was assigned the task of keeping a cheerful blaze in his room, for the weather had finally turned cold and drizzly. A picture of a smiling Madonna in a Florentine headveil holding the Child in her arms was hung on the wall.

Filippa also gave attention to the comfort of the other guests, and good-humoredly Mariotto remarked that they probably would never want to leave. At her request, he even brought forth the coffers of silverware which had been buried in the garden.

In a few days Casa Rucellai was ready to welcome her contingent of "barbarians" and make them feel at home.

The whole city was doing likewise, but for fear of reprisals. The Medici Palace was being hastily repaired in view of its occupancy by the "King of France and Emperor of the Orient." The San Frediano Gate, through which he was to make his entrance, was beautified with greenery and blue shields bearing golden fleurs-de-lys and inscriptions — in French — of eternal love.

Streets were sanded; carpets and tapestries displayed at windows and over balcony railings. Arches of triumph were hurriedly erected on the king's route and tableaux-vivants of biblical scenes decorated the heads of the four bridges. The population was directed to don their best clothes and shout with well-simulated fervor "*Francia! Francia!*" Shops were festooned with garlands of colored paper. Under severe penalties, candles were to burn all night in windows, as a symbol of the Florentines' delight at having the Great Crusader in their midst.

"This is not yet enough," remarked the *gonfaloniere*, Luca Corso, in a night session of the Signoria.

He went on to say that His Majesty had revealed himself an ardent admirer of Italian womanhood. Reports of his kissing Beatrice Sforza's ladies-in-waiting had spread through the peninsula. In every town he had visited, he had been greeted by the most beautiful local girls in scanty attire. Would Florence be the only city ashamed to display the comeliness of her maidens? What better way would there be to win the monarch's good graces but to send a cortege of the noblest and most seductive girls to meet him outside the city wall?

Their Magnificences agreed.

A mirthless, out-of-season-carnival was speedily organized with musicians, buffoons, acrobats on stilts, hilarious cardboard *giganti*, or giants. And, of course, a procession of gaily decorated floats or *trionfi*.

And so it came to pass that on the cloudy afternoon of 17 November 1494, Lisa de'Gherardini and two other novices stood, nude and shivering under flimsy veils, on the *Trionfo del Giglio*, or "Float of the Lily," representing the virtues of Faith, Hope and Charity, feebly waving olive branches as their cart lumbered through crowded streets to greet the king.*

The French stayed eleven days in Florence, to the twenty-eighth of November.

In this span of time, the Great Crusader visited the zoo, played badminton, rode horseback wearing a short green skirt over the cuissards of his armor, which made him look more ridiculous than ever, and an enormous hat of white felt with two ostrich feathers: one white, the other black. At first he demanded the reinstatement of Piero de'Medici, and an emissary was sent to Bologna to that effect, but too late. Piero had already left for Venice.

Reluctantly, Charles consented to revise the treaty he had

---

* A detailed description of the *Trionfo del Giglio* will be found in *L'entrée de Charles VIII à Florence* by Y. Labande.

signed at his headquarters. After several stormy sessions, he agreed to reduce to 120,000 the indemnity he was to receive. But he did not budge on any other point.

As to the Florentines, they soon had enough of "the barbarians." There was no large-scale raping or plundering, but the natives resented the presence of their uncouth and arrogant visitors and their 14,000 horses. Before long, stones began to fall from windows on marching soldiers; sentries were stabbed and thrown in the Arno.

In turn, things went very well at Casa Rucellai.

The bishop-minister of finances struck an immediate friendship with Mariotto. Like the two reasonable men they were, they soon exchanged confidences and deplored this senseless Italian campaign. The other French guests proved equally gracious. They, too, longed to be back home with their mistresses and their families.

Three days after they had moved in, Mariotto decided that their presence in the house was the best guarantee of safety for Lisa, who was brought back from the convent. She shed her novice's garb, gave a last glance to the pallet of straw on the floor that had been her bed, said goodbye to her cellmates, curtsied to the mother superior, and returned home with Tessa, once again in turban and bright calico blouses.

She found Casa Rucellai full of booted, bearded, and very polite "foreign devils." At once her services were required by her grandmother in the discharge of the unusually heavy household chores. She helped with the bed-making, emptied slop jars through windows, waxed furniture, and filled the wine decanter on the bishop's desk. When she learned that he had tried to have Piero and Giuliano reinstated to power, she grew fond of him and gave him her sweetest smile. He patted her cheek and let her kiss his ring.

She became popular among aides-de-camp and the younger guests. They made sheep's eyes at her, sought private encounters. Except for the fact that they were "barbarians" and did not speak Italian, they behaved exactly like young Florentines.

She struck up something of a friendship with the handsome

Pierre de Bayard, who did speak Italian and prided himself on the fact that all his ancestors had died in battle in the king's service. His dream was to follow in their footsteps, which she privately regarded as the proof that his brains had gone down to his boots.

At last, on 25 November, the king received a first installment of 50,000 florins on his "indemnity" and signed a treaty of peace with Florence. At the main altar of the cathedral, he solemnly swore to return all Tuscan towns he had seized on his arrival in Naples. He also publicly declared his "unswerving resolution" to depose and put in prison Pope Alexander, who had refused him the investiture as king of Naples. Finally, he pledged to depart the following morning: he, his men, his cannons, and his horses.

The signing of the peace treaty was the occasion of a farewell supper at Casa Rucellai. Bishop Briconnet wore his finest cassock and largest amethyst ring; the generals, their orders and gold-hilted swords. Mariotto himself had donned his red *lucco* and his gold chain of office as president of the Bankers' Guild. Filippa displayed her beautiful pearl necklace. As for Lisa, she wore her silver headband and looked charming in a blue brocade dress.

During the meal, the conversation was animated, but imbued with melancholy. The "foreign devils" looked back with longing on the days they had spent in the hospitable mansion. They had been awed and fascinated by such refined novelties as two-pronged forks and handkerchiefs, and they were eager to show their wives the samples they were taking back with them. Most of all, they dreaded pushing farther south on this inept campaign, trampling through muddy, winter-rutted roads in an increasingly hostile Italy.

Supper over, everyone passed into the formal living room, ablaze with candlelight. Lisa entertained the guests with her *spinettino* playing and performed a few *pastorales* and *bergerettes* which her music teacher had painstakingly taught her. At the sound of their native songs, the guests grouped around her and joined in the singing. She noticed that some of them had moist eyes and she concluded that they were not such barbarians after all.

The next day, however, Charles did not leave. He had forgotten his solemn oath in the cathedral the afternoon before and taken a liking to Florence. He wanted to go to the zoo once again and was very surprised when the Signoria reminded him of his promise. He was hurt to learn that the Florentines had had enough of him. They had seemed so happy at his entrance, had shouted "*Francia! Francia!*" with such fervor. He truly believed that they loved him and he wept when he found out that they did not.

Two days later, in an early morning drizzle, he finally made his exit through deserted streets.

The house seemed very quiet after the guests were gone. For the first time in nearly two months, Lisa had the opportunity to think about Giuliano and wonder where he might possibly be. At the same time, she could no longer escape the fears that had stirred up for some time in the recesses of her mind. The monthly blood smears which stained her bed sheets had not appeared and her anxiety grew daily.

Tessa, also, sensed that something was wrong. One evening, as she was preparing Lisa for bed, she mentioned the ride to Fiesole, and it did not take her long to learn what she already suspected. In gasping sobs, Lisa blurted out all she remembered of that fateful afternoon. This time, the slave did not launch into reproaches or wail about unladylike behavior and such. Instead, she took her *bimba* in her arms and let her talk and cry herself to sleep.

Only then did she let her heart overflow and tears roll down her ocher cheeks. For an instant she wept in silence; then, taking the candlestick from the night table, she went out of the room. Through the dark and silent house she and her shadow made their way to Donna Filippa's sitting room.

A moment later she came out, softly closed the door and retraced her steps to her room.

The next night Mariotto Rucellai walked, lantern in hand, to the house of Francesco del Giocondo. It was a blustery December night and snowflakes speckled his cloaked shoulders and the brim of his *cappuccio a foggia*.

His visit was expected and the door opened at his first knock.

"Will you have a goblet of hot wine?" asked his former son-in-law. "It is a beastly night."

Mariotto declined with a shake of the head, and without any further conversation took his place by the fireside.

"Francesco," he said, "In the name of the love you bore my daughter Camilla, I've come to ask you to marry my granddaughter Lisa."

They were married in the sacristy of Santa Maria Novella, late one January afternoon, in a furtive ceremony befitting the somberness of the times and the fact that the bridegroom was an aging, twice-widowered man.*

While the priest hurried through the service (mass had been dispensed with) Lisa knelt by Giocondo's side, eyes closed and hands joined before her face, in an attitude of devotion belied by the undevout thoughts whirling then in her mind.

Here she was, at fifteen, marrying this bulky, unhandsome man, old enough to be her father. Oh yes, he had given her a nice coral rosary and Camilla had assured her that he really was a good man. And she was properly grateful to him for rescuing her from social disgrace. Most grateful . . .

But you could not spend the rest of your life with a man you could never love simply out of gratitude, could you? Moreover, was he marrying her out of kindness of heart or lechery? How much gratitude did she owe to a man who was going to repay himself for his good deed by satisfying his lust on her delicious young body?

Would he at least respect her pregnancy? Even of that there was no certainty. For some men, nothing was sacred and he might be one of them. She still was slim in the waist and most

---

* Lisa's wedding to Francesco del Giocondo is confirmed by a score of Renaissance scholars. In his *Commenti*, the great Italian historian Gaet'ani Milanesi, whose manuscript can be consulted at the *Riccardiana Biblioteca* in Florence, wrote:

"Francesco del Giocondo, son of Zanobio and grandson of Bartolommeo, had three wives: Camilla, daughter of Mariotto Rucellai, whom he married in 1491; Tommasa de'Villani, daughter of Mariotto de'Villani, in 1493; and Lisa de'Gherardini, daughter of Antonio Maria, son of Noldo, in 1495 — and this is the beautiful lady whose portrait was painted by Leonardo da Vinci."

probably he would hurl himself at her the moment they would arrive at his house on Via della Stufa.

He now was her lord and master, and she was at his mercy. He could do with her as he pleased and, of course, she would submit, for she had no choice. With clenched teeth and death in her soul, she would swallow her tears, be his plaything, and let him have her body.

But her heart, he would never, never have.

It would remain inviolate, a shrine to Giuliano's memory where she would retire in the loneliness of the years to come. There she would come to recall every moment of their wondrous and tragic romance, every minute of that wondrous and fatal October afternoon in the olive grove. On such memories she would live until the end of her life.

She opened her eyes as the priest pronounced them man and wife and traced a hasty sign of the cross over them. Hand in hand, she and her new husband made their way out of the sacristy, followed only by her honored grandparents and Tessa, who had wept through the entire ceremony.

Not to attract attention, Mariotto and Filippa took their leave at the church's door while the newlyweds walked silently in the wintry dusk to Casa Giocondo, with Tessa following a good distance away. Lisa knew the house from the visits she had paid Camilla there. It was not patrician, but substantial and comfortable. She could not help noticing its spaciousness, the excellence of the furnishings.

As he led her to the dining room, the thought crossed her mind that at least she would be miserable in pleasant surroundings. It helped a little.

A light meal had been prepared and grudgingly she credited him for his consideration. At least he had restrained his lust long enough to provide her with some sustenance, a small point in his favor. Despite her apprehensions over the approaching ordeal, she ate with ravenous appetite. The food, she fleetingly observed, was delicious; the service faultless.

To create an illusion of conviviality, Giocondo made small talk about the weather.

"For the last two months we've hardly had any sunny days," he said. "We are still paying for those wonderful October days."

Discreetly he praised the elegance of her dress, implied it was exceedingly rare to find a woman of such tender years endowed with such a sure taste in fashion. She concluded he was more intelligent than he looked. At least he would not be one of these boorish husbands who never noticed what their wives were wearing. It pleased her that he had been so quick to observe her natural flair for clothes.

Dessert over, the manservant set a decanter of Malaga wine on the table, signaled the two serving maids to withdraw, and followed them out of the dining room.

Giocondo filled his goblet, took a sip, dabbed his lips with the tablecloth. This done, he looked thoughtfully at Lisa across the table for a few instants.

"Gentle wife," he began at last, "as you well know, we've been brought together by events that neither of us could predict or control. Camilla told me of your love for Giuliano and I shall not expect you to simulate towards me sentiments of devotion you cannot possibly experience. For my part, I shall respect your memories and will be content with your friendly companionship. Let's accept a situation we cannot change and trust life to grant us some small measure of happiness."

So saying, he rose from the table, led her to her room. At the door, he kissed her hand and walked away.

Their marriage passed almost unnoticed in the confusion that prevailed in Florence. The population had not yet recovered from the barbarians' visit. The town was still in shambles: her public squares littered with horses' droppings; her street shrines desecrated by drunken soldiers. Several mansions stood empty, their windows broken, their walls blackened by fire, their wrought-iron lanterns broken or stolen. On Via Larga, the plundered Medici Palace rose like the ghost of a splendid era, now forever gone.

Above all, Florence had lost her gaiety. No one whistled in the streets anymore; no one played the lute while waiting his turn at the barber's. The City of Flowers had become the City of Ashes and Thorns. She now had an unofficial but undisputed master, a Dominican monk by the name of Savonarola, who held crowds under the spell of his eloquence and his predictions of more calamities to come.

Cleansed of its Medici supporters, the Signoria had become the obedient instrument of his will. His suggestions became official decrees. The preacher had become statesman and lawgiver. In his cell at the San Marco Monastery, he was writing, under God's dictation, a new constitution that was to make Jesus the local lord and turn the sinful town of yore into a holy city, a model to the world.

Where greed and lechery had once bloomed, virtue now reigned. Singing was frowned upon; dancing forbidden. Dice or card players got ten lashes at the first offense; fifty at the second. Swearing was punished by piercing the blasphemer's tongue with a red-hot iron. Nothing like it to deter people from taking the Lord's name in vain . . .

Naturally, all social life had ceased. The town crawled with informers and even old friends avoided meeting in public. Former Medici officials were the object of constant police surveillance. For Lisa's sake, her cousin Jacopo de'Gherardini stopped seeing her, and so did Contessina.

Thus, Lisa was spared the traditional round of postwedding visits. Almost no one paid attention to the marriage of an insignificant society maiden to an unremarkable middle-aged silk merchant. Only a few matrons with marriageable daughters commented on Mariotto's astuteness in securing for his granddaughter the same rich husband he had already caught for his late daughter. And this, at a time when rich husbands were as rare as mosquitoes in winter.

"Count on a banker to strike a good bargain twice," they sighed.

Meanwhile, Lisa was adapting herself to her new life. Relieved from her fear of physical intercourse with the "fat old man," as she still called Giocondo in her mind, she resolved to show her appreciation by being an efficient housewife, a pleasant companion, a loving foster-mother to his son Bartolommeo. Except for her heart, which would always belong to Giuliano, she would try to be a good wife.

Dressed in black with the house keys at her belt, she now explored Casa Giocondo from top to bottom. She opened chests and cupboards, discussed daily menus with the cook, learned to give orders to servants, and grew used to being addressed by them as "Donna Lisa."

Of course, she no longer wore her hair streaming down the sides of her face, as in her maidenly days. A *giovinetta* might scamper about disheveled; but not so the young Donna Lisa de'Gherardini del Giocondo. Like all Italian aristocrats, Lisa retained her family name in addition to that of her husband.

After long sessions before her mirror and arguments with Tessa, she finally decided to wear her hair parted in the middle in two smooth, curving bandeaux which joined at her nape into a pleated coil. A cluster of false curls (Florentine ladies had a passion for false hair) cascaded over her ears. A black, diaphanous headveil maintained the headdress in place and added to the decorousness of the ensemble.

Between her various household chores, she climbed to the top floor where the nursery was and there she would play with Bartolommeo. He was now two and a half and in no time he held her in the palm of his tiny hand.

She had installed Tessa as his *bambinaia*, a decision she almost came to regret, for Meo worshipped his nurse from the start, gazed adoringly at her turban, played with her bracelets and brass necklaces. Tessa, for her part, fell instantly under his spell. Her liquid black eyes gleamed lovingly when they rested on the curly haired little boy.

This mutual rapture aroused Lisa's jealousy.

"With me you were very strict," she complained. "Always wagging a finger, always threatening to call a witch, but with Meo — oh, with Meo! — it's altogether different. He only has to smile at you and your heart melts in your chest, like wax in the fire. I think you want all his love for yourself."

"You soon will have a *bimbo* of your own," Tessa replied, "and I will love him, too."

Now and then, when Meo slept in his cradle, they would speak about Giuliano. For Lisa, he had become somewhat unreal, part of an adolescent world of laughter, quarrels, and kisses which had abruptly vanished.

"Sometimes I dream I hear his footsteps in the garden and he is throwing a pebble at my window, as he used to." Soon tears would well in her eyes. "If only I had seen him dead, I might have begun to forget. But I cannot get used to the idea that he is alive somewhere, yet out of my life."

"You still have your whole life in front of you," Tessa would say. "In time you will forget."

She spoke as though she were sure of it, and it annoyed Lisa, who retorted that other women might easily forget, but not her. Time would never erase her grief.

"When I give my heart, it is forever," she said with finality in her voice.

At the same time that she was adjusting herself to her new life, she was studying and discovering the man to whom she found herself married. Thank God, he was not a lecher as she had feared. He still kissed her hand on the threshold of her room, as he bid her good night. He even had, she conceded, a few good qualities. Camilla had told her he was patient and gentle, and this had turned out to be true. It also had come as a surprise to her, for he was a bulky man and she associated size with ferociousness.

As weeks went by, she began feeling more at ease with him. She greeted him in the house's courtyard on his return from the mill and wished him God's grace. During supper, he would tell her of King Charles's progress through southern Italy. She found it somewhat tedious, but it made time pass and it was better than silence.

After leaving Florence, it had taken the Great Crusader a little over a month to come in view of Rome, a journey usually made in five days. Camping under the wall of the Holy City, he had sent an emissary to the pope to inform him that he would make his entrance on 1 January. Then, on his astrologer's advice, he had changed his mind and entered the city the evening before when no one was expecting him. His soldiers had broken into the inhabitants' houses, turned out the men, and taken their places by the sides of their wives.

Charles and his entourage had taken possession of the San Marco Palace. A few surrounding houses had been blown to bits to make room for thirty-six cannons.

The Holy Father, for his part, had taken refuge in Castel Sant' Angelo after placing the Blessed Sacrament and the heads of Saint Paul and Saint Peter on its ramparts to remind the French that the fortress was not to be fired upon. These relics had not prevented a section of the wall from collapsing of its own accord, killing four sentries.

Superstitious as only a Spaniard could be, Pope Borgia had regarded this mishap as a warning to get out of his refuge before it fell on his head. He returned to the Vatican and was walking in the Belvedere gardens when Charles, who had been informed of his presence, appeared at the end of an alley and found himself face to face with the pontiff he had sworn to remove from office.

At the sight of the majestic old man, the Little King politely doffed his feathered toque and made two genuflections, which His Beatitude pretended not to see. He was about to bend the knee for the third time when Borgia let out a cry of joyous surprise, opened his arms and engulfed the Great Crusader in his bejeweled cope. For a few instants, the emperor of the Orient vanished from sight, crushed against the papal abdomen.

Naturally, there was no more talk of removing Pope Alexander from office. The two monarchs became great friends and their encounters exuded an air of extreme cordiality. When Charles asked his friend to appoint Bishop Briconnet cardinal, the pontiff obliged on the spot. Snatching the red velvet hat of one of his attendants, he personally clamped it on the bishop-minister's head, and that was it. Probably, the speediest, most informal investiture in the history of the Church.

Twelve days after his entrance, the Great Crusader started on his way to Naples. From a window of the Vatican Palace, Borgia watched him depart in his plumed helmet and sent an aerial blessing after him.

"By now," Giocondo remarked late in February, "he should be arriving at the final objective of his campaign."

Needless to say, with the expulsion of the Medici the traditional Florentine New Year's festivities did not take place. No more singing contest on Piazza della Signoria, dancing bears, acrobats. And, of course, no more dancing at night around bonfires.

On 25 March, a fine spring day, the new year arrived in a gloomy chanting of litanies through the streets, followed by one of Savonarola's gloomier sermons. For two solid hours the puny visionary monk stood in the pulpit of the cathedral, crucifix in hand, filling the immense and crowded church with the clamors of his discontent.

Nearly six months had passed since the Florentines had purged themselves of the satanic Medici tyranny; for nearly six months they had embraced the ways of the Lord; nearly six months ago he, unworthy as he was, had been chosen by the Almighty to lead them in the path of virtue. Yet, incredible as it sounded, there still were many among them who longed for the old sinful days.

Yes, there still were men vile enough to plot for the return of the Medici. It was the authorities' God-given duty to ferret out these traitors, these minions of Satan, and bring them to justice. Without mercy they should be put to death.

Do injustice, I tell you. . . . Off with their heads! Even were they the most prominent citizens, off, I say, with their heads!*

Despite the Florentines' predilection for sin and disregard for virtue, God's love for them was so great that He had communicated to him — unworthy as he was — His wish to have His own son govern them in person. No other population in the world had ever had had such unparalleled honor!

* This quotation and all subsequent ones are taken from Savonarola's sermons which were jotted down by a certain Lorenzo Violi, a notary by profession, who sat directly under the pulpit and transcribed them in a shorthand of his own as they were being pronounced.

Well, O Florence, God is willing to satisfy thee and give thee a head, a King to govern thee. This King is Christ. The Lord will govern thee Himself, if thou consent, O Florence. Jesus who is the king of the universe hath willed to become thy King in particular. Wilt thou have Him for thy King?

Dutifully, the crowd shouted back, "*Evviva il Cristo, il nostro Re!* — "Long live Christ, our King!""

As he turned the hourglass on the railing of the pulpit, he ran his glowing eyes over the faces lifted to him. This was what he lived for, the sight of these thousands of spellbound people who had placed their trust in him. Yes, he still had them in the palm of his hand. They still would do his bidding.

Reassured, he traced a large sign of the cross in the air and sent them back to their homes.

Lisa, who had been sitting in the garden, enjoying the early spring sunshine, heard the pealing of bells that announced the end of the service. Resting her sewing in her lap, she waited for Giocondo's return from the cathedral.

Idly, her eyes ran over the garden. This was the feature of Casa Giocondo she liked best. Its tidy flower beds and well-tended lawn were surrounded by a colonnaded gallery which made lovely circular shadows on the wall of the house. A few trees were already sprouting buds. Two cypresses reflected themselves in a blue-tiled pond, in the center of which a terracotta cherub dripped water.

As she saw her husband walking towards her she rose to curtsy but he signaled her to remain seated.

"And what did the holy friar have to say?" she asked, as Giocondo eased himself into a large wicker chair at her side.

"Apparently, we are still mired in sin," he replied with a well-feigned expression of dismay, "and a source of disappointment to our saintly leader. Six months after he has taken our destinies in hand, we are still wallowing in greed and debauchery. Some of us even regret the removal of the Medici tyrants. But everything is going to change, for he has had another vision in which God has informed him that, henceforth, His own Son would be king of Florence."

Suddenly, the banter went out of his voice.

"It is incredible that crowds still believe in this nonsense. How long will it take them to realize that their holy friar is a self-deluded, power-hungry fanatic tottering on the brink of insanity? Oh well, enough of that."

His good, plain face relaxed into a large grin.

"Let's speak about you, gentle wife. I believe it is time for us to move to the country."

Her pregnancy was becoming noticeable. Soon she would have to take to her bed. It would be unwise for her to go on doing the marketing or running about the house.

"You need rest and privacy," he said in conclusion.

He really was a kindly, considerate man, she thought. "I am at your command, noble husband."

"Not a command," he protested with a deprecatory gesture, "merely a suggestion. Turn it in your mind and see if you agree with it."

"I wholly agree with it. My only reservation is whether we may find a suitable midwife in the country."

He had thought of that, he said, and made arrangements for her *levatrice* to come and visit her once a week. Fortunately, the Giocondo villa was located at Settignano, a short distance from town. Later, when the time of confinement was at hand, the woman had agreed to live in the house in order to be with Lisa at any hour of the day or night.

Once again she was touched by his solicitude. Camilla had been right: he was a good man.

The following week they moved to the country.

The Giocondo villa was a squat, unpretentious building among old oaks and sycamores. Neither Giocondo nor his father who had built it had felt the need of adding one of those spiraling entrance staircases or some antique marble statuary — usually forgeries — at various places in the garden, as was the fashion among neighboring villas.

Plain as it was, the house had charm and Lisa liked it at once. The furniture was of hand-hewn, highly polished walnut. A few good paintings of religious scenes hung in the rooms. With surprise she discovered a *spinettino*.

"My sister Agnola used to play it," said Giocondo. "She was very fond of music."

Lisa's room (for here, also, she had her own room) opened on a balustraded terrace. There she spent much of the day, reclining on a lounge chair, listening to the screeching of grasshoppers which reminded her of Tithonus and Aurora, smiling at the laughter of Meo playing in the garden with Tessa.

From her chair she could see the outline of the forest where she and Giuliano had followed the cardinal's hunt less than a year ago. Once again, her mind returned to the hours they had spent lying side by side, kissing and caressing, while in the distance could still be heard the sound of hunting horns. But already the remembrance had lost some of its sharpness, growing blurred, almost unreal. At times, she could have sworn it had never happened at all.

And so the spring of 1495 went by, drowsy with eroding memories, vague regrets, and apprehension about the future. She was not yet sixteen and it seemed that her life had come to an end. She dozed and daydreamed in her chair, tried to welcome in her heart the child who had shattered her existence.

Time moved so slowly that she actually longed for the return of Giocondo at sunset. He would sit next to her, tell her what went on at the mill or in town – or in Naples where the Great Crusader had made another of his grand entrances in his plumed helmet under a canopy of blue velvet.

He had arrived on 22 February, at four o'clock in the afternoon, with the population shouting *"Francia!"* The Aragon king had fled from the palace two days before, but his artillery still held the surrounding hill and sprinkled the town with projectiles during the entrance ceremony.

The following morning a huge stone projectile crashed through the roof of a church during a Te Deum thanksgiving service, killing the organist, several choristers, and the officiant bishop. This went on for several days. Pedestrians were slaughtered while chatting on public squares, housewives while cooking lasagne, lovers while making love. It took Charles another three weeks to silence the Aragon batteries.

Then, just as he was about to celebrate this new victory, he came down with the measles.

As in Asti, laurel leaves were burned in his room, filling it with smoke. The bone of Saint Denis was set up by his bed. Once again, his physician peered at him from the doorway. Meanwhile, Charles scratched himself to distraction. Piteously, he wept through his bulbous blue eyes, now inflamed with conjunctivitis.

He vowed to lead a saintly life, and recovered. Four days later he was back on his spindly legs, alert and full of zest.

Spring was descending upon Naples. The sky was turquoise blue; the bay gold-sequined with sunshine. In the gardens of the royal palace, oranges hung like small, yellow balloons in the dark green foliage of the trees. Nights were fragrant with the perfume of flowers.

The earth itself seemed to be in ferment, and so were the novices of the Santa Chiara Convent. They opened to Charles like a parched land to a long-awaited rain.

Throughout April, Italy resounded with the echoes of his Neapolitan revels. There were badminton games, tournaments, hunting parties, suppers in the lantern-lit royal gardens at which comely serving wenches officiated, wearing only earrings and smiles. Between courses, they disappeared with guests into thickets.

Charles felt he had landed in heaven. He was twenty-four, at the peak of his sexual powers. Like a lascivious bee, he shuttled from girl to girl. After the Santa Chiara novices, it was the turn of the ladies of the former Aragon court to lie on his rose-spattered bed.

Dimly he sensed that time was short. As usual, he was without funds. His unpaid mercenaries compensated themselves by looting residences and churches. The population retaliated by stabbing or clubbing the invaders.

One day the dowager duchess of Malfi presented to His Majesty her daughter Leonora, and Charles drooled as he had never drooled before.

Leonora was seventeen and ravishing, an incomparable horsewoman. The monarch gasped at the things she could do on a horse; in bed, she was, if possible, even more spectacular. Soon, he thought only of her. She, in turn, thought only of her domain of Celano which he had appropriated and casually given to one of his courtiers. Between bouts of amorousness, she got it back.

And then, suddenly, disaster struck.

A mysterious, repulsive disease appeared among his troops like a galloping plague. It manifested itself in the form of purpulent pustules in the armpits and the groin. The ravages were frightful to behold. Some men lost their noses; others their lips or their toes. Occasionally, the stem of their manhood dropped to the ground like a rotten fruit. Army doctors declared themselves helpless. This was the first recorded appearance of syphilis in Europe. Its origins are still unknown, but no illness has received so many names. Among them, the Neapolitan disease, the French disease, the German disease, the Spanish itch, Venus's kick, Job's sickness, the Indian complaint, the great pox. Mortality was appalling. Of the 8,000 Swiss mercenaries in the French army, only 180 returned to their mountains.

At the same time, Charles learned that Ludovico Sforza, his former "cousin," and several other Italian rulers, had raised a powerful army which threatened to encircle him in his paradise. Already a Spanish fleet had landed in Calabria and was nibbling at his beautiful kingdom. His general staff, as well as Cardinal Briconnet, pleaded with him to return home while he still had a chance to do so.

Reluctantly, he agreed. Just then, it occurred to him it would look well to have himself crowned king of Naples in Naples. He sent an urgent message to his good friend the pope, asking for a brief of investiture. The pontiff did not even trouble to acknowledge his request. Undaunted, the Little King had himself crowned king of Naples once again, this time to the chimes of the Neapolitan churches.

The next day he presided over a staff meeting, left a garrison of 10,000 men to defend his capital, bid an affectionate goodbye to the Santa Chiara novices, whose portraits he had had painted during his sojourn and was taking home with him. The girls as well as the mother superior wept as he trotted away. He spent a last night of passion with Leonora who surpassed herself on this occasion. At sunrise, she gave him a last exhausted kiss, helped him into his armor, and watched him clipclop out of the royal palace. This done, she prepared to rejoin her husband who was awaiting her at their country estate.

On 20 May 1495, three months after his entrance, Charles started on the long trek northward, followed by the tattered and diseased remains of his once-powerful army, seventy cannons, and five thousand mules laden with plunder, the portraits of his mistresses, crates of oranges, his crown, and the bone of Saint Denis.

The day before, the French fleet had sailed home with the admirable bronze doors of the royal palace and other works of art valued at more than 1,000,000 gold florins, as well as "three hundred beautiful women, including several nuns." The fleet was captured by the Genoese in the Bay of Rapallo. Both loot and women were returned to Naples.

It was a piteous cortege that snailed its way up the Italian peninsula under a broiling summer sun. No longer did farmers wave their straw hats; no longer did their wives blow kisses to the returning invaders. Stragglers died, unattended, on dusty country roads.

On 4 July, for the first and only time, at three o'clock in the afternoon, Charles and his 9,000 worn-out men faced 30,000 fresh Italian troops across the Taro River, swollen by a diluvian rain the night before.

Before giving the signal to ford the stream, the Little King raised himself in his stirrups, unsheathed his sword, and thus addressed his staff: "Gentlemen, they are many times as many as we are, but God loves the French. With His help, I shall take you home."

He fought like a lion. Too shortsighted to see the enemy, too brainless to be afraid, he spurred his horse in the melee, killed a few people, had the visor of his helmet slashed off by a saber blow, and was not even wounded. That day, the drooling nitwit behaved like a knight of the medieval romances which had enthralled his sickly childhood.

The Battle of Fornovo lasted fifteen minutes and caused four thousand casualties. For a short while the conflict remained undecided. Enormous tactical blunders were committed on both sides. Then the Albanese mercenaries or *stradioti* in the Italian army threw themselves on the king's immense baggage train. Gone were his crown, his coronation mantle, the oranges, the Holy Thorn, the bone of Saint Denis, the portraits of the Santa Chiara novices; but the French had crossed the Taro River.

For the next three weeks Charles dawdled in Piedmont, for he had met an exciting girl by the name of Anna Soleri who had a son by him. He crossed the Alps in late autumn — a miraculous military feat — and finally entered the French city of Lyons to the blare of trumpets and the chimes of bells, bringing with him syphilis and five thousand haggard and gangrenous veterans. Over thirty thousand men lay in shallow graves all over Italy. As to his kingdom of Naples, it had collapsed even before he set foot in France.

"Welcome home, sire," said Queen Anne, when they were alone.

She thanked him for the Piacenza cheeses and asked if he had missed her a little.

"Madame," he lied stoutly, "even in the fray of battles, my thoughts were only of you."

She kissed his pocked cheeks, patiently listened to his spittle-flecked drivel about his great victories and grand entrances in Florence, Rome, Naples. While he prattled on, she reflected that the war had taught him nothing. He was the same irresponsible child he had been when he left. Perhaps this was why she loved him.

"My Neapolitan subjects are praying for my return," he assured her. "Next spring I shall go back to Napoli."

He meant it. Already he was talking about raising fresh troops, and building new ships when his three-year-old son, Orland, died.

At once he set out to sire another heir, for he could not leave his realm without assuring the future of his dynasty. The waiting was endless. He counted the hours. At last in September 1496, the queen brought forth another crown prince who was named François.

He lived five days.

Again and again, Charles returned to the task, but Anne remained barren. A sort of genetic rage descended upon him. He gave her no respite, exhausted himself in vain attempts to produce another dauphin.

Another winter arrived in sweeping gray veils of rain. All over France, peasants huddled around kitchen hearths and said that God was punishing *le roy* for bringing back the foul "Neapolitan disease."

Finally, Charles accepted defeat. His war projects receded into a dim and ever more improbable future. Although not yet twenty-seven, his youth was ebbing away. On the top of his head, his pate showed through his thin russet hair. Soon he would be bald. He felt old and tired. Even the act of love had lost much of its magic. Like Tithonus, he lived on memories.

As the year 1497 grew near and the queen showed no sign of pregnancy, the Little King sank into despondency. He spent much time in his room, watching rivulets of rain trickle down the window panes.

"In Napoli the sun must be shining," he would sigh. "Oh, Napoli!"

But in his heart he knew he would never see Napoli again.

It was now a little over two years since Lisa had become Giocondo's wife.

At the time of the Battle of Fornovo, in July 1495, she had given birth to a daughter who had been named Andoca and lived only one day, less than a day. She had arrived in mid-morning when Giocondo had already left for the mill and she was dead at sunset when he returned. She had breathed long enough to be anointed by the village priest and therefore would go to heaven.

She had been buried that same evening in the Settignano without any ceremonies.

Her time on earth had been too brief for Lisa to mourn her long. It almost seemed as though she had never lived at all. Poor little Andoca, she must have known she was the fruit of an errant hour and really did not belong in the Giocondo household. No doubt she was happier in the heavenly nursery under the Madonna's loving eye.

Two weeks later it occurred to her — suddenly, as she was musing on her terrace — that her marriage had lost its purpose. It had been intended to provide a name and a home for the forthcoming child. Now, the *bimba* was dead and in no need of either.

"Meanwhile," she thought bitterly, "I remain married."

It did not seem fair. Was she condemned, at sixteen, to spend the rest of her life bound to a kindly, but aging and unhandsome man for whom she felt only gratitude, an amiable stranger who kissed her hand on the threshold of her bedroom?

"Mind you," she confided to Tessa, "I am delighted we sleep apart, but nevertheless it is rather humiliating. It makes me feel unwanted. What was the use of all those massages you gave me, if I can't even kindle a gleam of covetousness in his eyes?"

"Last year you dreaded he might touch you."

"Last year things were different."

She had then been with child and had appreciated his restraint. Now she was slender again and pleasing to the eye. At least she thought so, and she would have appreciated some confirmation, even from her husband. Instead, he continued to look at her as though she were his daughter.

"I don't think you know what you want," said Tessa.

Hotly Lisa launched into a tirade from which it became clear that she would have liked Giocondo to make advances to her so that she might have the opportunity of rejecting them.

"Perhaps he knows what you have in mind," chuckled the slave.

It was no use trying to make her understand: she was too old, too simple-minded, without expertise in matters of love and the agonies of youth. Yet the problem left her no peace. She kept at it, like a dog at a bone.

She bathed in self-pity. Here she was, a desirable young woman, at the peak of her beauty, married to a man who did not even look at her. She calculated that by the time she was twenty, in four years, she would wither into a shriveled-up old hag, like Sister Perpetua, from lack of emotional and sexual fulfillment.

One day it suddenly seemed clear to her that her husband's restraint might be due to impotence. After all, he was past thirty-five, on the brink of old age, drained out by two previous wives. Thereafter, she looked upon him with a mixture of scorn and compassion.

It made her feel a little better, but not for long. Was she going to spend a lifetime with a man bereft of his manhood, a vertical corpse, you might say? She sought solace in a whirl of domestic activities. She prodded servants into endless waxing and polishing. No speck of dust escaped her attention. Housemaids and kitchen wenches trembled at her approach.

The spring of 1496 churned her inner turmoil. In dreams, handsome and muscular young men in skintight hose drifted slowly across the screen of her mind. In contrast to Giocondo, they grew taut with desire at the sight of her. They smiled at her and she smiled back at them. They engaged in amatory bouts from which she awoke panting and momentarily relieved.

The situation was becoming serious. Sleep no longer brought her peace. The ferment of spring quickened her pulse, brought sudden flushes to her cheeks. She was ripe for temptation.

It came one morning as she sat in the garden of Casa Giocondo spinning wool, a task that required almost no mental concentration. Her husband had gone to the mill, like the good, plodding, successful silk merchant he was. And here she was, with taut nerves and tension in her loins, facing another empty, restless day.

It was then that Satan whispered in her ear that she should consider a lover. At first, the thought made her gasp, but she soon overcame her qualms. Her health, Satan proceeded in a soft hiss, required it, as well as her peace of mind. Her youthful womanhood could not be indefinitely denied.

Something would have to be done, and she was ready to do it. Since Giocondo had married her out of pity and moreover was too old and feeble to provide the fulfillment she was entitled to, he certainly would not object to her seeking outside the house what she did not find in it.

Needless to say, she would be discretion itself. Her caution would be equaled only by her cunning. No one, absolutely no one, must suspect her infidelities. She would continue to be a model housewife, a delightful companion, a perfect mother to her stepson. In short, her unfaithfulness would save her marriage.

There remained only the problem of finding a handsome, virile, discreet, refined young man, the kind that appeared in her dreams. As the days of social functions and dancing festivities were past, churches were about the only places where men and women still convened. "Waiting-one's-turn-to-confession" was about the only custom that had survived from the good old, sinful Medici days.

Ladies arrived accompanied by their maids or women slaves carrying elegant stools. They gathered around coal *braseros* for warmth and a bit of gossip. Some chose secluded spots and entertained their suitors while nibbling candies. Peals of gurgling laughter rose from behind the statues of saints.

And so one June afternoon Lisa went to the cathedral, rented a chair and pew, and, opening her prayer book, pretended to read it. Through half-closed lids, her eyes swiveled back and forth over a number of kneeling young men waiting to confess their sins. Soon, several intercepted her glances and responded with meaningful winks and furtive smiles.

Alas, none of them appealed to her. Only one caught her fancy. He had lovely curly hair and a full red mouth, but the fool kept his nose in his prayer book.

She returned home in a dispirited mood.

It was not as easy to sin as it seemed, she brooded, as she neared the Giocondo house. Perhaps this was why so many women remained virtuous.

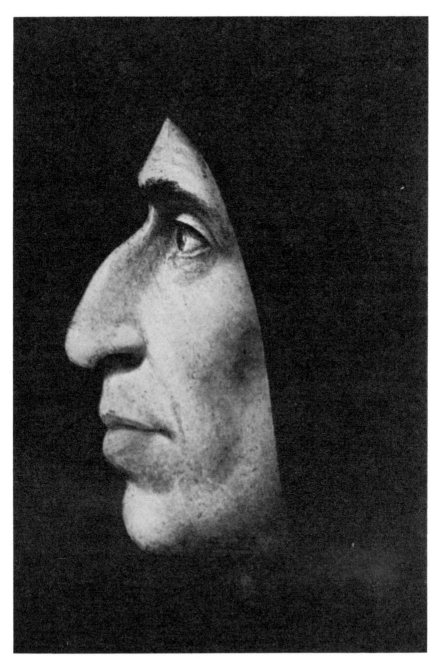

Savonarola by Fra Bartolommeo, *c.* 1498. *Courtesy of Museo San Marco, Florence.*

By God Possessed

 Lisa spent a troubled summer in Settignano, finding comfort only in the games she played with Bartolommeo. He was four and a half and called her "Mamma," and now that Andoca was dead, he filled her whole heart.

For her eighteenth birthday, Giocondo gave her a beautifully wrought gold chain which she twirled between the plaits of her bun. It was another of his delicate gestures that pleased her, yet increased her confusion. She had about given up trying to understand him or what to make of him. He could be so kind, yet so distant. There were times when she would have liked to cuddle up to him and say she really did not mind that he was old and not handsome. She only wished he would put his arm around her as she had seen him do once at "The Farm" with Camilla.

Another thing had come to her notice and this, also, added to her perplexity. One Sunday morning, as she was strolling through the garden, she had caught sight of him, bare-chested, axing down a tree. Never had she seen such a broad torso. Powerful muscles rippled in his sweat-glistening arms. And not an ounce of fat on him. A bull of a man, that's what he was.

The incident had made a deep impression on her. Instantly, her convenient theory of the feeble, impotent fossil had collapsed. Clearly, some thirty-six-year-old men could still swing an axe and he was one of them. It also occurred to her that his two previous wives had died in childbirth, which proved he was perfectly able to perform his conjugal duty. Then his reserve towards her could only derive from a total unresponsiveness to her charms.

"I simply don't appeal to him," she said to Tessa.

Instead of ingratiating herself towards him, she gave him icy glances, frosty smiles. The thought of taking a lover recurred to her, if only to show him that other men did not find her repulsive.

Vanity came to her rescue. Rather than admit defeat, she invented a mistress. Why hadn't she thought of it sooner? Yes, he had a mistress: a leech of a woman, jealous, devouringly possessive, who drained him of all manhood and sent him home exhausted, a shell of a man.

She began spying on him, sniffing for some trace of perfume, some revealing blond hair. She found no clue to any love affair and little by little the mistress theory crumbled.

Promptly she contrived another.

His indifference was motivated by cruelty. Beneath his kindly appearance, his gracious attentions, he was a heartless man. Never would he forgive her moment of passion with Giuliano; he would make her pay for her errant hour with a lifetime of chastity. This was the kind of man she had married: merciless, implacable.

What made it still more complicated was that she herself found it difficult to believe in his heartlessness. Now and then she would feel his eyes resting on her, gentle and patient, as though reading her thoughts and waiting for her to make up her mind.

By the time they left Settignano and returned to town, she no longer knew what to think. Through the winter she once again halfheartedly toyed with the idea of taking a lover and finally gave it up. No love affair was possible in the Florence of Savonarola, with everyone informing on everyone.

And so there was nothing to do but hope that the Florentines would finally get tired of the holy friar and chase him out of town. Then social life would return. There would be dancing, festivities, garden parties, and she would have the opportunity to meet some attractive young men.

On that February afternoon she sat by the nursery fire watching Meo humming contentedly to himself and playing in a corner of the room with his Christmas toys.

"Do you realize he will soon be five?" she remarked to Tessa. "How time flies!"

The slave went on mending a pair of the boy's breeches. "Already he is growing out of his clothes. In the spring he will need a new wardrobe."

Lisa turned her head aside and gazed out of the window at the gray afternoon. It had been on an afternoon like this that King Charles had made his entrance in Florence more than two years ago.

Most people had long forgotten about it, but it had remained embedded in her mind. She would never forget standing with her two companions, half-frozen and trying to smile, on the *Trionfo del Giglio,* each of them feebly waving an olive branch.

"What are you thinking about, *bimba mia?*" asked Tessa after a long silence.

"About the day the king entered Florence. Sometimes I wish you had not been there with all those blankets, and you had let me die of cold."

Unexpectedly she added, "It would have been better for everybody."

"What do you mean?" asked Tessa, perplexed.

It was very simple and anyone but Tessa could understand what she meant. "I would have spared much grief and shame to my honored grandparents. Giocondo would not have been forced to marry me. I wouldn't have to live, as I do, without the man I love or without the love of the man I live with."

"How do you know your husband does not love you?"

The reply came in a hot spurt of words. "Because he never says he does, because he never fondles me, never takes me in his arms, as he used to do with Camilla. He hates me, I can see it in his eyes."

"He is the kindest man who ever lived and he probably loves you very much. But you never give him a chance to prove it."

"How can you say such a thing!" exclaimed Lisa.

"You always thought the worst of him. At first, you said he had wed you out of pity or to vent his lust on you, or to please your honored grandfather. Now he hates you because he doesn't take you in his arms. You give him resentful looks and frosty smiles.

Do you expect him to hand you his heart, so you can stick darts into it?"

"So you too have passed to his side," sniffled Lisa, bursting into tears.

She had always known that some day Tessa would turn against her. Giocondo had probably bribed her into defending him, as he had bribed everyone else in the house to sing his praises. Servants, grooms, kitchen wenches had their mouths full of compliments for "the good master." Nobody knew him as he really was.

And now, her last friend, her own *bambinaia* had turned against her. The woman who knew all her secrets, who had seen her blossom from an infant to a full-grown woman.

"You are only eighteen," Tessa managed to slip in.

Yes, she was still young in years, but life had been so cruel that she had acquired much premature judgment. Now she had lost her last friend, and only the sweet, tender memory of Giuliano remained with her.

"The other day you said you couldn't remember him very well."

"I won't forget him, even if I don't remember him very well."

"How will you do that?"

Lisa thought she caught a gleam of amusement in the slave's eyes, and it made her furious.

"Oh, you don't understand," she flung back. "You never did. I have a good mind to sell you at auction or send you back to Turkey."

Tessa received the news with calm and went on mending Meo's breeches. Many years before Mariotto had freed her and given her enough money to start a new life in her native land. She had remained in Florence out of devotion to the Rucellai family.

"You won't need to," she said, biting off her thread. "I'll start packing tomorrow."

"You'll do nothing of the kind," snapped Lisa. "Your place is here, with us."

Now she berated Tessa for her lack of loyalty. How could she talk about going to Turkey when Meo needed her?

"And I need you."

She admitted having been tense, confused, restless in the past two years. Sometimes she even said things she did not mean; it was up to Tessa to guess when she meant what she said and when she didn't. "And I want no more talk about Turkey."

She made her swear she would never mention Turkey again, and dutifully Tessa swore.

"Now," she smiled, "you'd better go and wash your face. The 'terrible' master will soon be here for supper and you don't want him to see you with red and puffy eyes, do you?"

Lisa sprang to her feet, kissed Tessa's cheek, and ran to her room.

She was waiting in the courtyard when he returned from the mill.

"God's grace," she curtsied, as he walked towards her.

During the supper it began to rain, and she asked, "Do you really have to go to that evening sermon?"

He nodded resignedly. "I don't feel like it, but I'd better go. The friar's police watch for the men who do not attend, and we have to be more prudent than most."

Savonarola's private police, or sacred militia as it was called, had been one of his most effective instruments. It was composed of strapping young ruffians, clad in white shirts, who went about making sure that the monk's decrees were strictly enforced. On his orders, they had herded the local harlots and led them out of the city gates to fend for themselves. They also had attended to the expulsion of the "God-hating Hebraic sect." They had sacked Jewish *bottegas*, desecrated synagogues, expelled Jewish families from Florence, where they had lived peacefully for generations.

"I thank you for your concern," he went on, "but the reign of 'the holy friar' will not last much longer. He is losing ground every day. People are getting tired of him, his visions, his prophecies which turn out to be wrong."

Two things had struck a crippling blow to Savonarola's popularity.

Time and again he had proclaimed that "the Almighty Himself

had led across the Alps the Great Redeemer, the new Cyrus, by the bridle of his horse" for the express purpose of removing the infamous Pope Alexander from his throne. But "the Great Redeemer" had become a great friend of the corrupt pontiff. Savonarola's unfulfilled predictions had shaken the faith of many of his followers.

The Pisa war had brought another flagrant refutation of his prophetic powers.

Of all the absurd episodes of the French invasion, the Pisa war against Florence had been the most absurd, as well as the most tragic. It was due to Charles's ignorance of the Italian language and the uncontrollable trembling of his head.

On his march to Florence he had stopped to visit the City of the Leaning Tower, a tourist curiosity even then. After staring shortsightedly at the tower and wondering aloud how it managed to stand up, he had installed himself in the Medici Palace along the Arno and ordered a meal, for the morning ride had sharpened his appetite.

He was tearing his way through a breast of roast pheasant when his chamberlain had announced that a delegation of the town's prettiest ladies solicited the honor of an audience. Believing they merely wanted to feast their eyes on him, Charles had graciously acquiesced. Whereupon the lovely petitioners, dressed in their civic spirit and little else, had entered the room and fallen to their knees.

With clasped hands and bare, imploring arms, they had beseeched the glorious monarch to free them from the Florentine yoke and make Pisa a French city.

Charles, who had no idea what they were talking about, kept on nodding while continuing to eat. Interpreting his palsied motion as the granting of their request, the ladies had risen to their feet, blown kisses to the nodding nitwit and filed out of the room.

On that 10 November 1494, at the very moment when the Medici were being driven out of Florence, the Florentine regime was ending in Pisa. The marble lion which symbolized the Signoria's suzerainty was toppled from its pedestal and thrown into the river. The Florentine garrison abandoned its fortress and scurried out of the city, followed by the governor and other Florentine officials.

Even when Charles had returned to France with his diseased army, the Pisans had refused to return to their Florentine chains and declared war on Florence.

It was then that Savonarola had committed his second blunder. God had appeared to him, as He often did, and assured him in excellent Italian of the imminent conclusion of the conflict. On the strength of this heavenly revelation, the poor self-deluded prophet had rushed to his pulpit and made his fatal prediction: "I tell you this cloud will soon vanish and rain elsewhere. I pledge you my cloak on it."

That had been over five years ago, and on that February evening as Giocondo, lantern in hand, was making his way to the cathedral, the war was still on, and Savonarola's prophecy remained unfulfilled.

When the merchant entered the church, the preacher already stood in the pulpit, high above the crowd: a short, hooded figure of a man with a black cloak over his white Dominican habit, head bent and hands joined in prayer.

Dramatically, he pulled back his cowl and revealed his grotesque and tragic face. Savonarola was indeed ugly and puny-chested, with a low brow and an enormous, curved nose that plunged over thick and moist lips. His ugliness was startling, unforgettable, and made still more striking by glowing, deeply recessed eyes which could be those of a madman or a saint.

From early childhood, Girolamo Savonarola had been morbidly aware of his ugliness. It had poisoned his youth, embittered and unhinged his mind, and finally launched him on his tormented and violent life.

He had been born in Ferrara of poor but genteel parents. His grandfather had been private physician to the local sovereign lord: a position of prestige more than financial reward, the duke making a point never to pay his doctor.

Even as a boy, little Girolamo had been made aware of his ugli-

ness by the sarcasms of his classmates. He had asked his grandfather why had God made him so ill-looking. The pious old man
had replied that God had wanted to spare him the temptations of
comeliness, the flatteries of men, the smiles of women, so that he
might devote his whole heart to His service.

At sixteen, Girolamo was taken to a function at the ducal
palace. Quickly he noticed that girls winced at his approach and
young men jeered behind his back. On his return home, his
wretchedness had vented itself out in a poem of savage fury.
Those shapely girls and handsome boys who had cringed or
laughed at the sight of him, they soon would die. Their rotten
carcasses would crawl with maggots and their souls burn in hell.

The death of his grandfather increased his inner turmoil and
deepened his solitude. Although he lived with his parents, he had
little rapport with them. They wanted him to become a doctor
and help with the family's budget, but he had no thought of a
career. Why study for a profession when God had some lofty
mission for him? He prayed in his room, read the Bible until he
knew it by heart, and waited for God's sign.

Yet, on one occasion, he wavered.

A lovely Florentine girl, Laudomia Strozzi, came to live across
the street. From his room he could see her undress and bathe.
Dry-throated from desire, he gorged his sensuality with the sight
of her glistening body as she rose from the wooden tub. One day,
unable to control himself, he had cried out his love for her. She
had laughed, and the sound of her laughter never ceased ringing
in his ears.

This episode decided his fate. It was the sign that the world had
no room for him and God wanted his whole heart for Himself,
just as his grandfather had said.

One morning when his parents were out of town, he left home
and walked the sixty miles to Bologna where he entered the local
Dominican monastery. When his mother learned of this, she
wrote pleading for his return. In reply, he sent her a pamphlet of
his composition, "The Contempt of the World," together with
a long lecture on "the iniquities of men, the lusts, adulteries, rob-
beries, pride, idolatry and cruel blasphemies."

When his father joined his commands to her entreaties, Girolamo grew angry. What did he care if money was scarce at home?
Didn't they understand he had more important things to worry
about than the family's fortunes? Didn't they understand that
God had chosen him, unworthy as he was, to save thousands of
souls from eternal perdition?

His quill trembled as he wrote:

Why do you weep, you blind fools? Why do you lament and murmur, you who lie in darkness? What can I say to you if you grieve,
but that you are my chief enemies and I can only say *"Discedite a me!*
. . . Get ye behind me!"

After that they stopped writing and he now could devote himself to the pursuit of perfection. He flogged himself without
mercy, fasted so severely that he brought upon himself the stomach ailment that plagued his last years. He volunteered for the
most menial tasks, sang hymns while cleaning the monastery's
latrines. His piety awed his fellow novices. When he finally became a priest, he was already regarded as a saint.

His superiors, however, did not want saints: they wanted
preachers. Dominicans went out into the world to spread the
word of God. Preaching was their main function, and the reason
why Savonarola had chosen this order. His God-given mission, he
was sure, was to convert multitudes through his sermons.

He was given oratory lessons, taught the dramatic gestures, the
uprolled glances, the sighs, the gasps, the coaxing whispers and
thunderous clamors that constituted church eloquence in those
days. Earnestly, he practiced in his cell, preached to the crucifix
on the wall.

His efforts came to naught. His voice was tremulous and high-
pitched. In the pulpit he sounded as ridiculous as he looked.
When he was sent to preach in his native Ferrara, people laughed
in church. In 1482, when he was thirty, he preached a Lenten
season in San Lorenzo Church and lulled his listeners to sleep. By
the end of the season, his audience had dwindled to twenty-five.

His superiors agreed that he might be a saint, but a preacher he wasn't. Recalled to his Bologna monastery, he was appointed Bible teacher to the novices. In emergencies, he would be sent to some remote, snow-buried Apennine hamlet or sun-baked village in Lombardy. His absences grew longer, but no one seemed to miss him at the *convento*. Gradually, he was left to shift for himself and became a wandering monk.

For years he roamed through northern and central Italy in his frayed and dusty black-and-white robes, barefoot and staff in hand, living from the nuts and berries he garnered along the way, drinking from brooks, sleeping in haylofts or in the fields under the stars.

On Sundays, he preached in rustic chapels to handfuls of leather-skinned peasants and their gaunt, black-shawled wives. He talked to them in a way they understood, told them how Il Cristo had roved about the countryside in a torn and dusty robe, just like his, and preached to poor and weary *villani*, just like themselves. They, too, had been exploited by greedy, fat-bellied landowners who wore gold rings on their thumbs and roistered in their villas while their farmers toiled and sweated in the fields under a broiling sun.

But look what had happened! Now the poor farmers were in heaven, eating bellyfuls of pasta or eels in garlic sauce, taking long siestas under shady trees, singing and dancing around bonfires after supper. And the *padroni?* Well, they were writhing in hell, pitchforked into boiling cauldrons by red-horned devils.

After the service his listeners would invite him to share their meal, eat their chestnut bread. They would ask him to bless their children. At sunset they would make a pad of straw on the floor of the kitchen for him and he would sleep with the family. At dawn he would take his leave and start on another trek through dust or snow to some other village, another handful of peasants.

Gradually he was unlearning the gasps, the sighs, the upward glances of the oratory lessons. Unbeknown to himself, he was forging a preaching style of his own: plain, colloquial, vehement, effective. The range of his voice had increased. From thin and rasping, it had become velvet-soft or thunder-loud, at will.

In April 1490, he received a message from the Dominican authorities ordering him to proceed back to Florence. By a tragic irony, the request for his transfer to Florence had come from Lorenzo de'Medici, at the prayer of his friend and country neighbor, Pico della Mirandola.

He declined a horse-drawn cart a farmer had offered him and set out on his journey barefoot and staff in hand. One month later, on a lovely May morning full of skating swallows and chiming bells, he stood atop one of the hills surrounding Florence.

There she lay before him, that cruel City of Flowers where people had dozed at his sermons eight years before. God was giving him a second chance to fulfill His mission and wrench the Florentines from the claws of Satan. He would turn the City of Sin into a beacon of virtue, a model for the world to copy. This time, he would not fail.

Success had come to him almost at once. Soon the monastery's chapel became too small to contain the throng of his listeners. Less than a year after his arrival, he was given the pulpit of the cathedral. Four months later, in July 1491, he was elected prior of the San Marco congregation. From a lowly friar, he now had grown into an ecclesiastic personage of considerable importance.

He had not even thanked Lorenzo de'Medici for bringing him back to Florence. The man who had brutally cast aside his imploring parents did not suffer from an excess of gratitude. In the pulpit of the cathedral, he began to attack Lorenzo as a political tyrant, a lover of female flesh, a collector of indecent paintings and heathenish Greek statues. As long as the population remained devoted to this evil man, God would deny prosperity to Florence.

And so he poisoned Lorenzo's last months on earth, undermining his regime and that of his son Piero. He welcomed rapturously the Great Crusader in Italy and did his best to defeat Piero's policy of complete neutrality. With the expulsion of the Medici brothers, the Holy Friar became the undisputed master of Florence.

For three years the Republic of the Red Lily belonged to him. He gave her a new political constitution, which he presented as the work of God Himself and which proved cumbersome and impractical. The expulsion of the local courtesans had been followed by that of the Jews. Yet prosperity remained as elusive as ever. His private police, or sacred militia, encouraged people to inform against their neighbors. King Christ reigned over a city as rotten as in the days of the Medici — and much less happy.

During the sojourn of King Charles in Florence, Savonarola had occupied the limelight. Crucifix in hand, he had harangued the Little King to distraction until Charles had finally turned his back on the friar and waddled away.

But neither Savonarola's visions nor his prophecies seemed to improve the economic situation. The Florentines began to feel that their saintly leader was making them ridiculous in the eyes of the world. As for Savonarola, he sensed that the population was escaping from his grasp. At times he even wondered if, by chance, God was not making sport of him and his famous visions did not come from Satan himself.

Giocondo was struck by the look of exhaustion in the preacher's eyes. He was reputed to sleep only three hours and spend the rest of the night in prayer. An expression of despair spread over his gaunt, ugly face. He looked like a man who seemed to have reached the end of his endurance.

Yet his first words were of bitter reproach. He berated his listeners for their lack of gratitude. Once again he reminded them of his services at the time of the French occupation. It was he who had averted a conflict between the population and the barbarians; he who had held back the king's hand from giving the signal to open fire on the population.

Believe me, O Florence, that much blood was to have been shed . . .

After such meritorious services, he could have expected some love in return, some small appreciation. They might have given him their hearts or at least their trust. But, no! They had run to him in the hours of danger, they had filled churches with their laments and their tears. But, as soon as the danger was gone, they had forgotten about him or their fears.

O ungrateful people, you are like the crow in the belfry. When it first hears the bell, it takes fright and flies away. But when it has grown used to it, ring as you will, it sits on the bell and will not stir.

He lashed at everything and everybody: women — "those lumps of meat with eyes" — who still continued to display their nonexistent charms and spent fortunes on lotions of asses' milk for their complexion; men who still engaged in card games, lent money at usurious rates and coveted their neighbors' wives. He railed at artists for painting the Virgin in rich garments, like a courtesan.

I tell you she was robed like a begger. You, painters, do great harm. If you knew, as I do, the evil you breed, you would desist . . .

He then considered the subject of the forthcoming carnival which had Italy buzzing with activity. The spectacle of those men spending countless hours in the preparation of these brief and sinful revels sent him into transports of lamentation which bordered on incoherence.

Weep, O my heart! Weep, O my soul! Weep, O my eyes! Weep with me, great and small, women and men, sinners and just, rich and poor, religious and lay! Weep, Heavens! Weep, O stars! O Lord, I can bear it no longer! Sleep no longer on the cross, O Master! Put forth Your hand and prove Your power! O Lord, consider Your heart! Consider Your bowels! Consider Your compassion! Pity, pity, O my God!

He had lost the robust, sinewy oratory he had brought back from his wandering years and now spoke in whining jeremiads. The earthy, colloquial preacher to the peasants of Romagna and Lombardy had turned into a tiresome, verbal hemophiliac.

With the same repetitious, exclamatory grandiloquence he ranted against "the harlot Church," the cardinals with their racing stables, "their concubines or their boys," the lecherous Vatican prelates and, without yet daring to identify him by name, the pontiff himself. All those corrupt clerics jubilated at the approach of the Roman carnival, the most licentious in the whole of Italy.

But, he proceeded in a swelling voice, the Florentines would shun carnival and its rowdy frolics. They would turn these luciferan revels into pious festivals. Instead of the usual cortege of *trionfi*, buffoons and obscene masquerades, they would give the world the spectacle of wholesome, Christian merrymaking.

The zealous boys of the sacred militia would go from house to house collecting gold-encrusted toiletries, ivory chess games, indecent paintings, immodest gowns, lewd books, cosmetics, false hair. All such hateful vanities would be heaped into a monumental pyramid, soaked with resin, and set to fire.

This would show the world how the Florentines celebrated carnival.

"He's gone mad," said Giocondo when he finished telling Lisa about the friar's latest inspiration. "Or rather, he does not know what else to invent to rekindle his popularity and make King-Christ government function."

The man who had pitilessly criticized the Medici regime had discovered how difficult it is to govern. Since coming to power, he had tried all sorts of innovations, which were to bring prosperity back to Florence. At first, he had assured the population that things would immediately improve, if they only would stop eating meat. A vegetarian himself, he demonstrated that meat eating was a sure sign of decadence. The result was that he had ruined the town's butchers. Finally, the Butchers' Guild sent a delegation to the holy friar adjuring him to stop his tirades against meat eating — and he had toned them down somewhat.

Then he had turned the artillery of his eloquence on swearing and dice playing. If people would only stop taking the Lord's name in vain and rolling dice for drinks in wineshops, prosperity would bloom again. People no longer swore, no longer played dice, but prosperity did not bloom.

The closing of brothels on Via dei Preti, the expulsion of the local harlots, followed by the banishment of the "God-hating Hebraic sect" had likewise failed to lure the promised prosperity.

"Now we are told that if we burn our vanities," Giocondo went on with a mirthless chuckle, "God will finally be pleased with us and our trade will soar. It would make you laugh, if it were not so sad."

"Do you mean the sacred militia is going to come and search our home?" Lisa asked with alarm.

"I'm afraid it cannot be avoided; but at least we can prepare for it."

Naturally, everything of real value would be carefully hidden or buried in the garden. To avert a minute search of Casa Giocondo, Lisa might collect some silver trinkets, toiletries, perhaps one or two old dresses in a basket, and hand it to the boys of the sacred militia, together with two or three florins as alms to the poor.

As the time of their arrival was not known, she would do well to have a maid or two at the windows to watch for their coming.

"Above all, send a groom for me at the mill as soon as they begin searching houses in the street."

She followed his instructions and was ready when, a few days later, a maid came rushing in with the news that the white-clad boys were going in and out of neighboring houses, emptying bags and baskets into a train of waiting carts.

At once Lisa sent a groom to the mill. "And tell the master to hurry."

They arrived a moment later.

"Long live King Christ!" barked the leader of the troupe. "We've come for your vanities."

She duly handed him the prepared basket, as well as the alms for the poor. But instead of departing, as she hoped, the young rowdy and his companions pushed her aside and scattered through the house. In an instant, they were ransacking every room, pushing maids out of the way, seizing whatever caught their fancy.

With a sudden pang of terror, it crossed her mind that she had not concealed the inkwell her father had brought her from Venice and it still was on her *scrivania*, or writing table. She ran to her sitting room where she found four of the militia boys examining it and about to shove it inside one of the bags they carried.

"Not that!" she cried, snatching the box from the leader's hand. "There's gold on it, and gold is the devil's tool."

"Take anything else you want, but not that."

Threatening, they closed in on her as she retreated across the room. Disheveled, her back to the wall, she clutched the box against her chest when the door was flung open and Giocondo burst in, an awesome figure of wrath.

He seemed to have ten hands and ten feet and they all struck at the same time. He seized the leader by the hair at the back of his head, spun him around, heaved him up in the air and through the doorway. A few slaps and kicks sent the others scurrying for cover. Less than one minute after his intervention, the room was clear of militia boys.

With a sob of relief, Lisa pressed her face against his chest, as he circled a protecting arm around her shoulder.

He had brought with him half a dozen burly mill hands and they had not been idle. Soon the stairs were resounding with the patter of fleeing feet.

A moment later the house was quiet again.

Lisa and her husband spent an anxious evening expecting a retaliatory move from the regular city police. An assault on the boys of the sacred militia could have dire consequences.

The curfew bell rang, and still no one came.

"They probably will come in the morning," he said finally, shoveling ashes over the fire.

As usual, he accompanied her to her room and kissed her hand at the door. She undressed, went to bed, but did not sleep. The incident of the inkbox and Giocondo's intervention returned to her mind.

Indeed, he was a brave and strong man, and tomorrow he would be taken to prison for having saved her and her *babbo*'s inkbox. And now he was spending his last night in bed, alone, counting the hours until they came to fetch him. And what would they do to him? Put him on the rack, brand him with a red-hot iron? How could she leave him like this, without a word of comfort, a gesture of gratitude? . . .

It seemed so heartless that she got out of bed, slipped into a woolen wrapper, and, candle in hand, went to his room.

The searching parties had aroused the public's indignation. So numerous had been the complaints over earrings and necklaces taken forcibly by the militia boys that the city police had been instructed not to retaliate against the citizens who had resisted the depredations of the friar's emissaries. The members of the Signoria were beginning to weary of God's prophet, his white-clad ruffians, and his eccentricities.

Thus, Giocondo was not arrested. On the last night of carnival, he and Lisa were able to mingle with the crowd on Piazza della Signoria to witness the Burning of Vanities.

In the center of the square rose a huge octagonal pyramid of wood on which were piled, tier upon tier, the collected tools of Satan. The boys had done themselves proud. Masks, wigs, immodest dresses, mirrors, cosmetics, indecent paintings, exquisite and costly goldsmiths' artifacts, as well as books of amorous poetry and salacious tales were stacked on each step of the pyramid.

Savonarola, in his white and black cloth, sat in the Loggia dei Lanci surrounded by members of the Signoria and state officials. Once again he was tasting the heady wine of triumph; once again he had forced the Florentines to his will.

He clapped his hands.

At this signal, the white-shirted boys, wearing wreaths of flowers on their heads and chanting hymns, appeared in orderly rows, as a burning rag was flung into the pyramid. The resin crackled; bells pealed and trumpets blared. As the flames crept forward, the San Marco brethren linked hands with the boys and began dancing around the blazing tower. The value of the "vanities" destroyed that night must have been considerable, for a visiting Venetian merchant offered 25,000 gold florins for the lot. His offer was refused and he was burned in effigy.

Instead of rekindling his popularity, the Burning of Vanities dealt Savonarola another blow. He became a laughingstock throughout the Peninsula and it brought much ridicule on the Florentines. It angered the pope; it was resented by rich and poor alike. It increased the vocal opposition to the holy friar. Finally, it planted the seed of doubt about his sanity.

The popular disapproval expressed itself the following month by the election of a Signoria antagonistic to him. It was headed by a seventy-five-year-old venerable merchant, Bernardo del Nero, who had been a close friend of Lorenzo de'Medici.

As the monk's prestige dwindled, his political influence started to crumble.

Several of Savonarola's decrees were ignored or set aside. Blasphemers no longer had their tongues pierced; dice players were no longer flogged. A singing contest was held for the first time on New Year's Day, 1497. A few courtesans stole back into town and were unmolested. The police surveillance of Medicean families was relaxed. The Madonna's street shrines were once again abloom with flowers from lovelorn girls. "King Christ," Florence's personal ruler, was all but ignored.

Lisa shared in the general euphoria. As spring turned the hills green, she often sat in the garden, her face protected from the sun by a wide-brimmed straw hat. While her fingers diligently threaded her iron needle, her thoughts returned to the nocturnal visit she had paid her husband.

Never had a good deed been so richly rewarded. Having given herself out of gratitude (so she assured herself), she had discovered the delights of sex. Her astonishment at Giocondo's virility had only been exceeded by her enchantment at his expertise. For an old man of thirty-seven, Francesco (she no longer called him Giocondo in her mind) had given a splendid account of himself.

By tacit agreement, the one-night visit had turned into a daily custom. It seemed like the natural thing for them to walk to his room, undress, and lay side by side in the same bed. She was enthralled to discover that, like hunger, sex is reborn every day and yesterday's feast is but today's memory.

Her nervousness abated. She felt pleasantly relaxed. Servants now smiled at her approach. Even Tessa remarked on her good spirits.

She was embroidering a handkerchief one morning when the butler informed her that Messer Jacopo de'Gherardini della Rosa solicited the honor of paying his respects.

"Fair cousin," he said, kissing her hand, "it is wonderful to see you again."

"You will never know how much I missed you. But are you sure it is safe for you to come here? The friar —"

"Nobody pays attention to him anymore," he shrugged.

Her pleasure at seeing him kept her silent, her lips parted in an unbelieving smile. It was as though the past had suddenly returned and Giuliano himself stood before her. Memories rushed haphazardly to her mind.

"Remember the day we went to the storyteller and I made you miss your English lesson?" Then, without transition, "You haven't changed at all."

"Did you expect me to be bald and toothless and hobble on a cane? After all, it was less than three years ago that we met at Contessina's."

His words opened another floodgate of memories. The pre-wedding supper . . . her learning about his plans for a diplomatic career . . . her scheme of using him as a substitute for Giuliano . . . Tessa's vehement reproaches . . . It all was part of a world that had vanished and would never return.

"Let's sit down," she said.

She told him of the recent visit of the militia boys and her struggle with them over her father's inkbox. "I don't know what would have happened if my husband hadn't arrived. Shall we ever get rid of that confounded friar?"

"Sooner than you expect," he said gently.

"How do you know?"

His face assumed an inspired expression and he mimicked Savonarola's Ferrarese accent. "I had a vision. The Lord spoke to me, unworthy as I am, and whispered into mine ears, 'I'm getting sick of that chattering monk!' "

He had not changed. "Stop talking nonsense and tell me about your plans."

His hopes of a diplomatic career had evaporated. The fact that his father had been a Medici ambassador had lost him the promised position at the London embassy.

"But changes are sure to come," he went on. "The friar's stupid Burning of Vanities has opened the eyes of many of his supporters. I haven't given up and I still take lessons in the English language."

Meanwhile, he added, he made himself useful as best he could.

"Here is a little thing I brought you from Siena," he said, handing her a small, delicately painted wooden box.

"What were you doing in Siena?"

"I was there on business for my father."

She opened the box and gasped. Neatly coiled on a pillow of purple velvet was a lady's belt made of interlocking gold links and amethyst stones. She could not take her eyes away from it.

"Well, do you like it?" he asked after a long pause.

"I shall wear it at the first festivity we give in this house and we shall dance together."

That evening she told her husband about Jacopo's visit and showed him the belt. The merchant held it before his eyes for a moment.

"It is truly a beautiful thing and you will be able to wear it before long. And by the way, you may visit your friend Contessina if you wish. She is no longer under surveillance."

The next day Lisa hurried to Casa Ridolfi.

The two friends fell into each other's arms. Without effort they recaptured their past intimacy, recalled their happy summer days at Careggi, their whispered confidences in bed at night, their visits to the ladies' bathhouse on Via del Cocomero. Then, after Contessina's wedding, the black days with "the holy friar" in his pulpit, crucifix in hand.

"But God will soon punish him for what he did to my *babbo*," Contessina said, tears coming to her eyes.

Something in her tone caught Lisa's attention. "What do you mean?"

In whispers, Contessina told her about a plot to restore her brother Piero to power. Some of the most important men in Florence were involved in it, and the pope himself looked favorably upon it. At this very moment, Piero was in Siena waiting for the troops which Giuliano was bringing from Rome.

One morning two days later, Lisa was sewing in the garden when she recalled Contessina's confidence. She gave a sudden start and sent for Jacopo.

"Tell him it is most urgent," she said to the groom.

Jacopo arrived shortly afterwards, panting from the run.

"Why did you lie to me?" she snapped, even before he could talk. "I thought we were friends, but you lied to me."

He looked at her through his porcelain-blue eyes, wide and uncomprehending.

"Don't try to look innocent," she sputtered on. "You might deceive someone else, but not me."

"What on earth are you talking about?" he finally managed to say.

Pointing an accusing finger at him, she went on, "You didn't go to Siena on your father's business."

"Why not?"

"Because he has no business in Siena."

"Then why did I go?"

Her voice lowered and her eyes squinted angrily as she stressed every word of her reply. "Because you are involved in that stupid plot."

"What plot?" This with an expression of complete innocence. "I haven't heard of any plot."

"A great liar you are."

"I shouldn't have brought you that belt."

"Don't change the subject. I know everything." She repeated, "Everything."

She told him about her visit to Contessina and her learning of Piero's presence in Siena.

"At the time I thought nothing of it, but a moment ago it suddenly came to my mind that you went there to see him." Her glittering eyes bore into his. "It is true, isn't it?"

Her question hung in mid-air for a few seconds; then slowly he nodded. "I did not want you to know, so you could not be implicated. I was afraid —"

She would not let him finish.

Had he gone mad? Had his brains gone down to his slippers? What did he know about plots and such things? What right had he to risk his life?

"But, fair cousin, I do not risk my life. I merely carry messages."

"And what do you know about carrying messages?"

An impish smile flitted over his freckled face. It did not take much intelligence to carry a letter, and someone had to do it.

"Why you?" Her affection made her vehement. "Other people can carry messages."

"Most of them have wives and children. I have neither, and I want to be of some use."

He had spoken with unconscious nobility and she looked at him, torn between anger and admiration. He was a true Gherardini, one of those brave and foolish men her grandfather had told her about who had risked and occasionally lost their lives for something they believed in.

"Aren't you afraid of being caught and tortured?" The violence had gone out of her voice, only the anxiety remained.

Of course he was afraid sometimes, but not for long. As a rule, there was not even the semblance of danger.

She was not yet reassured. What about his honored parents? Did they know what he was doing? Did his father approve?

"My honored mother does not know," he admitted. "She would imagine things and worry too much."

In turn, his father knew and approved. "He only asks me to be prudent, and that I am."

To avoid suspicion, he usually rode out of town through different city gates. Occasionally, he merely walked across the drawbridge, as though bent on some innocent promenade, exchanging pleasantries with the sentries. Then, half a mile away, at some prearranged spot, he would find a saddled horse and gallop to Siena.

"Last time I crossed the gate disguised as a friar and riding a donkey. I pretended to read a prayer book and kept the cowl low over my face. I even blessed the sentry as I went by."

She knew it was useless trying to make him change his mind. "Be prudent, won't you?" she said softly.

He said he only had two or three more trips to make, as Piero was scheduled to march with his troops before the end of April. He promised to be most cautious and took his leave.

She did not see him for another week, when he appeared, early in the morning, dressed in spurred boots and a long traveling cloak. He apologized for the untimely hour of his visit and explained he was carrying a most important message. It was from the *gonfaloniere*, Bernardo del Nero, urging Piero de'Medici to postpone his march on Florence.

"This is my last trip, and I expect to see Giuliano. Do you wish to send him a note?"

She hesitated.

"Wait," she said and dashed out of the room.

She returned a few moments later with the *santelena* medal Giuliano had given her in the Fiesole olive grove on that memorable October afternoon over two years before.

"It is supposed to protect from dagger and poison," she said placing it on Jacopo's palm. "He may need it more than I shall."

"Anything else?"

She shook her head, leaned forward to kiss his cheek. "Now, go with God, and be careful — for my sake."

The next four days were an eternity of anguish. She burned countless candles before the statue of the Madonna. At night she dreamed of his being captured and tortured and she awoke screaming. She sobbed the whole story to Giocondo, who pressed her gently against his chest and soothed her fears until she finally fell asleep.

Jacopo returned, safe and smiling, one sunny morning as she sat in the garden trying to sew. He had given the medal to Giuliano who had asked a thousand questions about her. "I told him you were in good health and happily married."

As for the plot, he went on, everything was in readiness. Piero and his troops would arrive at the city gate any day now and would be welcomed by the population. Savonarola would be invited to depart and once again Florence would be ruled by a Medici.

Effectively, Piero de'Medici left Siena on the night of 26 April, with 1300 archers and 800 horsemen.

Traveling only under cover of darkness, he hoped to reach Florence without attracting attention, but on the second night of his journey, he and his men were observed by a farmer who galloped to town and warned the Signoria. At once the gates' drawbridges were raised, the ramparts bristled with bowmen. The element of surprise on which Piero had depended was lost.

Moreover, at the precise moment when he came in sight of the city, the sky cracked open in a deluge which lasted the whole day. The population, which was to welcome Lorenzo's son, did not venture out of their houses. By nightfall, rain was still coming down in buckets. With death in his heart, Piero had the trumpets sound retreat.

"If only he had waited a little longer," Giocondo commented, "the people would have begged him to return, as they did his great-grandfather Cosimo. But he could not wait, and his impatience cost him his opportunity. Fortunately, none of the conspirators has been caught, nobody has been hurt."

Although unsuccessful, the attempt to restore the Medici to power achieved what hundreds of Savonarola's tirades against the pope's private life and the corruption of "the harlot Church" had failed to achieve: it finally forced Pope Alexander, the least vindictive of men, to act.

On 13 May he dictated a brief of excommunication against "the babbling monk" as he called Savonarola, and pressed the Fisherman's Ring in the puddle of hot wax at the bottom of the document. Five copies were sent to Florence where they were read at night in the chapels of the town's five most important monasteries before the assembled brethren, standing, lighted tapers in hand, their faces hidden in the cowls of their habits.

To the mournful toll of bells the five priors read the edict of excommunication.

Wherefore we order you, on all festivals and in presence of the people, to declare the said friar, Girolamo Savonarola, excommunicate and to be held such by all men for his failure to obey our admonitions and commands.

Moreover, all persons whatsoever are to be warned they must avoid him as excommunicate and suspected of heresy, under pain of the same penalty.

At this point, the abbots as well as the assembled friars turned their candles upside down to signify the expulsion of Savonarola from the Holy Church.

The following day the papal decree was nailed to the doors of all the churches. In every district, clusters of men and women huddled around scholars who would read and translate the document in plain and familiar terms. With stupor, the listeners looked at one another, unable to believe that the man they called the Holy Friar, the God-inspired prophet, whose voice had filled the cathedral for nearly six years, was now a moral leper, an apostle of the Devil cast out of the Holy Church.

People still talked of nothing else when summer arrived and the Giocondos moved to Settignano, as usual.

Lisa had grown fond of the unpretentious villa with its hand-hewn furniture and waxed tile floor. It resembled her husband, she thought: outwardly plain, but satisfying inside. The servants also liked the relaxed daily routine that left time for games of *bocce* and restful moments in the late afternoon.

Giocondo returned from the mill at sunset, bringing news of the town. Savonarola's excommunication was still the main topic of conversation. Contrary to predictions, the holy friar had meekly obeyed the papal injunction and stopped preaching. He remained incommunicado in his cell in the San Marco Monastery.

"It must be terribly hard for a man like him to be forbidden to preach," Lisa remarked. "He loves so much to talk."

"If he had a flicker of common sense, he would remain silent."

"What would happen if he disobeyed the pope and started preaching again?"

"He would wish he had never been born."

The news from the mill was most comforting. While the wool industry continued to languish, the silk industry was flourishing. Giocondo was expanding his *stabilimento*. But while several of his competitors were turning to the manufacture of silk velvet or plush, he was planning to increase his production of *ciambellotto*, or silk camlet, which promised larger profits.

"Of course," he would muse aloud, "it calls for a large investment and new machinery, but it should bring in a great deal of money."

When he was not thinking about *ciambellotto*, he was already planning Bartolommeo's various apprenticeship stages.

"First, I shall put him with the *conduttori* or sorters of cocoons, then with the *calderai;* then with the —"

"Noble husband," she would smile, "don't you think he is still a little young to begin his apprenticeship? After all, he is only five and I must first teach him how to read and write."

Of course, he retreated hastily, it was still early to make plans, but in a few years Meo would be a strapping young man ready to enter the silk trade. "And I want him to become the best *setaiuolo* in town."

July sped by, as happy time always does. Lisa was content with her life, pleased with her husband. She thanked the Madonna for the felicitous conclusion of the Medici plot. Three months had already passed since it had taken place and already many people had forgotten about it. The police had failed to discover the identity of the conspirators.

Then, one day in August, Giocondo returned to the villa earlier than usual, his face ashen.

"They've arrested Jacopo," he told Lisa.

A certain Lamberto dell'Antrella had revealed the names of the six conspirators. All belonged to the most prominent families. Among them were Contessina's father-in-law, Niccolo Ridolfi; her cousin Lorenzo de'Tornabuoni; Gianozzo Pucci; and even the former head of the Signoria, the old and universally respected merchant Bernardo del Nero, whose sole part in the plot consisted in having warned Piero to postpone his plans. All had been incarcerated in the Bargello prison.

The trial was swift, secret, and merciless. The six men had been condemned to death, and none was allowed to appeal, a right solemnly guaranteed by the constitution.

On 17 August 1497, a star-studded midsummer night, Lisa and her husband stood among the silent spectators who filled the torchlit courtyard of the Bargello prison. Like all the other ladies present, she held a mask before her face to avoid recognition.

The Montanara Bell, which chimed curfew, began to toll. The seventy-five-year-old Bernardo del Nero was the first to enter the courtyard. Barefooted, he walked over the cobbles in a clatter of ankle chains, dressed in a long white shirt. Steadily he walked to the scaffold and gently smiled at the hooded executioner who fell to his knees and asked his forgiveness. The merchant traced the sign of the cross over him and calmly knelt down and placed his head on the block. The double-edged ax descended upon his neck with a hissing sound.

Then it was the turn of Lorenzo de'Tornabuoni, twenty-nine, one of the most handsome men in Florence. He walked, head high, a smile on his proud, aristocratic face. He was followed by Niccolo Ridolfi, Contessina's father-in-law, Giovanni Cambi, and Gianozzo Pucci.

Jacopo was the last.

He had been jolted out of sleep, the wonderful sleep of the young, blinking his blue eyes, as though half awake. In the glow of torches, his hair was flaming orange. Like his companions, he was chained at the ankles and clad in a long white sheath.

As he was passing before Lisa, she moved her mask aside and blew him a kiss. He stopped, turned to her, and his freckled face broke into a boyish grin. He was happy she had come to see him die and she would remember that he had shown no fear.

Savonarola refrained from preaching until Christmas. Inwardly, he was choking with frustration. He could not live without the sight of adoring crowds, their faces lifted to him. He paced the floor of his cell like a caged lion.

Yet he still tried to appease the man he had insulted in the pulpit. With sanctimonious insincerity, he wrote to the pontiff assuring him of his undying devotion.

Holy Father, I kiss the feet of Your Holiness, as a child grieving at having incurred the displeasure of his father. I fly eagerly to your feet and beg you to give ears to my cries and keep me no longer from your embrace. I beseech Your Holiness not to close against me the font of your kindness.

This letter remained unanswered. Weeks passed, and the brief of excommunication remained unrescinded. His despondency turned to fury. Advent, the season of his former triumphs, came and went. No word arrived from the Vatican. Six months had passed since the brief of excommunication had been nailed at the doors of the churches. Already he felt forgotten, and to him this was unbearable.

On Christmas Day, 1497, he exploded. Throwing away the mask of humility and obedience, he openly defied the pontiff whose feet he had been eager to kiss a few weeks before. Ignoring the papal brief of excommunication, he performed not one but three masses, led a procession through the cloister and, naturally, delivered a long sermon in the chapel of the monastery.

As always, his listeners fell under his spell. Incredibly, the Signoria took his side against the Holy See and gave him permission to preach in the cathedral. By February, he was back in his pulpit, eyes aglow and crucifix in hand.

Now he cast all caution aside. In words of fire, he defended his disobedience, declared his excommunication invalid, and called on the world's clergy to rise against "the Whore of Babylon," by which he meant the Holy Church.

O monks, black or white or brown or whatever color! O mendicant friars! O priests and nuns and monks! Christ wishes you to revive His Church. I call upon you.

A sort of madness descended upon him. He sensed he was spelling his own doom, but no longer did he care. He preferred death to silence. In rhapsodic, half-demented tirades, he clamored for martyrdom.

I seek neither mitre nor cardinal's hat. I only desire that which Thou hast given Thy saints. Death, a crimson hat, a hat of blood! . . . O Lord, Lord grant me, I pray Thee, Thy martyrdom and make me ready to die for Thee as Thou hast died for me! . . . I know the knife is already being sharpened for me . . .

He knew the pulpit would soon be taken from him, but he still wanted to shout a final malediction. His voice resounded through the immense church as he said,

I testify in the name of God that this Alexander is no pope, nor can he be considered such. I affirm he is no Christian and does not believe in God, which passes the limits of every infidelity.

He paused to catch his breath. Then, in a voice of thunder, he spoke the fatal words:

Therefore on him who gives commands opposed to charity, which is the fulfillment of the law, *anathema sit!*

Below, the crowd gasped. The friar was excommunicating the pope!

Instantly, he knew he had gone too far. In vain did he argue his cause, quote the Scriptures, the Fathers of the Church and, of course, God Himself Who spoke through his mouth, unworthy as he was.

It was too late. He had hanged himself with his tongue, just as Lorenzo de'Medici had predicted. Already people were leaving without waiting for the end of the sermon.

This time, the pope's answer was swift. By special courier, the Signoria was ordered to silence the rebellious monk or bring the sanction of excommunication upon the entire city. Memories of Pope Sixtus's ruinous excommunication nearly twenty years ago shook Their Magnificences back to their senses. On 17 March they enjoined the friar from preaching "anywhere in the city."

Yet "the incorrigible babbler" managed to climb once more the pulpit of the cathedral, this time in defiance of both the pope and the civil authorities.

He began with the usual self-eulogy. He was a godly man; he had "neither harlot, nor concubine." He lived on bread and water, fasted regularly, flogged himself with utmost severity. He preached to exalt, not to destroy the Church. Once again he proclaimed the invalidity of his excommunication, quoted the Scriptures and affirmed that his visions came from God.

The Word of the Lord has been with me like a consuming fire in my heart and my bones. I have been unable to restrain it. I felt myself aflame with the Spirit. O Lord, I pray Thee to have mercy on the good and delay Thy promise no longer.

These were his parting words. They fell on inattentive ears. He had lost his audience. They had wearied of him, his visions, his laments, his problems.

He had become a bore.

On that very same Sunday, a Franciscan preacher by the name of Francesco da Puglia presented his audience with an interesting proposition. "If Savonarola's excommunication is invalid, as he claims, why doesn't he submit to an Ordeal by Fire and let God — his friend God who was forever speaking through his mouth — proclaim his innocence?"

"For my part," added the preacher, "I shall willingly march through the fire with him."

The suggestion took the town by storm.

"Noble husband," asked Lisa, "what is an Ordeal by Fire?"

It was, Giocondo explained, an ancient form of trial to determine guilt or innocence between two litigants. Barefoot and clad only in a white shirt, they walked side by side along a narrow plank, fifty yards in length, between two walls of fire. The one who came out unscathed was declared a just and innocent man; the other, "a son of Satan."

This procedure had enjoyed great popularity in the Middle Ages. But, as both contestants usually lost their lives in the fire, it had fallen in disuse.

The Florentines, however, were eager to find out whether their friar was God's prophet or a charlatan. They wanted their ordeal, and great was their disappointment when Savonarola let it be known that "he was engaged in too great an undertaking to lose himself in such a miserable venture."

Coming from a man who recently had been clamoring for martyrdom and "a hat of blood," his reply was not appreciated by the population. It began to dawn in many of his followers' minds that their holy friar might well be a coward as well as a blabberer.

The matter was about to be dropped when a saintly and heroic Dominican monk, Domenico da Pescia, volunteered to replace his superior in his walk through the fire. Alas, the original Franciscan challenger would not hear of it. It must be Savonarola or nobody. Again the matter was about to be dropped when another Franciscan monk, a certain Rondinelli, declared himself ready to challenge Savonarola's substitute.

This time, the ordeal was no longer between the original contestants, but their subordinates. It was better than nothing. The date was set for the day before Palm Sunday, 8 April, at one o'clock in the afternoon.

Two mountains of brushwood had been built in the center of the square with a narrow passage, less than two feet wide, stretched out between them. City employees were spreading resin and gun powder to insure a violent conflagration.

Although the weather was cloudy with distant rumblings of thunder, a festive, jovial crowd sat on the ground around baskets of food in impromptu picnics. The prospect of a free *spectacolo* put everyone in high spirits and good appetite.

Savonarola, excommunicated as he was, could be seen in the Loggia dei Lanci surrounded by two hundred of his brethren. Domenico da Pescia, who was to walk through the fire, was calmly praying before a statue of Saint Dominic. The other half of the *loggia* was occupied by Franciscans, with their champion, Rondinelli, trembling in his white shirt more from fear than from the cold. The more he looked at the twin mounds of brushwood, the less he felt like walking through them. His teeth were chattering and tearfully he regretted his impulsive bravado.

Eventually, his brethren came to his rescue. They informed the members of the Signoria that Rondinelli would not walk through the fire in a shirt while his opponent was wearing a chasuble in which some devil might be hiding, thus protecting him from the flames.

A long debate ensued. Finally, the Dominican was stripped and sheathed in a white shirt like the other.

Everything was now in readiness. The city guards were about to fling the burning torches in to the brushwood when Savonarola demanded that his representative be allowed to carry the Blessed Sacrament. Naturally, the Franciscans replied this would give him an unfair advantage and turned down his request. Like the true Italians they were, the opposing monks were exchanging invectives when a deafening thunderclap drowned out the sound of their voices.

A deluvian cloudburst started to pour down from the heavens, emptying the square of its picnickers and transforming the twin pyres into dripping mountains of brushwood, too wet to ignite.

The cloudburst lasted only a few minutes, long enough to deprive the Florentines of their free *spectacolo*. Grumblingly, they started for home, blaming "the damned friar" for ruining their holiday with his last-minute request for the Blessed Sacrament. It had been another of his tricks, they said. Just like his visions, his prophecies.

Slowly they worked themselves up into a mood of violence which they directed against Savonarola. The rain had stopped and they no longer wanted to go home.

In tacit accord, they returned to Piazza della Signoria, milling aimlessly about the square, not knowing exactly why. Their anger swelled with each passing moment. It needed only a spark to explode, and it came at three o'clock. A Dominican monk from the San Marco Monastery, a certain Mariano Ughi, happened to be passing by with a few of his brethren on their way to Vespers.

"Go back to your house," shouted someone. "Go back, you cowards."

That was all it took.

A stone was flung at the clerics who fled in the direction of their *convento* followed by a rabble of men and women. Two of the friars were seized, beaten, and left bleeding on the ground.

The others reached the safety of their monastery in time to slam the door on thir pursuers. But the mob had tasted the ambrosia of revenge and would not disperse. Ominously they milled around, seeking a release to their mounting rage.

"Let's get him," shouted a voice. "Let's get the friar!"

A thousand throats took up the cry. Bundles of straw from a nearby stable were stacked against the monastery's doors. Ladders were leaned against the garden wall. On the roof, monks hurled tiles at the assailants.

As nightfall descended upon Florence, the siege of the monastery began. It lasted until three o'clock in the morning and caused over a hundred casualties. Assailants climbed ladders over garden walls, rampaged through the cloister and the cells. Monks fought back with crucifixes and lighted torches. Men ran, howling, their hair and clothes burning. Some were hacked to death before Fra Angelico's heavenly frescoes.

Gradually, resistance subsided. Several brethren slithered down to safety on ropes fastened to windows; others escaped through a secret tunnel. Finally, the chapel doors were splintered open and the invaders lunged toward the altar where Savonarola was praying, dressed in sacramental robes.

They did not go far.

A young German novice, a blond colossus named Brother Heinrich, had set his arquebus on the railing of the pulpit and fired with deadly accuracy while singing the Virgin's litanies. Finally he was killed, his face crushed by a rock.

Savonarola was seized, jerked up to his feet, almost blinded by torches. A hundred hands clutched him, pushed him along the arched galleries of the cloister and out on to the piazza, where a vociferating mob was waiting for him. They tore his chasuble off his back, spat in his face. They struck him, and soon rivulets of blood ran down from his mouth. Already they had him on his knees and might have butchered him on the spot when a detachment of helmeted city guards on horseback appeared from nowhere. The captain booted him up to his feet, and with prodding stabs of his sword made him stumble all the way to the Old Palace.

Only two weeks before, Savonarola had called for a Passion similar to that of Christ. In the dawn of Palm Sunday, 1498, amid the jeers and blows of a once-adoring crowd, it began.

He was incarcerated in the tower, slept for a few moments on the ground of his cell. Then he was awakened with a kick and brought before his judges.

As he refused to admit that his visions came from the devil, his wrists were pinioned behind his back. He was hoisted to the twenty-foot-high ceiling of the torture chamber by means of ropes and pulleys. Then, with an abrupt thud, he was dropped to a few inches from the floor. This was called the *strappado*.

When it was performed for the third time, the fall dislocated his shoulder. He fainted and was dragged back to his cell. So heartrending was his condition that his guardian, who had been a violent enemy of his, fed him a few spoonfuls of broth and let him rest his head on his lap.

The following morning torture was resumed. This time he was suspended over a *brasero* of burning coals, his soles less than one inch above the coals.

Still he did not recant.

It went on like this for five days. On Piazza della Signoria, burghers met after supper to discuss the trial. Although the proceedings were to be secret, some assistant notary or torturer could easily be bribed into revealing what had gone on during the day.

As the friar continued to maintain the authenticity of his visions and prophecies, a change of opinion spread among the population. The man they had called a coward was behaving like a martyr.

"Why do they keep on torturing him?" asked Lisa.

She, too, had been impressed by the friar's heroism. Her aversion to him had melted before his fortitude. "Why don't they kill him or leave him alone?"

"Because," replied Giocondo, "they know that a man can endure just so much, and if they hurt him enough, he will break down and confess to anything they want."

And so it happened.

Dazed with pain, he began wavering in his declarations, contradicted himself, blubbered incoherently about his visions. His words were transcribed by the tribunal's secretary, a certain Ceccone, and distorted into a recantation which the fainting man was made to sign.

The notary's report was immediately published, but it had been so flagrantly tampered with that no one would believe it. Another trial was ordered.

This time Savonarola was submitted to a new kind of torture.

An astrologer had predicted that "an hermaphrodite prophet" would appear, and the judges wanted to ascertain if, by chance, the holy friar might not be that double-sexed, satanic creature. Naked, he was bound by leather straps to a table, and for an hour a barber-surgeon thrust his knife and inserted iron pincers into his penis. At last he declared that the prior of San Marco was an ordinary male and departed, leaving him unconscious and blood-spattered on the table.

The human wreck was carried back to his cell, but no solace awaited him there. He was clamped into irons that scraped his raw-skinned ankles with every motion. In addition, doubt had now entered his soul. Had God really spoken to him or had his prophecies been whispered to him by Satan? Could his visions have been the inventions of his mind, born from his thirst for power? When he learned that his San Marco brethren had repudiated him and pronounced him a charlatan, he touched the bottom of the pit.

Now he was totally alone. There was no Christ to console him after the horrors of the torture chamber, no voice from Heaven to fill the silence of his cell with promises of eternal bliss, no prayers from his former disciples. He was disowned by God and man.

In the well of his solitude, he found the strength to hold a quill and give voice to his agony.

O unhappy wretch that I am, forsaken by all, wither shall I go? To whom shall I turn? Who will have pity on me? I dare not raise my eyes to Heaven for I have sinned against it. . . . I come to Thee, most merciful God, I come full of melancholy and grief for Thou alone art my hope, Thou alone my refuge. . . . Do unto me what must be.

On the fifth day of the second trial, he collapsed. As he was being strapped to be hoisted to the ceiling for the seventh time, he crumbled to his knees.

"Please, my lords," he stammered, "please, tear me no more."

Ceccone, the notary, grabbed his hand and made him sign a prepared confession. As he was putting quill to paper, Savonarola emerged from his daze, pointed a trembling finger at the notary, and predicted he would die within six months — which he did.

Then he signed, and it was all over.

For nearly one month he was left alone while two papal commissioners made their way from Rome. One was Giovanni Turriano, the elderly general of the Dominican Order: the other, Monsignore Remoline, a lecherous Spaniard who, as a welcoming gift, was given for servant a beautiful girl, "disguised as a boy."

Thus put in good spirits, the monsignore conducted the last act of the Savonarola drama with cheerful efficiency. The friar was brought before the commissioners and the judges, who promptly found him to be "a heretic, schismatic, and a seducer of the people." He was sentenced to be hanged and his body burned at the stake. With him were condemned two other San Marco monks: the saintly Domenico da Pescia who had volunteered to replace him in the Ordeal by Fire, and Sylvestro Marucci, a psychopathic sleepwalker who had accused him in the hope of saving his own life.

The triple hanging was performed early in the morning of 23 May 1498, on Piazza della Signoria.

A long wooden bridge had been erected six feet above the ground, ending in the center of the square with a circular platform that rested on a mound of straw and oil-soaked logs. A tall cross rose from it with a high ladder leaning on it, on which the hangman, while preparing the nooses, was clowning and joking, for which, after the execution, he was severely reprimanded.

By dawn, the piazza was already filled with people. But it was not the merry crowd that had come to witness the Ordeal by Fire six weeks before. This time, women carried no foodbaskets on their arms; men no wineskins on their shoulders. They wore black and did not speak. Some prayed on their knees; some wept over their rosaries.

At last Savonarola and his two companions emerged from the palace and walked to the table where sat the judges. A moment before the three of them had been "degraded," that is divested of their monachal robes. Now they wore long white shirts and, as always, chains clanked at their ankles.

The notary read the death sentence, but Savonarola barely heard it. His torn shoulder hurt so much that he longed for death. Patience, he told himself, it would be soon over. It would not take long to strangle on the rope.

He raised his eyes to the sky tinted with the tender blueness of early morning. Another day was being born, a beautiful May morning, like the one that had greeted him on his return to Florence eight years ago. In a flash, he recalled the fine blue-skied mornings he had known when he was roaming from village to village through Lombardy and Romagna . . . In His graciousness, God had permitted that he should die on a lovely spring morning.

The notary sat down and Monsignore Remoline rose, fresh from a night with his "serving boy." He announced that His Holiness had kindly granted a plenary indulgence to the three sinful monks, thus "restoring them to their pristine innocence and freeing them from purgatory."

With this final act of mercy, Pope Alexander sent the three monks to their death. In a jangle of chains they walked along the wooden bridge to the circular platform. Domenico da Pescia was the first to climb the ladder; then Marucci. The fire was lit below and soon flames leaped upwards as Savonarola reached the top of the ladder.

The *boia* slipped the noose around his neck.

"Friar, now is the time to make a miracle," he laughed, pushing him into space.

Convulsively, the man who had been the master of Florence swung and twisted as the fire reached his chained feet. Then, in a hissing gust of air, it engulfed his shirt, sheathing his body in a flaming shroud.

Then something extraordinary happened. Slowly, Savonarola's right arm was seen to rise in a ghostly benediction.

People crossed themselves and ran in all directions.

"O God," they cried, "we've killed a saint!"

Two weeks later, as Lisa was visiting her grandfather, she remarked, "This morning a peddler came to the kitchen with a sachet of the holy friar's ashes."

Mariotto grinned. "And naturally you bought it."

"He said it would protect everyone in the house from misfortune and illness."

"And of course you believed him. You should have had him thrown out."

"But, honored grandfather, many people say the holy friar was a saint."

"Many people say many foolish things."

She regarded the elderly banker with disapproval. "Do you mean to say you don't think he was a saint?"

"No, I don't. If he is, I hope I never go to heaven."

"But he blessed us from the cross. I saw it myself. Surely this is a great miracle."

"I am weary of hearing about this blessing from the cross. Men, my child, do strange things when they strangle at the end of a rope. They may even raise an arm. But, believe me, not in blessing."

She did not give in. "And what about his courage in the torture chamber?"

He remained unimpressed. Admirable as the friar's behavior had been, many scoundrels showed equal or even greater fortitude.

True, he went on, the friar had been treated harshly, but he himself had advocated the harshest treatment for those who did not agree with him.

"Have you forgotten how he recommended beheading for anyone who preferred the Medici regime to his own? Have you forgotten how he decreed that any swearing man should have his tongue pierced with a red-hot iron? This also is rather harsh, don't you think?

"No, my child, he was no saint, but a rebellious monk, a self-deluded, power-hungry fool who, like all fanatics, believed what he said. For this may God have mercy on him, as on all of us."

BOOK THREE

The Portrait

Mona Lisa (detail) by Leonardo da Vinci. *Courtesy of the Louvre Museum.*

Study for the Sforza Monument by Leonardo da Vinci. *Reproduced by gracious permission Her Majesty Queen Elizabeth II.*

The Very Strange
"Messer Lunardo Vinci"

Savonarola's execution marked the rebirth of a modest social life in the City of Flowers. After three years of King Jesus's reign, people longed for music and gaiety. None more than the nineteen-and-a-half-year-old Donna Lisa de'Gherardini del Giocondo.

After her discussion with her grandfather, she was no longer sure whether or not the friar had been a saint, and it didn't really matter. But one thing was certain: he had died not a minute too soon. A few more years of him, and he would have robbed her of her entire youth. As it was, she still had some remnant of it and she proposed to make the most of it before the decrepitude of middle age descended upon her.

Of course, this social renaissance could not be compared to the past splendors of the Medici years. Enfeebled by the decline of the wool industry, her treasury depleted by the "indemnity" paid to King Charles, exhausted by the ruinous and endless Pisa war, Florence was no longer a radiant commercial and financial metropolis, but a tired river town living mostly on memory.*

Memories of her Golden Age, that is, when Florence "floated on a lake of gold" and the great *stabilimenti* along the Arno worked at capacity and the world dressed in San Martino cloth. Memories of the recent years had left too many scars. The sack-

---

* Before returning to France, Charles had finally kept his word and ordered the commander of the French garrison in Pisa, Baron d'Entragues, to remit the fortress to the Florentine troops. Instead, the baron had read the king's letter to the Pisans who, for the sum of 12,000 gold florins, persuaded him to hand the fortress to them.

ing of the Medici Palace, the hysterical Savonarola years, the entrance of the French through the San Frediano Gate remained a nightmare that people wanted to forget.

They longed to wipe the slate clean and start a new era of peace and moderate prosperity. Their wish seemed to come true when news arrived from France that the Little King had died in April, on the day of the Ordeal by Fire.

His death had been as absurd as his life. On the way to a tournament, he had bumped into a door, violently struck his big, empty head, and collapsed. Immediately, he had sunk into a coma and breathed his last on a wretched pallet of straw, abandoned by the members of the court.

"Let's hope the foreign devils will stay behind their mountains," remarked Lisa, "and we may have a little happiness for a change."

Giocondo understood that she, too, was itching to dance and wear elegant dresses once again. She was entitled to some merriment and he certainly would not begrudge her a little gaiety.

"It is still a little too soon to celebrate the end of the Savonarola rule, but why don't you give a dancing festivity on our return from the country?"

She did, two weeks before Christmas, and the ball established her as one of the leading hostesses.

At first, she planned to wear the belt that Jacopo had brought from Siena, but courage failed her at the last moment. Instead, she wept thinking of him. How happy he would have been to dance with her! Dear Jacopo, now that he was dead, she finally could admit to herself he had loved her and she wished she could have loved him back. But in those days only Giuliano existed for her, and you could not command your heart.

So successful was her Christmas ball that informal gatherings brightened Casa Giocondo throughout the winter months ending with a much-sought-after garden party in June.

All these functions were pale replicas of the sumptuous festivities of yore. Gem-embossed gowns had vanished into pawn shops, and few ladies could still afford brocade or gold cloth. But the gaiety of these occasions made up for the impoverishment of costumes. As nearly everyone was poor, poverty had lost its sting. Dances were as lively as ever. Youngsters exchanged glances and smiles as tender as their elders had done.

Lisa's daily life now expanded to include a few mundane activities. As in the past, she did the marketing, discussed the daily menu with the cook, supervised the management of the house; but now, in the afternoon, accompanied by Tessa, she made a round of visits to friends and relatives. Her taffeta gowns and lace handkerchiefs were much admired. Her marriage to Giocondo had saved her from the penuriousness which afflicted much of the local aristocracy, still bound to the ailing wool industry. But she did not flaunt her prosperity and people forgave her good fortune.

On a specified day of each week, she received the visits of the same friends and relatives and they talked about the same things. It was all rather provincial and dull, but it created a semblance of social life.

Charity also had its place in her existence. She dropped in on pregnant ladies of her acquaintance, helped carry them to their hot baths, joined in the litanies to Saint Margaret. She succeeded her grandmother Gherardini as a patroness of the Orphanage of the Innocents and wheedled money from her husband to dower virtuous orphan girls. With Tessa, she went to the *stinche*, the city jail, and brought little sausages to the prisoners too poor to pay for their food.

She loved Giocondo, now florid and benevolent in the fullness of his middle years. She had long reconciled herself to his bulk, his unromantic looks. By moments, she felt he had always been part of her life. She liked the warmth of his body in bed, the reassurance of his presence. With him around, she felt safe and the house secure. She refused to believe that, once, she almost had hated him. She flirted with handsome young men, but merely to buttress her self-confidence in her good looks. A man's eyes, she learned, were the truest of mirrors.

At her side, Bartolommeo was growing up into a lively boy who preferred wrestling and racing to catechism and Latin grammar. At seven, he had entered the district school (Giocondo had vetoed the idea of a private tutor) and he often returned home bruised, his shirt torn, but excited at the prospect of another hand-to-hand scuffle.

"I fear he'll never be a scholar," lamented Lisa.

Giocondo told her that Florence was crawling with starving scholars. Meo might be weak in astronomy and theology, but he was learning to fight and defend himself.

"And believe me, gentle wife, this is more important than irregular Latin verbs."

And so the years flowed by, busy yet placid, unscarred by illness or regrets.

Despite the never-ending Pisa war, Florence enjoyed a period of relative tranquillity under the leadership of Piero Soderini, a fair and kindly man who had been elected *gonfaloniere* for life. He lodged at the Old Palace with his wife, Argentina, who could be seen watering her potted flowers on the building's single balcony. The one-handed clock in the tower was usually out of order, but that also had become a symbol of the relative quietude of the times.

On 25 March 1500, the fifteenth century died and the sixteenth began. In Rome, Pope Alexander, majestic in a bejeweled cope, proclaimed the advent of the jubilee year. Papal couriers galloped to the farthest frontiers of Christendom to announce the profusion of blessings and indulgences that awaited the pilgrims to the Holy City. Repentance was good for the soul as well as the local trade.

Lisa did not attend the New Year's festivities on Piazza della Signoria, for she was spending her days and many of her nights by her grandmother's bedside.

Helplessly, she watched the old lady's face wince in pain, her lips tighten to stifle her cries. The doctor came, squinted at her over the rim of his spectacles, muttered something in Latin, prescribed some potion, and departed decorously. The parish priest sprinkled holy water on her bed and spoke of God's wondrous but mysterious ways.

Filippa's sons and daughters dropped in whenever they could, but they had large families of their own or exacting business responsibilities. So they did not stay long, and it was mostly Lisa and her grandfather who provided company to the dying woman.

Sometimes Mariotto would silently hold her hand in his own for long periods of time, smiling or blinking back tears as they recalled their many happy years together. They only wished they could depart together and enter the unknown hand in hand. At last one evening she died and Mariotto was relieved that she had stopped suffering.

After her grandmother's death, Lisa decided that it now was her duty to watch over her surviving grandparent.

"Do you realize he is sixty-six?" she explained to her husband. "Now that he is all by himself, someone must keep his eye on him."

To which Giocondo replied that the elderly banker was strong as an ox and would probably outlive everyone. Moreover, he had several children, let alone a houseful of devoted servants, all of whom would gladly take care of him.

"Besides," she finished, "I am the only person with enough time and authority to keep an eye on him."

"What authority?"

"I tell him I won't bring Meo to visit him on Sundays if he doesn't do as I say."

Gently, he observed that this was known as blackmail, but she did not care. She was going to watch over him, whether he liked it or not.

"In short, you are like Savonarola who was going to save our souls whether we liked it or not."

Henceforth, her life included frequent visits to Casa Rucellai. She coaxed Mariotto into going to bed when the weather was cold or when it rained. If her pleas remained unheeded, she then turned to blackmail which usually proved effective.

In due time, she reached the age of twenty-one; then twenty-two, without visible changes in her appearance. Her face retained its youthful complexion; her figure its slenderness.

When she was twenty-three, her waist thickened somewhat and she gained a few pounds.

"It's your fault," she told Tessa who was massaging her. "You've lost your touch. In the old days you knew how to keep me thin."

"In the old days you did not eat so much *berlingozzo* cake."

"Is it my fault if it is my husband's favorite dessert?"

"Is that why you eat a larger slice than he does?"

By the time she neared twenty-four, she had grown slightly plump and she took solemn resolutions never to touch *berlingozzo* cake again. But as Giocondo seemed to like her as much as before, she weakened and forgot her good resolutions.

On the chilly afternoon of 4 March 1503, she sat by her grandfather's bedside, bent on an embroidery work. Mariotto, a nightcap on his head, lay in his silk-curtained four-poster, grumbling under his breath about the meddlesomeness of well-meaning granddaughters.

"Honored grandfather, are you saying something?" she asked, lifting her eyes from her work.

"I am saying that I feel perfectly well and have more important things to do than lie in this confounded bed."

"Would you prefer to stand in the *loggia* of the Exchange watching stocks and catching some noxious fever?"

"I've watched stocks for fifty years and never caught any illness."

"This is what my honored grandfather Gherardini used to say, but one day he did catch a pernicious fever and shortly afterwards he crossed the Great Sea." She rested her sewing in her lap. "However, since my presence is a burden to you, I shall depart at once. Of course, I won't be able to bring Meo next Sunday."

"And why not?"

"Because he would breathe the infectious air of the house and get sick. You wouldn't want that, would you?"

He gave her a feigned look of helplessness.

And so he said how much he enjoyed her presence and appreciated her solicitude. Profusely, he thanked her for taking time to come and visit an old man.

This done, he asked about Meo.

The boy was almost eleven and a more dutiful, loving, obliging, obedient boy did not exist in Florence. Alas, he thought only of wrestling and showed no desire to pursue his studies to the University. "Instead, he looks forward to starting his apprenticeship at the mill in October, when we return from the country."

"Praise the Lord!" exclaimed Mariotto.

He launched into an emotional tirade that Florence needed merchants instead of useless scholars who argued for hours over the sex of angels and the exact meaning of a Dante stanza. In his long business career, he had never had any use for Latin or Petrarch or theology. In his opinion, the economic decadence of Florence coincided with the craze of learning which had become fashionable in the past thirty years. The more ideas you put into a young man's head, the less likely was he to think about business.

He stopped abruptly and declared that this long speech had brought a parching thirst upon him.

"I should relish a goblet of wine," he announced.

She suggested a bowl of hot broth instead. Eyebrows aquiver, he declared that if he did not have a cup of Trebbiano brought him at once, he would jump out of bed and fetch the decanter from his study. The prospect of her honored grandfather running through the house in a state of total nudity ended the discussion.

Hastily she rose, pulled the bell rope, and ordered a tumbler of Trebbiano. Whereupon he regained his composure. She lit the candle on the night table and prepared to leave, for she made it a point to be home by the time Giocondo returned from the mill.

"Tomorrow I shall drop in to see how you are," she said, leaning down to kiss his hand. Meanwhile, she went on, he was to stay in bed, drink hot potions, and read a good book or recite a rosary. He promised to do so and watched her walk out of the room.

He waited long enough to make sure she had left the house. Then, with a loud ringing of the night-table bell, he summoned his valet and announced he was going to play cards at the guild. So saying, he jumped out of bed and began dressing.

As for Lisa, she was hurrying through the crowded streets in the deepening March twilight: an amiable, conventional, good-hearted, altogether unremarkable Florentine society lady. With her handkerchief pressed to her nostrils, she walked in short, rapid steps unaware that on that very day a bald, gray-bearded traveler had arrived in town, who was to play a memorable part in her life.

And make her immortal.

His name was Leonardo da Vinci.

Fifty-two years before he had been conceived on a star-spangled August night in some field or vineyard near the village of Vinci, where Caterina, a farm girl, and Piero da Vinci, a young notary, met after dark to kiss and make love.

She was sixteen, blonde, beautiful, and illiterate: he was twenty-four, selfish, ambitious, and the son of the village "rich man." One evening she sobbed out that she was with child and he stopped seeing her. Without delay he married Albiera Amadori, the twelve-year-old daughter of a Florentine notary, and brought her to Vinci.

As for Caterina, she returned to her mother's farm at Anchiano, a neighboring hamlet, and there on 15 April 1452, at eleven o'clock in the evening, in the glow of tallow candles, she gave birth to a son whom she named Leonardo.

For the next five years he grew by her side, while his father, the notary, ignored him and continued to live in the big Vinci house with his young wife Albiera, his father Antonio, and his brother Francesco.

One morning a sturdy young farmer by the name of Accatta-briga presented himself at the notary's house and informed him that he intended to marry Caterina, but did not want her *bastardo*.

"Leonardo is yours," he said, "and you'd better take him into your house."

The look in his eyes convinced Piero he should do as suggested.

Grudgingly, most grudgingly, he took his illegitimate son into his house.

He gave him food, a pad of straw to sleep on, but no love. In turn, Albiera, childless and unloved, fell head over heels in love with the beautiful blond farm boy. They pooled their solitude and lived in a world of their own. They played in the courtyard; at night, she pulled the blanket up to his chin and kissed him before blowing out the candle. Gradually, Leonardo forgot his real mother; the loving, brown-eyed girl with the smooth, dark hair parted in the middle became his real mamma.

On occasions, when the notary went to Florence on matters of business, Alessandro Amadori, Albiera's brother, who was studying to become a priest, would ride to Vinci to visit his sister. He would always bring some little toy for Leonardo who grew very fond of him. The three of them would walk through the countryside, sit on the grass, eat hardboiled eggs and have a fine picnic.

In this way seven years went by.

Albiera taught her stepson how to read and whatever little else she knew. With astonishment, she watched his mind awake to the wonders of the world and ask a thousand questions. What made flowers grow, birds fly, water run? She observed that everything interested him, but not for long.

Despite his insatiable curiosity and the swiftness of his mind, he did not do well at the village school. He felt impatient with his classmates' mental sluggishness, dozed while the priest droned through the rudiments of catechism, Latin grammar, and arithmetic. Before long, he played truant and roamed through the hills instead of attending classes.

Albiera died in childbirth at the age of twenty-four. Leonardo's universe crumbled with her. Something in him died as they took her to the cemetery. His father hastened to wed another childbride, Francesca Lanfredini, who was also a Florentine notary's daughter. She came to live in Vinci, but paid no attention to the silent and sullen twelve-year-old Leonardo. They remained strangers. Two years later she, like Albiera, also died in childbirth.

In the village, people whispered there was a curse on the notary and he would never have a child, for he had abandoned Caterina, the mother of his son, which was a great sin. They spat over their left shoulders when he went by. He felt their hostility and decided to move to Florence.

A cautious, methodical man, it took him two years to take the final step. Finally, in October 1468, he leased *una bottega con fondachetto* — a shop with a small basement— on Piazza Firenze for the yearly rental of twenty-four florins.

He was nearly forty years old, embittered by two unsuccessful marriages, his neighbors' dislike, his mediocre career as a village notary. He wanted to improve his lot, found a family, and make a new start.

Most of all, he wanted to unburden himself of the broody, almost illiterate youngster who reminded him of his youthful indiscretion. Piero da Vinci held a lifelong resentment against Leonardo. He never came to his assistance, either financially or morally; never recognized him and invariably listed him on his declaration of income as *figlio non legittimo* — illegitimate son. At sixteen, Leonardo showed no aptitude for anything, except drawing. On his return from his wanderings through the hills, he would make charcoal drawings of the plants, rocks, flowers he had seen. It occurred to his father that, with training, he might become a *dipintore*, a picture-maker. It wasn't much, but it was better than ploughing fields.

One day he went to Via dell'Acqua, or Water Street, where Andrea Verrocchio, a celebrated painter-sculptor, operated a *bottega d'arte*, where he sold his paintings and statues and taught the rudiments of painting to a dozen paying apprentices.

Round of face and rotund of girth, Verrocchio looked more like a pastry cook than the great artist he was. At a glance, he recognized Leonardo's innate mastery of line and declared he would be glad to accept him as an apprentice. To which the notary replied he was too poor to pay the tuition, but Leonardo might perhaps "earn his keep" by doing household chores.

Verrocchio's sister Tita, who managed his household (he was a bachelor), was called in conference. She said that she certainly could use an assistant, and on those terms Leonardo was accepted as an apprentice.

He was given an attic room in his teacher's house. He rose before the other apprentices in order to fetch water at the public fountain, start fires in the kitchen hearth and the classroom, sweep the floor, help Tita scour with sand the boarders' wooden bowls, pots, and pans.

His arrival at the *bottega* caused something of a sensation. For one thing, he was sixteen, several years older than the average art student. Moreover he was tall, strikingly handsome, blond and blue-eyed, which made him conspicuous among his short-legged, brown-eyed and dark-haired classmates. Behind his back, they laughed at his peasant's awkwardness, his Vinci accent.

But the laughter stopped the moment he started to draw. The fact that he was left-handed made his skill smack of sorcery. Verrocchio vaunted the exceptional talent of his pupil among his colleagues at the Saint Luke's Brotherhood, which functioned more or less as the artists' guild of Florence. Well-known *dipintori* came to the *bottega* to watch Leonardo draw. In the wineshops where they convened, there was much talk about the extraordinary gifted country boy.

Four years after his arrival in Florence, Leonardo was ready to launch on a career as a picture-maker.

"Of course," said Verrocchio, "you will have to pass the test of the Saint Luke's Brotherhood, but that won't give you any trouble. Then you will open your own *bottega* and go into business for yourself."

Leonardo passed the guild's tests with disconcerting ease, became a member of the Saint Luke's Brotherhood, but did not open a *bottega* of his own. He did not want to become a picture-maker, but a great scientific savant. As an inventor, he would gain fame as well as riches. A fever of learning had taken possession of the boy who used to play the truant to roam through the hills.

Now, after helping Tita with the dishes, he climbed to his attic and pored over his Latin grammar, for scientific books were written in Latin and he wanted to read them all. He also dabbled in mathematics, chemistry, mechanics, geometry, physics, botany, and astronomy. War engines fascinated him and he dreamed of building exotic killing-machines. Like a drunken bee buzzing from flower to flower, he shuttled from one science to another, spurred by a compulsive, pathological curiosity that was to remain with him for the rest of his life. He procured a copy of Vitruvius's *De Re Militari*, copied most of it and fancied himself a military inventor.

Despite his laborious attempts at self-education, Leonardo never mastered Latin, or even Italian, for that matter.

In his study *Man Without Letters*, Giorgio di Santillana, professor at the University of Rome and Harvard, noted: "Leonardo writes exactly as the peasants of his time wrote and as they still write today. His spelling is that of the servant girl. . . ." Likewise, his knowledge of mathematics remained rudimentary. George Sarton, Professor of History of Science at Harvard University, states, "In spite of what has been claimed to the contrary, Leonardo was not a mathematician. . . . Genius though he was, he could only grope his way, like a blind man."

As to his revolutionary war engines, a recent study proves that "most of his military designs are not original."

Verrocchio would gently remonstrate. "A devil has entered your head, Leonardo. What good will it do you to read all those books?"

To revive his interest in art, he appointed him *fattore* or studio foreman at the salary of one florin per month. Now Leonardo circulated among the apprentices, showing the beginners how to grind pigments into stone cruets, sand picture panels or prepare tempera paint with the sap of the fig tree.

Whenever he had a free moment, he would sit at his easel and finish some of his teacher's works. He is supposed to have added an angel in Verrocchio's "Baptism of Christ." It was then common practice for apprentices to complete their masters' pictures by painting the background, costumes, draperies. This practice has given rise to the legend that, in his student days, Leonardo painted in their entirety splendid works which should be credited to Verrocchio or others. In the evening he returned to his room, his Latin grammar, his mathematics, his war engines. Four more years went by in this way. He still did not leave Verrocchio's *bottega*.

Then, on the morning of 8 April 1476, two men from the Office of the Night and Monasteries — Florence's vice squad — presented themselves at the studio and placed Leonardo under arrest.

Pandemonium broke loose in the classroom. Apprentices left their cruets and easels to crowd around the police officers. Verrocchio himself burst out of his adjoining workroom and appeared, a clod of clay in hand, *berretta* askew, asking what the tumult was about.

He was told that an anonymous note had been found in the "denunciation box" fastened on the wall of the Old Palace, accusing Leonardo of "sodomitic acts and other such sad goings-on" — "*altre tristezze*" — with the seventeen-year-old Jacopo Saltarelli, an artist's model, and three other young Florentines.

Verrocchio let out a gasp.

Such lies he had never heard! Why, Leonardo had lived eight years in his house and he was like a son to him. No better foreman could be found in Florence, even if he spent half of the night making calculations which the devil himself would not understand.

The guards replied that their instructions were to bring in the accused for questioning. And so on this April morning, one week before his twenty-fourth birthday, Leonardo was marched to the Bargello prison where he was duly interrogated and locked in a cell.

News of his arrest aroused the public's interest because of the notoriety of his father who had finally become a successful notary and because homosexuality had become rampant in Florence. At the university, Greek scholars taught Socratic philosophy and vaunted the charms of Socratic friendship. In the San Marco gardens, languid youths with rouged cheeks and dyed hair traipsed at dusk among marble statues of naked and virile gods. In their Sunday sermons, preachers deplored the prevalence of sodomy. Alarmed parents clamored for sanctions.

The authorities decided to make an example, and announced

that a thorough investigation would be conducted into the charges against Leonardo and his codefendants, its results to be made public in June when sentence would be pronounced.

Two months later Leonardo was brought before the red-robed judge, who exonerated him of all wrongdoing. Not a speck of evidence had been found to support the charges against him.

He was released and returned to the *bottega*. He resumed his duties as foreman, but he was a changed man. Prison had left scars that would not heal. He had lost faith in God and man, for both had failed him in his hour of need. Even his father had not answered his call for help. An all-embracing pessimism descended upon his soul like a noxious mist.

He returned to his nocturnal studies and plunged back into his laborious solitude. He knew, or thought he did, the author of the anonymous note that had sent him to prison and he hungered for revenge. Not an ordinary *vendetta*, of course, a dagger thrust in an ambush or some such banal vengeance. No, he would dispose of his enemy in some uniquely clever, undetectable way.

He began injecting poison in the sap of fruit trees in the hope of producing beautiful but lethal fruits. He would exult at the prospect of inviting his delator to taste some luscious peach and watch him writhe in agony at his feet.

As a diversion, he took up juggling and magic and became proficient at both. He discovered he had a fine singing voice and taught himself to play the lute. Music became the companion of his loneliness.

Eighteen months after his release from prison, he was still at the *bottega*, showing no desire to enter on a career as a picture-maker. Secretly he dreamed of wealth, fame, fine clothes, and exalted social contacts, and art promised none of these. He had no stomach for the precarious existence of the free-lance *dipintore*. Even the most celebrated and industrious of all — Botticelli, Verrocchio, Ghirlandajo — lived from hand to mouth.

None of that for Leonardo.

Fortunately, he was a scientific genius; of that he had no doubt. Science would make him rich and famous. He would invent some epoch-making industrial device or terrifying war engine and his fortune would be assured. Some great and generous prince would be eager to secure the services of so valuable a military engineer.

Meanwhile, he lacked courage to face the penurious existence of a free-lance artist. His teacher sensed it and in December 1477, he braced himself to ask Lorenzo de'Medici, for whom he had done many works, to give Leonardo some little commission. With his usual generosity, Lorenzo had bestowed upon him the commission of an altarpiece for the Signoria's private chapel in the Old Palace. A stunning sign of goodwill towards an unknown painter of twenty-six.

A contract was drawn, signed, and sealed; an advance of twenty-five florins was paid to Leonardo. Twenty-five florins! Enough to live on for a year . . .

This time, Leonardo had no more excuse to remain at the *bottega*. He gathered his astrolabe, compasses, models of machines, and moved to a modest room in an unfashionable district, for he had a villager's thriftiness.

This done, he set out to work on the San Bernardo altarpiece.

Well, not exactly to work . . . After all, creation must be preceded by a period of gestation, and with him gestation could take an awfully long time. Which was understandable, for his altarpiece was going to be different from all previous altarpieces, a breathtaking masterpiece that would stun the members of the Signoria and the world.

Four months later, in April 1478, when the Pazzi Conspiracy exploded and Lorenzo's brother was murdered in the cathedral, Leonardo was still cogitating. He was pulled out of his musings by Pope Sixtus's declaration of war. This was the opportunity the great military engineer had been dreaming about. At once, all thought of the altarpiece was cast aside. He ran to the Old Palace to show Their Magnificences the sketches of his wonderful war engines.

To his astonishment, the sketches failed to impress the magistrates, who remarked that his inventions were either chimerical or already in use. The *gonfaloniere* observed that his beautiful

scythe-equipped chariots had been used in the second century before Christ by the Persians with disastrous results to themselves.
Kindly, Their Magnificences advised the young inventor to con-
centrate on the San Bernardo altarpiece.

The frustrated inventor came out of the Old Palace a very
angry young man. What did those merchants know of military
matters? How could they be expected to recognize his genius?
Florence was filled with fools. Never would he be given his due
here . . . For the first time he began thinking about moving to
some more appreciative city. But he was as afraid of the unknown
as he was of poverty. He remained where he was and continued
to live on the advance he had received for the altarpiece. He
merely forgot about the altarpiece.

He became a man of mysterious habits, a bohemian lost in a
thousand dreams and incapable of any achievements. He took
long walks through the countryside with a notebook and an inkhorn at his belt. As in the days of his childhood, he lay on the
grass and watched clouds sail across the sky. He jotted down observations about "the blue vapors of the atmosphere," the transparency of leaves in sunshine, and wondered whether or not there
was water on the moon. He stood on the Trinita Bridge and
studied the flow of the river below, noting that "a stone thrown
into water forms various circles, so a sound spreads through the
air."

He struck a friendship with the *beccamorte*, or gravedigger,
who collected amputated limbs from the surgery room of the
Hospital of Santa Maria Novella. At low prices, he provided arms,
legs, hands, feet — now and then a whole corpse — to Leonardo,
who dissected them in a remote candlelit room in the basement of
the hospital.

One day the *beccamorte* arrived with a grin of carious teeth on
his stubbly face and an object wrapped in a bloodsoaked sheet. It
was the trunk of a pregnant woman. Leonardo exulted at the
prospect of delving into the most secret parts of what had recently been a young woman.

Impervious to the stench, he spent enchanted hours, scalpel or pencil in hand, cutting ligaments, scraping bones and making drawings of surpassing beauty.*

At the same time, he gave instructions to himself to follow in his investigation.

Cut the kidneys and note well where the blood separates from the urine. . . . Observe the uterus where the spermatic vessels originate. . . . Show the anus and its five muscles. . . .

His excitement grew as he advanced in his task.

I am revealing to men the origin of the prime and maybe the secondary cause of their being. I want to make miracles! *Voglio far miracoli!*

It was all very interesting, but it did not bring him any money. Three years after leaving Verrocchio's *bottega,* the San Bernardo altarpiece was still nonexistent, the advance spent long ago. As a last recourse, he turned again to painting.

In March 1481, he signed a contract for another altarpiece, this time an "Adoration of the Magi" to be hung in the Chapel of the San Donato Convento. As in the case of the San Bernardo altarpiece, a contract was drawn up and an advance paid.

Again he plunged into cogitation, for he intended that his "Adoration" should eclipse an admirable "Adoration" that Botticelli had recently completed and that had been greatly admired. To this end, Leonardo made myriad preliminary drawings, each more complex than the previous one.

Gradually, these preparatory studies turned into a maelstrom of bearded old men in crawling attitudes of stupor, angels floating about for no apparent purpose, an arched stairway ending in mid-air, strolling nude young men, rearing horses, a crouching camel, a bemused Saint Joseph, and a world-weary Bambino giving a blessing in a gesture that vaguely resembled a military

---

* Some of the magnificent sketches he made of this pregnant woman can be seen on a double page in the Schlossmuseum in Weimar, Germany.

salute. Its meaning grew so vast, cosmic, esoteric, and profound that finally it meant nothing at all.

Seven months after signing the contract, he had not begun the painting and already he was sick of it.

The monks fretted, and threatened to sue. To placate them, he painted the monastery clock with blue and yellow colors which, naturally, they had to provide. Under pressure, he consented to trace an oil outline of his "Adoration" in bituminous brown. Further he would not go. He simply had had enough of it. Neither blandishments nor threats had any effect. He laid down his brushes and forgot about the San Donato altarpiece as he had the San Bernardo one.

In fact, he forsook painting altogether and took up music.

He acquired a music pupil, an attractive boy named Atalante Miglioretti, and together they performed at social functions in a juggling/magic/singing and lute-playing act. Endowed as he was with a keen sense of showmanship, Leonardo soon realized he needed some major attraction that would set their act apart from others.

He set out to build a lute that was like no other lute ever built. To begin with, it was made of silver instead of wood and in the shape of a horse's skull. It was decorated with ram's horns, eagle's claws and a piece of nondescript fur. On top of all, it was played upside down.

As he hoped, this contraption aroused a great deal of curiosity. Somehow it caught the eye of Nannina Rucellai, Lorenzo de'Medici's sister, who urged him to look at it.

Lorenzo was anything but keen to meet the man who had defaulted on his San Bernardo altarpiece while keeping the advance payment, but finally he sent for Leonardo. He examined the freakish instrument, strummed a few chords and offered to buy it, not for himself, but as a trifling gift for Ludovico Sforza, duke-regent of Milan and an ardent music lover.

Someone, of course, would have to go to Milan and show the duke how to play the freakish instrument. To Leonardo, this was a providential opportunity to escape from unappreciative Flor-

ence and the vindictive San Donato monks who were threatening
to take him to court over the unfinished "Adoration."

In his haste to be off, he chose to brave the ten-day journey in
the dead of winter. On a snowy January morning, he and his
pupil, Atalante, rode through the northern gate, followed by a
mule carrying their meager belongings.

As they plodded across the frozen Lombard plains, the travelers
discussed the brilliant careers that awaited them in Milan.

Atalante would be content to be taken into the duke's orchestra. Leonardo, also, yearned for employment at court, but of
course he aimed higher, much higher. He had prepared a letter
which he planned to read to His Excellency. In it, he listed his
various military inventions as well as his multifarious talents as an
engineer.

"It won't take long for Duke Sforza to realize how valuable I
could be to him," he told his companion, "After all, his father and
grandfather were great generals."

The vertiginous rise of the Sforza family was one of the greatest
Renaissance success stories.

It had begun in 1382 when Muzzo Attendolo, a Romagna
peasant, having grown tired of tilling his stony field, flung his hoe
away and joined a band of roving mercenaries. Uncommonly
handsome, brave, and intelligent, although illiterate, he had taken
to military life like bow to arrow. His prodigious strength had
earned him the nickname of Sforza — "Force" — which he
adopted as his patronymic.

Rapidly, he was promoted to captain; but, as he wanted to become a *condottiere* with a band of mercenaries of his own, he deserted one night, taking most of his men with him. He drilled
them into an efficient fighting unit and offered their services as
well as his own to Queen Joanna II of Naples, an oversexed lady
who took an instant liking to her general.

For several years he served her well in battle and in bed. In
turn, she gave him many kisses, a trunkful of decorations, and
much money. Unfortunately, she was jealous. When she discov-

ered that he scattered around the bounty she wanted all for herself, she clamped him in jail. It speaks well for him that he profited of this enforced leisure to learn how to read.

He might have become a scholar, had she not recalled him to active duty.

Again he protected her realm and fulfilled her ravenous sensuality. Between battles and jousts of love, he also managed to marry thrice and sire thirteen children, six of them illegitimate.

His bravery was his undoing. As he was leading his troops across the Pescara River swollen by torrential rains, his horse stumbled, taking him into the churning waters. Twice he raised his mailed fist in a call for help, and Muzzo, who should have learned to swim instead of how to read, was no more.

He was succeeded by one of his bastards, Francesco, who was, if possible, even braver and more handsome than his father. Queen Joanna implored him to remain in her service, both public and private. But by now she had grown somewhat decrepit, and he politely declined.

Taking his men with him, Francesco went to Lombardy where they were hired by Filippo Visconti, the last duke of Milan.

The Visconti claimed to be descended from Venus and a Trojan prince, the wedding having been performed by none other than Jupiter. Their crest showed a huge snake in the process of eating a man. As a clan, they combined intelligence, exquisite manners, a passionate love, with a chronic treacherousness and a streak of sadism.

These shortcomings did not prevent them from marrying into the most aristocratic families of Europe. In 1387 Valentina Visconti, Bernabo's daughter, had wed the duke of Orleans, brother of the king of France: a marriage which, a century later, was to have disastrous consequences.

Filippo Visconti was the last of this distinguished and neurotic clan. An enormously fat, broody, and timorous recluse, he seldom ventured out of his castle for fear of being assassinated. He lived in dread of thunder. At the first distant rumble, he would run to a double-walled room he had built for that purpose, and there he would wait for the storm to pass while saying his beads on his knees.

Besides being a coward, he was so treacherous that he betrayed friends and foes alike with equal pleasure. In an age when duplicity was regarded as the soul of diplomacy, he was acknowledged a master diplomat. Behind locked doors, he would weave schemes so intricate that on occasions he trapped himself in them.

Filippo was a self-made widower, so to speak, having had his wife beheaded on suspicion of adultery with one of her pages. To fill the void she had left, he had maintained a number of concubines, one of whom had presented him with a daughter, Bianca, whom he loved tenderly.

This was the man to whom Francesco Sforza, freshly arrived from Naples, attached himself. So well did he serve his new master that the duke pledged him the hand of his daughter Bianca, then aged eight. Then he had changed his mind and pledged her to someone else, only to change his mind again and promise her to Francesco once again. When he changed his mind for the third time, Francesco left his service.

He had no trouble finding employment for himself and his men, for by then he had become a famous *condottiere*. For a while he served as *generalissimo* of the papal army, but the pope took a dislike to him and tried to have him murdered.

Then Francesco became a free-lance soldier of fortune, fighting for whomever would pay him and his troops. As his tactical skill equaled his prudence, he survived many campaigns without a scratch and earned the love of his soldiers.

In the course of one of these campaigns, he came to grips with an army composed entirely of women.*

They looked beautiful, these women, in their shiny armor, their black manes flowing out of their helmets. When they charged on their steeds, they were a sight to behold, but they were no match for Francesco. After the battle their commander, Camilla Rodolfi, went to his tent to discuss the terms of surrender. When they emerged, they had become staunch friends. Likewise, his men and her women found much to talk about. Soon they

* See *The Story of the Sforzas* by L. Collison-Morley.

shared tents and war tales. Tears were shed on both sides when the rains came and the war ended.

It was now seven years since Francesco had left the service of Duke Filippo, who had inveigled himself into such a labyrinth of treacheries that he no longer knew where to turn. In despair, he called on his former general, offering him a huge raise in salary and, once again, the hand of his daugter Bianca, now a succulent fifteen.

Francesco flew to his rescue, but he had learned his lesson. He began his service by raping Bianca, who was so delighted by this outrage that she informed her father that she would marry none but her ravisher. Grudgingly, Filippo consented to the wedding and died shortly afterwards.

As he left no male heir, the throne of Milan remained vacant. Francesco longed to sit on it. He was growing old, bald, and pot-bellied. He had wearied of camp life. The prospect of becoming the ruler of one of the richest Italian states appealed to him. It seemed an appropriate way of ending his military career. His father, he felt, would thrill in his watery grave.

He knew, of course, that his wife, being illegitimate, had no claim to the crown. He also was aware that there existed a perfectly legal heir to the duchy, and this was Velentina Visconti's son, the French Duke Charles of Orleans.

But Charles was far away in his French chateau of Blois, writing poetry. He had not much money, no army. Francesco, on the other hand, had much money, a powerful and loyal army. Best of all, he was in Milan.

Thus, when a delegation of the guilds and the citizens came to offer him the Lombard crown, he accepted with alacrity.

He endeared himself to his new subjects by giving them a good government and the pageantry they loved. He also found time to beget nine children from Bianca and eleven bastards from various other ladies. He was sincerely mourned when he died in 1466, after a reign of sixteen years. His widow flung herself on his lifeless body, covered his face with kisses, spoke of joining him in the grave. When reminded of his countless infidelities, she proudly replied that "wenching comes naturally to men" and resumed her weeping.

He was succeeded by his eldest son, Galeazzo, who was handsome, courtly — and a sadist. In him, the peasant Sforza blood and the Visconti neuroses combined into a monster of cruelty and debauchery. He enjoyed raping his friends' wives or sisters, preferably in their presence. He liked strangling prisoners with his own gloved hands, hanging them by the genitals, or pushing them into roaring ovens. A poacher caught on his hunting preserve was made to eat a live rabbit, fur and all — an experience from which he died. He had his valet put on the rack for nicking his chin while shaving him. A courtier who had inadvertently brushed against his mistress had his arm amputated.

With all that, he maintained the finest choir in Europe, and sang with them in church. His hunting dogs were fed human flesh, and his favorites wore diamond collars.

His good looks and courtly manners had won him the heart and the hand of the young Duchess Bona of Savoy, whose sister was queen of France. Her love for him remained steadfast despite the flaws in his character.

The Milanese endured him ten years until at long last, on the day after Christmas, 1476, he was stabbed to death on the steps of San Stefano Church. The population let out a sigh of relief, but his widow gave vent to the most spectacular grief, even by Italian standards. For days she remained locked in a black-draped room — *la salanegra* — rending the air with her wails, refusing food, bumping her head against the walls. Never were so many tears shed for such an unworthy object.

As she feared — and with excellent reasons — for the salvation of her husband's soul, she petitioned Pope Sixtus IV for "a posthumous absolution": an extraordinary dispensation available only to the superrich. Fortunately, Bona was one of these. She wrote His Holiness, imploring him to let her monster of a husband into the kingdom of Heaven. In exchange, she pledged to lead a saintly life, wear a hair shirt, fast three times a week, and distribute large alms among the churches of Milan. *Papa Sisto* replied, approving of the saintly life, the hair shirt, the fasts. As for the alms, he directed that they be sent directly to him.

The sinister Galeazzo had left an heir: a blond, angelic-looking boy of seven named Gian Galeazzo, or Gian for short. He was duly crowned His Serene Highness of the sovereign duke of Milan in the cathedral amid the thunder of the organ and the pealing of bells. When he stood before the altar wearing the ermine mantle and the Lombard crown on his silky locks, every woman in the audience longed to hug him in her arms. To them he became *il duchetto* — "the little duke" — and they longed for the day when he would sit on the throne.

As he was too young to rule, Bona, his mother, assumed the regency. She plunged into her duties with the zeal of her passionate nature, devoting her days and much of her nights to affairs of state. Tirelessly she toiled at her desk, barely taking time to eat a crumb of stale bread or recite a rosary between audiences. To all, she was an inspiration.

Chastity, however, lay heavy upon her. Whatever his drawbacks, Galeazzo had been a superb lover and the memory of his embraces kept her tossing in bed at night. She lost weight; her face turned white as a pearl. Her eyes receded in their sockets. Her moans could be heard through the door of her bedroom. Everyone felt sorry for the bereaved duchess.

Then, one day when she was not fasting, she noticed that her young meat-carver, Antonio Tassino, was remarkably handsome. In his waist-high, skintight hose he looked good enough to eat. Soon she was eating meat every day just to watch him carve. Before long, she was spending all her time with him. Color returned to her cheeks; sparkle to her eye. The moans which seeped at night through her bedroom door no longer were those of despair.

Meanwhile, affairs of state were falling into neglect. Ambassadors cooled their heels in antechambers while waiting for audiences. Important documents gathered dust on her desk; urgent dispatches remained unanswered.

Something had to be done.

Stealthily, her brother-in-law Ludovico seized the reins of

government. While she frolicked with her meat-carver, her relative received ambassadors, answered dispatches, and ruled the duchy with the administrative talent he had inherited from his father. When he felt secure in his position, he packed Antonio Tassino off to his native Ferrara and the merry widow to a secluded castle, deep in a forest.

Bona's grief at the loss of her lover was, if possible, even greater than that at the death of her husband. At night, she walked along the ramparts howling at the moon, calling Antonio's name and keeping sentries awake.

Prayer and the healing hand of time finally brought her some measure of resignation. She returned to her fasts and hair shirt. She made friends with loneliness and at last peace descended upon her too-loving heart.

Meanwhile, Ludovico, now in full control of the regency, began making plans to seize his nephew's throne. In the Renaissance, such an ambition offered no serious difficulty. A pinch of poison, a strong hand clamped over the boy's neck at night, a pillow pressed on his face while he slept — any of these devices would have achieved his purpose.

But it was all too simple, too direct for Ludovico, who had inherited the complicated treacherousness of his grandfather, Filippo Visconti. Instead of simply murdering the child, he chose to corrupt his morals, blunt his mind, and make him incapable of founding a family or ruling the state.

And so the beautiful little duke was taken away from his mother, relegated to the Castle of Pavia several miles from Milan, left to the care of servants and the companionship of vicious boys, with the result that he grew up into a spineless, barely literate nonentity, a homosexual and a drunkard to boot.

Leonardo and his companion reached Milan, tired but buoyant with hope.

After a good night's sleep at an inn, they went on a tour of the city, which overwhelmed them by its spaciousness, the number of elegant carriages driving through its wide streets, the sight of its cathedral in process of construction, the life-size wax dummies in gleaming helmets and breast plates displayed in armorers' windows.

In the ice-cold January morning, Milan buzzed with activity. Signs of prosperity were everywhere. With its 300,000 inhabitants, 14,000 shops, 18,000 houses (Paris had only 13,000), Milan was one of the most impressive cities in Europe. Next to it, Florence was a speck of a town. In his heart, Leonardo knew he had come to the right place.

They went to the ducal palace, the immense Castello Sforzesco with its many buildings, high red walls and round towers, deep twin moats, and sixteen drawbridged gates guarded by halberded sentries. There Leonardo presented Lorenzo de'Medici's letter of introduction and was told that he would be informed of the day when His Excellency Duke Ludovico would receive him in audience.

Two days later he was escorted to the palace and ushered into a stately room with frescoes on the walls. Behind a marble railing, there was a canopy of mulberry-red velvet under which sat the duke-regent with his greyhound, Baretta, crouched at his feet.

He had an impassive tallowy face from which jutted a thin curved nose, not unlike a shark's fin. His dark, smooth hair ended in a short fringe across his forehead and rolled down to his shoulders. His eyes, black and opaque, gazed steadily under heavy, half-closed lids. Although only thirty-one, he was already stout, like his grandfather Filippo Visconti. He gave an impression of massiveness without strength, as though his body had neither bones nor muscles.

His manner was courtly but distant. He spoke slowly, with few gestures and long pauses between sentences. There was something unctuous, faintly sacerdotal about him. In his robe of crimson and gold brocade, he brought to mind those fat, ceremonious cardinals who ambled majestically along the Vatican galleries.

He read Lorenzo's letter of introduction and signaled Leonardo to play his lute. A thin smile of amusement lingered over his lips as he listened to the freakish instrument. The performance over, he spoke a few gracious words and motioned to an attending page to take the odd-looking lute from the visitor's hands.

He was about to terminate the audience when Leonardo swiftly pulled out of his sleeve's cuff the letter he had prepared and asked permission to read it. The duke nodded and the musician began reading aloud the prologue of his missive.

Having sufficiently considered by now, Most Illustrious Sir, the experiments of all those who are reputed masters and contrivers of war instruments and having found that, in character and working, said instruments do not differ from those which are in general use, I shall endeavor to divulge and explain my secrets to Your Excellency.

This famous letter gives a precious insight into Leonardo's opinion of himself. It reveals his immense conceit and naïve self-delusion about his talents as a scientist. It is also a good example of his involved and grandiloquent style, the earmark of the half-literate man that he was.*

These secrets which he was willing to divulge consisted of "light and movable bridges," tunnels that he could bore "without making any noise," bombards "that were loaded from the rear," catapults "of the most beautiful design," blunderbusses "of marvelous efficacy," and finally, "ships that would resist fire, powder and smoke."

Breathtaking as they were, these achievements concerned only the things he could do in time of war.

In time of peace, methinks I can give the best satisfaction, well bearing comparison with anyone else, in architecture, in the designing of buildings, whether private or public, and in conducting water from one place to another.

Coming from a man who had never built anything, these were brave words indeed. But there was more to come.

I shall carry out sculptures in marble, bronze, and clay, and similarly paintings of every possible kind to stand comparison with anyone else, be he who he may.

* The above quotation as well as all subsequent ones are taken from his manuscripts.

As the duke's face remained expressionless, Leonardo played
his last trump.

It will also be possible to put in hand the bronze horse which will be
an immortal glory and eternal honor to the happy memory of your
honored father and the illustrious House of Sforza.

This, he thought, should do the trick . . . Like everyone else
in Italy, he had heard of the colossal equestrian statue Ludovico
wanted to erect to the memory of his father, the famous *condottiere* and usurper of the throne of Milan. Many prominent
sculptors had been approached for its execution. All had declined,
because the specified size of the monument made its casting in
bronze impossible.

Leonardo had no such qualms. Although inexperienced in
sculpting, he felt certain he could solve the casting problem if he
only applied his mind to it. Besides, this was no time for details.
So keen was his desire to obtain a position at court, he would have
promised to fly to the moon.

As he spoke, he was aware of Ludovico's stony gaze upon him.
Not even the trowelful of flattery about "the immortal glory and
eternal honor of the illustrious House of Sforza" had brought a
gleam of interest in the duke's hooded eyes. A premonition of defeat ran through the petitioner.

Quickly, he finished reading the letter.

And if any of the aforesaid works should appear to anyone to be impossible of execution, I am ready at any time to put it to the test in
your park or at whatever place shall be convenient to Your Excellency, to whom I most humbly commend myself.

So saying, he bowed and waited.

After a while Ludovico broke his silence. In his halting manner
of speech, he thanked the visiting lute player for bringing his
various talents to his attention. Alas, he already had a military
engineer, an architect, a sculptor, a painter — all of whom gave

him complete satisfaction. Thus, there was no position available for him at the palace.

Then, with a flip of his white, pudgy hand, he terminated the audience.

Leonardo rejoined Atalante who was waiting for him at one of the palace's gates. A glance was enough for the young man to sense the crumbling of their beautiful plans. On their way back to the inn, they surveyed their situation. It was grim, not to say desperate. Traveling expenses had nearly exhausted Lorenzo's money. The last few florins would allow Atalante to return to his family. Leonardo had no family, and no wish to face the irate San Donato monks.

With tears in his eyes, he watched his pupil start on his way back to Florence. He now was alone and penniless in an alien town.

For him the remainder of the winter of 1482 was a nightmare. He walked aimlessly through the streets, warmed himself at the *braseros* in churches, waited in line for the soup the nuns ladled out at the door of their convents.

In March a chance encounter brought him in contact with the Predis brothers, three local craftsmen of small talent, but with keen business acumen. They quickly saw the profits they could derive from an association with such a gifted and indigent man. They entered into a sort of partnership and invited him to live with them in their house near the Ticino Gate.

Almost immediately, Ambrogio, the eldest of the brothers, secured for him an important commission: an altarpiece for the Chapel of the Immaculate Conception.

The monks knew what they wanted and they listed their specifications in a long and detailed contract. God the Father was to be represented surrounded by the Virgin, several angels and at least one prophet, preferably two. The Bambino, also, was to be there in His cradle "amid a mountainous background." Everyone was to wear a halo. The agreed price was two hundred florins, an uncommonly large fee. Delivery was to be made twenty months hence, by December 1484.

An advance was paid, and Leonardo set out to work. That is, he took long, solitary walks through the countryside, for spring had come to Lombardy. He dozed under shady trees, munched blades of grass, and cogitated.

One day the vision of "The Virgin of the Rocks" coalesced in his mind. The Madonna, her little boy, and his cousin Gianbattista, had come to rest in a cool and dim grotto where flowers grew in abundance. With them was an angel, the most bewitching female ever painted, who served as a sort of *bambinaia*. It was an improbable, tender and enchanting family scene. He held it on the screen of his mind long enough to let it imprint itself in his memory. Back at the Predis home, he sanded a large picture panel, and for the next three weeks he worked assiduously. Rapidly the masterpiece came to life.

By now, summer had come and the plague broke out in Milan. Bonfires were lit in public squares to purify the air. Processions snaked through the streets. Men and women flagellants ran about the city naked, lashing themselves. People died like flies. Their clothes were burned; their corpses piled high on red carts by hooded men with long iron pincers and then dumped into common graves. Duke Ludovico gave large alms to hospitals and prudently moved to his country estate of Vigevano.

Leonardo decided to look into this matter of the plague and relieve the suffering humanity of this dreadful, recurrent scourge. He would be the genial, ever-blessed conqueror of the plague. In heaven, Albiera would be proud of him; on earth, his father ashamed of himself.

All this, of course, was much more important than a mere altarpiece. He laid down his brushes and concentrated on the problem of the plague. In a short time, he had the solution. It was wondrously simple. All that was to be done was to raze Milan to the ground and replace it by ten cities of thirty thousand inhabitants each, built to his specification.

He had never built a chicken house, but the prospect of building ten cities did not daunt him at all. Excitedly, he wrote the duke of his plan.

In this way, you will distribute the masses of humanity which live together like herds of goats, filling the air with stench and spreading the seeds of plague and death.

Having thus reminded His Excellency of his existence and his desire to be of service, the self-appointed architect began drafting his ten ideal cities. They would rise along the Ticino River which would provide a natural sewer. Manure, offal, and the contents of slop jars would be emptied into the stream through a web of subterranean ducts or *vie sotterane*, as he called them. What would happen in summer when the Ticino dried up, he refused to contemplate.

Another imaginative feature of his model cities was that they would be partly built underground. The rich would live in the houses' upper floors and breathe fresh clean air. The poor — well, the poor would dwell underground, carry on with their menial tasks far from the sight of their betters, breathe their own fetid air in the unventilated ill-lit galleries, and probably go blind.

He was quite pleased with his brainchild and never tired of extolling its merits to the duke.

Each of these cities will be a symbol of beauty and great value in its yield and will bring you everlasting fame. Give me authority for all this to be done. . . .

None of his letters received any reply, but he continued to forge ahead and tackled the problem of latrines.

It was his considered opinion that Milanese latrines left much to be desired, and he proposed to improve this deplorable state of affairs.

Privvies need not be filled with their usual stench. But in order to attain what I promise, these places must be, contrary to the usual custom, kept clean and sweet.

He recommended that they be provided "with holes for the vapors to escape." As an illustration of what could be done in this field, he invented a toilet with a movable seat "like the little window in monasteries." Finally, in order to discourage the Milanese from their habit of relieving themselves on landings between floors, he advocated the construction of spiral staircases.

And so it went, while the peerless "Virgin of the Rocks" gathered dust on his easel.

As he never received any answer from Vigevano, he finally concluded that Duke Ludovico was not yet ready to raze his capital to the ground. He stopped writing, but did not resume work on the altarpiece. Instead, he launched into the study of wall fissures, indirect chimney drafting, the tensility of wires, the strength of arches and beams. As a diversion, he invented an ingenious screw for the loading of cannons.

In December 1484, the monks asked to see their alterpiece, as stipulated in the contract. Naturally, it was far from finished, but the prior insisted on coming to look at it. Loudly, he expressed his displeasure. His specifications so minutely listed had been disregarded altogether. Where was God the Father? And the prophets, where were they? And why was Jesus sitting on the ground instead of lying in His cradle? And the halos — where were the halos?

Scornfully, he offered twenty-five florins for the painting. Leonardo held out for one hundred. Strong words were exchanged. The dispute degenerated into a quarrel, the quarrel into a lawsuit which was to last twenty-three years.

The Predis brothers were not overly sympathetic. Bluntly, they told Leonardo that he would have to "earn his keep" if he wanted to go on eating their food and living under their roof. Reluctantly, he began making sketches of the "Virgin and Child" variety from which Ambrogio dashed off "commercial" pictures of dubious artistic merit. At night, Leonardo returned to his Latin grammar, his drawing of machines.

And so three more years went by. He now was thirty-five, still obscure and lonely. Dejectedly, he admitted being as much of a failure in Milan as he had been in Florence. His dream of a position at court seemed more remote than ever.

Once again he longed to go away, far away, to some exotic

town where some perceptive sultan would recognize his genius and reward it adequately. But he realized that his fancies would never come true. He was a timorous man. His adventures were only of the mind. He knew he would never leave Milan and would spend the rest of his life there, poor and friendless.

Then, in the spring of 1487, the tireless Ambrogio de'Predis secured for him another important commission: the portrait of the duke's mistress, Cecilia Gallerani.

She was seventeen, well-born, and slenderly pretty. Ludovico really loved this wisp of a girl and she was fond of him. Their relationship was pleasant, placid, almost conjugal.

She lived at the palace, and the sittings gave Leonardo the opportunity to discover the luxuriousness of her apartment. He thrilled at the Persian carpets on the floor, the tapestries on the walls, the window curtains of crimson brocade. For the first time he saw members of the court at close quarters. He gaped at the men's velvet doublets and elegant manners; the ladies' gowns of rustling silk. Just to be near them was almost too much to bear. He vowed that some day he, too, would be part of this glittering, enchanted world.

He applied himself and caught the sparkle in Cecilia's eyes, the impish half-smile at the corners of her lips. (Today the portrait hangs in the Czartoryski Museum in Krakow, Poland, under the title "Lady with an Ermine.")

The portrait delighted Cecilia; it impressed the duke who often came to visit her during the sittings. Gradually his suspicions against the bombastic lute player he had received in audience five years before disappeared. The man was truly a remarkable *dipintore*. Could he by chance be also as good a sculptor as he said he was?

"Are you absolutely certain you can execute the Sforza Monument?" he asked one day on an impulse.

"Give me two years and Your Excellency will have it standing in the Honor Courtyard of the palace."

The duke believed him. Then and there he entrusted him with the commission of the colossal monument.

As in a fairytale, Leonardo's life changed. He moved to the

palace where he was allocated three rooms in the "Old Court" — the servants' quarters — as well as a shed on the ground floor where the statue was to come to life. At the same time, the ducal treasurer, Gualtieri, informed him that he would receive a monthly salary of five florins, the same as the court's architect, Donato Bramante.

Of course, it was a long way from the prestigious, highly paid position of Chief Army Engineer he had coveted on his arrival in Milan. But he was too happy to argue. He had lodgings of his own and a regular salary. Better still, he had entered the enchanted world of the Sforza Court.

Now all he had to do was create the largest bronze statue in the world.

True, he had not the faintest idea how to go about it, did not know how to cast it in bronze if and when he ever finished, did not like sculpting (which he regarded as a dirty and inelegant craft), did not feel inspired by the subject: an aging, paunchy soldier of fortune on a horse. Nonetheless, he looked with assurance upon the task which had frightened the most experienced sculptors. After all, he had two years to do the confounded thing and in that period of time he would have solved whatever problems might arise along the way.

One thing was certain: he would stun the world. After a few rapid calculations, he announced to a panting world the dimensions of the forthcoming masterpiece. In those days, the average equestrian statue stood about ten feet in height and weighed about two thousand pounds. His, he predicted, would weigh one hundred thousand pounds with the horse alone (without the general) rising twelve ells or forty-five feet in the air. Moreover, the animal would stand on its hind legs without any frontal support, by a miracle of mathematical balance.

These pronouncements sent a ripple of astonishment through the peninsula. In Florence's wineshops, artists talked of nothing else. The painter-juggler-magician-singer-lutist had revealed himself the most daring sculptor the world had ever known.

Having rocked the artistic world on its foundations, he then withdrew into creative solitude.

Two years later Ludovico came to the shed, unannounced, and found his sculptor in residence ankle-deep in broken, two-inch wax models of rearing horses. The confounded beasts which reared so beautifully on paper invariably collapsed the moment they became three-dimensional.

The duke departed without saying a word, but that evening he took aside the Florentine ambassador, Pietro Alamanni, and beseeched him to write His Excellency Lorenzo de'Medici to send "one or two masters who might be equal to the task."

For Leonardo, the summer of 1489 was a nerve-racking period of anguish. He had been unmasked as a braggart, a *fanfarone*, in the eyes of his fellow artists. He trembled at the prospect of his forthcoming dismissal from the duke's service. His heart sank at the thought of it. He had made a few friends among the ducal employees; he had become attached to his cozy lodgings, his cluttered study with the hooded chimney and the table where he sat by candlelight to fill his everlasting notebooks during the long solitary evenings. At the thought of saying goodbye to all that and resuming his wandering, hand-to-mouth existence he was filled with despair.

In an attempt to placate the duke he wrote an apology, not a humble plea for mercy, but a grandiloquent justification which, for greater effect, he had translated into Latin:

I am no Lysippus or Apelles or Polycletus or Zeuxis or Myron, noble in bronze; I am the Florentine Leonardo, a son of Vinci, admirer and grateful pupil of the Ancients. All that I lack is the ancient symmetry. I have done what I could. May posterity grant me its indulgence.

He was saved from dismissal by an event which occupied Ludovico's attention at the time: the wedding of his nephew Gian.

Before long, he calculated, he would reap the reward of his machiavellian plan. At nineteen, Gian had grown into a strikingly handsome adolescent, a confirmed homosexual, and a doltish drunkard. The population ignored all of this. They wanted their *duchetto* to marry some beautiful princess, sire many boys, and take in hand the reins of government. Chuckling to himself, Ludovico agreed heartily with them and promised to find him a suitable bride.

By refinement of cruelty, he chose his own niece, Isabella of Aragon, daughter of his sister Ippolita and granddaughter of Don Ferrante, king of Naples.

The wedding was celebrated in February 1489 with appropriate pageantry, thirty-six priests, squadrons of cavaliers in gold helmets, and a white carpet stretching all the way from the ducal palace to the cathedral. The bride had golden skin, blue-black hair and the ardent temperament of Neapolitan women. She was seventeen, eager to love and be loved. The moment she saw Gian, she gave him her heart, wholly and forever. As the bridal couple rode side by side away from the cathedral, people said they were the fairest couple in Europe.

The nuptial festivities were postponed until the following year because of the sudden death of Isabella's mother. By then, however, the court's *festaiuolo* or master of revels, Bergonzo Botta, fell ill, and Leonardo was asked to replace him.

In January 1490, he presented his first *spectacolo*, a ballet named *The Heavenly Feast*. Its immense success restored him to the duke's favor. Once again his talent for frivolities had come to his rescue. Just as his freakish lute had salvaged him from the laggard painter of the Adoration for the San Donato monks, his *Heavenly Feast* redeemed the incompetent sculptor.

As for him, he had found his métier. He felt at ease in the make-believe, tinsel world of masquerades and *divertimenti*. He was a *festaiuolo* born with an inexhaustible gift for costumes, hilarious skits of grotesque instruments, choreographic ensembles. Other festivities during the winter season confirmed his reputation. His position at court was now secure. Servants doffed their hats to him in the palace's courtyards when he passed by.

Success breeds success. He was the man of the hour. Ladies asked him to organize festivities in their homes, sought his opinion of their dresses. Suddenly he was regarded as a great architect.

General Sanseverino, commander in chief of the nonexistent Milanese army, commissioned him to draw the plans of a stable for his Arabian horses. This horse stable, and another one he drew many years later for Giuliano de'Medici, constitute the sum total of his architectural works that ever were realized.

Meanwhile, disturbing rumors had begun to trickle from Pavia where the newlyweds had retired after the wedding. Gossip had it that His Highness refused to touch his bride Isabella, who was still a maiden and was forced to sleep with one of her ladies-in-waiting. Her timid advances were brutally rejected by her husband who preferred the company of pretty boys. Tales of drunken and pederastic orgies spread consternation in Milan. At public fountains, housewives wondered if, by chance, their beloved *duchetto*, grandson of the memorable Francesco Sforza — he of the twenty children! — might not be a *sodomista*.

These reports were, of course, music to Ludovico, who carefully fed them while pretending to ignore them. Inwardly he exulted. The time was approaching when the population would beg him to accept the crown his nephew was unworthy to wear.

In his impatience to hasten that day, he committed an irreparable blunder.

He summoned his nephew before an assembly of prominent citizens presided over by the archbishop of Milan and lashed into him with a vehement pretense of surprise and indignation. Was it true that Her Highness Isabella was still a virgin? Was it true that he shamed and scorned her in public? Didn't he know that her grandfather, His Majesty Don Ferrante, threatened to recall her to Naples, demand the refund of her dowry, and declare war on Milan?

He waxed eloquent and gave a superb performance, ending with a ringing peroration in which he declared Gian unworthy of the Lombard crown.

Through it all, the handsome young prince stood, head bowed, his face livid with rage. The session over, he galloped to Pavia, grabbed Isabella by the wrist, flung her on a bed and did what he should have done long before. Nine months later to the day, she gave birth to a son who was named Francesco.

Ludovico was aghast. Now there were two obstacles between him and the throne. Worse still, rumors were now circulating about *him.* Here he was, almost forty, and not yet married. Could anything be wrong with him?

Realizing he must marry as soon as possible, he remembered that he had been more or less engaged to the duke of Ferrara's younger daughter, Beatrice d'Este. She had been five at the time of their engagement; she was now fifteen. He sent an ambassador to Ferrara with instructions to conclude the wedding negotiations as soon as possible.

On 29 December 1490, Beatrice, swathed in sable fur (a gift from Ludovico), emerged from her father's palace in a gaily decorated sleigh with her buffoon, Fritella, cuddled at her side. Behind came the members of her retinue, also in festooned and beribboned sleighs, and a train of wagons carrying her trousseau.

As the cortege slid over the frozen Po River, she dreamed of the exciting life that was awaiting her as the wife of the Duke Ludovico Sforza. She knew almost nothing about him, except that he was very, very rich and maintained the most sumptuous court in Europe. To her it meant a never-ending whirl of balls, masquerades, plays, and hunting parties. And, of course, countless gowns and furs, coffers filled with gems.

Her disappointments began with her wedding night. After doing his duty by her, Ludovico politely excused himself, and joined his mistress, Cecilia, who lived in the apartment on the floor below.

This first disillusion was followed by others.

Her husband, she found out, was not the Prince Charming she had fancied on her sleigh journey, but an aging, huge-bellied, courtly stranger who paid scant attention to her. Nor was he duke of Milan, as she naïvely believed, but only duke-regent, a sort of prime minister who governed in the name of his nephew Gian, a pervert and drunkard. Still harder to swallow was that the real duchess of Milan was her cousin Isabella, daughter of the crown prince of Naples.

Beatrice vowed that she would detach her husband from his

mistress. She would inflame his lust, conquer his heart, and bend him to her will. It was an almost impossible task, but she tackled it with iron determination. This short, pudgy, apple-cheeked country girl turned into the most seductive of courtesans. In a few months she dislodged Cecilia from the palace.

Now in possession of the battlefied, she went after Isabella. With the approval of her doting husband, she outdressed her rival, wore the state jewels which by right belonged to her cousin. Never did she let an opportunity pass to humiliate Her Highness.

An undeclared war began between the two young women.

It did not take long for Leonardo to guess that Beatrice would win the contest and wisely he sided with her. She, in turn, took him under her wing.

She did not ask him to paint her portrait, but she spent hours with him going over the details of plays and masquerades. She trusted his taste and asked his counsel on her dresses and coiffures. At his suggestion, she changed the color of her window curtains. When she learned that he had a fine voice and played the lute well, she had him entertain the members of her intimate entourage.

She made a courtier out of him, and never was there a more assiduous pupil.

He began dressing in silks of purple and scarlet, his favorite colors. Over his balding head he wore a dashing beret of black velvet. He perfumed his beard and waxed the tips of his moustache, for the Milanese had a passion for scents and washed their clothes in perfume.

He cut a handsome figure with his graying long beard and fine garments. Beatrice introduced him in the circle of ladies and noblemen who revolved around her. He aped the manners of the aristocracy and soon bowed from the waist and fluttered his hands with the best of them.

Tenaciously, he toiled to erase all traces of his humble origins and lack of formal education.

By candlelight, he pored over Pulci's *Vocabolista* and laboriously copied seven thousand Italian words: long and impressive ones, such as syllogism, rhetoric, sophism, ostentation, which he later used in his conversation. His pride at learning all those fine words was touching and so great that he could not refrain from revealing his jubilation.

I now possess so many words in my mother tongue that I am more likely to have trouble with the right understanding of things than from lack of words with which to express my mind's conception of them.

To please Beatrice, he even tried becoming a raconteur. Painstakingly he copied fables, maxims, witticisms, which he later offered as his own during the long winter evenings by the fire when no play or masquerade was being presented.

He told about "the siren who sings so sweetly that she lulls the mariners to sleep, then climbs aboard and kills the sleeping navigators"; the ant "who, by natural instinct, provides in summer for the winter"; the unicorn "who sleeps in the lap of a pure maiden and can be captured only in this way"; the salamander "who lives in the fyre"; the chameleon "who flies above the clouds"; the oyster "who symbolizes treachery."

His efforts were well rewarded. The son of Caterina the farm girl now exchanged repartees with noblemen, received confidences from contessas, knew the palace's gossip, and delivered secret amorous missives. He was not quite "accepted," but he was useful. He also gave medical advice, and recommended a potion of his own composition to dissolve kidney stones. His singing and lute playing added to his popularity.*

Having mastered the art of social climbing, he felt it his duty to pass on to future generations of social climbers the secret of his success.

---

* His exertions as a courtier and entertainer won him more applause than his achievements as an artist. Paolo Giovio, a contemporary of his and his first biographer, wrote of him: "He was a rare master, inventor of pleasing stage spectacles, skilled also in music, playing upon the lute and singing most sweetly. He became dear in high degree to all the princes who knew him." There is no mention of painting or sculpture.

Avoid at all times the words that do not please the ear of a listener or fill him with tedium or annoyance. You may see sign of it in that such listeners emit copious yawns. Accordingly, in talking to men whose goodwill you wish to enlist, when you see such signs of annoyance, cut short your words and change the subject. . . . When you see he no longer yawns, you may be certain that this subject is the one in which he takes pleasure.

Still he found time to dissect more corpses and make anatomical drawings of surpassing beauty.* He even had the courage to resume work on the Sforza Monument, but this time there was no more nonsense about a rearing horse, forty-five feet high. In the course of a journey to Pavia, he had admired the equestrian statue of Gisulf, king of the Goths, and he had been deeply impressed by his horse which managed to look martial, yet stood on three legs. When he went back to his *cavallo*, Leonardo had Gisulf's horse in mind, and this time the work proceeded rapidly. It had shrunk to twenty-six feet and become a placid, big-bellied palfrey.

With zest, he slammed clods of moist clay over the frame of the statue, kneading them into shanks, legs, shoulders. In a few months he had the horse's front quarters. He was starting to work on the middle when, in January 1493, Beatrice gave birth to a boy who was named Ercole, after her father.

From that day onward, she was like a woman possessed. No longer was it enough to humiliate Isabella, she must destroy her, seize the throne for herself and her boy. The fact that Isabella also had a son did not matter.

More disturbing was the fact that Isabella's grandfather, the king of Naples, had the most powerful army in Italy and threatened to march upon Milan. But Beatrice happened to read the letters from the Milanese ambassador at the court of France and from them she learned of King Charles's impatience to "regain" his stolen kingdom of Naples.

* Yet even there his mastery of draftsmanship is combined with baffling errors, as in the famous "Coicion Figure" in which his drawing of the penis is shown with two canals: one for the sperm and urine, the other "for the soul."

This was the solution.

If the Little King and his terrible army could be lured to Italy, they would push Don Ferrante into the sea and deprive Isabella of her only ally. Her stupid husband Gian would be easily persuaded to abdicate in favor of Ludovico. Thus Beatrice would become the sovereign duchess of Milan, succeeded by her son and his sons until the end of time.

She won Ludovico to her scheme, masterminded the bribing of the French court officials, and knew the headiness of triumph when the drooling nitwit set foot in Italy. Leonardo's festivities at the Annona Castle had marked the peak of Beatrice's triumph.

Alas, the honeymoon had been short. Charles had proven an autocratic, expensive, and erratic ally.

Ludovico had begun having second thoughts about his wife's scheme. His last illusions vanished when Duke Gian died of natural causes a few weeks after the French had entered Italy. Naturally, Isabella and her son were pushed aside. Beatrice and Ludovico were duly crowned duke and duchess of Milan. During the ceremony, Ludovico reflected bitterly on the immense sums of money he had spent to seize the crown which would have descended upon his head of its own accord, if Beatrice had only waited a few months.

He hungered to hurt back and he did so where it hurt most, her pride. He took one of her ladies-in-waiting, Lucrezia Crivelli, as his mistress and flaunted his new love before the court.

It was Beatrice's turn to taste the humiliations she had heaped on her cousin. She was now the sovereign duchess of Milan, but she had lost her husband.

If Leonardo felt sorry for his benefactress, he did not waste a single word of compassion over her downfall in his notebooks. He painted the portrait of the new favorite and ingratiated himself with her, as he had with Beatrice.

He had worries of his own. His position as the court's *festaiuolo* which had seemed so secure, now hung by a thread. To recoup some of the money he had so unwisely spent, Ludovico drastically curtailed festivities. To give Leonardo something to do, he commissioned him to paint "The Last Supper" on one of the walls of the refectory of the Santa Maria delle Grazie Monastery.

He had never liked to paint and he liked it even less now. He had lost all religious faith and "The Last Supper" ignited no emotion in him. But he trembled at the prospect of being dismissed from the duke's service. He was forty-three, with almost no savings. He had taken into his lodgings a beautiful street urchin whom he called Salai, or "Little Devil," and who cost him nearly every *soldo* he earned.

Salai was the love and despair of his life. In his notebook, the aging *festaiuolo* vented his desolation: "He is thievish, lying, obstinate, gluttonous. He steals money, yet it is impossible to wring a confession from him."

What would become of the two of them if Duke Ludovico discharged him?

He accepted the commission, signed a contract stipulating a date of completion. This done, he went to the monastery and gazed at the thirty-foot blank wall he was expected to decorate.

He had never done a mural, but already he planned to make his one of the world's wonders. To begin with, it would not be painted in fresco technique which required that the color be applied in a thin coat of fresh plaster. It would be painted in gleaming oil paints of his composition. When finished, his "Last Supper" would glow like an immense sheet of enamel.

He worked intermittently on it for three years, and it was not, naturally, completed on the stipulated date. A note dated June 1497 from Duke Ludovico reminds his minister, Stanga, "to ask Leonardo, the Florentine, to finish his work on the wall of the Refectory, which he stipulated in an agreement signed by his own hand, to finish within a certain time." It was finally completed — almost — in the spring of 1498.

Many things had happened during this time.

Beatrice died. In the last months of her life, she had become a haggard shadow of her former self. Her bulging eyes were bloodshot, her cheeks waxen. Although in the last stages of pregnancy, she insisted on dancing until dawn or going boar-hunting with a trained leopard crouched behind her saddle.

On the night of 2 January 1497, she supped with a few friends in her apartment, laughed very loud, drank a great deal. Then, the orchestra began a lively tarantella. While the revelry proceeded, she collapsed, and for a while no one noticed her lying inert on the floor. At midnight she was dead, after giving birth to a stillborn daughter. She was twenty-two.

Meanwhile, Leonardo was working furiously on a thousand inventions. He had had enough of ballets and masquerades, enough of painting, this wretched profession that brought neither fame nor riches. His decision was irrevocable; he even had put it in writing in his notebook. *"La mia arte la quale voglio mutare."* . . . "This profession of mine which I want to change."

He would go into business for himself, earn a fortune from his inventions. He would become an industrialist.

On the night of 1 January 1496, he happened to invent a needle-sharpening machine that, in his opinion, would revolutionize the textile industry and make him enormously rich.

As he sketched the device, his enthusiasm grew. This time he would be shrewd; he would manufacture his invention and let no one else fatten on his genius.

Already he computed the gigantic wealth that would soon be his:

A hundred times an hour with four hundred needles each time makes 40,000 an hour and in twelve hours, 480,000. But let us say 400,000 which, at five *soldi* per thousand, gives 20,000 *soldi*, that is in all 1,000 *lire* every working day, and with twenty working days on the month it is 240,000 lire or 60,000 florins a year.

Tomorrow, 2 January 1496, I shall have a model of the strap made. . . .

Sixty thousand a year! More than most people ever earned in a lifetime. At long last, colossal wealth was within his reach.

But he did not have the model of the strap made the following morning. Because — well, because it was snowing and he did not feel like trudging through the snow for a strap. "After all, I am not going to build my factory tomorrow, am I?"

Anyway, he had just thought of another, even more profitable invention. A cloth-warping machine this time. Why settle for 60,000 florins when he could earn more, much more? Yes, he would manufacture both his needle-sharpening and cloth-warping machines. But already a third invention was bursting out of his ever-fertile brain. A roller-bearing machine this time, which promised untold riches . . . Why think in thousands when it was just as simple to think in millions?

When he was not calculating his forthcoming wealth, he wrote in his right-to-left handwriting (which he fancied undecipherable) about his most secret thoughts. In a delirium of disorderliness, he jotted down helter-skelter chemical formulas, geometry theorems, aphorisms, household accounts. He railed at the priests "who have naught but words and water"; he scoffed at the "unhappy women who, from their own free will, confess to men their most shameful and secret deeds." He described Jesus as "a man who died in the East"; he, the painter of Madonnas, laughed at the cult of Mary. He mocked astrology and fortune-telling and later admitted having spent six *soldi* to have his fortune told — *per dir la ventura.*

Above all, he lashed at those who called him "a man without letters" because of his lack of formal education. He denounced those who denied the importance of his inventions.

I know well that, because I have no literary education, there are some who will think in their arrogance that they are entitled to set me down as uncultured. The fools! They go about, puffed and pompous, in fine raiments and bejeweled, not from the fruits of their own labors, but my own labors they refuse to recognize. They despise me, the inventor, but how much more are they to blame for not being inventors, but trumpeters and reciters of the works of others.*

---

* Leonardo has often been described as a superhuman, olympian scientist who invented practically everything, from the ballpoint pen to the submarine and helicopter. This awe-inspiring legend is somewhat impaired by the fact that we are never sure which of his machines are truly original and which are not.

In his study "On the Relation between Leonardo's Science and Art," Kenneth Clark writes, "Of the hundreds of machines scattered through Leonardo's notebooks, which are inventions and which are simply drawings of things seen?"

Along the way he kicked at courtiers, the same courtiers he had so assiduously copied and entertained with song and lute; he struck at the clergy, "those greedy Roman wolves with their thousand spurious relics." Even his fellow artists knew the sting of his venom. Antonio Pollaiuolo, who had tried to help him with his Sforza monument, was castigated for his nudes "which are wooden and without grace, resembling sacks of nuts or, indeed, a bunch of radishes." Nor was he more lenient with Botticelli's admirable "Annunciation" in which "Our Lady looks as though she wanted to throw herself from the window." With equal severity, he censured the painter of "Primavera" for his "very poor landscapes" – *"tristissimi paesi."* There was very little milk of human kindness in Leonardo.

No one found mercy in his eyes. His bitterness swelled into a wish for cosmic cataclysm and the extinction of Man.

O Earth, why dost thou not open and engulf in the fissures of thy crevasses and caverns this ruthless monster.

He did not even like children. To a friend who informed him of the birth of a son, he wrote, "You have provided yourself with an enemy waiting for the freedom which will come to him only with your death."

Amid the permanent cerebral eruption in which he lived, he managed to finish his "Last Supper" which was very much admired. Meanwhile, in Florence Savonarola's reign was coming to an end with the Ordeal by Fire and the siege of the San Marco Convento. On the same day, King Charles removed himself from the earthly scene by colliding with a door.

The news of his death shattered Ludovico, for Charles's successor was none other than Louis of Orleans, grandson of Valentina Visconti, the last legitimate heir to the crown of Milan. And Louis's first pronouncement on becoming king of France had been, "I shall soon go to Italy and regain my duchy of Milan."

Leonardo loved to sleep late in the morning, and to correct himself of this habit, he had invented an ingenious device which served him more or less as an alarm clock.

At the foot of the bed, a pipe slowly dripped water into a basin set upon a tubular lever which was held down by another basin of water. When the first basin reached a certain weight, it sank, lifting the other end of the tubular lever. The shallow water basin emptied. Brusquely, the lever pushed up the feet of the sleeper who bounced out of bed and went about his business.

Under the sketch of this contraption, he had sententiously written:

This is a clock for the use of those who watch jealously over the use of their time.*

He seldom used it for, like everything else, he preferred his bad habits to his good resolutions. Only in times of great stress had he turned to it, as when he had to organize some important festivity.

No festivity was scheduled for that April day of 1499. Yet shortly after sunrise he had got out of bed without the help of his alarm clock. Now, as the sun slowly spread over the Old Court, he was leaning on the sill of his bedroom window gazing unseeingly into the cloudless sky.

Like everyone else at the ducal palace, he knew that the end was not far away. In a few weeks the French would trample over Lombardy on their march upon defenseless Milan. He shuddered at the prospect of the dreaded *écorcheurs* butchering the duke's officials and employees.

"Then what will become of me and Salai?" he asked half aloud.

As he formulated the thought, he was filled with pangs of regrets. Why, oh why hadn't he gone into business for himself, as he had planned? By now the manufacture of his needle-sharpening and cloth-warping machines would have made him a millionaire. Instead, here he was, forty-seven and looking almost ten years older, with little chance of finding employment and almost as poor as when he had arrived in Milan seventeen years before.

How much did he have exactly? Suddenly he wanted to know the precise amount of his savings.

* Both the sketch and the remark are in Manuscript B in the library of the Institut de France in Paris.

He pulled away from the windowsill, passed into the adjoining study, pulled out one of the bricks in the fireplace, and took out a small money-box. He counted its contents. Two hundred and eighteen lire.

Not much, was it, for his countless ballets, masquerades, his "Last Supper" and his beautiful clay horse of the Sforza Monument which was still standing in the Honor Courtyard, looking like marble from afar, but now gray with dust and slowly crumbling away. Not much, indeed!

He replaced the money-box in its hiding-place, walked to his writing table, and, sharpening his quill, entered the date and amount in his notebook.

Today, on the first of April, 1499, I found myself with 218 lire.

Gradually, his shock swelled into anger. For two years his salary had not been paid and *per Bacco!* he wasn't going to be cheated out of his just wages! It seemed that the duke needed every *soldo* to prepare for the forthcoming French invasion. Well, that was too bad, but it was none of his affair. Nor did he care if no one else at the palace had been paid either. Let them be fleeced if they chose. As for himself, he was going to demand his money.

Three times he drafted the letter and three times he crumpled it and flung it away. Finally, he had it. Forceful, subtle, clever, just as he wanted it.

Sir,
Knowing the mind of Your Highness to be fully occupied, I must ask pardon for reminding you of my small affairs. Gladly would I undertake immortal works, but I am obliged to earn my living. My life is at your service; I am ready to obey your commands. . . . But, as Your Highness is aware, two years' salary is owing to me. . . . I will say nothing of the horse, because I know the times.

Painstakingly he copied the letter, read it aloud to himself, and found it perfect.

He rose, peered into the bedroom to make sure that Salai was still asleep on his cot, his lovely profile pressed against the pillow. Noiselessly he closed the door, threw his long purple cloak over his shoulders, and went to the office of the treasurer, Gualtieri, in the administration building.

"Ha, another letter!" exclaimed the official with well-feigned cheerfulness. "If you painted as diligently as you write, I wouldn't have to send you those sharp little notes reminding you of your obligations."

He let out a jovial, forgiving chuckle, straddled a pair of spectacles over his nose, and perused the letter.

"You are absolutely right," he said, resting it on his lap. "Your wages are long in arrears, and no one deplores it more than myself. But, as you know, His Highness is preparing the duchy against the imminent French invasion. Cannons cost a great deal of money and we who have lived for many years at the palace must make sacrifices."

The cordiality went out of his voice. "If, however, you find your lot unbearable you may leave the duke's service at any time."

Leonardo had not foreseen this eventuality. Hastily he declared that his dearest wish was to go on creating immortal works for His Highness.

The grin returned to the treasurer's lips. "In this case, I have another little task for you."

He explained that Duchess Isabella, widow of the lamented Duke Gian, had moved to the Castello Sforzesco. Like most southern ladies, Her former Highness had remained very fond of hot baths. It would greatly please her if Leonardo would install a hot-water duct into her bathroom.

Leonardo remained silent, but his face flushed with humiliation. Was this "the immortal work" he was offering to create?

But already the treasurer was proceeding.

"For a scientist of your stature," he went on, keeping his eyes on the crestfallen *festaiuolo*, "the matter should present no serious problem, I am sure, and it will give you something to do for the next few weeks."

Leonardo was seething when he walked out of the treasurer's office. A plumber, that's what he had become! Was this going to be his future status? A sort of handyman who would install hot-water ducts in bathrooms, hang window curtains, do plastering or carpentry tasks when required?

Again he felt a stab of regret for not having gone into business for himself. But what could he do, where could he go with 218 lire in his money-box? Oh, poverty, hideous poverty!

Such were his thoughts as he walked aimlessly through the city. Suddenly he found himself in the vicinity of the Santa Maria della Grazie Monastery. He needed to feast his eyes on his "Last Supper," replenish his stock of self-assurance by the sight of his masterpiece.*

Over a year had passed since he had seen it last. It still glowed as when he had finished it. Gradually, however, as his eyes adjusted to the dimness of the refectory room, he became aware that small pieces of the mural were flaking off the wall. No doubt his assistants had made some mistake in the application of the resin primer he had especially composed for it. The blemishes were very small and few people would notice them. Perhaps the peeling would stop of its own accord. Anyway, it still was an impressive work and he felt proud of it.

Back at the palace, he began making preliminary sketches for the duchess's bathroom. This plumbing problem required as much cogitating as a work of art. By the end of April he was still turning it in his mind when he was summoned to Duke Ludovico's office.

The strain of the last few months had ravaged the prince's impassive, slablike face. It now guttered down in flabby folds that

---

* "The Last Supper" has received ecstatic praise; it also has been called a very bad painting, bereft of all religious feeling, full of theatrical agitation, mathematical miscalculations, and faulty drawing, especially in the hands. The celebrated art scholar, Bernard Berenson, compared it to a "deafening, fatiguing squabble on a Neapolitan market-place."

Today it can be said that Leonardo's work no longer exists. Lord Clark points out that a few years after its completion, the mural was already a hopeless wreck. "The painting we see today is largely the work of restorers. The coarsely painted grimaces are all that time and restoration have left us and would have horrified Leonardo."

The monks did not help matters by cutting a door in the mural.

shook when he spoke. His hair had turned gray. Shadows of sleeplessness circled his eyes. He had become very pious in adversity and gave large alms to atone for his past sins. For a moment he remained silent, tapping Leonardo's letter in the palm of his hand.

"Your complaints about your unpaid wages are justified, but your remarks about the bronze casting of your horse are out of place and in bad taste. It may come as a surprise to you, that the Sforza Monument was intended as a tribute to our honored father. You haven't done or even begun his statue, and yet you have the effrontery to expect me to squander 60,000 pounds of bronze on a riderless animal. Moreover, all the experts are of the opinion that the casting operation would be unsuccessful."

His expression softened.

"All of us are led astray by vanity," he said gently, "and we can only hope in God's mercy."

He then spoke of the imminent arrival of the French in Lombardy and their probable entrance in Milan. But even if they captured the city, they would never seize the ducal palace with its double moat, its sixteen fortified, drawbridged gates, its ramparts bristling with guns, its immense stocks of food and ammunitions.

"We want you to make it still more impregnable," he said, and right then and there appointed him *ingeniere camerale* in charge of the palace's defenses.

Leonardo assured him that his military talents were at his service. Ludovico thanked him with a smile and assured him that while the French would exhaust themselves trying to enter the *castello*, he would raise a powerful army of German mercenaries and force the invaders to retreat behind their mountains. Then his wages would be paid in full and everything would return to normal. He only asked for loyalty and a little patience.

"Meanwhile," he added, "here is a token of our esteem."

So saying, he handed him the deed to a vineyard near the Vercilian Gate.

Dutifully the new engineer inspected the palace's ramparts and jotted down this observation.

Since the power of artillery has increased by one third, the ramparts
should be made one third stronger.

He did not pursue the matter any further and returned to the
duchess's bathroom. In August he made a note that "three parts
of hot water to four of cold" would make a pleasantly warm bath.

He was still immersed in plumbing when the French approached Milan. Nowhere did they meet with any resistance. The
commander in chief of the Milanese troops, General Sanseverino
(for whom Leonardo had built that beautiful horse stable), fled
at night even before his men had to face the enemy.

Ludovico sobbed at the news. On 31 August he drew up his
will, specifying that the money he had extorted "from the Jews
be spent on good deeds." This done, in the presence of the entire
ducal household in the Honor Courtyard, he handed the keys of
the palace to the garrison's commander, Bernardino da Corte,
who received them on his knees. With tears rolling down his
cheeks, Bernardino swore to defend the *castello* to his last breath.
With its 1,800 cannons and 2,800 men, he vowed that the fortress
would defy the barbarians forever.

On these comforting assurances, Ludovico informed his household that he was leaving for Innsbruck in the Tyrol, and would
soon return with a powerful German army.

Three days later the French entered Milan, but did not even
attempt to besiege the *castello*. The following week, without having fired a single shot, Bernardino let the French commander in
chief know that he could have the palace for the sum of 30,000
gold florins.

He got them, and the French entered the impregnable fortress
to the sound of trumpets. A month later King Louis XII made his
entrance in Milan to the cries of "*Francia! Francia!*" and the pealing of church bells.

This was the happiest day of his life. At thirty-seven, the dream
he had nursed for so many years had finally come true, and a
euphoric grin creased his scrawny, bilious face. From his earliest
childhood, he had heard of that fairylike Italian city which belonged to his family and which had been "stolen" by a rowdy

Italian *condottiere* by the name of Francesco Sforza. Once, during Charles's Italian expedition, Louis had attempted to seize Milan with a small contingent of his own men while the drooling nitwit was frolicking in Naples with the Santa Chiara novices. He had failed, and it would have been easy for Ludovico to dispose of his rival once and for all. On an unwise impulse of generosity, he had released his prisoner and let him return to France.

Today Louis was reaping the reward of Ludovico's folly and tasted the ambrosia of revenge. As the crowds waved their hats and women blew kisses at him, he admired the wide tree-lined avenue, the stately palazzi of the local aristocracy, the magnificent, still unfinished cathedral. Leonardo's "Last Supper" made an overwhelming impression on him. He wanted nothing less than to bring to France the wall on which it was painted. Great was his disappointment when he was told it could not be done.

On learning that the creator of the mural was the same man who had molded the huge clay horse standing in the Courtyard of Honor, he demanded to have this extraordinary artist brought to him. Leonardo was at his best. He performed the three ritual genuflections, swept the floor with his velvet beret, and accepted with becoming modesty the compliments King Louis showered upon him. He assured the monarch that he was ready "to undertake immortal works" and bring "eternal glory" to his reign.

After that, he found himself in high favor with the barbarians. The young Seigneur de Chaumont, who was to remain as viceroy of Milan after the king's departure, summoned him to a private audience. He, too, mentioned painting commissions, architectural plans for a summer residence, and, of course, the organization of brilliant festivities for the coming winter season. Again Leonardo pledged his total devotion to the French.

On top of all this he was escorted to Cesare Borgia's apartment. The twenty-four-year-old cardinal had renounced the trappings of his high ecclesiastical rank for a doublet of white satin which set off his short auburn beard. He now had become the French duc de Valentinois and wore the sash of the Order of Saint Michael, the highest French decoration.

This transformation was due to the astuteness of his honored genitor, the Holy Father Alexander VI. King Louis had repudiated his wife, Jeanne of France (who was canonized in 1957), in order to marry Charles's widow, Queen Anne. To do this required several papal dispensations which Pope Alexander had granted on fulfillment of three conditions: (a) that his son Cesare would be made a French duke; (b) that he would be given a French princess as a bride; (c) that he would receive assistance in men as well as money in the achievements of his military aspirations: the carving for himself of a kingdom in central Italy.

"I have greatly admired the *castello*'s fortifications," began the former prelate, "and I understand you had much to do with them."

Modestly, Leonardo admitted he had been Ludovico's military engineer, but did not go into further details.

"I, too, have some military plans of my own," continued Cesare Borgia, "and I hope to avail myself of your services at the proper time."

Leonardo swore his unfaltering devotion to the Borgia family and returned to his lodgings blessing the Providence for bringing to Milan these wonderful and appreciative conquerors. His salary was being paid again. He still had his lodgings, his beloved Salai, and the future, so bleak a few weeks before, was now rosy and secure.

King Louis remained exactly one month in Milan. He was recalled to France by the news that during his absence Queen Anne had been safely delivered of a daughter. More than anything he wanted a son, but he swallowed his disappointment and hurried back home to resume the pursuit of an heir to the throne.

No sooner had the monarch gone, than Leonardo found himself involved in an absurd cloak-and-dagger intrigue.

During King Charles's Italian invasion four years before, count de Ligny, his *compagnon de lit*, had married the Neapolitan Princess Altamura, who owned extensive estates. Since then the princess had died, but the count was resolved to recoup her vast domains — by force, if necessary.

To this end, he planned to lead a small army of his own across Tuscany and needed to learn about the system of Florence's military defenses. And who could better give expert information on this subject than the great military engineer who happened to be a Florentine?

Henceforth, he wallowed in clandestine meetings, passwords, coded messages, barely audible whispers. He could not, however, refrain from writing of his secret activities, but he multiplied his precautions. Besides his inverted writing, he now used names only in anagrams. Ligny became "Ingil"; Roma "Morra"; Napoli "Ilopanna." The child in him was having a wonderful time.

Then everything collapsed in December, when news reached Milan that Ludovico was returning at the head of a strong German and Swiss army. The French, who, in three months, had made themselves detested by the population, began packing their loot and returning home. Count de Ligny abandoned his harebrained Neapolitan adventure and resumed the command of the French cavalry.

Abruptly, Leonardo was again in a pit of despair. Ludovico, who had given him a vineyard and depended on his loyalty, would not appreciate his fervent "collaboration" with the enemy. He had no alternative but to sneak out of Milan.

He discussed the subject with a friend, Luca Pacioli, a Franciscan monk who was professor of mathematics at the University of Pavia and had often helped Leonardo in his calculations. Luca was going to Venice. The two men agreed to travel together, at least until Mantua.

On 31 December 1499, on a gray, snowy dawn, they rode out of the southern gate, followed by Salai, half awake on his saddle.

The days of shelter and security were over; the days of wanderings had begun.

Leonardo da Vinci, probable self-portrait (1512). *Reproduced by gracious permission Her Majesty Queen Elizabeth II.*

Like a Leaf in the Wind

Under the ramparts of Mantua, the friar-mathematician reined in his horse.

"You will soon hear from me," he told Leonardo. "The Venetians are at war with the Turks, and in desperate straits. No doubt they will welcome a military engineer of your ability. You will shortly hear from me."

Leonardo spent the month of January in Mantua waiting for Luca's letter and trying to elude the advances of the local marchioness, Isabella d'Este, Beatrice's sister, who wanted him to paint her portrait. Finally, she cornered him into making an uninspired red-chalk profile of her. He was about to transfer it to a picture panel when he received the long-awaited letter.

The Venetian authorities implored him to come and save the floating city from the heathen Turks, whose fleet was anchored in the lagoon. Leonardo departed at once and alone, for Salai had returned to his native Pavia. Despite the February rains and the poor condition of the roads, the great naval engineer arrived in Venice in less than three weeks.

He was overwhelmed by her beauty.

"This is the most triumphant city I have ever seen," he wrote in his inseparable notebook.

But there was no time for sight-seeing. He was received like a conquering hero, actually addressed the Venetian Senate and assured everybody that he would sink the fleet of Reis Kemal Pasha with a revolutionary invention of his.

What it was, he would not say, but he described it at length in his papers. It consisted of a "diving dress" fitted with a glass mask, an elephantlike trunk connected with the air-filled bladder of a lamb and provided with "a receptacle for urinating." A man in this "diving dress" could swim under water for a span of four hours: ample time for him to bore a few holes in the hulls of the Turkish vessels. (There existed already a diving apparatus in the notes of a fifteenth-century Sienese scientist, Giacomo Mariano.)

Somehow, the diving dress did not live up to its inventor's expectations. The Turkish fleet did not sink. One month after his jubilant arrival, Leonardo fled Venice at dusk, glancing nervously over his shoulder for the sight of the pursuing police gondolas.

He safely reached the mainland and, as he had no other place to go, he made his way to Florence.

He now was a stranger in the town he had left eighteen years before. Of course, after the splendors of Milan and Venice, Florence seemed small and provincial. Nevertheless, it was good to be back. But the cost of living was high in the City of Flowers. Even at three and four to a bed, inns were grievously expensive. The Venetian venture had been a financial disaster. In some way or other, he must earn money.

The solution to this problem presented itself two days later when a jovial, thickset man recognized him in the street and rushed to him, hands outstretched. This was Filippino Lippi, a colleague of his in the old *bottega* days and a former pupil of Botticelli.

Over a tankard of wine, Filippino offered to transfer to him the commission of an altarpiece he had just received from the Servites monks of the Annunziata Monastery.

"They'll be proud to have you do it," he declared. "After all, everyone has heard of your wondrous 'Last Supper.' "

To his delight, Leonardo learned he had become famous as a painter during his absence. He replied that he would love to paint the altarpiece, especially if he could be given bed and board at the monastery while he painted it.

"Let me handle it," said the Good Samaritan. "I'll let you know in a few days."

As he had predicted, the Annunziata friars were thrilled at the prospect of having Leonardo paint their picture. Gladly they gave him a cell as a studio, another as his living quarters, besides a substantial advance.

One year later their houseguest was still living in the monastery, together with Salai who had returned from Pavia and passed as his apprentice. By then, the prior timidly asked to have a glimpse at the masterpiece in progress. Leonardo, who had not even begun the work, showed him a charcoal study he had made in Milan, assuring him that this was the preliminary sketch of the altarpiece.

It was a lovely drawing, and the prior had it exhibited in the monastery's visitors' room.

Another year went by. The prior was becoming somewhat impatient. For his part, Leonardo had wearied of the monks' fare and their tiresome habit of singing matins in the middle of the night. Salai was bored and wanted to return to Milan. Once again, Leonardo found himself in a quandary. The time had come to move somewhere else.

But where?

For the hundredth time, his guardian angel came to his rescue. A letter from Cesare Borgia invited him to join his service as a military engineer.

A little over two years had passed since they had met in Milan. Since then, the former cardinal had performed astonishing feats. With the help of French troops and money, he had appropriated four Church states on the Adriatic side of the peninsula, as well as the town of Piombino on the Mediterranean coastline. He planned to join the two segments into a central Italy kingdom by annexing Tuscany and the Florentine territory.

Cesare's proposition held the promise of an exciting and well-paid profession. One morning, as the lay brother was bringing breakfast to the celebrated painter and his young apprentice, he noticed that the doors of their cells had been left ajar. A peep inside sent him to the prior. The two honored houseguests had flown the coop.

Naturally, there was no altarpiece.

On arriving at Piombino, a tranquil seashore village, he found

Cesare Borgia's instructions to supervise the draining of the local marshes. He had never drained anything, but he designed two intricate networks of ditches which emptied into canals which, in turn, emptied into the sea.

Under the drawing, he wrote, "This is the way to drain the Piombino marshes."

Whether it was or not, he never knew, for just as the digging was about to begin, he was urgently called to Arezzo, some hundred miles away. It was an arduous journey for a man who had just passed fifty. But he was now in the army and orders were orders. Dutifully he took to the road.

Another of Florence's vassal cities, Arezzo was in the throes of revolution against the Signoria when he arrived. One of Cesare Borgia's lieutenants occupied the town and planned to march upon Florence. For that, he needed topographical maps. Leonardo the Florentine produced them for him, and they were very beautiful.

No sooner had he laid down his quills and brushes than he was ordered to blow up the Arezzo fortress which had remained loyal to the Signoria. From cartographer, Leonardo now became an explosive expert and developed a blasting powder which, fortunately, refused to ignite.

Two weeks and one hundred impotent explosions later, the fortress still stood when, from its own accord, the garrison decided to surrender. At last Borgia's lieutenant began his march on Florence with Leonardo the Florentine on his staff. But a few miles from Arezzo, at Borgo San Sepolcro, fresh instructions from Cesare ordered him to ride posthaste to Urbino, a fortified village on an inaccessible peak in the Apennines.

By now it was July and the sun beat mercilessly on the aging traveler as he climbed the mountainous slopes. He was becoming tired of his constant wanderings. All his life he had dreamed of a military career, but now that he had come in contact with the realities of war, he found it a most bestial folly — *una bestialissima pazzia*. Already he missed the peaceful days in the Annunziata Monastery and, further back, his cozy rooms in Ludovico's palace. Poor Ludovico, who had lost his duchy for the second time and was now languishing in a French prison.

On the day of his arrival in Urbino, Leonardo was received — at night, as was his custom — by Cesare Borgia.

Tall and lean, the pope's son was dressed entirely in black, and, by candlelight, his shoulder-length hair and short beard glinted like gold. At twenty-six, he stood at the peak of his power. By an act of treachery, he had just seized Urbino and its surrounding duchy. The kingdom he dreamed about for himself was within his reach. Already he was making grandiose plans for the future.

"I asked you to come here to study the magnificent Urbino palace which I propose to copy as my residence in the capital of my choice. I want you to familiarize yourself with its most distinctive features and make sketches of them."

Leaning over a map spread on the table, he pressed his finger on various Romagna towns, listing the works he had in mind for Leonardo in each of these cities.

"This winter we shall go over your plans together, and next spring you will begin their execution."

He then handed him a rolled parchment in which he instructed all his "deputies, castellans, captains, *condottieri*, soldiers, and subordinates to allow free passage and give assistance to his excellent servant, architect, and engineer, Leonardo da Vinci."

The following morning he was gone.

Leonardo stayed a few days in Urbino to visit the palace's three hundred and sixty-five rooms. He took a few measurements, walked along the colonnaded galleries where lingered the kindly ghost of Duke Federigo of Urbino who had refused to capture Florence when she lay at his mercy. He met Giuliano de'Medici who was spending his years of exile in a wing of the castle. They had a long and fateful talk. He also made a lovely sketch of a pigeon house which, for some unknown reason, he carefully dated: "July 30th. 1502. The dovecot at Urbino."

During the remainder of summer, he traveled through Romagna. His interest in military matters had waned altogether. He paid no attention to arsenals and fortifications, but he browsed in libraries, sketched balconies, wrought-iron lanterns, graceful marble fountains.

He spent the autumn at Imola with Cesare, drew plans of canals, buildings, draining devices. Borgia took a liking to the old man. One day on an impulse he tossed him his gold-embroidered short tunic which the architect-engineer admired effusively.

By November they were both in Rome, where Leonardo had an opportunity to study the papal court in the final debasement of the Borgia pontificate. It did little to restore his long-lost respect for the Church. During the winter, he slowly reached the decision to abandon his military position and leave Cesare's service. Even painting was better than these endless rides in all weathers.

Moreover, he now had a good reason to return to Florence. It might yet not be too late to start a career as a portrait painter. In Florence they did not know that his "Last Supper" was already dying. He had a great reputation as a painter. He might still achieve fame and fortune.

On 3 March 1503, as Lisa sat by her grandfather's bedside, watching over his health, Leonardo was walking through Florence, stopping here and there to ask the way to the Giocondo Mill.

"This afternoon I had a most interesting visitor," began the merchant as he sat down at supper.

The man's name was Leonardo da Vinci, and he cut an impressive figure with his tall stature, his long gray beard, and flashy clothes. He had long been employed as a painter at the Sforza court, and in this quality he had painted several portraits, as well as a large mural, "The Last Supper," in the refectory of a local monastery.

For the past three years, since the French had occupied, lost, and occupied Milan again, the picture-maker had moved about a great deal and done all sorts of things.

"His last employer was Cesare Borgia, and in the course of a trip to Urbino last summer, he met Giuliano de'Medici who commissioned him to paint your portrait."

"My portrait!"

He nodded. "That is, of course, if you have no objection."

"You mean Giuliano asked him to paint my portrait?" she repeated incredulously. "Why?"

"Because he has not forgotten you and would like to have your likeness in remembrance of your youthful friendship."

"What did you tell the picture-maker?"

"I'd let him have your reply in a few days." During the silence that ensued, he added, "Personally, I have no objection to it, but it is for you to decide."

She did not reply and nibbled her lower lip in perplexity. After a few minutes she came out of her musings and declared she was inclined to reject Giuliano's request.

"For several reasons," she went on.

First, it was almost ten years since they had seen each other. Both had been very young and immature at the time. She had been a reedy, angular *giovinetta*, while she now was a sedate housewife of twenty-four. "He wouldn't even recognize me."

Moreover, she was too busy, much too busy, to sit for her portrait. What with the supervising of the household, doing the marketing, keeping accounts, fetching Meo from school, visiting the orphanage, she did not have a single minute to herself, let alone any time to sit for her portrait.

"And on top of all this I have to start organizing our garden party in June."

"Why don't you sleep on it before giving your final answer?" he suggested.

There was no need, she replied. Her mind was made up, and when her mind was made up, she never changed it.

"As you wish, gentle wife. Tomorrow I shall send a note of regret to the picture-maker, and that will be the end of it."

To change the subject of conversation, he inquired about Mariotto's health.

"If I didn't keep an eye on him, he would've crossed the Great Sea a long time ago."

"I hope he duly appreciates your solicitude."

"Not in the least," she replied petulantly.

Far from being grateful, her honored grandfather regarded her as a meddlesome female. "Men never appreciate what women do for them." Then, without transition, she said, "Just the same, it is rather touching of Giuliano to want my portrait after all these years. Don't you think?"

"It proves that he is a young man of deep feelings," remarked Giocondo, draining his glass of wine.

They passed to her sitting room and he spent a few moments poking at the fire logs.

"Moreover, you two are cousins and it seems rather ungracious to reject a kinsman's request."

"I had not thought of that. Besides, I really haven't changed that much, have I?"

"Not in the least," he lied lovingly.

This was exactly the right thing to say. A smile came into her eyes. Encouraged, he elaborated, expounded about those women who neglected their appearance after marriage. "But not you. As a matter of fact, I think you look better than when you knew him."

This was also her opinion, and she marveled at his perceptiveness. How nice it was to be wed to a man who appreciated his wife and had the wisdom to tell her so now and then.

For a moment she watched little blue flames tiptoe along the glowing logs.

"It shouldn't take long to paint my portrait, should it?"

"No more than four or five sittings, I should say."

He explained that, as a rule, portrait painters sketched only the face and the hands of their subjects, leaving to apprentices the task of painting the background, the folds of the dress, the ornaments. "The whole thing shouldn't take more than a month at the very most."

And, he added, it would give a great deal of pleasure to Giuliano. At the same time, it would give Messer da Vinci a chance to earn his money, for he had already received the price of the painting. "So, you see, you would be helping a poor painter as well as obliging your kinsman."

She hesitated a few instants and again nibbled her lower lip. In her opinion, she stood now at the peak of her loveliness. She rather liked the idea of showing Giuliano how delectable the scrawny little girl he had known had become.

"You are right, noble husband. It would be most uncharitable of me to refuse a kinsman's request. And since it won't take long, somehow I shall manage to find time for a few sittings."

Two days later Leonardo presented himself at the Casa Giocondo.

Somehow she had expected a typical Florentine *dipintore* in paint-spattered clothes, a wineskin on his shoulder, a sheaf of drawing paper in his hand. She was astonished to see an elderly dandy in a maroon velvet doublet and silk hose. Halfway into the sitting-room, he removed his black velvet beret and bowed from the waist with the skill of a seasoned courtier. In flowery sentences, he expressed his delight at finding himself in the presence of the illustrious Donna de'Gherardini del Giocondo, justly renowned for her beauty as well as the prestige of her pedigree. The term "Donna" was the equivalent of Madonna or Madame, the title by which society ladies were called in the Renaissance. "Mona" was a diminutive of "Madame," a somewhat less formal appellation used mostly for young matrons. Thus "Mona Lisa" means "the young Madame Lisa."

This sort of hyperbolic compliment was not appreciated in Florence. Coming from a stranger and a lowly picture-maker, it was altogether distasteful. For an instant, she regretted having consented to have her portrait painted.

She did not invite him to sit down and explained she had little time for sittings.

"As a matter of fact," she went on, "I had hoped you might start today."

This, he replied, would be a grievous mistake. Oh yes, most picture-makers would be content to paint a likeness of her. But he aimed higher, much higher. Not only did he want to capture her lovely features, but her soul as well.

"A likeness will do," she countered somewhat tartly. "I have no intention to send my soul to my kinsman."

He assured her that he could paint with great speed when necessary, and the portrait would be ready by the end of June.

She then inquired whether he wished to paint her portrait indoors or in the garden.

"In the garden," he said, "if it is agreeable to you."

She led him out of the house. He expatiated on the charms of the garden with its blue-tiled pond, its neat flower beds and budding trees. He described how he planned to represent her sitting between two columns of the covered gallery, with her shapely hands crossed on her lap.

He announced that he would immediately sand and prime a picture panel, grind oil paints of his own composition and make brushes of the finest fur.

"By the beginning of April," he said as he was taking his leave, "we shall be ready to begin the sittings."

One morning early in April two attractive youths arrived at Casa Giocondo carrying a three-legged easel or *cavaletto*, a small panel of poplar wood, a handful of brushes, and an assortment of small ceramic jars containing pigments finely ground in linseed oil.

They set the paraphernalia under the gallery and waited for the master, who presently appeared, wearing Cesare Borgia's gold-embroidered tunic. He approved of everything while removing his gloves and then dismissed the youngsters.

A few minutes later Lisa entered the scene dressed in her usual dark house garments with the muted wine-coloured blouse and sleeves. Leonardo performed his courtly bow and, amid elegant chitchat, began adjusting her pose. This required much frowning, squinting, stepping back and forth, and twirling of his moustache.

At last he pronounced himself satisfied. Walking to the easel, he then pulled out a pair of iron-rimmed spectacles from a leather case, straddled them over his sharply curved nose, and peered at her over the lenses. For a few instants he remained motionless, holding a stick of charcoal in his left hand.

He was about to start sketching when she let out a cry, "Wait!"

In rapid gestures, she pulled the rings from her fingers, removed the ebony combs from her elaborate coiffure, unfastened the cluster of false curls over her ears. With a toss of her head, she sent her hair tumbling down her shoulders.

"My kinsman never saw me with my hair up or with rings on my fingers," she explained. "I will try to look as I did when he knew me or he might not recognize me."

Quickly she resumed the pose, and the sittings began.

He had promised to finish her portrait by the end of June, before she left for Settignano. He meant to keep his word, and throughout that spring of 1503 he worked assiduously.

Gradually, her annoyance at his foppishness, his fawning manner, his pretentious yet ungrammatical speech vanished before the evidence of his immense talent. He truly was an outstanding picture-maker, she thought.

As the weather grew warmer, she would order refreshments. They would call a recess from the sitting and drink lemonade while listening to the dripping of the fountain in the pond and the twittering birds.

Like most solitary and lonely men, he unconsciously longed for someone in whom he could confide. As he looked at the young lady who smiled at him through her gentle brown eyes, the remembrance of Albiera took form in his mind. With every sitting, the resemblance grew stronger. By moments, he almost believed that Albiera was alive again and had returned into his life.

One day he no longer could hold his thoughts to himself. He told Lisa about her: their happy years together in the Vinci house, their play in the courtyard, their walks through the countryside with her brother, Alessandro, who studied to become a priest. "She wore her hair parted in the middle, as you do, and she had large brown eyes, like yours."

There was sorrow in his voice when he described her brief, fatal illness at twenty-four.

"And I am twenty-four," said Lisa. "Perhaps this is why I remind you of her."

That day a new relationship was born between them. Through some mysterious alchemy, she became for him the reincarnation of Albiera. She, in turn, brought back to life the twelve-year-old boy he had been at the time of his foster mother's death. The aging adventurer, so bitter and secretive, opened to her the recesses of his mind and heart.

He told her about his father's neglect and unforgiving resentment, recalled his years at Verrocchio's *bottega*, his household chores, his evenings in his attic room laboriously poring over a Latin grammar by candlelight, groping through the arcane world of mathematics which he yearned to master.

Soon Lisa came to know his pathetic conceit and self-delusion, his compulsive curiosity which lured him from one science to another, his psychotic incapacity to ever finish anything, his habit of signing contracts he did not fulfill, keeping advances he had not earned.

To Lisa, it became increasingly clear that Albiera's death had deprived him, at twelve, of the love, the firm and tender guidance which might have kept him anchored to a career in art where his outstanding talent would have brought him, if not riches, at least honorable success. With Albiera gone, he had become a rudderless ship, darting hither and yon with every gust of his fancy.

The incomparable artist had become an entertainer: juggler, magician, singer, lute-player, and, finally, by a kindly twist of fate, a *festaiuolo* or master of festivities. But his insatiable ambition to win fame and riches had never left him. All his life he had tried to stun the world as a sculptor, an architect, an engineer, a mural painter, and finally a manufacturer of his own inventions.

Now, at fifty-one, having failed at everything, he was at last back where he belonged, with a brush in his hand and painting an admirable portrait. At long last he had returned to the path he had been born to follow. It would be easy to find portraits for him to paint and make a comfortable living at it.

"Just among my friends," she thought, "I shall find him many commissions."

And so spring wore on. By the end of May he had finished the face, and it was a miracle of sensitivity as well as craftsmanship. The hands also were well advanced. He had kept his promise. The portrait would be ready before her departure for Settignano.

"You have done a remarkable work," she said. "You soon will be able to send the portrait to Urbino and my kinsman will be very pleased with it, I am sure."

And then it all collapsed.

He arrived one morning in a state of great agitation.

"Donna Lisa," he announced the moment he entered the room, "I'm going to do it."

"Do what?"

"Change the course of the Arno."

"What?"

In the autumn of 1502, while in Cesare Borgia's service, he had met a certain Niccolo Machiavelli, who had come to visit the duke on a diplomatic mission. The two Florentines had sympathized and become good friends.

By chance, Leonardo had run across Niccolo a few days before. The official had now become the Signoria's secretary, a post of the highest importance, as well as an adviser to His Excellency Piero Soderini, the life-*gonfaloniere* or chief of state. They had repaired to a wineshop where they had talked of the endless Pisa war which, according to Machiavelli, was exhausting the contestants on both sides.

"I casually mentioned that the reason the Pisans continued to fight was that they received food and ammunitions through the Arno River which crossed the city. Change the course of the river, and the starving Pisans would soon be suing for peace."

Machiavelli had been struck by the ingeniousness of the plan. When Leonardo has assured him that he could easily swerve the course of the river away from Pisa, he had grown enthusiastic. He submitted the plan to the magistrates, who also endorsed it.

"You are going to change the course of the Arno?" Lisa asked with dismay. "How then will you be able to finish my portrait by July?"

He wouldn't, but on his return to Florence in October he would finish the portrait.

"By then, my canal will be finished and the war over," he said with tranquil self-assurance. "By Christmas, your portrait will be in the hands of His Lordship Giuliano de'Medici. You have my word on that."

Two days later, in company of Giovanni Cellini, the town's piper and father of a four-year-old boy named Benvenuto, he departed for the headquarters of the Florentine army in a carriage drawn by six horses. His spirits were high. He had no doubt that he would change the course of the Arno and bring an end to the Pisa War, practically single-handedly. The old dream hung once again in his mind: his engineering genius would bring him fame and riches.*

At first, the general staff laughed at his notion of lifting the Arno from its bed, but a stern message from the Signoria silenced the guffaws. Military engineers obediently placed themselves under his orders. Surveyors traced the itinerary of the proposed canal. Laborers were hired at the extravagant wages of ten *soldi* per day and began digging. Sentries were set upon them to make sure they worked hard.

Thus, Leonardo's plan went into operation.

Meanwhile, the fountainhead of all these activities left the supervision of his undertaking to subordinates and escaped in long, solitary walks. Staff in hand and wearing a wide-brimmed straw hat, he wandered along meadow lanes, his inseparable inkhorn and notebook dangling from his belt.

Now and then, he would sit on the grass and fill his eyes with the surrounding beauty. Briefly, the artist revived in him.

* Experts disagree over Leonardo's standing as an engineer, as they do over everything else concerning him.

In his *Engineers and Engineering in the Renaissance*, W. B. Parsons writes: "If Leonardo contributed nothing more to engineering than his plans and designs for the Arno Canal, they would place him in the first rank of engineers of all times." Another great Renaissance expert, Ralph Raeder, refers to these same studies for the Arno Canal as "a page of labyrinthine calculations, an incoherent record of mathematical delirium."

A. Koyré, member of the Institute for Advanced Studies in Princeton, states that "though Leonardo has been depicted as a great scholar, modern historians have rejected this interpretation almost unanimously." In the same vein, Kenneth Clark remarks: "Leonardo's engineering schemes were wholly beyond the technical powers of his time."

Leaves assume the transparency of green glass when struck by sunshine. . . . The shade of cypress is nearly black while that of a pear tree is yellowish green. . . . At noon, the landscapes are of the loveliest blue. . . .

Occasionally, he thought about Lisa and her uncanny resemblance to Albiera. It was more than a likeness of features, it was a similarity of expression and personality. In her last year of life, when she was twenty-four, his foster mother had looked, talked and smiled as Donna Lisa did.

With anticipation he mused about his return to town at the end of summer. It would be nice to resume his visits to the Giocondo house, leisurely finish the portrait of the gracious lady who had come into his life. He would share with her the triumph that would crown the completion of his canal.

In this way July and August went by. Then September arrived, setting the trees on fire.

One day as he was watching the clouds move slowly across the sky, he was struck by one of his lightning thoughts. His idea of starving the Pisans into surrender was worthless; his canal was all wrong. What Florence really needed was not one, but two canals. One would link it to the sea and permit the shipping of wares directly from the mills; the other would meander through Tuscany, pass through Prato, Serravalle, and Pistoia and give these landlocked towns access to the sea. What a boost for the Florentine trade!

So great and sincere was his confidence in the success of his new project that he communicated it to the members of the Signoria when he returned to town at the end of September. Disappointed as they were to learn that the canal under construction was still unfinished, they soon fell under the master promoter's spell. They, too, became entranced with the vision of Florence's vassal towns reaching out to the sea. Craftily, he fanned their enthusiasm with the promise of a yearly profit of 200,000 gold florins. By the time he finished talking, he had won their approval.

"I shall start next summer," he told Lisa excitedly.

Of course, an undertaking of such magnitude was fraught with technical difficulties. At Serravalle, for instance, his canal would have to climb to a height of 470 feet. Never mind! He would build a huge suction pump that would lift the water to the desired height. Tunnels would have to be bored, but he was not afraid. Already he had drafted a gigantic excavating device that broke ground into chunks weighing 2,240 pounds. In many places, he would substitute oxen for laborers. Beasts, he remarked with a chuckle, worked harder than men, took no siesta. Best of all, they didn't get paid.

She listened, a finger to her cheek, in discouraged silence. He was off in another *ghiribizzo*, another one of his whimsies. Her hope of keeping him at his painting trade would never come true.

"With so many things to do," she said wistfully, "you won't be able to finish my portrait by Christmas, as you promised."

"I see you do not know me well, as yet," he replied with a teasing smile. "Have no fear, Donna Lisa. Everything will be done."

Without any hesitation, he declared he would find time to finish the picture which was already well advanced and have it ready by Christmas.

"You have my word on it, Dona Lisa," he added. "I shall welcome the relaxation of painting between my mathematical labors."

She did not see him for a few days when, unexpectedly, he reappeared one morning, his face flushed with excitement.

He had been commissioned by the Signoria to decorate the walls of the Great Council Room with murals of the great Florentine victories.

"The first subject is to be the Battle of Anghiari," he announced. This was the memorable battle the Florentines had won over the Milanese in 1440, at the cost of *one* casualty: one of the Florentine cavalrymen had fallen from his horse and been trampled to death by his fellow horsemen.

He went on to say he had been granted a salary of five florins per month as living expenses and lodgings at the Santa Maria Novella Monastery where the prestigious Pope's Room or *Sala del Papa* was to serve him as a studio.

"Now I am sure you won't be able to finish my portrait by Christmas," she sighed.

This time he did not protest. He admitted that between his calculations for the canal and his preliminary studies for "The Battle of Anghiari" he simply would have no time to finish her portrait by Christmas. But in the spring he would be ready to transfer his cartoon for the mural to the wall, and while the priming mixture of his own composition would be drying, he then would be able to give the finishing brushstrokes to her portrait.

"It will be ready by Easter," he said. "You have my word on it."

Three months passed before he called again, on a cold January morning, at Casa Giocondo. He was radiating prosperity and self-confidence and wearing his splendid gold-embroidered tunic. His beard was perfumed, his moustache carefully waxed to a point.

He apologized profusely for his long absence. He had been living under extreme pressure, what with his preliminary studies for "The Battle of Anghiari," his labor-saving devices for the canal, his frequent consultations. He implied that Their Magnificences sought his advice on all kinds of subjects.

"For instance, can you guess where I spent the morning?" he asked, enjoying her inability to answer the question.

Finally, she admitted she could not guess where he had spent the early part of the morning, and he answered his own question. With Botticelli and a few other painters and sculptors, he had been in Michel Agnolo Buonarroti's shed where the young sculptor was finishing his statue "David."

"A fine work," he conceded in the tone of a benevolent master speaking of a talented young colleague. "A truly fine work, even though the left hand is somewhat too large."

Over twelve feet in height, the block of white marble showed a nude young man with flawless classical features and a magnificent physique. From the sling on his shoulder one might think of him as some young Greek god sent on some hunting lark. "He should have been called Apollo or Young Hercules, but never David."

"And why not?"

His tone became professorial. David was a Jew, and Michel Agnolo's hunter was not circumcised. Moreover, according to the Bible, David was a mere boy armed only with "five smooth pebbles." He had vanquished Goliath solely because God was on his side.

"David is the symbol of human weakness that becomes invincible through God's assistance. Michel Agnolo's young athlete seems capable of toppling Goliath without God's or anyone else's assistance."

"I hope you did not say all this to him, for I understand that he is a brilliant young stone-carver, but inclined to violent rages."

Leonardo gave her a reassuring smile. Several years at the court of Milan had taught him to refrain from making unwelcome remarks. "Anyway, we were not there to appraise the work, but merely to advise on its location."

Botticelli and the other artists had suggested various emplacements. For his part, Leonardo had recommended that "David" be set in the Loggia dei Lanci, on Piazza della Signoria, where it would be protected from the weather as well as the commotions of the populace in times of turmoil.

This innocent and well-meant suggestion had earned him the hostility of Michel Agnolo who wanted his work displayed at the entrance of the Old Palace.*

"I did not want to displease him," he added. "I only meant to protect his work."

"Don't worry about it," she said comfortingly. "You spoke for his own good. He should be grateful for your suggestion. Now tell me about your 'Battle of Anghiari.' "

It was advancing satisfactorily. He had been given until May to finish the preparatory cartoon of "The Battle of Anghiari" and already he had made several studies and solved the problem

---

* Michelangelo's choice prevailed, yet Leonardo's suggestion remained a sounder one. The sculptor's vanity almost brought disaster upon his masterpiece. In 1512, it was struck by lightning; in 1527, in the course of a popular *tumulto*, the left arm was broken in three places.

Since 1873, "David" has been located at the Accademia. Various replicas of it are scattered throughout the city.

of composition. Because of the two windows which opened in the wall, the mural would be divided into panels. The one at the left would represent Saint Peter appearing to the Florentines before the encounter and promising them victory: a bit of pious nonsense which the Signoria wished to perpetuate; the one at the right would show the Milanese cavalry fleeing in billows of dust. "The central panel will depict 'The Struggle for the Flag.' "

It would be a maelstrom of savage fury in which wild-eyed horses bit one another while their shouting, grimacing riders slashed the air with their swords.

"This will be the first panel I shall paint." Imprudently, he added, "The preliminary cartoon is already well advanced."

"I shall come to see it tomorrow." She caught the look of panic in his eyes and guessed the truth. "There is no 'Battle of Anghiari,' is there? No Saint Peter, no 'Struggle for the Flag' either?"

He gulped, and fingered his beard while groping for excuses. "Well, you see, Donna Lisa—"

"No preliminary sketch? Nothing?" she pressed on. "For three months you've been given a salary, living quarters, and a beautiful studio and you haven't done a single thing. Have you no sense of obligation?"

Under her unflinching gaze, his confusion increased. He floundered in a morass of words. Every minute of his time had been taken by conferences with the authorities, calculations for his canal, cogitation about the mural.

She would have none of it.

"Don't make the chickens laugh," she snapped. "You have no sense of responsibility. It's like my portrait. You will never finish it."

He raised an arm in a vague semblance of an oath. He would resume work tomorrow and this time he would not leave it until it was finished.

She saw he meant it, and her annoyance began to thaw.

"Tell me the truth," she said more gently. "What on earth have you done these past three months?"

He hesitated, groping for some last-minute excuse, but her eyes remained on him and finally he took the plunge.

"I've been working in anatomy," he said.

All his life, he explained, anatomical research had fascinated him. Even as a youth he had been burning with curiosity about the inner working of the human machine. In the old days, when he was living in Florence, he had become acquainted with a *beccamorte*, a gravedigger who collected amputated limbs from the surgery room of the Santa Maria Novella hospital. By chance, this man had reappeared in his life and provided him with more legs and arms at very low prices.

"And what are you doing with such things?" she asked wincing.

"I dissect and make drawings of them. You have no idea how wonderful is the human body!"

Now he spoke like one inspired. Under his bushy eyebrows, his blue eyes glittered with mounting enthusiasm.

She looked at him in despair. He could not help himself. He had forgotten about his mural, his Arno canal, the tunnel he was going to dig under the Serravalle hills. He had thought only for his chunks of putrefying flesh.

"What will you gain from all this cutting up of dead people? Don't you know that the Church forbids it and you may incur the most severe punishments?"

"The Church!" The words exploded out of his mouth. "What do those ignorant priests know of the marvels of the human body? It is because the Church forbids dissection that medicine has made almost no progress in fifteen hundred years."

"You may be right," she broke in, "but one of these days the Signoria will want to see your cartoon of 'The Battle of Anghiari,' and you won't have anything to show. What then?"

Her words jolted him back to reality. In a flash he realized the consequences of his folly. No more salary, no more lodgings, no more canal. More wanderings in search of employment . . .

"You are right," he nodded repentantly.

He now was full of good resolutions. He was going to sever all relations with the *beccamorte*. No more limbs, no more corpses. From now on he would work day and night on "The Battle."

"You have my word on it, Donna Lisa," he said with a hand on his heart.

In long, rapid strides he returned to the Santa Maria Novella hospital, descended the rickety stairs to the basement, and groped his way to his dissecting room.

And there the *beccamorte* was waiting for him.

"Such a wonderful piece I have for you today!" he whispered excitedly. "A corpse, a whole corpse!"

Through his friendship with the hangman, he had obtained the body of a freshly executed *bandito*. To his stupefaction, Leonardo discovered that the corpse's penis was in a state of erection. The temptation was too great. At once all his good resolutions vanished.

He bought the corpse, slipped on his blood-spattered leather apron and began dissecting the genital organs, interrupting himself to scribble observations in his notebook.

Of the virile member when it is hard, it is thick and long, dense and heavy. This should not be adjudged to the addition of flesh or wind, but to arterial blood. I have seen this in the dead who have the member (*la verga*) rigid.

He was in luck. The following week the gravedigger brought him the whole corpse of a woman. Now Leonardo could dissect, compare and illustrate the male and female genito-urinary system, a field for which he had a distinct predilection. With delight he discovered that the sexes are homologous. Every male sexual organ had its female counterpart. To the urethra corresponded the vagina; to the testicles, the ovaries; to the spermatic vessels, the ovarian vessels. And so on.

Quill in hand, he moved in the dark world of urology. The female sexual organs received only his cursory attention; but the penis moved him to poetic praise.

The penis has a life of its own. This animal has a soul and an intelligence which are independent of the man. Although man's wish may be to arouse him, he remains stubborn and acts according to his own will. Sometimes he moves of his own accord, without permission or thought from the man, whether asleep or awake, doing as is his wont. . . . Yet man is ashamed of naming or showing him; he covers and hides him, whereas he should be adorned and displayed with solemnity, like a minister. . . .

This was not yet enough for such a soulful and intelligent "animal," and further down the page he proceeded with unabated fervor:

The origin of the penis is situated on the pubic bone, so that it can resist its active force on coition. If this bone did not exist, the penis on meeting resistance would turn backwards and would enter more often in the body of the penetrator than into that of the penetrated. . . . The rigid penis has a gland — *testa*. When it is not rigid, it has a whitish appearance. . . .

Once I saw a mule which was unable to move owing to the fatigue of a long journey under a heavy burden and which, on seeing a mare, suddenly its penis and all its muscles became so swollen that it multiplied its forces as to acquire such speed that it overtook the speed of the mare which fled before it and which was obliged to obey the desires of the mule. . . .

And so he lived in his fetid hole, the happiest of men, while above the sky turned blue and spring descended upon Florence.

In May Lisa's prediction came to pass. The members of the Signoria demanded to see the cartoon of "The Battle of Anghiari," and he had nothing to show.

Their Magnificences did not like that; they did not like it at all. He was summoned before the council and told some scathing truths. For eight months he had collected a salary, lodged in quarters granted him by the Signoria and produced nothing in exchange.

Again he was all repentance. He gave his word that thereafter he would work on "The Battle" without respite. They appreciated his pledge, but would prefer a contract.

Their Magnificences were beginning to know their man.

He ran to Lisa and reported the episode, hoping for sympathy and understanding. He got neither.

"I warned you this would happen," she snapped. "They should have thrown you in jail."

In vain did he extol the scientific importance of the homology of sexes, the double curvature of the spine. She was adamant.

"You defaulted on your obligation to the Signoria as you did on your engagement to deliver my portrait by Christmas, then Easter." Brought up in a world of merchant aristocracy in which one's word was one's bond, she was incensed by his casualness in money matters. "The truth is that you don't like painting!"

He protested that, on the contrary, he loved painting, that it was the highest of arts, "the supreme intellectual analysis."

The year before she might have been impressed by these oracular profundities, now they merely increased her impatience. She had run out of forgiveness for his vagaries, his petty larcenies, his dubious business ethics.

"If you love painting so much, where is the San Bernardo altarpiece which Lorenzo de'Medici commissioned out of the kindness of his heart to start you on a career? And the 'Adoration of the Magi,' where is it?"

He defended himself as best he could, but she was like an angry wasp and gave him no respite.

"And the Annunziata altarpiece for which you filched two years of free bed and board, where is it?"

"Well, you see, Donna Lisa, I was immersed in geometry —"

She shrugged impatiently. "Geometry, anatomy, mathematics —anything is a good excuse for you to avoid painting."

Her annoyance turned to anger. At that instant she disliked everything about him. "And this tunic — where did you buy it?"

"Duke Borgia gave it to me. Beautiful, isn't it?"

"Much too beautiful for a person of your age and condition. You shouldn't wear the discards of other men. Buy a plain *lucco* of brown or maroon wool and look like a modest, honorable merchant."

She considered him as if searching for some new target of criticism.

"And stop using perfume," she said brusquely.

"But, Donna Lisa, in Milan —"

"I know. In Milan they wash clothes in perfume, but here we like our men to be clean and smell of soap. Now, go to work on the cartoon of your 'Battle of Anghiari' and try to keep your word for once."

That day she dismissed him without giving him her hand, and he looked so perplexed and ashamed that she almost felt sorry for him.

"I probably will never see him again," she told Giocondo that evening. "He is the most unreliable, exasperating man I've ever known!"

Yet she did see him again, and only a few days later.

This time he was soberly dressed in a wine-colored *lucco*. His face was parchment-white. So great was his emotion he could not bring himself to speak.

"Sit down," she said gently, "and tell me what's grieving you."

A few moments before he had been crossing Piazza della Trinita. In front of the Palazzo Spini, a group of scholars were debating the correct meaning of a Dante stanza. One of them had asked him his opinion of it.

"Just as I was about to reply, I noticed Michel Agnolo, unkempt and lost in thought as usual, entering the piazza. 'Why don't you ask him,' I said, 'for I hear he is learned in matters of poetry.'"

The sculptor had come out of his musings and turned to Leonardo. "Explain it yourself," he had scoffed angrily, "you who made a clay model of a horse that could not be cast in bronze. And those fools of Milanese entrusted such a task to you!"

"That was most uncouth of him," said Lisa.

"Why does he hate me so?" he asked her with despair in his eyes. "He is a great sculptor, but I am old enough to be his father. Shouldn't he have some respect for my years?"

Patiently she reinflated his ego. The only thing for him to do was to ignore Michel Agnolo's ill-bred remarks. "Your answer will be your Arno canal and your beautiful mural."

Gradually his self-confidence returned. By the time he was about to leave, he had shed his despondency.

"I shall show him what I can do," he said, a challenge in his voice.

The following month, in June, "David" was moved to its new location at the entrance door of the Old Palace. When its protective boards were removed and the statue appeared in all its virile splendor, the crowd let out a gasp of admiration. Suddenly maidens revealed a keen interest in art and cast long glances at his smooth, muscular thighs.

Meanwhile, Leonardo finished his drawings of labor-saving devices. He even found time to resume work on Lisa's portrait and brought it virtually to completion.

Once again he was in a confident mood. His calculations left no doubt as to the success of his canal.

"By the time I return, it will already be in operation," he assured Lisa, as she was leaving for Settignano.

The day before his departure for the site of operations, he learned of his father's death and made a note of it.

Today, at 7 A.M. Wednesday, 9 July, 1504, Ser Piero da Vinci, my father, notary of the Podesta, died at seven in the morning. He was eighty years old and left ten sons and two daughters.

His notation is remarkable for its inaccuracies. He had the date wrong: 9 July was a Tuesday, not a Wednesday; his father was not eighty, but seventy-seven.

He attended the funeral, not with the family, but with the hired weepers and representatives of the Guild of Notaries. The following morning he drove to the canal in the company of Giovanni Cellini.

The sight of thousands of antlike men digging his canal filled him with optimism. The work, already in progress since mid-April, was well advanced. In August an attempt to divert the

Arno into a completed section of the canal was crowned with success. Thereafter, he felt so confident in the outcome of his project that he lost interest in it and took up the study of astronomy.

This period of euphoria came to an abrupt end in late summer. A heat wave descended upon Tuscany. The Arno dwindled to a trickle, refused to flow into Leonardo's canal, and perversely returned to its bed.

This was regarded by the laborers as a sign that God did not approve of the canal. They crossed themselves, dropped their tools, and ran away at night. Those who remained demanded to be recalled. Even the supervising sentries deserted in droves. In Florence, criticism of the venture swelled into a clamor.

Yet, in the face of mounting opposition, the Signoria ordered the operations to be continued. God's answer came in the form of a deluge. Digging became impossible. The trenches, so laboriously excavated, dissolved in a sea of mud. Before the Almighty's hostility and the public's disapproval, the Signoria capitulated. Orders were sent to abandon construction of the ill-starred canal.*

"Was it my fault if it rained so much?" he asked Lisa in a voice of despair.

"Of course not," she said tiredly.

---

* One of the reasons advanced to explain why Leonardo undertook the creation of the Arno canal was his conception and creation of the admirable port-canal linking Cesena with the sea, still in operation and traditionally credited to him. In fact, he had nothing to do with it, as demonstrated by the eminent scholar Professor Ladislao Reti, in his *Leonardo da Vinci and Cesare Borgia.*

The key to Leonardo's disastrous career as a sculptor, engineer, architect, and chemist was his "irresistible power of persuasion," already mentioned. Incredible as it seems, he was able to convince some of Italy's most astute rulers and governing bodies of his ability to fulfill spectacular undertakings for which he had no qualification whatever and which all ended in failure: the Sforza Monument for Ludovico; the destruction of the Turkish fleet for the Venetian Senate; the blasting powder for the destruction of the Arezzo fortress, and finally the Arno canal for the Signoria of Florence.

The clue to his promotional success must be sought in his own self-delusion, the fact that he himself believed what he said.

Was it his fault if those ignorant laborers had got into their stupid heads that God frowned upon the canal? The enterprise would have been a great success but for the jealousy of his sub-ordinates who had conspired to cheat him of his triumph. Was it his fault if the army engineers were envious of his genius?

She looked into the blazing October fire, patiently listening to his self-justification. Of course it was not his fault, she repeated. It all had been an unfortunate, most unfortunate, turn of events.

She tried to put some warmth in her words, but with little success. She had lost her faith in him as a great engineer. At Settignano, during the long summer afternoons, Giocondo had told her of his misgivings over the success of Leonardo's project. As the major guilds of Florence were expected to provide funds for the payment of the canal, the various boards of directors had conducted discreet inquiries into Leonardo's engineering career. The results had been devastating. The great engineer was mostly a great talker.

"Why, I wonder, does this man persist in doing things he knows nothing about," the merchant had sighed, "when he could be the greatest painter in the world?"

His words returned to her as she tried to comfort the heart-broken old man.

"Your only chance to redeem yourself is to paint a magnificent 'Battle of Anghiari,'" she said. "You must not lose a minute and make sure that the cartoon is ready by February, as stipulated in the contract."

He nodded broodily, swore that every moment of his time would be devoted to the preliminary study of the mural. But she sensed he was mostly motivated by his fear of having to refund his wages in case of default on his engagement. His enthusiasm for "The Battle of Anghiari" had evaporated. He dreaded the prospect of toiling for months on a project which no longer aroused his interest.

Even more so, he was hurt by the unfriendly atmosphere now surrounding him. Innocent in his own eyes of the canal's failure, he could not understand the alteration in his relationship with the authorities and the public at large. Gone were the officials' bows and smiles, the deferential hat-doffing of strangers in the streets.

The "miracle worker," who only yesterday was going to end the Pisa war and revive Florence's prosperity, had become a bombastic old fool. The population resented the immense amount of public money spent on his absurd venture, his *ghiribizzo*. Urchins jeered at his astrologer's beard.

Before long he was given a shattering proof of his diminished status. Michel Agnolo was commissioned to paint the wall opposite that of "The Battle of Anghiari" in the Great Council Room.

The gesture had clearly been intended as an affront to Leonardo and he was deeply wounded by it. For once, he could not deceive himself on the artistic stature of his adversary. Michel Agnolo would prove as great a painter. His "David" had established his fame. Although not yet thirty, he was acknowledged the greatest artist in Florence. He might be ugly, irascible, slovenly in dress, but he was a true miracle worker. Already the popular verdict favored him in the forthcoming duel between the two artists.

"I shall be sneered at as a painter, as I am as an engineer," he said despondently.

Once again Lisa comforted him, made him promise to work assiduously on his cartoon — and did not see him again for a long while.

She began to worry.

"I think I should go and see him," she told Tessa. "God knows what he may be doing."

To her delight, she found him hard at work on his "Struggle for the Flag." For nearly an hour she watched him draw in forceful, unerring charcoal lines. Once again she measured the magnitude of his talent. There was nothing, she thought, that this man could not do in painting, if he set his mind to it.

"You have nothing to fear from Michel Agnolo or anyone else," she said, as she rejoined Tessa. Softly she added, "I am proud of you."

Incredibly, the cartoon was ready by February, as stipulated in the contract. The members of the Signoria judged it beautiful and their admiration tempered their hostility. He was complimented, given until May 1506 to finish the mural. He was allocated two assistants, in addition to "a boy to grind pigments." A rolling scaffold of his own design was built in the Great Council Room and in March the wall was primed with a binding mixture, especially prepared by him.

Suddenly he had time on his hands, and during the spring he returned to Casa Giocondo and worked on Lisa's portrait. She felt it was finished and urged him to send it to Urbino.

"Do you realize it is over two years since you started working on it? My kinsman must be impatient to see it."

He pleaded with her to let him work on it a little longer. He was not entirely satisfied with the smile.

"Most people smile with their lips," he said, "but you smile with your eyes."

She gave in, and they saw a good deal of each other that spring, while his binding mixture reached the correct amount of adhesiveness. He still went through a pretense of working, squinted at her over the rim of his spectacles, applied a few thoughtful brushstrokes. But it was make-believe and both knew it.

They enjoyed their visits in the sunniness of the garden. While sipping refreshments, he told her about his days at the court of Milan and the festivities he had organized in honor of King Charles and how the Great Crusader had trembled and drooled from excitement.

He also told her of his plans for his "Struggle for the Flag." He would not use the fresco technique but a very ancient method of wax painting, named encaustic, which produced works of great and lasting brilliance. By the greatest hazard, he had found the formula in a book by Pliny the Elder, a famous Roman scholar.

"Of course, I shall improve on it," he said complacently. "I have begun experiments which promise the greatest success."

His words sent a tremor of uneasiness rippling through her. What on earth was brewing in that head of his?

She made him promise to transfer his cartoon to the wall as soon as the binding mixture was dry enough. He gave his word. A few days later Michel Agnolo announced that he had already completed the cartoon for his "Battle of Cascina," another great Florentine victory.

This time the Signoria's troops had been surprised by the Pisans while bathing in the Arno, but so swiftly had they scampered out of the river that, naked as they were, they had managed to win the day. Michel Agnolo's cartoon was an enormous, 280-square-foot affair with sixteen nude male figures to Leonardo's six helmeted and breastplated warriors.

The news rocked the town. Excitement grew daily at the prospect of the two enemies working back to back in the same room. Then it was learned that Michel Agnolo had been called to Rome by Pope Julius, who wanted him to carve his tomb.

Thus Leonardo was left in sole possession of the battlefield.

Lisa prodded him to take advantage of the situation and transfer his cartoon to the wall as soon as possible. He received her suggestion with well-feigned enthusiasm. But he explained that his binding mixture was not quite dry enough. Moreover, he felt tired after such a strenuous winter. He had a whole year to paint his mural. There was no hurry. He longed to stroll through the hills.

"Spring is the best season of the year," he said, "and I think best when I walk."

"What will you be thinking about?"

He tried to elude her question, but he was no match for her. Finally, he admitted he was planning to write a treatise on the flight of the birds.

"Flight!" she cried in alarm. "Are you going to try to fly?"

"And why not?"

His manner became doctoral. From the beginning of time, many men had tried to fly. All had failed, but he had studied the problem and solved all the difficulties which had defeated his precursors.

"My name will live forever as the conqueror of the sky."

A few months ago she might have tried to dissuade him from

his folly. Now she knew it was no use. No one could help him. A devil had got into him.

The poor man had gone mad.

For Leonardo, that spring of 1505 was bewitched with the growing certitude of realizing his lifelong dream of flying.

For the first time he had the freedom, the money, the place to build his flying machine. Better still, he had found the man to build it with. He was none other than Alessandro Amadori, Albiera's brother, who as a young cleric had come to Vinci now and then.

He now was a kindly old man in his early sixties and the parish priest of Fiesole. He had not gone very far in his career. No miter or red hat for him, no ruby ring or gold pectoral cross: he had made his humble way in the service of God and man and found peace of mind along the way. Now he was finishing his days in a tile-roofed rectory on the edge of the village, tending his small garden, doing his priestly duties, enjoying the companionship of his dog and that of an elderly and grumbling housekeeper, in that order.

Leonardo had met him in the course of a stroll through the hills, and they had recognized each other at once. At the rectory they shared a cup of wine under the sun-dappled pergola while reminiscing about the past and, of course, Albiera. They took a walk through the garden, ate figs from the trees. Leonardo noticed a large and secluded empty shed at the end of a small vineyard. The perfect place, Leonardo had reflected, to build his "great bird," as he called it.

As though this were not enough, he found the ideal launching site for his flying machine: a plateau atop Swan Mountain — *Monte Ceceri* — ending in an abrupt cliff.

Jubilantly he had made a note of it in his usual cryptic and bombastic way:

Upon the back of the great Swan, the great bird will make its first flight and fill the world with amazement, filling all records with its fame and bringing eternal glory to its birthplace.

His visits to the rectory became more frequent. In June, Alessandro invited his "nephew," as he called him, to move in with him for the summer. In no time, the "great persuader" had him spellbound with his notions of a flying machine. Throughout the summer, the two old men worked in the garden shed, building "the great bird" that was to bring "eternal glory to its birthplace." Diligently they bound its light but sturdy reed frame, stretched coiled linen over its sixty-foot bat-shaped structure.

The awkward-looking contraption was ready in September, but by then it had started to rain. Leonardo had to postpone his dream of fame and riches and return dejected to Florence and his mural.

He transferred the cartoon of the "Struggle for the Flag" to the central wall between the two windows. Remembering the penalty clause in the contract, he clung diligently to his task. By May 1506 he had it finished, and a magnificent work of art it was. Already rumors of the masterpiece circulated through the town. Milan might boast of his "Last Supper," Florence would have his "Struggle for the Flag." The masterly artist had redeemed the incompetent canal-builder.

But there seemed to be something wrong with his binding mixture. The wax colors glowed as expected, but they would not dry. By his order, two large *braseros* were lit under the mural — and what was bound to happen did happen. As the heat wafted up the wall, the mural began to disolve into multicolored rivulets.

As the work of the past eight months vanished before his eyes, a sort of madness came over him. He remained motionless, unable to speak, as his assistants ran about trying to douse the fires. Already he heard the sound of angry voices as the news of the catastrophe spread through the Old Palace and officials came rushing into the room. In words of outrage or sarcasm, they berated the fool who did not know that heat would melt wax.

But he was nowhere to be seen. Profiting from the confusion, he slipped out unnoticed.

It was a fine spring day, and it did not take him long to gallop to the rectory.

With the help of the old priest and a few peasant neighbors, he carried his "great bird" to the top of the Swan Mountain. Gripping the wooden bar in his white knuckled hands, he sprinted to the edge of the cliff and thrust himself out into space.

For an unforgettable moment he soared with an upward gust of wind and his lifelong dream came true. But not for long. A wing collapsed. The air hissed by his ears as he felt himself plunging at increasing speed towards the valley below.

Then, all went black.

He awoke three days later at the rectory and found the old priest at his side.

"Albiera protected you from heaven," said Alessandro, raising a spoonful of broth to his mouth. "Tomorrow you will be well enough to walk for a while."

Leonardo did not reply. He closed his eyes and wished he had died in the crash. He had hoped to be acclaimed for his glorious flight, instead he would have to endure the sneers and the jibes of the populace. Once again fate had denied him the rewards of his genius. Once again he had failed — and not through his fault. He never would stun the world: he was born unlucky.

What would now happen to him? Would the Signoria demand the refund of the monies he had received? Would he be thrown into prison? In either case, he was a ruined, broken man. Why, oh why had he ever returned to this cruel, ungrateful town? Oh, to be back with those nice and generous Frenchmen! Barbarians they might be, but they paid his salary regularly, heaped commissions on him, showed him respect . . . If only he could induce the French viceroy, Seigneur de Chaumont, to request his immediate transfer to Milan! The Signoria would not dare to refuse his wish.

As the month of May wore on nothing was heard from the magistrates. Finally, towards the end of the month, he received an official message summoning him to the Old Palace.

At the appointed time he was ushered into the presence of Their Magnificences. His Excellency the *gonfaloniere*, Piero Soderini, considered him through cold, but not vindictive eyes. He then informed him that a letter had arrived from the French viceroy in Milan requiring his immediate journey to the Lombard capital. (Whether Leonardo secretly beseeched the French official for his immediate recall to Milan, which seems likely, is not known.)

"We cannot deny such a demand from the representative of His Majesty the king of France," he went on. "Therefore, you will be granted a three-month leave of absence."

But, he went on, Leonardo had defaulted on his obligations. For two years he had received a salary as well as free living quarters and he had produced nothing in return. The council expected him to repaint his mural or paint it anew. Furthermore, to make certain he would return at the stipulated time, he would have to deposit a sum of 150 gold florins with the chancery.

"Should you fail to return in three months, you will forfeit this sum."

He dismissed Leonardo, who bowed to the stony-faced magistrates. That morning he withdrew a hundred and fifty gold florins from his dwindling bank account and deposited them with the chancery. Early that afternoon he signed a contract pledging on his honor to be back in Florence by the first of September.

This done, he went to Casa Giocondo.

Lisa was shocked by his appearance. She asked no questions, but her heart went out to him.

"Sit down and have some wine," she said.

Politely he declined. He was leaving in the morning and still had many things to do. He then asked permission to take her portrait with him.

"On my way, I shall stop at Urbino," he said, "and deliver it myself in the hands of His Lordship, Giuliano de Medici."

"You won't forget, will you?"

He gave her a sad, reproachful glance. She, too, had lost faith in him.

"You have my word on it," he said formally.

Silence fell between them. There was no use trying to recapture the old intimacy. Fate, which had brought them together for a moment, was now pulling them apart. Once again they had become strangers.

"At least Giuliano will finally have his portrait," she told her husband that evening.

"I hope so," he said with a tinge of doubt in his voice. "Personally, I shouldn't count on it too much."

She soon forgot about him in the preparation of her garden party. Then there was the annual wrestling contest at the Giocondo mill. For weeks she heard about nothing else from Meo, who was taking part in it.

These athletic events were a tradition among Florentine factories and provided opportunities for demonstration of good fellowship between the workers and their masters. During the year a series of elimination matches were held, ending with the gala ceremony of the final contest at the end of June.

Throughout winter and spring Bartolommeo had declined all social invitations in order to practice armlocks, butting, tripping and other holds and falls of the games. He now was fourteen: a proud *calderaio*, or sorter of cocoons, in the second year of his apprenticeship. His devouring ambition was to win the apprentices' wrestling championship. Nothing else mattered. His private hero was Milo of Crotona, a Greek athlete of the sixth century before Christ, who had carried an ox on his shoulders and been crowned Olympic wrestling champion six times.

The previous year Meo had been eliminated in the semifinals, but this time he had vowed to win the trophy.

"You will see, Mamma, I'm going to win," he told Lisa.

Secretly she burned a few candles to the Madonna, for the Virgin had much influence in sports as in everything else; no less secretly, Tessa had recommended him to Allah.

On the day of the contest, the courtyard of the Giocondo mill was festooned with greenery and decorated with the red-lily flags of the Republic. An orchestra of fifes and sackbutts filled the air with lively strains of popular marches. Above, the cloudless June sky stretched out, calm and blue. The firm's officials and their families occupied the benches of a specially built tribune while the mill workmen stood on three sides of the courtyard.

The contest began with a short address by the parish priest, who assured his listeners that God was watching the tournament from His heavenly throne. Then there was some more music.

The program began with the wrestling match between the first-year apprentices. Then it was Meo's turn to climb on the roped and sanded platform, bare-chested, a confident smile on his lean face. He bowed to his father sitting on the tribune with his board of directors, smiled at Lisa and Tessa, and, turning around, waved at his fellow *calderai*.

At a signal from the referee, he froze into a half-crouching position, and his opponent, the current champion, did likewise. The match began with a few lightning feints and counterfeints. Then the two boys came to grips and tumbled to the ground, writhing and rolling. For a while the fight appeared undecided. Gradually, however, Meo's superior technique prevailed over his adversary's greater strength. With a sudden stranglehold, he almost choked him and swiftly pinned his shoulders to the sanded floor. Amid general applause and a burst of fifes and sackbutts, he was proclaimed the victor.

His face and chest were lacquered with sweat and his black curls clung to his cheeks as he walked up to the tribune where his father, after pronouncing a short complimentary address, handed him a silk purse containing two florins. Lisa smiled tearfully as Meo turned to her and kissed her hand. From the last row of the tribune, among slaves and family servants, Tessa watched the scene through moist eyes.

A week later the family moved to Settignano for the summer.

Through the years Lisa had become very fond of the plain country house with its vast garden and gently rustling sycamores. She liked the drowsy afternoons on the terrace listening to the crowing of roosters in neighboring farms or the distant chimes of the village church.

Summer was the lazy season, and for three months she gave in to her inclination to daydream. She would lay on a lounge chair, a book forgotten on her lap, recalling small episodes of her youth, wondering about the future, lovingly thinking about Bartolommeo.

The news of his wrestling championship had spread to Settignano and endowed him with a brawny clamor that attracted young girls. Proudly they palpated his biceps, exclaimed at their firmness and size. They fluttered their lashes at him and he enjoyed the shy admiration in their eyes.

He was entering the choppy seas of adolescence and confided his most secret feelings to his young stepmother. He admitted to having kissed (mostly out of curiosity) Tita and Faustina on the lips, and found no difference between them. Tita was prettier; Faustina had more sense. It was hard to decide which one he preferred.

Then, in August, he met Esmeralda, the daughter of a wealthy *sensale* or stockbroker, and there was no one else in the world for him. Esmeralda had soft brown eyes and dimpled cheeks. Thereafter, Tita and Faustina, who had obligingly let him kiss their lips, ceased to exist. He thought only of Esmeralda, who was not impressed by his biceps, refused to kiss him, and seemed to enjoy watching him suffer.

At Lisa's suggestion, he brought her a lovely bouquet of flowers, and to his delight, her resistance evaporated. She let him kiss her on the lips, assured him that he was her best friend. But, she added, he would do well to ask his honored father to have her pledged to him, for she was thirteen and a half and of marriageable age.

To Lisa, it all sounded vaguely familiar. It was not so very long ago that she, too, had urged Giuliano to have her pledged to him or lose her. Life, indeed, repeated itself. Successive generations experienced the same fears, the same joys and pains; they played the same games, spoke the same words.

Meo was in the throes of puppy love. The prospect of Esmeralda marrying anyone else but him, sent him into fits of homicidal fever. Passionately he confided to his "mamma" that he would kill any rival, then stab himself in the heart. She assuaged his alarms as best she could. She explained it was still a little early to ask for Esmeralda's hand, but she promised to keep close watch and make sure she would not be wed to anyone else.

And so summer went by.

The family returned to town. Meo entered his third year of apprenticeship and joined the *acquaioli* and *torcitori* who sprayed and twisted raw silk. At the same time he began training for the forthcoming wrestling contest in June. At his father's suggestion, he read about the history of the silk industry.

Excitedly, he told Lisa how, in the year 550, two monks had arrived in Constantinople from China, bringing with them some silk eggs and worms concealed in a bamboo, which they had presented to the emperor. From these humble origins, the silk industry was born. In time, it had spread to Greece; then to Spain through the Moors, and, finally, to Sicily.

With so many things to do and to think about, Meo had less time for Esmeralda. Gradually she receded into the background of his life. Of course, he still loved her, but she demanded too much of his time. She wanted him to serenade her when he had to practice wrestling. Females did not understand that men had other things to do besides thinking about love. No longer did he urge Lisa to keep close watch on her, and he even hinted that he would survive if she married someone else.

Now and then Giocondo brought news about Leonardo da Vinci. Naturally, he had not returned to Florence by September, as promised. Another letter from the viceroy had requested a one-month extension of his leave of absence, which had been grudgingly consented to by the Signoria. In October, Leonardo had again failed to appear. This time, His Excellency, the life-*gonfaloniere*, had written an angry letter to the French viceroy.

Leonardo da Vinci has not behaved as he should toward this Republic, for he has taken a good sum of money and scarcely begun an important work that he was to do.

There was an exchange of acrimonious letters between Florence and Milan. Finally, the Signoria had confiscated the hundred and fifty florins Leonardo had left with the chancery and let the matter drop. They had had enough of him.

To Lisa, Leonardo's greatest misdeed was that he should have broken his promise to her and failed to deliver her portrait to

Giuliano. Contessina had told her that her brother was still waiting for it.

"He had given me his word," she kept repeating incredulously, "and I thought we were friends."

Giocondo attempted to explain that artists could not be judged by ordinary standards. His words remained without effect.

"He is a thief," she said, "a plain thief."

What made her anger still more acute was that, according to news received from his Milan agent, Leonardo enjoyed great popularity among the French "barbarians." He did not begrudge them the fact that Gascon archers had taken his great clay horse as a target and destroyed what he confidently believed to be an immortal piece of sculpture. Neither did he resent the transformation of Ludovico's palace into a pigsty, plundered of its most precious works of art. The finest tapestries and paintings had been appropriated by the viceroy and sent to his French estate of Meillant. "*Milan a fait Meillant*" had become a rueful witticism among the population.

This dishonest, drunken, and lecherous proconsul had taken Leonardo under his wing. Not only had he reinstated him in his functions of *festaiuolo*, but he had entrusted him with the plans of his future summer residence.

Naturally this villa would be like no other in the world. Water traps would be concealed in various places, so that unsuspecting visitors would be doused with water sprays from all sides. The sight of elegant ladies caught in unexpected showers promised to be a rib-splitting spectacle.

Another delightful novelty was the windmills Leonardo proposed to install throughout the viceregal garden, which would create "a constant wind" and set into operation several instruments of his invention, thus creating music without musicians.

He was so pleased with this latest brainchild of his that he simply had to write about it to his patron.

And so you will have music at all times mixed with the scent of flowers, cedars and citrus.

While working on these absurdities, he also painted the second version of "The Virgin of the Rocks."*

As if this were not enough, he began writing his *Trattato della Pitture*, or *Treatise of Painting*. After a high-blown preface, he disserted at length on Light, Darkness, Solidity, Color, Form, Position, Distance, Propinquity, Motion, and Rest.

This done, he delved into the comparative size of the body's organs.

The width of the palms is the same as that of the foot. . . . The length of the longest toe is equal to the width of the mouth. . . . The width of the heel is equal to that of the wrist. . . . The foot is as long as the whole head of a man. . . . From the navel to the genitals is a face's length. . . .

And so on and on and on . . .

In June 1509, Pisa capitulated, and the fifteen-year-old war came, at least, to an end.

Born from the Little King's uncomprehending nod, it had exhausted the two adversaries, but it had taught the Florentines some measure of common sense and humanity. This time there was no branding of Pisan women on the cheeks, no mutilating of old men. The victors opened their arms to the vanquished. Like an old couple too weary to quarrel any longer, Pisa and Florence buried their grievances and tried to live in peace once again.

"Thank Heaven," observed Giocondo, "we shall be at peace for your thirtieth birthday. Gentle wife, what would please you most on this occasion?"

"What would please me most," she replied, "would be for everybody to forget about it."

This, she discovered, was impossible. Men were implacable in their kindness and insisted on publicizing an event that she joyously would have left unmentioned. With dismay, she learned that

---

* On 27 April, when he still was in Florence, he had been sentenced by a Milan tribunal — after twenty-three years of litigation — to paint another version of the same subject, this time with a halo on each personage's head. The work hangs today in London's National Gallery.

her grandfather had made arrangements for a banquet in her honor. Already many members of the Gherardini, Rucellai, and Giocondo clans had sent in their acceptance.

The dinner took place at "The Farm" in the late-summer dappled sunshine of the *boschetto*. It was duly festive, enlivened with song and lute — and she hated every minute of it.

She hated the food, which was excellent, the countless toasts to her health and long life. Most of all, she hated her elderly women relatives, who, with sweet smiles and compassionate glances, welcomed her into their ranks.

Thirty, they said, was the gateway to the sunset years. Middle age, they insisted, offered many compensations for vanished youth. No more iron corsets, no more plucking of eyebrows, elaborate headdresses, long makeup sessions. The overrated pleasures of sex were replaced by those of the table. You no longer had to worry about becoming a few pounds overweight, for men no longer looked at you with eyes of lust.

Lisa felt as though she were attending her own funeral and wished a pox on her well-meaning cousins. No, she would not listen to those decrepit old witches, their talk about the joys of middle age and sunset years. She would go on plucking her eyebrows, rouging her cheeks, remaining young, desirable, and enjoying sex. For her, time would make an exception and stand still. She wanted men to go on looking at her with eyes of lust.

In her nervousness, she managed to prick her tongue with her two-pronged *forchetta*. Inwardly, she cursed these new-fangled, dangerous instruments with which you were expected to spear your food and perilously bring it to your mouth. In her heart, she pined for the good old days when people ate reasonably with their fingers, without risk of piercing their tongues.

Suddenly it flashed through her mind that she was fretting over progress and lamenting the past.

Like an old woman, she thought, a thirty-year-old woman.

And for the first time that day she smiled.

The following year her husband reached the age of fifty. Although his complexion remained florid, his eyesight keen, and his gait firm, this made him officially "an elder."

Lisa began seeing him as a very old man living on borrowed time. He became dearer to her than ever and she vowed to watch over him, as she already did over her honored grandfather who, thanks to her vigilance, had reached the incredible age of seventy-six.

That winter she coaxed Giocondo into wearing a fur chest-warmer and pressed hot potions on him when he returned from the mill.

While "keeping an eye on her two beloved elders," she also watched and guided her stepson, now eighteen. His apprenticeship had come to an end and he was now his father's assistant, as well as his secret critic.

"My honored genitor is old-fashioned," he would confide to Lisa. "I told him what great profits we could make in the production of silk velvet, but he said the firm is big enough as it is. Now, if I were directing the mill —"

"But you aren't," she would cut in. "In a few years when you return from your silk-buying journey, you may try your ideas. For the moment, be content to learn, observe, and obey."

When he was not telling her about silk velvet and other innovations he planned to initiate, he told her about girls. Now they took precedence over wrestling. They caused immense pleasure as well as abysmal pain. One moment you wanted to kiss the ground they walked on, the next you would like to strangle them.

Esmeralda had vanished from the scene. After her father's death, she had moved to Verona, her mother's native city. Her departure left Meo unmoved. He recently had met Ginevra, and once again he wallowed in the ecstasies and agonies of adolescent love.

Ginevra was the most beautiful girl in the world, but she had a stone in place of a heart. Not only was she cruel, but capricious. At times her eyes would turn into pools of liquid sweetness; her smile promised the most heavenly rewards. Then in a flash she was merciless again. It was enough to drive a man to distraction.

Lisa watched Meo's emotional ups and downs, his periods of suicidal despair and his moments of ecstatic happiness. Between her husband, her stepson, and her grandfather, her heart was full. Nearly fifteen years had passed since she had wed Giocondo. The fearsome stranger had become infinitely dear to her. She trembled at the thought that he was such an old man, with so little time left before he crossed the Great Sea. She did not dare to think what would become of her when he died and left her a widow. Secretly she burned candles to the Virgin to keep him in high spirits and good health.

As for Giuliano, he had ceased to be a presence, or even a memory. On a few occasions she had entered the inner shrine that she had devoted to him and had found it empty. Only two or three childhood episodes had survived from the past: her pushing him off the bridge, their trip to Pisa, the memorable October afternoon in the olive grove.

Now and then she heard about him from Contessina. He still lived at the Urbino Palace, as a guest of Duke Guidobaldo. He took part in courtly literary debates, wrote poetry, and patiently waited for the wheel of fortune to turn and bring his family back to power.

She had tried to keep his memory green and found it impossible. No love could survive endless separation. Anyone you could not hear or touch became as remote as a star. She now realized that the relationship which had enthralled and tormented her adolescence had merely been the first and awkward stirrings of awakening sensuality. They had mistaken the bud for the flower. Nothing remained of their kisses and caresses but the melancholy fragrance of an avid, bygone youth.

During the next two years Lisa clung to her resolution to remain young and desirable.

She found the task increasingly tedious, time-consuming, and unrewarding. Dutifully she continued to pluck out her eyebrows while bathing, to rub unguents in the net of fine wrinkles that spanned out from her eyes when she laughed. With stoic fortitude she declined the *berlingozzo* cake she loved so much in order to remain slim.

These hours of toil and these privations brought unsatisfactory results. People praised her personality, her elegance, the graciousness of her manners, her charity, the charm of her smile, but few men — except her dear old husband, God bless him! — looked at her with eyes of lust.

At first she wept in secret at the evanescence of her youth. What was the use of being a woman, if not to be coveted? Tears flooded her eyes at the remembrance of the "undressing" looks she had so pleasurably endured while walking down the streets. Where had those wonderful days gone when Tessa accused her of having "as much modesty as a cat"? Now men stepped aside to let her pass, doffed their hats, and resumed their conversation. Before her lay the long, forlorn years of middle age with the family crypt at the end of them. For a few minutes she wished she were dead.

Her mind returned to the sunny days of her adolescence. She recalled the minute of happiness paid for by hours, sometimes days, of uncertainty, jealously, waiting, disappointment, lonely sobs at night. Had it really been worth it? She thought of Meo going through periods of despair over the merciless Ginevra. Suddenly it struck her that youth was wonderful mostly in retrospect.

This discovery made her feel much better. That day she had a double portion of *berlingozzo* cake and enjoyed every mouthful of it. The following week she stopped plucking her eyebrows — and no one noticed it.

Another factor contributed to divert Lisa's thoughts from her ebbing youthfulness. Once again Florence was threatened with excommunication and war. This time by Pope Julius.

His predecessor, Alexander, had been a great lecher, but he had remained a gentleman to the end, something Julius had never been. In his youth he had been an onion peddler; all his life he was a foulmouthed, drunken vulgarian. The stench of unwashed flesh, mingled with the fetor of purulent syphilis, was such that dignitaries were excused from kissing his feet, as prescribed by etiquette.

Like his unlamented uncle, Pope Sixtus, he retained the manners and speech of the Savona waterfront all his life, lied by instinct, turned against those who had helped him; like him, he had children and was suspected of strong "sodomite inclinations"; like him, he fell into fuming rages in the course of which he struck the bishops and cardinals in his entourage with his cane, calling them *bastardi* (which in many cases was true) and "miserable clowns."

He chewed little onions and spat plum pips during audiences, curtailed the mass ritual to suit his convenience, and drank so much wine in the morning that by early afternoon he was unable to discharge his duties. For these reasons, he was nicknamed *"Il Mezzo-Papa,"* or "Half-Pope."

For eleven years he had hated his Borgia predecessor, Pope Alexander, with a passion bordering on mania. In the hope of having him removed from office, he had prodded King Charles into invading Italy. With money given him by King Louis, Charles's successor, he had bought his election to the papal throne. He also had used French troops to recover some lost Church territory and to defeat the Venetians. In that last undertaking, the French had won one of the most costly victories in their history, sacrificing the flower of their knighthood and several thousand men.

Whereupon Julius, for whom the battle had been fought, turned against his benefactor. The contemptible pontiff became a patriot and swore to expel the "barbarians" whom he had first invited.

With the help of the Spanish army, which already occupied the Kingdom of Naples, he destroyed the French domination in Italy and replaced it with that of Spain.

In the spring of 1512, the exhausted French crossed back over the Alps and returned home. Julius could then turn his undivided attention to the Florentines, whose only crime was to have remained faithful to the king of France. The pontiff unleashed the soldiery of Ferdinand the Catholic upon defenseless Prato, a few miles from Florence. The Spanish "barbarians" demonstrated they were in every way the equals of the French *écorcheurs*.

On 29 August 1512, the champions of the Holy See burned churches, ravished nuns, and killed six thousand people — nearly the whole population.

After this sample of warfare, the Signoria could only plead for mercy. Julius demanded an "indemnity" of 100,000 gold florins and ordered the revocation of the chief of state, Piero Soderini, who, disgusted with Christians, took refuge in Turkey. The pontiff also insisted that the Medici be returned to power.

And so it came to pass that on 1 September 1512, after eighteen years of separation, Lisa saw Giuliano again as he made his entrance into Florence.

It had taken all of Giocondo's persuasiveness to make her ride all the way from Settignano to look at a man whom, she said, she would not even recognize.

"True, gentle wife, but he is your kinsman and you owe him this mark of courtesy."

As she stood on the balcony of her house, she almost did not recognize the youngster she had known in the tall, pale man dressed in black who smiled and waved from his saddle at the clamoring crowd.

"He does not look well," she remarked. "Contessina told me he coughs a great deal and has inherited his mother's evil chest humors."

The following day she returned to Settignano: its garden, its rustling sycamores. The sight of Giuliano had revived a handful of memories, but no emotion. Time had done its work. The past was dead.

From Giocondo, she learned that he had retaken possession of Casa Medici and started the necessary repairs. He seldom went out, saw few people. Time and again he repeated that he had no wish to take part in politics; he only asked permission to live in Florence as a citizen and be permitted to buy back the works of art that had been stolen during the sacking of the palace.

The citizenry, who had expected retaliations, breathed a sigh of relief. Once again the Florentines went through one of their recurrent fits of democratic fever. Everybody babbled about liberty; everybody demanded more rights. No one mentioned duties. A new *gonfaloniere* was elected. A council of eighty was elected, no one knew for what purpose. Work began on still another constitution. An epidemic of strikes crippled the already faltering economy.

For one month the Florentines demonstrated once again their congenital incapacity of governing themselves.

It all came to an abrupt end early in October when Don Raimondo Cardona, commander of the Spanish army, arrived in Florence. Followed by a retinue of helmeted and breastplated guards, he rode to the Old Palace, eased himself into the *gonfaloniere*'s velvet-backed chair, and, flapping his crop against his spurred boots, addressed Their Magnificences with straightforward candor.

He began by saying that there would be no new constitution, no more speech about it. The old Medici laws would be restored, all power placed in the hands of His Excellency Giuliano de'-Medici, who would replace his honored father, the late Lorenzo, as chief of state.

He added that the magistrates would do well to send a sum of 80,000 gold florins as a token of their love and affection to the king of Spain, another twenty thousand to him. Whereupon he rose, bowed to the councillors, and stomped out of the room.

And so, at the command of the pope and the Spanish general, and in answer to the pleas of his brother the cardinal, Giuliano took over the reins of government, revealing a genuine talent for statesmanship. In a short time he succeeded in winning the trust and affection of the Florentines. Like his father, he went about the town without an armed guard, stopping to chat with shopkeepers. At the public ovens and fountains, black-shawled housewives crossed themselves and said that their beloved Lauro of their youth had returned from the grave.

One day Lisa received a visit from Contessina. The events of the past few weeks had brought a distinct change in her friend's appearance and manner. Gone were the pallor of her cheeks, the homemade garments of the penurious years, the look of fear in her eyes. The sable coat she casually tossed on the window seat left no doubt as to her present prosperity.

"It's a gift from Giuliano," she said. "Oh, *cocolina*, how wonderful it is to be rich again!"

And this was only the beginning, she added. After its long eclipse, the Medici star was on the ascent again. Old Pope Julius was ailing, drunk most of the time and more cantankerous than ever. He was not expected to live long.

"And mark my word," she went on with confidence, "this time my brother Giovanni will take his place."

Already she was making plans. Immediately after the election, she would move to Rome and become the Vatican's official hostess, so to speak. She would be the channel of all benefices and preferments.

"To begin with, I'll have my son Niccolo made a cardinal."

Meanwhile, in addition to his duties of state, Giuliano was buying back the manuscripts and works of art so lovingly collected by his father. The palace's rooms assumed once more their former stateliness. The rare onyx cups, the precious Greek and Roman coins, the Botticelli paintings, the Luca della Robbia ceramics reappeared in the places they had once occupied. The past was coming back to life.

Giuliano announced the resumption of another Medici tradition, the Christmas diplomatic ball.

Lisa and her husband were among the people invited to the function. On that cold, crisp winter night, the Medici Palace glowed with candlelight and resounded with music, as in the great days of yore.

Only towards the end of the evening did Lisa have a few moments alone with Florence's new ruler.

"Fair cousin," he exclaimed with a happy smile, "it is good to see you again after all these years."

She was about to plunge into a reverence, but he reached out for her hand and gently pulled her up to her feet. "No need of ceremonies between us. After all, you did try to drown me."

"And you pulled me down with you."

For an instant they stood in their minds on the rickety bridge over the Mugello: two carefree youngsters who did not suspect what fate had in store for them.

"I pushed you off the bridge involuntarily," she lied, "but you pulled me down from sheer malice."

He protested that nothing could be further from the truth. Their make-believe argument covered whatever embarassment they might have felt at being together again. She noticed he had not changed as much as she had thought at first. His hazel eyes still had their teasing gleam, but his face was drawn and pale. Several times he pressed his handkerchief to his lips to stifle the dry cough which brought a momentary flush to his cheeks.

She sensed that he really was happy at seeing her again. Gently he drew her to a corner of the room, away from the crowd. He admired the amethyst belt she was wearing that night, and she told him it had been a gift from Jacopo.

For an instant the boyish, freckled face floated in her mind and her eyes moistened when she said how bravely he had died.

"He always had faith in your return."

She almost told him about Andoca, but decided against it. Some memories were better left dormant. Instead, she asked him about his years of exile at Urbino. He described the peaceful routine in the immense castle, his friendship with the young Duke Guidobaldo, his encounter with Leonardo.

"By the way, did you finally receive my portrait?" she inquired.

No, he said with an indulgent smile. Perhaps Leonardo had tried to reach him. "But for the past three years I've been engaged in the wars against the French."

They danced once, decorously and in silence. She thought him a handsome, charming, kindly man: the sort of man that a woman with a vacant heart might fall in love with. But her heart was filled with love for Giocondo and Meo. There was no room in it for anyone else.

In January a new Signoria was elected and, to his surprise, Giocondo found himself among the eight appointed magistrates.

He protested that he was a merchant, not a politician, and much too old to meddle in public affairs. Lisa joined him in his laments.

"I see with your eyes in this matter," she said with well-feigned dismay. "I don't understand why people do not let you alone."

Of course, she went on, should he refuse to serve and shirk his civic duty, his ancestors would weep from shame in their graves. The members of the Giocondo clan would go about with heads bowed down, and Meo would lose face in the eyes of his friends.

"As for myself," she added with lowered lids, "I wouldn't dare show my face in the streets."

She let that sink in.

"But don't let these considerations hold you back," she pressed on. "After all, you are a feeble old man who should not be expected to attend to difficult and important matters of state."

At once she knew she had hit the target. Testily he remarked that every day he faced problems more complex than any political issue.

"Moreover," he added, after a thoughtful pause, "you are right, gentle wife. It wouldn't be right for me to shirk my civic duty."

The following day, after Sunday mass, they bought a very beautiful, very expensive gold chain of office in one of the goldsmith shops on Ponte Vecchio. As the craftsman adjusted the chain on Giocondo's ample chest, Giocondo muttered words on the extravagance and hollowness of political honors. Especially when he should be preparing for his crossing of the Great Sea instead of buying foolish trinkets.

"You will have me end my days at the alms' house," he predicted.

To which Lisa replied that she would be right by his side and together they would reminisce about their opulent days.

For a moment they felt very close and happy and young again.

In February, Pope Julius died. Four months before he had revealed to the world Michelangelo's fresco on the ceiling of the Sistine Chapel. As crowds flocked to gasp at the 10,000-square-foot masterpiece with its three hundred and forty-three figures, Julius basked in the achievement of the artist he had tormented and humiliated beyond endurance. Once the foulmouthed, evil-smelling pontiff had the supreme artist appear before him on his knees with a rope around his neck, as a sign of repentance. Twice he forced him to interrupt his work and ride the 250 miles to Bologna to beg money for pigments to finish the ceiling.

This same discerning art lover did not hesitate to strip Roman monuments of their marble coverings for his Saint Peter Basilica which nearly bankrupted the Church, outraged Luther, and played an important part in the Protestant Reformation.

No sooner had he exhaled his last onion-smelling breath, than Cardinal Giovanni de'Medici left Florence to attend the conclave and proceed to the election of a new pope. Because of a painful anal fistula, the prelate traveled in a silk-curtained, slow-moving litter. The journey over winter-rutted roads was slow and excruciating. His fellow cardinals had already been five days in session when at last he arrived in Rome.

So great were his sufferings that his colleagues were touched to compassion. A barber-surgeon was admitted to the conclave room — a fact without precedent in the history of the Church. With skill, he lanced the rectal abscess and performed the delicate operation, which filled the room with such intolerable stench that the cardinals promptly elected the young and obviously dying cardinal in order to get out into the fresh air.

As he climbed down from the operation table, Giovanni learned that he had just been elected to the highest office on earth. Immediately, he felt better. The walled-in window of the conclave room was broken open. The waiting multitude on the square below heard the news that the Church had a new pontiff and his name was Leo X.

Cautiously, most cautiously, he was hoisted on the *sedia gestatoria* and carried to the Lateran Basilica on the shoulders of eight strapping young men. As the cortege was making its way, someone observed that the new pontiff had never been ordained priest. Four days after his election, on 15 March, Pope Leo celebrated his first mass.

The coronation took place on 11 April 1513. For hours the cortege meandered through the city to the chiming of bells and the booming of cannons. The corpulent, thirty-seven-year-old *pontifex maximus*, wearing his gold-rimmed monocle, rode majestically his white horse, blessing the kneeling crowds as he went by.

A week later it was Giuliano's turn to leave Florence, at the summons of his brother the Holy Father.

The day before his departure he paid a short visit to Casa Giocondo. He thanked the merchant for serving his two-month term on the Signoria and took his leave from Lisa. This time they knew they would never see each other again and their emotion expressed itself in long, wistful silences. Finally, he rose, kissed her hand, and departed.

During the following weeks news reached town of the great ceremonies that had marked Giuliano's entrance into Rome. His brother, who loved him as he loved no one else, had given him the splendid Belvedere Palace in the Vatican gardens as his residence. There he lived surrounded by a court second only to that of the pope himself. There was talk of making him king of Naples. Meanwhile he had been named commander in chief of the papal army.

"He probably wishes they would leave him alone," Lisa remarked. "He has his mother's illness and will soon cross the Great Sea."

At Settignano, she heard little about him, and once again he receded into unreality from which he had emerged for a few months.

Lisa's thoughts were now occupied by Meo's silk-buying journey which had been scheduled for the next spring.

"I hate silk," she told Tessa one afternoon as they reviewed the list of the dangers he would meet in his travels.

A wool-buying trip would have taken him to France, England, Flanders — all Christian and more or less civilized nations. But silk would take him to savage, heathenish countries like Greece, Turkey, Egypt, and there was no telling what perils he might encounter there.

She harassed Giocondo with questions. Did they have apothecary shops, did they have physicians in Constantinople? Was it true that people rode camels instead of horses? Were there many lions in the countryside? She had heard that Egyptian rivers were full of crocodiles – huge water lizards with mouths full of sharp teeth. And the Arabian wenches, would they steal Meo's purse and leave him penniless in some Egyptian forest rampant with snakes?

He reassured her as best he could. In Constantinople, Meo would work three months in a silk factory to learn Turkish methods of fabrication; he would live with the owner's family and be treated as one of their boys. As for apothecary shops and physicians in Greece and Alessandria, they were far better than those of Florence. Oriental women offered no real danger, for they covered their faces in the streets and lived apart in their own section of the house. Meo would probably never speak to a single Turkish or Arabian woman.

In this way, he assuaged her fears, and summer went by.

One week after her return to town, Lisa was informed by a maid that Ser da Vinci was waiting in the drawing room and asking for permission to present his respects.

She had been sitting at her writing table going over the household accounts and gave a start of surprise. She thought she would never see him again and there he was, waiting for her to receive him. Maybe he would tell her why he had not delivered her portrait. She told the maid to usher him in.

He looked very old and tired. Thin wisps of grey hair fell over his ears and vanished into his prophet's beard. His enormous forehead was rutted with deep furrows. Even his bushy eyebrows had turned white. He had lost several teeth. She felt sorry for him.

Suddenly she forgot her resentment and waved him to a chair.

He apologized for presenting himself in a traveling cloak and spurred boots, but he was stopping in Florence a few hours only.

"I came to tell you that on my arrival in Rome, my first care will be to deliver your portrait to His Excellency Giuliano de'-Medici. You have my word on it."

She wanted to laugh. His word! . . .

He caught the glint of skeptical amusement in her eyes and launched into a tirade of self-justification.

He had been unable to deliver her portrait, as promised, for the simple reason that no sooner had he reached Milan than he had been submerged in work, overwhelmed with commissions. To begin with, he had drawn the plans for the viceroy's summer villa which would have been one of the world's wonders — if only it had been built.

"The one with the water traps and musical windmills?" she asked tartly. "Surely this nonsense did not take all your time?"

He gave her a hurt look. These mirthful devices might seem like nonsense to her, yet they had required long and difficult calculations. Moreover, he had organized many palace festivities. It was not easy to draw masquerade costumes, choreograph ballets, build mechanical lions who advanced by their own power and opened their mouths to release a bird or flowers or a French flag.

And then there had been the numerous pictures he had painted at enormous cost of time and effort.*

"What are you planning to do in Rome," she asked, "besides delivering my portrait?"

Nothing definite at the moment, but he had various projects in mind. Rome had now become the art center of the world, and he had no doubt that his services would be in great demand. Because of his reputation as an engineer and architect, he might be asked to participate in the construction of the Saint Peter's Basilica. He might be invited to decorate the Vatican Palace with some immortal mural. Or he might simply limit himself to painting portraits of papal dignitaries, perhaps of His Holiness himself.

In addition, he had developed a keen interest in distorting mirrors, optics, and centrifugal pumps, and planned to make extensive and profitable researches in those fields.

Sadly, she looked at him in silence, marveling at this brilliant man's capacity for self-delusion. He had left Milan when the French had been chased out of it and he had lost his livelihood.

* His painting output during this second, seven-year Milanese period consists of the London version of "The Madonna of the Rocks," the pyramidal "Saint Anne, the Virgin and Child," remarkable for the beauty of its coloring and some startling anatomical errors; an ectoplasmic, unwholesome "Saint John"; an androgynous, cross-legged "Bacchus" (sometimes called "John in the Wilderness"): all highly controversial works; all painted with the assistance of apprentices; all bearing the identical dulcet, one-sided smile which had become the tiresome trademark of his declining years.

He was now in search of some new patron who would give him lodgings and a good salary. He still dreamed of stunning the world, acquiring immense riches. The poor man did not want to admit that everyone knew that his "Last Supper" was already crumbling, that his soot-blackened "Struggle for the Flag" still decorated the Great Council Room, and everyone in Italy had laughed at his disastrous Arno canal.

Undaunted by his countless failures, he went on making extravagant projects, fancying himself the greatest inventor in the world, retaining his unshakable self-confidence.

Perhaps that was what kept him going.

"I am certain you will meet with great success in Rome," she said, rising from her chair.

He bent over her hand and turned around. With a slow shake of the head, she watched him walk out of the room and out of her life.

A few weeks later she learned that he had entered the service of Giuliano, who had given him lodgings in his own Belvedere Palace as well as a lavish salary of thirty-three florins per month.

At last, she thought, Giuliano will finally have received the portrait.

Good-hearted as he was, he had taken pity on the errant old man who had found every door closed to him, and commissioned him to draw the plans for his stable of Arabian horses. He even had obtained from his brother a painting commission for Leonardo. But the pope did not have Giuliano's charity. One day when he was leaning on the windowsill of his apartment in the Vatican, he noticed the elderly painter collecting flowers to make some new varnish of his own composition. Setting his gold-rimmed monocle into his eye socket, he watched him for a while.

With an amused grin, he turned to his companion and said, *"Costui non è per far nulla"* . . . "This man will never get anything done."

Before long, Leonardo vanished from Lisa's mind. Through that winter and early spring, she thought only of Meo's approaching departure. Her fears increased with each passing day.

In vain did Giocondo swear that there were almost no lions in

Turkey, and none whatever in Constantinople. Snakes were equally rare. As for crocodiles, they lived farther south in parts of Africa where nobody ever went.

She remained unconvinced. At night she dreamed of Meo being pursued by Arab *banditi* on galloping camels or lost in some snake-infested Egyptian forest.

Clearly, Meo would need protection, a lot of it. She recalled her grandfather Gherardini telling her in his *studiolo* how he had been lured into dowering an orphan girl to insure Antonio's protection.

"Twenty-five florins it cost me," he had sighed, "but the Virgin brought him back home safe and sound."

That was what Lisa wanted. She broached the subject with Giocondo, who remarked that twenty-five florins would buy a great many masses. And what better protection could there be than that of the Almighty himself?

Lisa shook her head. She had no faith in the Almighty as a travel insurance agent.

"My tutor, Maestro Bernardo, told me that the Crusaders were promised God's protection, but they all died on their way to Jerusalem."

"Not all, gentle wife. A great many, but not all."

The odds did not appeal to Lisa. She wanted Meo back safe and sound, and for that there was no one like the Virgin.

Her husband did not object and she went to see the mother superior at the Orphanage of the Innocents. When she handed her the twenty-five florins, the old nun shook her head. Yes, in the olden days a virtuous orphan could find a husband if she brought a dowry of twenty-five florins, but no more. Now it was thirty-five florins or she had to go on remaining chaste.

When she learned that Meo's journey would take him through savage countries with lions and snakes everywhere, the mother superior said she could not guarantee the Madonna's full protection — and nothing else would do — for less than an additional fifteen florins.

"But then," she said, "you may sleep at ease. The Virgin will be with him every step of the way."

When Lisa told her husband of the mother superior's request, he let out a sigh. "Apparently the protection costs more than the journey."

But he gave her the money and was glad he did. From that moment onward she regained her peace of mind. Even after Meo had left, she no longer dreamed of lions and crocodiles. She knew that with the Madonna at his side "their" boy would come back safe and sound, for she always kept her word.

Now all that remained was to wait and count the days until his return.

The Giocondo family tomb. *Santissima Annunziata Church, Florence.*

The Curtain Falls

 After Meo's departure, Lisa put away her clusters of false curls and the delicate headveil which she had worn out of vanity. She replaced it with a small white coif, similar to the one her grandmother Gherardini had worn. It covered her hair and ended in two small pointed wings. This was her farewell to youth and she gulped when she looked at her reflection in the Venetian mirror. No man would now ever look at her with lust.

Her iron corset followed shortly afterward. She gave up the dabs of rouge in her nostrils and the blue unguent on her eyelids. Her skirts were no longer slit at the sides; her necklines rose to the neck.

Quietly she put an end to her social activities, even her traditional Christmas ball. She simply had no heart for laughter and dancing while Meo was away. She now really preferred spending her evenings with her husband, either in the garden in late spring, or by the fire when the weather turned cold. He would warm his palms before the flames while she sat in her chair, her skirt trussed up to mid-thigh. To pass the time, he would read and reread aloud Meo's letters they received from Constantinople. Although heathens, the Turks were very polite and friendly. They washed their feet before entering their churches. Meo was in very fine health, and so was his manservant. He was learning all sorts of valuable devices for the fabrication of silk velvet and painting on silk.

"On his return, it will be time for him to take a wife," remarked Giocondo one evening.

Lisa said she would "keep her eyes open" for a suitable bride.

Now and then news would reach Florence from Rome where Giovanni de'Medici was revealing himself the most prodigal of pontiffs. His personal household counted nearly four hundred people. Although he fasted twice a week, he had become very fat. His white pudgy hands glittered with diamond rings. His morals were unblemished. This tall, bulky man had the temperament of a eunuch. Nonetheless, he played cards for huge stakes, and when he won, he would fling fistfuls of gold coins over his shoulders to his attendants. He had begun to ride to hounds at the age of nine and continued to indulge in his passion for hunting. Once he had hunted for thirty-seven days in a row. He still loved music as much as ever and still sang and played the lute in bed at night.

Next to him, the most important personage in Rome was his brother Giuliano, who had won great popularity thanks to the simplicity of his manners. Ten years after having commissioned it, he finally had received Lisa's portrait and hung it in his room. Unfortunately, his health did not improve and the sweltering Roman summer did not agree with him. He was often confined to his bed.

As for Leonardo, he continued to keep in the limelight more by his eccentricities than by his achievements. Florentine travellers returning from Rome reported his latest pranks, or, as they were called, *ghiribizzi*.

Except for Giuliano, he was totally friendless. Neither Bramante, his former colleague at the Sforza court, now the architect of Saint Peter's; nor Raphael, who had one time been his protege and whom he had allowed to make a copy of Lisa's portrait, seemed to remember him or to have anything to do with him. Yet, he had resumed his sartorial flamboyance and went about in purple velvet doublets, maroon hose, and, of course, the inevitable gold tunic.

"How sad to see a man of such great artistic talent behave like a pretentious fool!" Lisa would say with a sigh.

Then suddenly, in October 1514, came news from France that, for a while, superseded anything that came from Rome.

Louis XII, a widower and, at fifty-two, still without an heir, wed Mary Tudor, the sixteen-year-old, ravishingly beautiful sister of Henry VIII of England. She landed in France with a splendid retinue which included her lover, the earl of Suffolk, and Anne Boleyne, then aged eight, her future sister-in-law and queen of England.

The news of the marriage between the adolescent, sensuous English princess and the doddering French king aroused many sniggering comments in the marble galleries of the Vatican. King Henry enjoyed much popularity for he still was a loyal son of the Holy Church and had sent shiploads of tin for the roofs of the Basilica of Saint Peter. High stakes were wagered on the probable duration of the marriage between the French royal couple.

And yet another princely marriage occupied the public's attention with the announcement that Giuliano was to wed Filiberta, daughter of the duke of Savoy. This purely political union had been negotiated by the pope several months before.

Sadly, Giuliano removed Lisa's portrait from the wall and handed it to Leonardo.

"It would not be proper for my bride to see another woman's portrait in my room," he said. "I know you are much attached to it. Keep it in memory of me."

He left for Savoy a few days later, and Leonardo, once again anxious about his future, made a note of his departure.

The Magnifico Giuliano de'Medici left town on the 9th of January at daybreak to take wife in Savoy on the same day the death of the king of France took place.

As a matter of fact, Louis had died on January 1. It had taken Mary Tudor less than three months to dispose of him.

He was succeeded by Francis I, a young giant with a tremendously long nose, small, slanted eyes, an erratic disposition and the reckless courage of the brainless. A great swaggerer and lady killer, he would have made a perfect cavalry officer. It was France's misfortune that he became king.

Scarcely had he assumed the throne, than he began making preparations for a third invasion of Italy.

"Our country has become the obsession of French kings," remarked Giocondo bitterly.

In April, Giuliano returned to Rome with his bride Filiberta, a quiet, unobtrusive girl of seventeen. They had been married only two months, and already they were deeply in love with one another, as if they knew they had only a short time to live. Giuliano would die less than a year later, in March 1516; Filiberta never married again and died at twenty-six, on 24 April 1524.

As Filiberta happened to be the aunt of Francis I (who was four years older than she), her wedding marked the entrance of the Medici family into European royalty. For this reason, the pope ordered extraordinary festivities in honor of the newlyweds in which they partook with cheerful resignation.

Giuliano's tuberculosis was entering its final stage and with a broken heart, his bride watched life ebb slowly out of the man she loved. They hungered for each other's company, quiet walks in the spring-blossoming countryside. Instead they had to endure the acclamations of the crowds, the blare of fanfares and the sight of the papal elephant, Aymone, who had been trained to kneel before them.

Meanwhile, in France, the new young king was preparing for another descent upon Italy. He had mustered an army of 35,000 men and invincible artillery. He coveted the throne of Milan and eventually that of Naples too. Pope Leo, who owed the restoration of his family's fortunes to the Spaniards, had no choice but to side with them. Thus, his troops joined them, and Giuliano, as commander in chief, left Rome to confront his bride's nephew and his formidable army.

Less than a month later, in May 1515, Lisa learned of Contessina's death. The news aroused a cloud of half-forgotten memories. Poor Contessina, her dream of wealth and influence had been a short one, but at least she had seen the splendor of her House restored.

No sooner had Giuliano reached Florence than he fell desperately ill and had to relinquish the command of the papal troops. As his condition did not improve, his young wife hurried to his bedside, bringing Leonardo among the members of her retinue. While she nursed her husband, her nephew, King Francis, invaded Lombardy. In September, after a furious two-day battle at Marignano, in the course of which thirty thousand men died in twenty-eight hours, Francis I made a victorious entrance into Milan amid familiar cries of *"Francia! Francia!"*

Once again, Milan had become a French city.

As the monarch threatened to march on Rome, Pope Leo suggested they meet in Bologna. In November, while waiting for the arrival of His Holiness, the sovereign conferred upon the dying Giuliano the title of duc de Nemours. This magnanimous gesture towards the man who technically was his enemy prompted Filiberta to thank her towering nephew in person.

It was on this occasion that Leonardo was presented to the monarch. In excellent Italian, which he had learned from his mother, Francis complimented the elderly painter on his "Last Supper." Having heard many wondrous things about him as an engineer and architect, he declared he would be pleased to have him enter his service.

These were the very words Leonardo had hoped to hear. With Giuliano at death's door, his generous, unexacting patronage would come to an end. Gone would be the generous monthly thirty-three gold florins; gone his lodgings at the Belvedere palace. At sixty-three, he was once again facing the specter of unemployment.

With sincere emotion he declared himself ready to perform "immortal works" and bring "eternal glory" to his reign. He had said these same words so many times to so many people that they now fell of their own accord from his lips.

An agreement was concluded on the spot. He would organize court festivities as he had done for the late Duke Ludovico, and serve as a consultant on architectural and engineering matters. For this he would receive the munificent salary of 700 crowns a year. His servants and assistants would be equally well provided for. On top of all, the small, elegant manor of Cloux, a stone's throw from the royal residence at Amboise, would be placed at his disposal and that of his household.

Waves of gratitude passed through his mind as he visualized the splendid future awaiting him in that distant, foreign land. He would have liked to travel with the king who would soon return to France, but various things had to be attended to before. He could not in all decency leave Giuliano who had only a few weeks to live. And then he wanted to gather his precious notebooks, an enormous bundle of nearly 35,000 manuscript pages which contained the fruits of his life's labors. Also his compasses, astrolabe, scientific instruments and three finished paintings. And, of course, his stylish wardrobe.

He decided he would accompany Princess Filiberta when she returned to France, after her husband's death.

But he did not accompany her when she returned to her native Savoy, a heartbroken widow. At the last minute, he was seized by one of his fits of indecision that had paralyzed him at various stages of his career. He feared this distant, foreign land and the perilous crossing of the Alps. He dreaded the solitude of exile in a country whose language he did not speak. Most of all, he apprehended the tasks that would be heaped upon him. In his years of service to the French in Milan, he had learned that they expected value for their money.

Suddenly he was seized by a last desperate hope that he might still find some generous and indulgent patron in Rome, another Giuliano. Moreover, he had entered the competition for the façade of the church of San Lorenzo in Florence, and he was confident that his plans would be judged the best. What a revenge over Michel Agnolo who, also, had entered the competition! The results had not yet been announced and he wanted to stun the world, one last time, with the belated proof of his architectural genius. This made it worth staying in town.

Weeks passed. Leonardo once again lived in his rent-free quarters at the Belvedere Palace, flittering, as usual, from one science to another. Unfortunately, he also returned to his scalpels, bone saws and his corpses. But dissection was a dangerous hobby in the city of the Holy Inquisition.

When someone denounced him, terror cut short his hesitations. Trembling at the prospect of the *strappado* and the rack, he packed hurriedly and departed from Rome.

It was August and the countryside was baked by the summer sun. As he drove his baggage wagon along dusty roads, he filled his eyes for the last time with the beauty of his native land. Silently, he bid farewell to the harvested wheat fields, the hilly vineyards waiting for the vintage, the pink-roofed villages huddled around their chapels.

In Florence, he learned of the death of his friend, Donna Lisa de'Gherardini del Giocondo. He did not ask for details and proceeded on his northward journey.

Because of the lack of vital statistics concerning women, we do not know the exact date of Mona Lisa's death. It probably occurred in the spring of 1516, when she was thirty-seven, for in June of that year her husband commissioned Domenico Pulego to paint a large painting for his funeral chapel at the Sant' Annunziata Church. It represented Saint Francis (Giocondo's patron saint) receiving the Stigmata.

In the Renaissance, such commemorative pictures were regarded as expressions of mourning over the recent demise of some important and beloved member of the family. This painting was later transferred to the Pitti Museum. It is now lost.

The Giocondo Chapel can still be seen behind the main altar.

Eight years later, in 1524, Francesco del Giocondo was still living in his house on Via della Stuffa.

He was corpulent as ever and mentally alert, but he suffered from rheumatism. On his physician's advice, he bought a costly sapphire ring which he wore on the third finger of his left hand. It had been guaranteed to work miracles, but the wretched thing had failed to bring him any relief. His faith in doctors, never strong to begin with, abandoned him altogether. He slipped off the ring and learned to live with his affliction.

He had retired from business and entrusted the mill's direction to Meo on his return from his journey to the Orient. It was one of his deepest regrets that Lisa had not lived to see how well he looked. Indeed, the money spent to insure the Virgin's protection had proved a sound investment. It would have pleased Lisa to hear about his long treks on camels through burning deserts, and she would have loved the beautiful parrot he had brought her as a gift.

No sooner was he put in charge, than Meo had inaugurated various profitable innovations and added the production of plush or silk velvet to the mill's range of fabrics. Occasionally, Giocondo rode to the *stabilimenti*, pored over ledgers, toured the factory, talking to old employees and waving to apprentices. The mill, he felt, was in good hands.

Then, followed by his groom, he would ride to the headquarters of the Silk Guild on Via Capaccio to play cards or reminisce with former rivals. Then, back home.

In due time, Meo married the girl Lisa had chosen for him. Tita proved to be a pretty, loving bride, an expert housewife, and a good mother. Soon she presented Giocondo with a grandson and a granddaughter. The last he could have done without, but one must accept whatever God chose to send. A grandson then made up for his sister. In a few years, it would be time to start him on his apprenticeship.

One of the saddest things about growing old alone, Giocondo felt, was that you were watching the disappearance of your contemporaries. Each year friends, colleagues, competitors, relatives crossed the Great Sea. Gradually you became a stranger among the members of the succeeding generations. They might be polite and show respect, but you no longer were one of them. They paid you compliments on your good appearance, as they would soon put flowers on your grave.

Historical or social events lost much of their immediate interest for you knew you would not see their conclusion. You came to the sad conclusion that future generations would repeat the blunders that yours and all previous ones had committed since the beginning of time. Wisdom, apparently, always came too late.

And so, to pass the little time Giocondo still had on this earth, he turned back to the past where he had left most of himself and those whom he had loved. He tried to recall their gestures, the sound of their voices, the way they smiled, the way they frowned. They continued to live in his mind and heart.

In this way, he sometimes remembered Tessa. She had seen Meo return from his journey and this had been her last joy. She had thanked Allah for protecting him from lions and crocodiles. She had died shortly afterward and rejoined Lisa. As she had no tomb of her own, Giocondo had buried her in the family crypt, for this was what Lisa would have wanted.

Two years later, in 1519, he learned of the death of Leonardo. Fate had been kind to him. The perennial houseguest had ended his days in a little manor of his own, almost adjacent to the royal castle of Amboise, surrounded by the admiration and respect he craved so much.

"He was well advised to go to France," Giocondo told Lisa that evening in one of those imaginary conversations he often had with her. "In Italy, people knew too much about him. Despite his immense talent as a painter, he had deceived too many people, defaulted on too many commissions. People had lost confidence in him. He would have died in the poorhouse."

"I fear you are speaking the truth, noble husband," she would have agreed ruefully. "He did not even win the competition for the façade of San Lorenzo Church. He would have been so happy to leave some important work of his in Florence."

The fact is that he was given many opportunities to leave important works in Florence, starting with the San Bernardo altarpiece for the Signoria. Yet he had not achieved a single one. It is questionable whether he would have been more successful in this instance. After all, he was no more an architect than he was an engineer and that's why the commission went to Michel Agnolo.

Fortunately in France they did not know about the altarpieces, the "diving dress," the blasting powder that wouldn't blast, the Arno canal. They only saw a tall, white-bearded old man, dressed with care and lost in thought. Because the king came to see him now and then, they fancied him some great foreign lord and called him "Maystre Leonard de Vince." As usual, Leonardo has been credited with various engineering and architectural master-pieces while in France, notably the admirable openwork spiral staircase tower of the castle of Blois. No report, not a single note of his own, not a single sketch in his papers connects him with it.

In turn, he drew plans (never executed) for the rebuilding of the royal Amboise Castle into a palace *à la mode d'Italie,* a vast network linking the various royal residences and ending in Italy. This also was never built.

On occasion he was called upon by some important personage, which raised his prestige still higher.

Thus, it happened that on 10 October 1517, he received the visit of the cardinal-prince, Louis of Aragon, illegitimate grand-son of the king of Naples and former husband of one of Pope In-nocent's two daughters. As was to be expected, the prelate was accompanied by a brilliant retinue of clerics and men-at-arms, in addition to his private secretary, a young moon-faced monk by the name of Antonio de'Beatis who left a famous description of this memorable visit, which still can be seen at the National Li-brary of Naples.

Messer Lunardo Vinci, a Florentine of more than seventy [he was only sixty-five] and a painter most excellent for one so old, showed three paintings to His Illustrious Worship: one of them that of a cer-tain Florentine lady which he had painted from life at the urgent re-quest of the Magnificent Giuliano de'Medici.

The truth of this statement is attested by the fact that it was made in public at a time when Giuliano's widow was living a few steps away at Amboise Castle, when his brother, Pope Leo X, was still reigning; when Lisa's grandfather, Mariotto Rucellai, and her husband, Francesco del Giocondo were still alive — and it was de-nied by none of these.

Leonardo's statement also strengthens the assumption that Lisa was dead in 1517, for he would never have dared make it had she been alive at the time.

Leonardo played host with consummate grace. He had his

young apprentice, Francesco de'Melzi, bring his anatomical drawings and manuscripts from carved coffers and shown to the visitors. But it was the three paintings he had brought from Italy that aroused their enthusiasm: the "Saint Anne, Virgin and Child," the disturbing "Saint John," and Lisa's portrait, then in its pristine freshness.

After the cardinal's departure, Lisa's portrait was brought back to Leonardo's room where it usually hung. A moment later the old master himself returned to his place by the fireside as the October afternoon ebbed away into dusk.

His mind was filled with memories of Lisa. He recalled the sittings in the garden, the way she smiled when she was pleased with him, how her eyes glowed when she berated him for "cutting up dead people" and frittering his time away on a thousand and one things, instead of concentrating on painting.

Suddenly he realized how right she had been. He had served the God of science who promised fame and riches. The scientist he was not had killed the artist he was born to be. His bony hands cupped over his face. As he reviewed his long, crowded and disorderly life, he was overwhelmed with remorse and regrets.

He rose from his chair, lit his water lamp on his desk and laboriously wrote in his notebook:

"I have wasted my hours."

From that day onward, he was a changed man. He stopped dreaming of machines; he abandoned his project of waterways spreading over France; he tossed into a chest his plans for the reconstruction of Amboise Castle. He spent much of his time sitting in the sunshine, his spotty hands on the knob of his rustic cane, gazing at the restful Loire countryside. The peasant in him was being reborn.

It was too late to repair the errors of a lifetime, but not to implore God's forgiveness. That winter he learned to pray again. He who had laughed at Christ and Mary now held a rosary in his hand and muttered the prayers of his childhood.

As months went by, he grew increasingly feeble. A stroke paralyzed his left arm; yet he lived another year, mostly in bed. From it he could see Lisa's portrait smiling at him from the wall. He was pleased with it. He had not lived entirely in vain after all. It was nice having her with him during the long, lonely hours while he waited for death to come. She did remind him of Albiera and the two women blended into one in his mind.

When spring returned, he had himself helped out of bed by Francesco and his French housekeeper, Mathurine, and brought to his chair by the window. On 30 April, he wrote his will, commending his soul to God, the glorious Virgin, His Lordship Saint Michael, all the blessed angels and saints in Paradise. He gave detailed instructions for his funeral, stipulating that his body be followed by "sixty poor men from the town of Amboise, each carrying a burning torch." Thirty low masses were to be said for the repose of his soul. Tradition has it that King Francis bought the Mona Lisa for the astronomical sum of 4,000 gold crowns (five thousand dollars). Curiously, Leonardo who noted the price of a loaf of bread or a dozen eggs, made no mention of this sum in his will. Possibly Francis purchased the painting from Francesco de'Melzi, who was Leonardo's main heir.

The next day, he confessed, knelt on the floor to receive communion. The following morning, 2 May 1519, as the sun rose in the sky, he peacefully fell asleep for the last time.

In the course of one of their imaginary conversations, Giocondo informed Lisa that her portrait had been purchased by King Francis for his private art collection. She was pleased. It meant it would not pass from hand to hand and die, forgotten, in some rat-infested attic.

It would be safe and well taken care of, and it would show future generations what a fine picture maker he was.

The following year, in 1520, Mariotto Rucellai finally crossed the Great Sea at the incredibly old age of eighty-six.

He and Giocondo had become close friends in the last few years. They met at each other's house to play chess and recall the great days of Lorenzo de'Medici over a tankard of hot wine. Florence was no longer the capital of commerce and culture she had been, but she had had her "hour of the Lion." For a few years, civilization had dwelled within her walls and she left an incomparable legacy of art. Few cities could claim as much.

In October 1524, Giocondo was again elected to the Signoria. This time he really did not want the honor and said so to Lisa in one of their imaginary conversations.

"As you can see, gentle wife, I am too old and feeble to dabble in politics."

He saw her sitting at her usual place, her face rosy in the glow of burning logs, her hair concealed in the white pointed coif, her skirt trussed up above the knees. Her features were set in what he called her "Gherardini" expression: a mixture of sweetness, cunning, and mulishness that came over her face when she wanted him to do something he did not want to do.

He could hear her answer in his mind: "Indeed, noble husband, you are heavy with years, but your mind is as sprightly as a robin in spring. The Signoria could use a man of your wisdom and experience."

He replied that his ancestors had long turned to dust and could not possibly care whether or not he served again on the Signoria.

"Remember that I am a sick man, enduring grievous rheumatic pains," he said, groping for sympathy.

He got none. But he did comfort himself with the thought that to serve on the Signoria would take his mind off his affliction.

"I have a good mind to take a stick to you," he said, forgetting he was arguing with a ghost.

But suddenly, the ghost of Lisa turned to him and said pleadingly, "Then, do it for me."

His ill humor vanished.

And so, he donned once again his red robe and his beautiful gold chain of office and for the second time served on the Signoria.

He returned home in December. And there, two weeks later, he died, knowing that he had made Lisa happy as she was waiting for him at the gate of that remote province of Heaven that looked so much like Tuscany, with open arms and a smile on her lips.

Bibliography

Acton, Harold. *The Lost Medici*. London: Methuen, 1932.

Ademollo, Agostino. *Firenze al tempo dell'assedio*. Vol. 5. Firenze, 1845.

Baily, Auguste, *François Ier*.

Balcarres, Lord. *Donatello*. New York: Scribners, 1903.

Beach, Mrs. Hicks. *A Cardinal of the Medici*. New York: Macmillan, 1937.

Bellonci, Maria. *Beatrice and Isabella d'Este*. New York: American Heritage, 1961.

———. *Lucrezia Borgia*. New York: Harcourt Brace, 1953.

Belt, Elmer. *Leonardo the Anatomist*. Lawrence, Kansas: University of Kansas, 1955.

———. *The Story of the Manuscripts of Leonardo da Vinci*. Pasadena: Ward Ritchie Press, 1957.

———. "33 Anatomic Firsts of Leonardo da Vinci." Spectrum, 14 (1966).

Berenson, Bernard. "An Attempt at Revaluation." In *Leonardo da Vinci: Aspects of the Renaissance Genius*, Morris Philipson, ed.

Bosanquet, Mary. *Mother of the Magnificent*. London: Faber and Faber, 1960.

Breton, Guy. *Histoires d'Amour de l'histoire de France*. Paris: Editions Noir et Blanc, 1956.

Brion, Marcel. *Laurent le Magnifique*. Paris: Editions Albin Michel, 1937.

———. *Michelange*. Paris: Editions Albin Michel, 1939.

Brunetti, Gino. *Cucina Mantovana di principi e popolo*. Mantova: Instituto Carlo d'Arco.

Burckhardt, Jacob. *The Civilization of the Renaissance in Italy*. New York: Mentor, 1960.

Cantor, Norman. *Mediaeval History*. London: Macmillan, 1969.

Cartwright, Julia. *Beatrice d'Este*. London: Dent and Sons, 1926.

———. *Isabella d'Este*. 2 vols. London: John Murray, 1903.

———. *The Painters of Florence*. London: John Murray, 1902.

Castelot, André. *Le génie de Léonard de Vinci*. New York: Orion Press, 1964.

———. *Les grands heures des cites et châteaux de la Loire*. Paris: Librairie Academique Perrin, 1962.

Clark, Kenneth. *Leonardo da Vinci*. Cambridge: Cambridge University Press, 1939.

———. "Mona Lisa." *Burlington Magazine* (March 1973).

———. "On the Relation between Leonardo's Science and His Art." In *Leonardo da Vinci: Aspects of the Renaissance Genius,* Morris Philipson, ed.

Collison-Morley, L. *The Early Medici.* New York: E. P. Dutton, 1936.

———. *The Story of the Borgias.* New York: E. P. Dutton, 1933.

———. *The Story of the Sforzas.* New York: E. P. Dutton, 1934.

Cronin, Vincent. *The Florentine Renaissance.* London: Collins, 1967.

———. *The Flowering of the Renaissance.* London: Collins, 1969.

Curtis, Edmund. *A History of Mediaeval Ireland.* London: Methuen, 1938.

Dennistoune, James. *Memoirs of the Dukes of Urbino.* 3 vols. London: Longman, Brown, Green and Longmans, 1851.

Didier, C. de Cherrier. *Histoire de Charles VIII.* Paris, 1870.

Duffy, Bella. *The Tuscan Republics.* London: G. P. Putnam's Sons, 1893.

Durant, Will. *The Renaissance.* Vol. 5 of *The Story of Civilization.* New York: Simon and Schuster, 1953.

Eissler, K. R. "Psychoanalytic Notes on Leonardo da Vinci." In *Leonardo da Vinci: Aspects of the Renaissance Genius,* Morris Philipson, ed.

Fitzgerald, Brian. *The Geraldines.* New York: Devin-Adair, 1960.

Freud, Sigmund. *Leonardo da Vinci: A Study in Psychosexuality.* New York: Knopf, 1947.

Fumagalli, Giuseppini di. *Eros di Leonardo.* Milan: Garzanti, 1952.

Gamurrini, Fra Don Eugenio. *History of the Noble Family de'Gherardini of Tuscany* (1671). Manuscript in the Library of the Royal Irish Academy.

Grousset, René. *The Epic of the Crusades.* New York: Orion Press, 1970.

Guicciardini, Francesco. *The History of Italy.* London: Macmillan, 1969.

Hare, Christopher. *Ladies of the Italian Renaissance.* New York: Harper, 1904.

Hart, I. B. *The World of Leonardo da Vinci: Man of Science, Engineer and Dreamer of Flight.* New York: Viking, 1962.

Heim, Maurice. *François Ier et les femmes.* Paris: Fallimard, 1948.

Henry-Bordeaux, Paule. *Louise de Savoie.* Paris: Librairie Plon, 1956.

Hommage à Lenard de Vinci. Paris: Musée du Louvre, 1952.

Hours, Madeleine. *Secrets of the Great Masters: A Study of Artistic Techniques.* New York: Putnam, 1968.

Irigo, Iris. *The Merchant of Prato.* London: Jonathan Cape, 1956.

———. *Pope Pius II.* New York: American Heritage, 1961.

Joliffe, John, ed. and trans. *Froissart's Chronicles.* London: Harvill Press, 1967.

Kendall, Murray. *Louis XI: The Universal Spider.* New York: Norton, 1971.

Ketchum, Richard M., ed. *Book of the Renaissance.* New York: American Heritage, 1961.

Kuhner, Hans. *Dictionaire des papes.* Paris: Buchete Chastel, 1958.

Lacroix, Paul. *Louis XII.* Paris: Georges Hurtrel, 1882.

Lansing, Elizabeth. *Leonardo, Master of the Renaissance.* New York: Thomas Y. Crowell, 1942.

Lefrance, Abel. *La vie quotidienne au temps de la Renaissance.* Paris: Librairie Plon, 1888.

Loth, David. *Lorenzo the Magnificent.* New York: Brentano's, 1929.
Lucas-Dubreton, J. *The Borgias.* London: Staples Press, 1951.
——. *La vie quotidienne à Florence au temps des Medicis.* Paris: Hachette, 1958.
McHardy, George. *Savonarola.* Edinburgh: Clark, 1911.
Maguire, Yvonne. *The Women of the Medici.* London: G. Routledge and Sons, 1927.
Mattingly, Garret. *Machiavelli.* New York: American Heritage, 1961.
Mazzoni, Mario. *San Gimignano.* Florence: Casa Editrice Toscana, 1955.
Menil, Dominique de. *The Renaissance Popes as Patrons of the Arts.* Houston: University of St. Thomas, 1966.
Merejcovski, Dmitri. *The Romance of Leonardo da Vinci.* New York: Heritage Press, 1938.
Moller, E., and Pedretti, Carlo. *La Gentildonna dalle Belle Mani di Leonardo da Vinci.* Bologna: Eziaioni d'Arte, 1955.
Moody, T. W., and Marin, F. X. *The Course of Irish History.* New York: Weybright and Talley, 1967.
Morgan, Charles H. *The Life of Michelangelo.* New York: Rexnal, 1966.
Muntz, Eugene. *La Renaissance.* Paris: Firmin-Didot, 1885.
Neret, Jean-Alexis. *Charles VIII.* Paris: Les Editions de Paris, 1947.
——. *Louis XII.* Paris: Editions J. Ferenczi et Fils, 1948.
Passerini, Luigi. *La genealogia dei Rucellai,* Table 8. Columbia University.
Pater, Walter. *The Renaissance.* New York: Mentor, 1959.
Pedretti, Carlo. *An "Arcus Quadrifons" for Leo X.* Milan: Raccolta Vinciana, 1964.
——. *Dessins d'une scene executes par Leonardo da Vinci.* Editions de Centre National de la Recherche Scientifique.
——. *La machina idraulica.* Milan: Raccolta Vinciana, 1964.
——. *The Royal Palace at Remorantin.* Cambridge, Mass.: Harvard University Press, 1972.
Pernoud, Regine. *Eleanor of Aquitaine.* London: Collins, 1967.
Perosa, Alessandro, ed. *Giovanni Rucellai e il suo Zibaldone.* London: Warburg Institute, 1960.
Philipson, Morris, ed. *Leonardo da Vinci: Aspects of the Renaissance Genius.* New York: George Braziller, 1966.
Reti, Ladislao. "The Double-Action Principle in East and West." *Technology and Culture,* 3 (1970).
——. "Leonardo da Vinci and the Graphic Arts." *Burlington Magazine* (April 1971).
——. "Leonardo on Bearings and Gears." *Scientific American* (February 1971).
Reumont, A. von. *Lorenzo de' Medici.* London: Smith, Elder, 1876.
Ridolfi, Roberto. *The Life of Girolamo Savonarola.* New York: Knopf, 1959.
Roeder, Ralph. *Lorenzo de' Medici.* New York: American Heritage, 1961.
——. *The Man of the Renaissance.* London: Meridian Books, 1960.
——. *Savonarola: A Study in Conscience.* New York: Brentano's, 1930.
Roscoe, William. *Life of Leo the Tenth.* 2 vols. London: Henry C. Bohn, 1846.
——. *Life of Lorenzo de' Medici.* London: G. Bell and Sons, 1891.

Ross, Janet. *Lives of the Early Medici as Told by Their Correspondence.* Boston: Gorham Press, 1911.

Sabatini, R. *The Life of Cesare Borgia.* New York: Brentano's, 1915.

———. *Torquemada and the Spanish Inquisition.* New York: Brentano's, 1913.

Sanminiatelli, Bino. *Vita di Michelangelo.* Edizioni Nanni Canesi, 1964.

Santillana, Giorgio de. "A Man without Letters." In *Leonardo da Vinci: Aspects of the Renaissance Genius,* Morris Philipson, ed.

Saponaro, Michele. *Michel-Angelo.* New York: Pellegrini and Cudahy, 1966.

Schevill, Ferdinand. *The Medici.* New York: Harper Torch Books, 1949.

Singleton, Esther. *Florence.* New York: Dodd, Mead, 1910.

Sizeranne, Robert de la. *Beatrice d'Este and Her Court.* New York: Brentano's, 1934.

———. *Les masques et visages à Florence et au Louvre.* Paris: Hachette, 1926.

Staley, Edgcumbe. *Famous Women of Florence.* London: A. Constable Ltd., 1906.

———. *The Guilds of Florence.* London: Methuen, 1906.

———. *Tragedies of the Medici.* New York: Scribners, 1908.

Steinitz, Kate. *Leonardo da Vinci's "Trattato della Pittura."* Copenhagen: University Library.

Taylor, Pamela. *The Notebooks of Leonardo da Vinci.* New York: Mentor, 1957.

Thomass, John. *Leonardo da Vinci.* New York: Criterion, 1957.

Truc, Gonzague. *Léon X et son siècle.* Paris: Grasset, 1941.

Valentiner, W. R. "Leonardo as Verrocchio's Co-worker." In *Leonardo da Vinci: Aspects of the Renaissance Genius,* Morris Philipson, ed.

Vallentin, Antonina. *Leonardo da Vinci: The Tragic Pursuit of Perfection.* New York: Viking, 1938.

Vasari, Giorgio. *The Lives of Painters, Sculptors and Architects.* 4 vols. London: J. M. Dent and Sons, 1963.

Wallace, Robert, ed. *The World of Leonardo.* New York: Time-Life, 1966.

William, Charles. *The Earls of Kildare.* 3 vols. Dublin: Hodges, Smith, 1858–1872.

Young, G. F. *The Medici.* 2 vols. New York: E. P. Dutton, 1909.

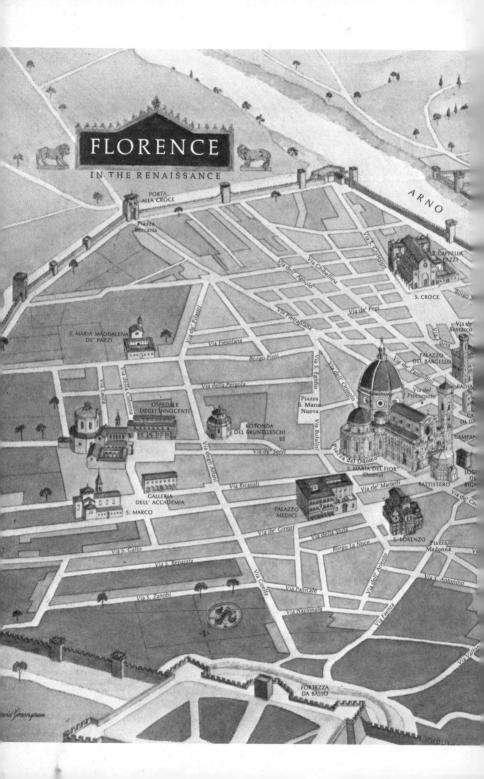